LORI WICK

TO KNOW
HER BY NAME

HARVEST HOUSE PUBLISHERS

EUGENE, OREGON

All Scripture quotations are from the King James Version of the Bible.

Cover design by Terry Dugan Design, Minneapolis, Minnesota

Cover photo © Richard Nowitz/National Geographic/Getty Images

This is a work of fiction. Names, characters, places, and incidents are products of the author's imagination or are used fictitiously. Any resemblance to actual persons, living or dead, or to events or locales, is entirely coincidental.

TO KNOW HER BY NAME

Copyright © 1997 by Lori Wick
Published by Harvest House Publishers
Eugene, Oregon 97402
www.harvesthousepublishers.com

Library of Congress Cataloging-in-Publication Data

Wick, Lori.
  To know her by name / Lori Wick.
    p. cm. — (Rocky Mountain memories series)
  ISBN-13: 978-0-7369-1820-6
  ISBN-10: 0-7369-1820-5
  1. Frontier and pioneer life—Rocky Mountains Region—Fiction. 2. Man-woman relationships—Rocky Mountains Region—Fiction. I. Title. II. Series: Wick, Lori. Rocky Mountain memories series.
PS3573.I237T6   1997
813'.54—dc21   96-51683
                                                                    CIP

Printed in the United States of America

        07 08 09 10 11 12 13 / BC / 10 9 8 7 6 5 4

One of my favorite books for one
of my favorite people, Roxie Carley.
I'm not sure what I would do without you,
dear friend, and I hope I'll never have to find out.
This dedication comes with my love and prayers.

The Author

LORI WICK is one of the most versatile Christian fiction writers in the market today. From pioneer fiction to a series set in Victorian England to contemporary writing, Lori's books (over 5.1 million copies in print) are perennial favorites with readers.

Born and raised in Santa Rosa, California, Lori met her husband, Bob, while in Bible college. They and their three children, Timothy, Matthew, and Abigail, make their home in Wisconsin.

Other Books by Lori Wick

A Place Called Home Series
A Place Called Home
A Song for Silas
The Long Road Home
A Gathering of Memories

The Californians
Whatever Tomorrow Brings
As Time Goes By
Sean Donovan
Donovan's Daughter

Kensington Chronicles
The Hawk and the Jewel
Wings of the Morning
Who Brings Forth the Wind
The Knight and the Dove

Rocky Mountain Memories
Where the Wild Rose Blooms
Whispers of Moonlight
To Know Her by Name
Promise Me Tomorrow

The Yellow Rose Trilogy
Every Little Thing About You
A Texas Sky
City Girl

English Garden Series
The Proposal
The Rescue
The Visitor
The Pursuit

The Tucker Mills Trilogy
Moonlight on the Millpond
Just Above a Whisper
Leave a Candle Burning

Other Fiction
Sophie's Heart
Pretense
The Princess
Bamboo & Lace
Every Storm

Acknowledgments

Each book is a process and an adventure. Each book is a journey. This page is for just a few, out of the many, who have traveled that road with me.

I wish to acknowledge Helen Wick, my mother-in-law. You challenge, encourage, love, and support me. Your ear has never been too busy to listen, and even when it's difficult, you speak truth to me. Your example in Christ has helped me move mountains. Thank you for remaining ever faithful.

And for Jane Kolstad, my sister-in-law. Your time and efforts on behalf of each manuscript have helped me grow as a writer. Thank you, Jane, for all your help and for loving me unconditionally.

And to the memory of my maternal grandmother, Mabel Strebig. You were so fun, Grandma. My childhood memories of you are sweet, filled with love and caring. I will miss you.

And finally to my husband, Bob. Who would have thought that our journey would be the sweetest of all? I am often guilty of underestimating God, but never so much as where you're concerned. I am blessed beyond measure because I'm married to you.

The Civil War officially ended on May 26, 1865,
when General Edmund Kirby Smith surrendered the
last Confederate troops still in the field.
The war to preserve the American Union was finished.
Even so, it was ofttimes weeks or months before men could
muster out and reach their homes across the country.

The journey to that end is where this story begins.

Prologue

Colonel Nick Wallace stood outside the brick building in St. Louis, Missouri, the documents in his breast pocket forming a lump under his jacket. He moved swiftly up the steps, his aide, Peter Crandall, just a step behind him. The rest of his depleted regiment were garrisoned at the temporary barracks on the west side of the city.

"The general is waiting for you, Colonel," the private at the door, saluting smartly, said as soon as the two men came into view. The colonel returned the salute and stepped in as the door was opened.

"Colonel Wallace, sir," a second private announced him, and Nick now saluted his commanding officer.

"Come in, Nick." The general returned the salute but became familiar as soon as the door was closed. "Have a seat."

"Thank you, sir."

Nick reached into his pocket, handed the papers across the desk, and then made himself comfortable in the wooden chair.

The general nodded his approval over the documents and then set them aside. "Thank you for bringing these, Nick. What happens from here?"

"My regiment is ready to head out. We'll be leaving today. Some are done with their tour of duty; others will serve out their papers after we get to Denver."

"And yourself?"

"I'll stay in Denver, sir. Work with the treasury department awaits."

"Not to mention your wife," the general commented, a glint in his eye.

"Her, too," the colonel smiled, the thought bringing him extreme pleasure.

The general nodded and stood. As much as he would have enjoyed talking to Wallace, he had others waiting to see him. He came around the desk and shook the colonel's hand.

"I wish you Godspeed, Nick."

"Thank you, sir."

The men saluted again, and Colonel Wallace made for the door. As had come to be the pattern of the last few months, Peter Crandall was immediately by his side, eyes watching and ready for every command. Nick saluted the private at the door and led the way out, Peter following silently in his wake.

Once on the street, Nick spoke.

"I'm headed home, Peter."

"Yes, sir."

They walked along, their long legs eating up the yards and eventually many blocks.

"What about you? Where do you head after Denver—a new regiment?"

"I have my discharge papers, sir. I'm going home."

Nicholas slowed and finally came to a complete stop as he realized he'd never asked the boy where he was from. There had been so little time for pleasantries.

"Where is home for you, Peter?"

"Boulder, sir."

"Let me see your papers, son."

Peter surrendered them willingly and stood respectfully as the older man read them.

"You're free to travel home from Denver certainly. Do you have a plan to get there?"

"No, sir, not at this moment."

Nick looked at him. There was nothing attention-grabbing about him—just another young soldier who'd seen more pain and suffering than any man his age ever should. But Peter was the most intelligent aide he'd ever had. Not everything was done to perfection—he tended to be messy—but nothing in his service had been wanting since he'd joined the colonel's regiment some time before Christmas. He'd worked hard, but like so many others, he would soon be forced to make a life for himself outside of the military.

"How old are you, Peter?"

"Eighteen, sir."

"And you do have family in Boulder?"

"Yes, sir."

Nick's mind was made up. He would take him to his home in Denver.

"Come with me, Peter."

"I always do, sir."

A smile lit the colonel's eyes, and he laid a hand on Peter's shoulder. So alike in stride and thinking, the men turned and continued on toward the west end, first to the camp where the regiment rested, and then to the train station.

Many weeks later Peter stood and witnessed a tearful reunion between the colonel and his wife, his heart clenching as he thought about seeing his own parents.

Nick and Camille Wallace urged Peter to stay more than one night, if not several days, but eager to see his family, Peter was up and gone early the following morning. His destination was the Boulder foothills. Nick had offered Peter a job in Denver with the treasury department but believed he'd seen the last of him. Peter surprised the older man by showing up just two weeks later.

"Peter," Nick spoke with delight and surprise as the housekeeper showed the young man into the parlor.

"Hello, Colonel. I hope I'm not imposing."

"Of course not. How is your family?"

"My mother is well, sir, but my father died while I was away." The words were spoken quietly.

"I'm sorry, son."

"Thank you, sir. I came back because you'd mentioned a job."

"Yes, my offer still stands. I always need more clerks. The pay won't be first-rate—cutbacks across the countryside. You know all about that, but I can use you."

"Yes, sir, but would the offer still stand . . ." Peter hesitated, "that is . . . I'm not 18 as I said I was."

Nick smiled. How many young men had lied their way into the service? The colonel did not condone such actions, but he'd seen Peter at work: A brighter young man he'd yet to encounter.

"I'm not too worried about it, Peter. How old are you?"

"Just 16, sir."

Nick nodded his head. "I can still use you."

"Can you still use me if I'm a girl?"

This time Nick did not smile or speak; he felt incapable of either for many minutes. But at the moment there was no need. Peter was speaking again, and all the colonel could do was listen. It wasn't many minutes later that the older man decided he still had a job for his aide.

1

Boulder, Colorado
April 1878

Travis Buchanan came from the post office, a stack of correspondence in his hand. As he walked toward the wagon, which was already loaded and ready for home, one of the letters caught his attention. He stopped and read, his eyes studying the signature at the bottom before continuing down the street.

His wife, Rebecca, was expecting him home, but suddenly Travis decided that he had to look into this. He climbed onto the wagon seat, turned the team around, and headed farther down the street. He stopped in front of the Boulder Hotel and jumped down to go inside.

"Well, hello, Travis," Mel Doyle, the hotel's proprietor, greeted him.

"Hi, Mel. How's business?"

"Busy, but no complaints."

Travis smiled. "Have you got someone registered by the name of McKay?"

He consulted the register. "We surely do. Room 14."

"Thanks, Mel. I'll head on up."

Travis' long legs took the stairs two at a time, his mind busy as to who this man could be, or if he'd ever seen him before. He didn't have long to speculate. No more than a few seconds after he knocked, the door to room 14 opened.

"Mr. McKay?" Travis questioned the man inside the room. He received a kind smile.

"Actually, it's Harrington. McKay Harrington. You must be Travis Buchanan."

"Yes. You left a letter for me at the post office?"

"I did. Thank you for coming up. Won't you come in?"

Travis stepped inside, not planning to stay overly long, but finding himself fascinated. He moved across the threshold and turned to study the man.

McKay Harrington wasn't as tall as Travis' 6'4" frame, but Travis guessed him to be very close to 6'. His hair was dark and his face clean-shaven, a squared-off jaw giving him a stubborn look. The eyes he turned to Travis were warm brown, friendly, and open. He dressed in a combination of styles— riding boots and denim jeans, with a dress jacket lying across the bed and a string tie hanging loosely below the collar of his crisp white dress shirt. Travis took all of this in in a moment, knowing that at the same time he was being measured as well.

Finally Travis asked, "Have we met?"

"No, we haven't. I work for the treasury department based in Denver, and I'm here in town on business. Your name was given to me as a possible contact for this area."

Travis' brows rose slightly. "But I've never done any work for the treasury department."

"That doesn't matter. Your name was given to me because of your reputation in this town. I was told that even if you can't give me the information I seek, you would stay quiet about our meeting."

Travis was intrigued but didn't forget the time. The men talked for a moment longer, McKay briefly explaining what he had in mind. Travis would not be overly involved. Still he did not give an answer. Instead he agreed to get back to the treasury man. They shook hands, and Travis swiftly made his way from the hotel. He was already later than he told Rebecca he would be.

"Is everything all right?" Rebecca asked when she saw him. Travis smiled. At one time their marriage had been anything but a loving partnership, but it had grown so that even if he were only preoccupied, she noticed.

"Yes, everything is fine, but I met someone in town," Travis said, aware of their twin sons playing on the floor. "I'll tell you about it later."

Rebecca let it go, but as soon as the boys were in bed and she and Travis were settled in the living room, she looked at him. He smiled, knowing what was on her mind.

"Was there something you wanted to talk about tonight?" he asked innocently.

Rebecca knew that to laugh or even smile would encourage him to tease her more, but she couldn't seem to help herself. Travis saw that smile, even though it didn't reach her mouth, and leaned over to pull her very close.

"Whom did you meet in town?" she asked when she was comfortable against him.

"It was a treasury man, but I don't think I'll tell you his name right now."

Rebecca now shifted and looked at him. "That was cryptic."

"It was, wasn't it?" Travis admitted. "I was contacted by this man from the treasury department today about some work he wants to do in this area. I didn't have time to question him thoroughly, but he wanted to meet me in the morning."

"Did you agree?"

"No, I told him I had church and would get back to him. He'll be around until Tuesday."

"What will you do—have him come out here?"

Travis' hand spread on the swell of his wife's stomach, and he pulled her a little closer. Their baby was due in just three months. His mind also went to the little six-year-old boys sleeping upstairs.

"No," he told her. "Not now and maybe never if I don't get the answers I need."

"So you think it might be something dangerous."

Travis kissed her temple. "I just don't know. He didn't make it sound that way. I will tell you this: I was very impressed with him and would help if I could, but how that would come about at this point is any man's guess."

They were quiet for a time, and then Rebecca said softly, "Boulder *is* growing, Travis. I'm sure it's because of our new statehood, but along with the growth, crime has stepped up. I heard a woman in the hardware store this week. She says it's the alcohol. Did you know there are ten saloons in Boulder? Now I ask you, Travis, why does any town, especially one with less than 3000 residents, need ten saloons?"

"I certainly agree with you, but growth is not all bad."

"No," she agreed swiftly. "The paper just said that the university will be ready to open in the fall, and the new building going on all over town is wonderful. Boulder is turning into a beautiful place. But it still wouldn't surprise me if your mystery man is here to investigate crime."

Travis stared at her. It was an excellent point. She was probably right. And if that was the case, did he want his family involved at all?

"I must have gotten you to thinking."

"Yes, you have," Travis admitted. "But I still don't have any solid conclusions."

"Well, how could you? You don't really know anything."

Travis stared at her, a tender light in his eyes.

"You're certainly full of answers tonight, Mrs. Buchanan."

Rebecca smiled contentedly and snuggled a little closer to him. The conversation shifted to the day and how the boys had behaved for her. At one point Travis scolded her for not lying down to take a rest, but Rebecca continued to lay comfortably in her husband's arms until it was time to head upstairs for the night.

On Sunday morning McKay Harrington slipped into the rear pew of the church and almost immediately spotted Travis Buchanan; he was sitting with two little boys. McKay prayed that the man would not take overdue notice of him and made himself comfortable as the service got underway. He stood for the singing and bowed his head for the prayer, but his mind was elsewhere.

McKay didn't care for this new assignment. Tracking down criminals and bringing them to justice was nothing new to him—he'd been at it for years. He just liked knowing everything before he started out. This time it hadn't been possible. He'd been ordered to move and move swiftly. Govern Hackett had eluded them once again, and this time McKay's superiors were angry. They didn't really want Govern, or his brother, Jubal, but they suspected that the Hackett brothers led to a much bigger fish, and he was the man the treasury department was after.

McKay's eyes went to the back of Travis Buchanan's head. What kind of help could he be? McKay knew from his report that Travis had lived here for years, but that didn't mean he could shed any light on the Hackett brothers. Indeed, if the truth be told, the brothers lived a very secretive life somewhere in the hills around Boulder. Their files didn't hold half as much about them as McKay's boss, Carlyle Crawford, would have liked.

"What is on your heart today? What is it that's weighing you down?" McKay suddenly heard the pastor ask, and realized he hadn't been attending at all. In the next few seconds he gave his case to the Lord and turned his heart toward the sermon.

" 'Casting all your care upon him, for he careth for you.' Now, isn't 1 Peter 5:7 a familiar verse? But have you looked around that verse? It's so easy to center on just that one, but look one verse above it to verse six. 'Humble yourselves therefore under the mighty hand of God, that he may exalt you in due time.'

"How do we humble ourselves before God? Again I quote verse seven to you and add one word, '*By* casting all your care upon him, for he careth for you.' Did you catch it, my friend? Is your heart humble before God? It is if you've given your anxiety to Him, if you're trusting Him completely for every aspect of your life."

McKay had to keep himself from smiling. He certainly had *not* been casting his cares upon the Lord. He'd been worrying over them and carrying them around with him like a burdensome satchel. The pastor continued, but McKay's head remained bent as he studied the verses in the small Bible he'd brought with him. He had committed verse seven to memory as a child, but had not automatically put verse six with it. He worked at doing so now. In fact, he was so intent on his task that he nearly missed the end of the service. He was eager to hear the pastor's closing remarks, but he needed to be on his way before he attracted too much attention, and that meant not milling around after the last song. When the congregation stood to sing the closing hymn, McKay slipped out the door and made his way down the street to his hotel. It would have been nice to fellowship with some of the other people in church, but having to skip that was part of his job.

The rest of the day was spent wandering around town, looking like any other person on the street, but McKay was mentally collecting information to be documented once he was back in his room. He slept well that night, with plans to check some leads on Monday, including Travis Buchanan. McKay's family lived in nearby Longmont, and he planned to go to see them first thing Tuesday morning. However, there was a telegram for him at the hotel desk when he went downstairs on Monday. Clearly from his boss, the message was a bit hard to grasp, but McKay thought he understood. He also thought he might have to put off the trip to see his family. The telegram was the very lead for which he'd been looking.

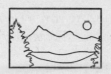

2

Pup Jennings had been going about her business for the whole day, but her mind was only half on the work. She had a feeling that trouble was afoot. She was low on supplies and hated to leave her cabin in the hills unless she absolutely had to, but dreading the trip to Boulder was not her problem. Not normally given to flights of fancy, Pup could not shake the feeling that something was going to go wrong.

The feeling lingered all day, but nothing out of the ordinary happened. She ate a solitary supper and went to bed at the usual time. However, her premonition came to light just at daybreak, as her brother burst swiftly through the front door of the cabin. He was greeted with a shotgun aimed at his face, and a sister none too happy to see he'd arrived.

"What are you doing here, Govern?" She wasted no time in pleasantries.

"I need money, and I need it fast." His voice was a growl.

He looked as if he hadn't slept in days, but Pup felt no compassion.

"I don't have any," she told him, only now lowering the gun. The calm action infuriated him, but he was careful not to show it.

"You always have money." He just managed to keep his voice calm. "I won't stay if you'll give it to me."

Pup eyed him dispassionately. They were so different. Not in looks, for both sported full heads of crow-black curls and dark, serious eyes, but their goals and desires in life were worlds apart.

"You can stay as long as you like or leave now," she spoke as she set the gun against the wall, "but you won't get any money out of me."

"You arrogant little mutt," he gritted, his true nature coming to the fore. "Mama would be ashamed if she could see the way you treat me!"

Pup laughed. "You're something, Govern Hackett—I just don't know what. Standing there telling me that Mama would be ashamed when you and Jubal are involved in all kinds of disgraceful trash."

Govern glared at her, but Pup stayed calm.

"Whom are you running from this time, Govern, Colorado law or local authorities?"

It was the worst thing she could have said. With a nearly savage growl of rage, he began to prowl the cabin, searching madly for the money he knew his sister had hidden. Wishing he would leave, Pup stood still. She dreaded the mess she would have to deal with when he did. Talking would do no good, and she was content to remain silent until he opened the front door and began throwing things outside.

"Knock it off, Govern!" she bellowed at him, but was ignored.

"Hey," she tried again when one of her few kitchen chairs sailed out the door, but again her brother took no notice.

Pup moved toward the door to close it, but he only came at her. He threw it open and tossed a few more things outside. When Pup heard a dish break on the rocks, she headed outside. Dodging another flying object as she went, she turned to look back inside and was relieved to find Govern heading into the extra bedroom and away from the glassware in the kitchen.

With a weary sigh she began to gather the mess in the clearing at the front of the cabin, stacking it against the log siding. She could hear Govern inside, loudly yelling at her as he tore things apart, but Pup stayed where she was. Govern was still crashing around inside when she heard movement in the bushes. Alarm slammed through her when a man stepped into the clearing. Pup was calling herself every kind of fool for coming out without her gun when the man spoke.

"Govern inside?" the voice asked loudly.

The sun was in her eyes, but Pup still caught sight of the rifle in his hand. It had gotten very quiet inside.

"What did you say?" she tried to stall for time.

She was sure the man was going to answer, but he wasn't given time. A shot rang out from inside the house, and the man dove for cover. Pup was doing a little diving of her own. She dropped to her belly, the ground hard and unforgiving as she stayed low and tried to think what to do.

"Come on out, Govern," she heard the man shout. "I'm not leaving without you."

Her brother's answer was another bullet, and then things fell to pieces. Shots were being fired every few seconds when she began to crawl, inching along on her stomach, to the side of the cabin. She stayed flat until she was completely out of range, and then sprang to her feet to race around the back. Unfortunately that was all she could do. The windows were too high off the ground for her to reach, and there was no back door. Her eyes went to the lake, just 30 yards away, but she'd never hid a gun or weapon outside.

Her mind was racing when the shots stopped. Still flattened against the back of the cabin, she now inched her way toward the other end, the end where the mystery man with the gun could hide. She never arrived. More shouts sounded, accompanied by glass breaking, and then the bullets began to fly again.

I thought there might be trouble, she thought wildly, *but I didn't suspect this!*

In the midst of her thoughts, the shots died out again, only to start up just a few minutes later. Pup finally sank to the ground, her legs drawn up, her back against the logs. She didn't think this man was here to do away with her. Clearly he was after her brother. But it could be her life if she put herself in their way. Not to mention the fact that Govern was angry enough right now to try to use her as a hostage.

Once again the shots died off. Pup tried to determine how much time had passed, but she was a complete blank. She only now realized how she was trembling. Her hand went to her mouth as the silence continued, and she realized that she'd been heading the wrong direction. Moving as softly as she could, she retraced her steps to the far end of the cabin. All along the back and halfway up the side, there were still no more shots. Pup inched her way to the front, peeked her head out and quickly drew back. Nothing. No sound, no movement. She tried it again, this time withdrawing her head, but putting it right back out again. Still no sound or movement.

With a deep breath she eased around to the front of the cabin. Her eyes scanned the trees and bushes in all directions, but she saw nothing. Still keeping her back very close to the cabin wall, she made her way to the porch. She kicked a pitcher she'd set down and froze as it banged against a rock, but nothing moved. She was at the porch now.

"Govern?" she tried quietly.

No answer.

"Govern, can you hear me?" she called again, this time a bit louder.

Nothing.

She brought her voice up. "I'm coming in, Govern. Don't shoot. If you're hurt I'll help you, but don't shoot me."

With movements just as quiet and careful as she could manage, Pup navigated the front steps and small porch. Her foot caught on the wood strip that ran across the threshold, tripping her just slightly. Again she froze, but there was still no movement or sound.

The main room in the cabin, which served as living room, dining room, and kitchen, was a shambles, but there was no sign of her brother. She had seen Govern heading into the spare room but wanted to keep her back to the wall. She moved carefully toward the kitchen and then popped her head into her own bedroom. There was no sign of him.

Going to the other bedroom meant walking in plain view of the living room windows, but she had to check. She spotted him almost immediately. The bullet had clearly caught him off-guard as it flew through a window. He was dead, a bullet hole in his temple, the gun he'd been attempting to reload, open. Pain clenched at her heart as she stared at the blood. Govern had not been a wonderful person, but he had been her brother, and she never would have wished him to die so violently.

Pup was on the verge of going to him when she heard a noise outside. How could she have forgotten the other man? Nearly holding her breath, she went for the rifle that had dropped out of Govern's hands. Loading it as swiftly and silently as she could manage, she inched her way to the doorway, giving her a full view of the living room. There was no sign of life at the windows or at the front door which still stood open, so Pup eased her way along. She shot a glance out the front door and would have withdrawn her head, but she froze. Standing in the clearing was the man with the rifle. The front of his shirt was soaked with blood, and his rifle hung limply from one hand.

Pup watched as he began to raise his free hand, but the act proved too much for him. Without a word, he crumpled into a heap. The gun still ready, Pup moved toward him. Her eyes darted to the trees yet again, but it seemed they were alone. Her hand went to the stranger's throat. He was still alive.

It wasn't the way Pup had planned to spend the day, but she was a woman accustomed to rising to every occasion. Her dead brother was wrapped in a sheet on the living room floor, and there was a man in the spare room who would probably die as well. The bullet had gone into his upper chest, lodging below his left shoulder. Pup knew some doctors supported the idea of leaving the bullet while others urged removing it, but the stranger had been bleeding profusely, and she had never liked the thought of a man living with lead in his body. Figuring he would die anyway, she gritted her teeth and dug the bullet out. The bleeding had slowed some, but it did not look good.

However, he was lying peacefully now, and she knew the next job had to be done today. It was unlikely that the night would be very restful for her, but she refused to go to sleep with a dead man in her living room. Her mouth set in a grim line, Pup went for the shovel and started to dig a grave, careful not to upset the two plots already in the small cemetery some yards off the lake.

Hours later, Govern Hackett lay next to his mother and father. Pup stood for a long time and stared at the fresh dirt. It wasn't very pleasant to picture his body in the ground. He had not even had a coffin. She didn't have the skill to make one. With a weary sigh she turned back to the cabin. She hadn't eaten a thing all day and now felt overwhelmed with hunger, but curiosity over the man in her spare room sent her to him.

Surprisingly enough, he was still alive. She had divested him of his clothing, but only now thought about the fact that he must have come on horseback. The light was fading fast, so she grabbed the gun again and went out. From where he'd appeared in the clearing, it was not hard to know where to look. Not ten minutes later, she found his horse, half asleep, tied to a bush. Pup led the roan gelding to her own small stable and made him comfortable for the night. Her own horse, Ginny, took little notice. She gave her some extra oats, picked up the stranger's saddlebags, and went back inside.

Again she checked on the man. She knew better than to remove his dressing, but she added to it and was thankful he seemed to be lying still. Again she found herself shaking and knew she could not wait any longer to eat. The bread and cheese, along with a tin of peaches, tasted like the best she'd ever had. She brewed a large pot of coffee, starting to drink it while it was still very hot, and tried not to dwell on the events of the day. She was contemplating a bath in the lake when she spotted the saddlebags. She had thrown them on the sofa and promptly forgotten them in her hurry to eat.

Without a twinge of conscience, she began to go through the contents. It would be nice to know why this man was hunting her brother, but since she knew he was going to die, her main concern was finding a name and possibly a lead to his family. She found both. The small card she finally discovered read:

McKay Harrington
Longmont, Colorado

Pup stared at the card for a long time, her eyes going to the doorway of the spare room and then toward the windows, looking at nothing in particular.

"McKay Harrington," she said the name out loud, her mind moving over the possibilities. The coffee had sounded so good, but now the rest of her cup sat ignored and growing cold. Indeed, the cabin itself grew chilly before Pup roused enough to build up the fire. Things were already growing warm when she took a kitchen chair and a lantern into the sickroom.

She made herself comfortable by the side of the bed, the lantern low as she looked into the pale face of her patient.

"Are you going to live, McKay Harrington?" Pup heard herself ask softly. She was a woman who had seen a lot of things and believed with all her heart that man made his choices. McKay Harrington had decided to come up the mountain after Govern, but now the choices had clearly been taken out of his hands.

3

Pup woke in the chair, her neck aching slightly. The lantern was turned low but still burning. She could see as well as hear that her patient was no longer lying quietly. His arm thrashed a little. Pup simply placed her hand on it, her actions calm and unhurried. McKay lay quiet for a moment, but then murmured something incoherent. Pup kept her hand on him and watched as he settled back into sleep.

She wondered absently if the mind registered pain when the body was sleeping. She didn't have any firsthand experience on which to fall back, at least not with a gunshot wound. She thought about it for some time but didn't come to any solid conclusions. Her patient was moving again, so she again put a hand on him and watched as his eyes opened. She could tell he wasn't really awake, so she stayed quiet. A moment later his lids dropped. He thrashed a little more, still mumbling at someone or something, but then grew very quiet. Were it not for his even breathing, his chest rising rhythmically, Pup would have thought he was gone.

She rose slowly and stretched, her nose wrinkling over the smell of herself. The mingled odors of blood, sweat, and dirt reminded her that she'd missed her evening bath. She looked into McKay's sleeping face and knew that sitting there was not going to keep him alive. With movements quiet and swift she went to her room, and slipped out of her filthy garments and into her pale yellow robe. When her rifle was in her hand, she headed for the door.

There was no moon this night, but Pup knew the path to the lake as well as she knew her own face. She didn't linger but slipped into the icy waters and scrubbed furiously with her bar of soap. It felt glorious. Once her hair was clean, she lay on her back in the water and looked up at the sky. Cold as it was, she was tempted to stay out much longer, but McKay's pale features floated into her mind.

She swam toward shore and sought her robe, the feel of it like the comfort of a friend. The gun felt heavy in her hand as she walked back to the cabin, and Pup suddenly realized how tired she was. She wondered if she would hear McKay from her bedroom if he started to move about, but then sternly reminded herself that she couldn't keep him alive.

Her bed was still torn up from Govern's searching, and she'd dropped her dirty clothing in a pile on the floor, but all of this was ignored. She fell onto her bed and slept within a minute.

Dawn was just breaking when Pup woke. It never seemed to matter when she went to sleep; she always woke with the morning's first light. Her shoulders ached, and her nose felt a little stuffy, but she knew all of this would pass. Ignoring the mess around her, she climbed from the bed and went to the spare room. McKay had thrashed some of his covers off, but he was still sleeping, his breathing even. Pup laid a hand on his forehead and found him slightly warm. She covered him again, making him as comfortable as possible, and debated whether or not she should look under the dressing. However, she heard a noise in the yard before she could decide.

"You in there, Pup?" a gravelly voice called.

Pup secured the belt at her waist and opened the door.

"Hey, Mud," she greeted the man in her yard.

"You got coffee?"

"Not yet. You want to wait?"

"Nah." He looked disgruntled and also like he'd been out all night.

"How's the claim?"

This earned her a scowl. "You know very well how the claim is, or I wouldn't be standing here with a hangover."

"You were supposed to tell me when you were going to town, Mud," the woman chastised him. "I've got a list."

"I forgot."

She frowned at him. "You'd better get home. Percy'll be having a fit."

"I bought him a book," Mud said by way of explanation, and Pup nodded.

Percy and Mud Dougan were her closest neighbors. They were brothers who worked the creek about half a mile away. Some weeks they were loaded with gold, and others they starved. Percy hated to go to town, content to pan the creek bed and read in the evening, but Mud was different. If he had money, he sought whiskey and company. At times they were like two fussy old women. Percy would hide the gold. Mud would find it and spend it all on liquor. But then he'd buy Percy a new book to placate him. Pup didn't know how they survived.

"I'd better go."

Pup didn't bother to tell Mud that she'd already suggested this.

"I'll see you later."

"All right."

"Tell Percy I might be up to borrow a book."

"He won't let you have any of his new ones."

"That's all right. Anything will do."

Without bothering to say goodbye, the prospector, who looked old beyond his years, turned and moved away. Pup turned back inside.

In the few minutes of exchange, the sky had lightened even more, and the mess Govern had left behind became clear to the eye. Pup would have her work cut out for her. Even before she made coffee, she began to put her home and yard to rights.

McKay woke to a burning in his shoulder that no movement could ease. He was cold, colder than he'd ever been, but couldn't tell if he was in water. Something was wrong—something was very wrong—but he couldn't put his finger on the problem.

Hackett! His eyes opened as the name exploded in his mind, and as if he'd actually conjured him up, Govern Hackett approached and stood above him.

"Hackett," he tried to say, but nothing came out.

"It's all right," Govern assured him in an odd voice.

McKay told himself to get up and fight, but there was nothing—no energy, no strength—to fall back on. He felt as weak as a child.

"Where am I?" he managed, wondering what bizarre twist had put him at the mercy of his prey.

"You're in bed. You've been shot."

"What drug," he began, trying to ask the question he dreaded, the one his mind couldn't quite form. He'd been given something; he was certain of it. He'd been shot before, and it hadn't felt like this. Govern Hackett had drugged him. He had to stay awake. He had to fight.

A long-fingered hand was placed on his forehead, and the desire to fight went out of him. The hand was cool. It felt like his mother's hand on him when he was sick as a child. He told himself to open his eyes and make certain it was Govern, but he couldn't manage it. The sea was rolling back in again, and this time he didn't even have the strength to swim.

Pup stood above McKay's bed and looked down into his flushed face. She'd been working on some breakfast when he'd cried out. His head was so hot, but he calmed down the moment she placed her hand on him. She went for a cloth then, soaked it in cool water and laid it across his forehead. The chair was still at the side of the bed so she sat down.

He had clearly thought that she was Govern. What would McKay say when he found out he was dead? Had they wanted Govern for questioning? Or was there a reward? Pup admitted to some ignorance on this matter, and also admitted that she hadn't wanted to know everything her brothers were up to. She didn't like to go into town, but when she did, she had learned to turn a deaf ear to rumors about the Hackett brothers. It was odd. Here she had a half-dead man in her spare bedroom, and he was the first one to think she looked like her brother. No one else had ever connected them. What would McKay say when he woke up?

Pup shook her head and stood up. She was tired of asking questions that had no answers. And besides, she still had a cabin to clean.

"You in there, Pup?"

Pup's brows rose as she left her tub of dirty dishes. Mud's calling on her twice in one day was unprecedented.

"I'm here," she spoke as she opened the door and stepped onto the porch. He was cleaned up now, face shaven and hair in place. It was funny to her that he didn't care how he looked for town, but to pan gold he cleaned up. Then again it probably wasn't Mud's idea. Percy insisted on neatness.

"Percy sent you a book."

Mud held the volume out, and Pup took it without studying the cover.

"He said he heard shots," the man went on.

Understanding hit Pup like a bullet.

"I'm fine."

"I told him you were."

"I've got a wounded man in the spare room. I didn't shoot him. My brother did and he's dead now, but I'm fine."

Mud's eyes widened, but he didn't ask anything else.

"Did you want some coffee?" Pup offered the drink as though it were any other day.

"No, I gotta get back. Are you—" he began but cut off. Pup was the most private individual he'd ever known. Countless times he had come by her place, still half-drunk, and poured out his life story of panning gold with his brother and then drinking it all away. She never talked, only listened. Indeed, she'd never given a hint about her own life until now when she had calmly told him that she had a shot-up man in her spare bedroom and that her brother was dead. Mud hadn't even known she had a brother.

"I hope you enjoy the book," he finally managed, hating how foolish it sounded.

"I'm sure I will. Tell Percy thanks."

"I'm sorry about your supplies."

"It's all right. I'll probably head down tomorrow."

"What about the man?"

Pup shrugged. "I've got to eat, and my sitting by his bed isn't going to keep him alive."

It was exactly the type of remark he would expect her to make, and somehow it comforted him. She was still Pup. She had told him she was fine, and clearly it was true.

"Well, I'm off."

"Thanks again," Pup called after him, but he was already on his way.

She finally looked down at the book in her hand. *Pride and Prejudice* by Jane Austen. She had heard of this book but not read it. Laying the volume on the kitchen table, she went back to the dishes. The water was cold as she finished them, stacking them to air dry.

She hadn't checked on McKay in more than an hour, but felt no urgency since she was headed in there to work on the broken glass. She had made certain there was none on the bed and then ignored the rest. The amount of bleeding he'd been doing when she had dragged him had been too heavy on her mind.

Now with broom and dustpan, she went to work. She poured the glass and wood splinters into a metal bucket. The sound was like a bell in the quiet room, so she took the bucket to the living room to muffle the noise. It was on her way back into the room at one point that she spotted McKay's eyes on her.

"I've been shot?" His voice was rusty, but she caught the words.

"Yeah." Her voice was soft. "In the shoulder. The bullet is out, but you've lost a lot of blood."

"So tired," he managed.

"Here," she had moved to his side, "sip a little water." She helped him without speaking, and McKay finally put his head back with a satisfied sigh. He looked at the woman standing above him.

"Where's Govern?"

"Dead."

"How?"

"You shot him."

McKay frowned at her and told himself to keep his eyes open. Could it have been her? At the moment he didn't know where the question came from or what it meant, but something wasn't right.

"Think you can manage a little broth?"

"I'm hot."

Pup put her hand on his head. His skin was warm but not on fire.

"There's a breeze coming through the window, but you don't want to get too cold."

She watched him try and push the covers away, but he didn't have the strength. However, it wasn't a minute before he said, "Where are my pants?"

Pup didn't need to answer. His eyes were already closing. A man couldn't lose that kind of blood and pop out of bed like nothing happened. Pup touched his head once more, and again the action seemed to calm him. He moved slightly under her touch, but the anxiety was gone. Pup didn't hear from him the rest of the day.

4

Pup was gone from the cabin long before daybreak the next morning. Govern had been right about the money. Pup had cash on hand—she always did—but Govern would never have found it in the various places between the logs of her bedroom walls. She had put large saddle bags on Ginny and was now headed in for supplies. If she moved right along, she'd be back up the mountain by mid-afternoon.

McKay had been awake when she checked on him, and had even accepted some broth from a spoon. She'd left him resting quietly. Pup wasn't exactly thrilled to leave him on his own, but they had to have food. It had been her plan to tell him where she was headed, but he'd fallen back to sleep. Supplies could not wait another day.

The ride into town was uneventful, and so was the shopping trip. Pup eyed the produce and canned goods dispassionately but still chose a good variety. Her patient was on her mind for most of the trip, so as soon as she finished filling her saddle bags she made a stop at the bank and headed back up the hill.

McKay woke slowly, feeling like he'd been dragged behind a horse. His shoulder was still on fire, and the rest of his body was sore to the bone. His head hurt, so he tried not to move much. The back of his head deep in the pillow, he let his eyes roam his surroundings. From his vantage point there was nothing pretentious about the room. It was square with a low ceiling, and only the bed, nightstand, and one chair served as furniture. No pictures hung on the walls, and there were no curtains at the window. Indeed, one window was boarded up, casting a shadow across the bed. His mind still fuzzy, McKay wondered what had happened.

He shifted his head to the left side. Now he was able to look out the open door to the room beyond. He thought he could see the edge of a table and some chairs, and with his head in this direction he also caught sight of a cup of water that had been left for him. Only about 18 inches away on the nightstand, it was like reaching for the moon. McKay was gasping with pain by the time he managed to maneuver the cup to his lips, and he splashed himself before getting anything into his mouth. He finally let his head fall back, feeling as if he'd run a race. The cup was empty in his hand.

"Anyone out there?" he croaked, but was only met with silence. "Hey," he tried again, his voice little more than a whisper. "Is someone there?"

His hostess, or whoever she was, was obviously out. McKay had a dozen questions, and he was determined to stay awake to ask them, but he couldn't make it happen. He fell back to sleep, not even stirring when the cup rolled from his hand and landed with a small thump on the rug beside his bed.

When McKay woke again he was assailed by the smell of meat cooking. His stomach clenched in hunger, and he rocked his head to squint out the door. He could tell by the shadows that the day was long spent, but there was still plenty of light in the sky. He hadn't cried out this time, but his movement brought the woman with the head of dark curls. She stopped in the doorway but came forward when she saw he was awake.

"How are you feeling?"

"I've been better."

"Water?" Pup filled the glass she'd retrieved earlier and held it up.

McKay nodded and she helped him drink. Their eyes met when he lay back.

"Where am I?" he asked.

"You mean in the hills above Boulder, or the cabin?"

He didn't answer. "You live here?"

"Yes."

"What's your name?"

"Callie Jennings."

McKay was not at all surprised that Govern Hackett would have a woman living with him in the hills, but she was different than he would have imagined—clearly small town and down to earth. If rumor could be trusted, Govern enjoyed the big cities and women who'd seen a little more of life. Not that McKay could tell what this woman had seen—her dark eyes gave nothing away.

"Can you eat something?" she asked without emotion. "I've got some rabbit stew on. I can cut it into small pieces for you."

"That sounds good."

She left without a word, and when she returned it was with a small bowl and spoon. Steam billowed from the top of the bowl. She was almost to the bed when she tripped on the edge of the rug and slopped a little onto the bed covers. Without a sound, she set the bowl on the nightstand and went for a towel. She cleaned up the mess without comment, pulled the chair close, picked up the bowl, and held out the spoon.

McKay realized in that instant that he hated being flat on his back, weak as a child. It was humiliating. He couldn't tell her that he could manage on his own, since it hurt to even move his shoulder, and Callie Jennings did not look large enough to help him into a sitting position. But it was true—he hated this helplessness.

37

"Are you the woman I saw outside the cabin?" he asked between bites.

"Yes," she answered before putting the spoon back to his mouth.

"Where's Govern?"

"He's dead," Pup supplied calmly, feeling no need to remind him that they'd covered this the day before.

"Did I shoot him?"

"Yes."

This time McKay didn't take the food she offered. He'd eaten all of four bites, but it had cost him.

"Had enough?"

"So tired."

"You're going to be, with all the blood you lost."

"How'd I get in here?" he asked, slurring his words.

"I dragged you in."

"Bullet," he began, his eyes barely staying open.

"It's out," she told him, but she didn't think he heard. She set the bowl aside and picked up the cloth. She tenderly wiped his mouth and chin as well as the little bit of stew that dripped onto the sheet. It wouldn't be long before he'd be wanting a bath. Pup remembered how heavy he was and didn't relish the thought. It seemed that he was going to make it through, and she couldn't help but wonder how long he'd be laid up. He didn't interfere too greatly with her lifestyle, in fact not at all, but she had her own life and didn't enjoy the idea of a stranger living in her home indefinitely.

It would be dark soon, Pup thought absently as she cleared away the bowl and towel and left the sickroom. As she did the dishes, she decided she would take a bath and turn in early. Days spent going to town and back always made her tired; it felt good to finish the dishes and sit down. With the little bit of light left in the sky she picked up the copy of *Pride and Prejudice*, the book from Percy. It was very good. She read until the light faded, lit her lantern, and readied for her bath. McKay was doing surprisingly well, so she took as long as she liked, letting the cold water clear her head and cleanse her body. She then did as she'd planned and turned in early, thankfully sleeping the whole night through.

McKay's fever was up the next day. He was in and out of coherency and hot to the touch all day. He was not overly demanding in his needs, but each time he surfaced he had questions.

Where is my horse? Did you get my saddlebags? What day is it? Where's Govern? What was your name again? What time is it? How long have I been here?

None of it was unreasonable, but Pup was a woman who could go for days, even weeks, and not talk to anyone. McKay's constant questions were wearing her out. However, there was an upside. Each time McKay woke over the next three days, it was for a little longer period. Pup knew that he was gaining strength. She hoped he would be on his feet soon, not just for her sake, but for his as well. However, she hadn't reckoned with the man—McKay Harrington. She didn't know him well enough to realize that as he improved he also grew more frustrated with the fact that he wasn't back to *full* strength. He woke up on Tuesday morning, just seven days after he'd been shot, his body still weak as a child's, but his mind moving in 40 different directions.

5

"Miss Jennings," McKay called to his nurse as soon as he heard movement in the next room. He figured he'd been awake for more than an hour, just waiting, his mind still moving much faster than the rest of him. It was a relief to hear someone else stirring.

Pup didn't have any trouble hearing McKay's voice, but she'd never been called Miss Jennings before. She went to the door.

"I take it you're feeling better?" she asked kindly from the threshold.

"Yes, thank you." His voice was all business, and he wished he had the strength to sit up. However, that was not going to stop his mission. "I know you've gone to a lot of trouble," he began, "but I need a favor."

"What is it?"

"I need you to go to town. I need you to send a telegram."

"I was just in Boulder," Pup said calmly, thinking this was all the explanation necessary.

"I need you to go back."

Rather surprised that he would argue with her, Pup took a moment to respond.

"I don't like going into town," she said simply. "Did you want some breakfast?"

"No, but I—" McKay wasn't given a chance to finish. His hostess had already moved from the doorway.

He lay staring at the ceiling, asking himself how the conversation could have gone so badly. It was certainly true that Callie Jennings didn't owe him anything, but she hadn't even been willing to hear what he had to say. It didn't occur to McKay that he hadn't been listening either. He was so dead set on having that telegram sent that he didn't care whether she liked going to town or not.

He heard the rattle of pans and knew Callie would be making breakfast. He was hungry, but his mind was so centered on sending word to Carlyle that he easily put his appetite aside.

I'm still with the treasury department, Lord. I can't put my position on the shelf just because I'm injured. Please help me to rest in You, but also help me to make Miss Jennings see that she needs to do this for me. It's important, Lord, I believe this with all my heart. Help me make her understand.

The sound of an opening door, assumably at the front of the cabin, broke into McKay's thoughts. He was fairly certain Callie must be gone because things in the cabin were now quiet. Outside and from a distance he thought he heard the chopping of wood. It was such a common sound that it drove him crazy. The world was going on in a normal fashion, and he was stuck in this bed. A moment earlier he'd prayed for peace, but now all such thoughts flew out of his head. Feeling almost desperate, he shifted the covers slightly and tried to sit up.

Pain ripped through his shoulder, but that wasn't the worst of it. There was nothing there—no energy, no tensing of his muscles for action—nothing. It was as if every ounce of strength had been drained away through a small bullet hole. Defeated and breathing heavily, McKay fell back against the pillow. He heard the door open again but didn't move. After a moment his eyes shifted and he found his hostess watching him from the other room.

"You all right?" she asked solicitously.

"I tried to sit up," he admitted.

Pup moved toward the bedroom door, stopping when she was next to the bed.

"I imagine it will take some time. It would probably help if you ate, but it's up to you."

She started away, but McKay caught her hand, his hold light because he could manage no more. Thinking he now wanted food, Pup was surprised when he said, "If you would just listen to me, Miss Jennings, I *need* you to go to Boulder. It really is a matter of—"

"No one calls me Miss Jennings," Pup inserted calmly.

"What?" McKay was completely caught off-guard by this statement.

"I go by Pup, and sometimes Callie. Be sure and let me know if you change your mind about breakfast."

She turned and walked away before McKay could utter another word. The laid-up man was flabbergasted. Was the woman stupid? She didn't appear to have heard a word he said. Or maybe she was just completely unreasonable. He was torn between confusion and outrage, but over all of this was determination. He simply had to make her see. His mind racing, he called her name again.

"Miss Jennings?"

Pup appeared in the doorway a moment later.

"I'm sorry to trouble you, but I would like to eat now."

Pup didn't answer but moved off, her expression giving nothing away. She was back inside of three minutes, carrying a steaming plate of fried potatoes, eggs, and salt pork in one hand, and a cup of hot coffee in the other. She tripped on the rug as she came in and dumped a little of the coffee in the plate, but made no apologies and didn't hesitate in her delivery. The plate and cup were set down, the chair was pulled up, and she handed McKay a fork.

"I'll hold the plate for you," she offered calmly, "if you can manage the fork."

He didn't say anything as he started on the food, but he choked painfully on the first bite.

With no pomp or ceremony, Pup set the plate aside, bent over McKay and carefully put another pillow behind his head. She then picked up the plate again and held it over his chest. The position was awkward for the injured man, but he knew he would not choke again. He ate the food slowly, not really tasting it because his mind was on other things. The plate disappeared at one point as Pup offered him the coffee; McKay barely noticed what he drank.

"I've had enough," he said when the plate was half empty, "thank you."

"You're welcome," Pup said and stood. She handed him a napkin and waited until he wiped his face. McKay was on the verge of speaking when Pup cut him off.

"I have some neighbors up the mountain—both men. I can get one of them to help you clean up or I can help you, whichever you want."

This was the last thing McKay expected. He blinked at her stupidly but thought fast and said, "I think if you'll just bring me a rag and towel, I can manage."

Pup left but was back with a basin of hot water, a towel, a small cloth, and a bar of rough soap just five minutes later. She used the small cloth to soak up some of the water, wrung it out, and handed it to McKay. The warm, wet cloth felt wonderful to the bedridden man. His eyes slid shut as he held it along the line of his beard, and then ran it down the front of his neck and around the back.

His hostess stood calmly by during all of this but took the cloth just as it was cooling. This time she soaped it before handing it back and waited again while McKay slowly scrubbed his face, neck, and arms. He was about halfway through when he began to talk.

"I suppose you have questions. I mean, it would only be natural, and I'd be happy to answer them, but the only thing on my mind right now is your getting a message to Denver for me. I came up this mountain on business, and whether or not I can get out of this bed, I have to see the job done."

Pup took the cloth at that point, rinsed it, soaped it again, and handed it back to him. In those few seconds, McKay took in the state of her dress—torn in places and stained.

"I'd make it worth your while," he offered when she looked back at him. Her dispassionate stare made him think he'd offended her so he was quick to add, "I didn't say that as an insult—I just want you to know how badly I need this job done. I'm willing to pay you because there are people counting on me and—"

"You're healing fast."

McKay took a moment to catch her meaning, but catch it he did.

"Even if I get out of this bed by the weekend . . ." McKay began, but his voice trailed off and he was silent for a moment.

"How long *have* I been here?" he asked, having just realized he didn't know.

"A week."

His whole body jerked. "A *week?*" His voice was incredulous as pain slashed across his face.

"Are you done washing?" Pup reached for the cloth.

"You've got to understand how important this is. I've got to get word to Denver."

Pup took the cloth from his hand and turned toward the basin. She handed him the towel. He ignored it.

"I need you to go to Boulder."

"Has anyone ever told you what a nag you are?"

"I am not a nag!" McKay was caught off-guard one more time and completely indignant over her comment.

"You're not a nag?" Her tone was clearly skeptical.

"No." He was still angry.

"What do you call a person who won't take no for an answer?"

"I didn't hear you say no."

"I said I don't like going into town."

"Yes, but that was before I had a chance to explain how important this is."

45

Unaware that he was getting more out of Pup than most people did, McKay didn't realize that he was pushing way beyond the limit.

"Your having a cause gives you permission to nag?"

"I am not nagging," he told her again, as if explaining to a slow child. "I've just got to make you see."

But Pup was done. She left the towel on the bedside table and lifted the basin.

"Miss Jennings, please, if you'll only—"

"I go by Pup or Callie." Her voice was quiet, but it got through. "I'd appreciate it if you'd remember that."

Anger and defeat washed over McKay as he watched her walk out the door. His eyes lingered on that empty doorway for a few seconds and then lifted to the ceiling. He knew he had a lot of praying and confessing to do if he wasn't going to lose his mind lying in that bed.

"What brings you up here, Pup?" Percy asked his nearest neighbor, his voice none too friendly.

"I need to return your book and ask Mud a favor."

"Mud is working," Percy informed her in a way that warned her not to disturb him.

"I don't need him right this minute," Pup said calmly, not feeling the need to remind Percy that he was not Mud's keeper. "I'll just find him myself." She held the book out. Percy took it, his face showing his displeasure, and Pup, finding it easy to ignore him, walked on. A few minutes later she found Mud by the stream. He was bent over the sluice box, his face intent as she approached. He spoke without looking up.

"I don't want you checking on me, do you hear me, Percy?"

Pup stopped, a smile lighting her face.

"Get on outta here, Percy, or I'm going back to bed. I swear I will."

"What put the burr under your saddle, Mud?"

The man's head shot up. "Oh, Pup, it's you."

"Nice to see you, too, Mud."

Mud shook his head, his expression irritated. "Percy's been a royal pain today. Banged around in that kitchen 'til I thought I would lose my mind." He stopped and studied her. "What brings you up here?"

"My houseguest. Any chance you're headed to town in the next few days?"

"Not if Percy has anything to say about it."

"Well, if you do, the man has a message he wants telegraphed to Denver."

Mud didn't bother to ask her why she didn't go herself because he already knew: Pup hated town as much as Percy did. Mud couldn't understand either one of them.

"It won't be tonight, but I'll stop by if I go soon. There's no guaranteeing that the telegraph office will be open when I get there."

"Well, at least you can say you tried." She started away but turned back. "He could also use a bath."

Mud grimaced. "Well, I'll be sure and rush down to take care of that."

Chuckling at his sarcastic reply, Pup turned away but didn't comment. She walked back down the mountain, her rifle held loosely in one hand. There was no promising that Mud would show up, but at least if he came by it would get McKay off her back.

"Could I please talk to you a moment," McKay called as soon as he heard the front door open. Pup went straight to the door of his room, three dead rabbits dangling from one hand, the rifle still in the other.

"Did you say you prefer Callie or Pup?"

"It doesn't matter."

"Pup must be a nickname."

Pup only nodded.

McKay had never encountered such an uncommunicative woman; for a moment he fell silent.

"Did you find my saddlebags with the horse?"

"They're out here. Do you want them?"

"Please."

Pup went for them immediately, laying them on the bed next to him. She was turning away when he said, "It really is important."

Pup turned and looked at him. "I'm sure it is."

They stared at each other. The rabbits and gun were gone, and McKay's hand rested on the leather bags.

"Why haven't you asked me why I came after Govern?"

"I assumed I'd find out sooner or later."

"But you're not that curious?"

Pup didn't immediately reply. "I knew what Govern was like. I'm sure you were hunting him for a good reason."

McKay's face was a mixture of regret and resignation. "There was a good reason, but I'm still sorry he's dead. I really thought I could reason with him."

"Then you didn't know Govern at all," Pup said softly, and this time moved out the door.

6

"This is Mud," Pup said by way of explanation the following afternoon.

McKay stared up at the grubby-looking man and then at Pup, but she had no other comment for him.

"There's hot water on the stove, Mud, and I'll be in the yard if you need me. Be careful around that wound or he'll be bleeding again."

McKay could not believe his ears when she said this, walked from the room, and shut the door behind her.

"Did she mean something by that?" McKay asked with quiet incredulity the moment they were alone.

"Pup said you needed a bath and a message sent." Mud took a step toward the door as he said this since he was not exactly thrilled with his task. "If she was wrong, I'll be on my way to town."

McKay was surprised, but he wasn't about to let this opportunity slip away.

"As a matter of fact I would enjoy cleaning up some, and I'm quite desperate to send word to someone in Denver."

Mud nodded, his face resigned. "I'll get some water. You got any shaving gear?"

"In the saddlebags," McKay told him, and the two of them went to work. It wasn't without its embarrassment or pain, but Mud cracked a few jokes to lighten the mood, and the job got done. McKay was well spent by the time he wrote out his message, but he managed the words.

"The office might be closed," Mud warned him as he put the scrap of paper in his pocket.

"All right." At the moment McKay was too tired to care. His voice said as much. "At least I tried."

Mud's heart was wrung with compassion. To be shot and weak and living with Pup Jennings, who didn't say two words in a month, must be almost more than any man could bear.

"I'll get there as soon as I can."

"Thanks. If you think of it you could also let that livery know that I haven't stolen their horse."

Mud nodded and stuck his hand out. McKay shook it, a smile lighting his tired features.

"I'll stop back and let Pup know if I got the job done."

McKay's brow creased with thought. "Why do people call her Pup?"

Mud's head went back with laughter, showing a surprisingly even line of teeth. "You stick around here long enough, and you'll figure it out."

He exited on those words, and McKay was left on his own to ponder what he might have meant.

"He's all set," Mud said by way of greeting when he found Pup hanging clothes. As a child he'd known what day of the week it was by the jobs his mother did. She always did laundry on Mondays, and always first thing in the morning. Pup did laundry when her clothes were dirty. And if they didn't dry before dark, she left them out all night.

"Is he bleeding again?"

"No, but that dressing needs to be changed. I concentrated on the rest of him. He gave me a note."

"Good."

"Do you want to read it?"

"Why would I need to do that?"

"He's living in your house, Pup! Don't you care?"

She didn't answer, so Mud took the paper and thrust it into her hand.

"I'm not delivering no message that brings even more people to this mountain than we've already got—so read it!"

Pup's eyes dropped to the paper that she held lightly in her fingers.

Carlyle Crawford
Denver Colorado.
GH dead. Laid up in Boulder.
Will contact when able. MH.

She handed the note back to him.

"Send it," Pup said simply. "If it draws a crowd, then we'll deal with it."

Mud pushed the note back into his pocket and turned away. He'd tied his horse to a tree branch, and now went and climbed into the saddle. He spoke just before he rode out.

"He's weak, but it won't be long before he's up and around."

Pup nodded. "Then he can be on his way."

"Is that what you really want, Pup?"

"What do you mean?"

"He was better looking after I shaved him."

Pup laughed at this, and Mud grinned at her before heeling his mount down the path.

"I've got some rabbit in the pan out here," Pup said as she went to McKay's door much later that day. "Do you want some?"

"Yes, please."

She started away, but McKay's voice stopped her.

"Callie?"

"Yes?"

"Thank you for sending Mud."

"You're welcome."

She left, and McKay was given a few more moments to ponder how quiet she was. He had a sudden idea.

"I can try to manage this plate on my own," he said as soon as she came back, "if you want to bring your own food in."

"I'm not hungry right now," she informed him calmly. "Do you want help with this?"

"I can do it on my—" McKay began, but he stopped short. "Yes, thank you," he finally managed, and watched as she settled down with the plate, holding it competently so he could eat.

Tonight the food was different. She had not thrown everything into a stewpot as usual. The plate held mashed potatoes, pieces of rabbit, and an unidentified green, leafy pile. The rabbit took some chewing, and the potatoes were only half-mashed and very dry. The green leafy stuff was not completely tasteless, but even after McKay had it in his mouth he did not recognize it. The coffee, however, was delicious.

"You make good coffee."

"Thank you."

McKay chewed for a moment. "You don't say much, do you?"

"Not if I don't have anything to say."

He wasn't at all surprised by her logic. Having spent only a few days in her presence, McKay was still certain that he had her figured out. She was clearly a simple woman with simple tastes. She hadn't been willing to go into town for him, but she'd found someone who was. Even if she hadn't done that, he could not fault her care of him; he would have certainly died without her intervention.

"Do you mind if I ask you some questions, Callie?"

"No."

"How long had Govern been here when I arrived?"

"Not long. Twenty minutes, half an hour at the most."

"What was he doing?"

"Looking for money."

McKay stopped to take a bite, his face thoughtful.

"What day is this again?"

"Wednesday. You were shot a week ago yesterday."

"And I bled a lot?"

"Yes."

"But the bullet's out?"

"Yes."

"What are the chances Mud will actually send that telegram?"

"If he can send it, he will."

"And the horse—if Mud gets to the livery—is the owner going to come looking for his horse?"

"Where'd you go? Mickey's?"

"Yeah."

"He'll be fine. He'll charge you for every day, but he doesn't rile easily."

"Have you seen Jubal lately?"

If he had planned to surprise her, it didn't work.

"No."

"Do you know where he is?"

"No."

"What's he going to say when he learns that Govern is dead?"

"I can't say as he'll be too happy, but he won't be surprised."

"Do you know Jubal very well?"

"About as well as I knew Govern."

"And you don't have any clue as to where he might be?"

"No."

She continued to hold the plate, offering the coffee once in a while. McKay began to know real pity for her. What a lonely life she led, but then maybe it wasn't. In truth she didn't appear to be all that bright; she showed so little curiosity or interest in things. Maybe it was like that when you were so cut off from town. If this were all she'd ever known, then she probably wasn't lonely at all.

"Do you want more?"

"No, I'm done. Thank you."

"I have some berries if you'd like something sweet."

McKay looked into her face. Her voice was kind and so were her actions, but her face was so difficult to read.

"I appreciate the offer of the berries—they sound good— but I've had enough. Thank you."

She nodded, and McKay felt at a loss to say more. Pup left a moment later but was back swiftly, clean rags in her hand to change his dressing. Neither one of them spoke while she worked, but McKay's mind was busy. He lay looking at the door for a long time after she left. His Bible lay on the bed next to him, and without opening it he placed his hand on the cover. There was really no way for him to repay Callie Jennings for all she had done, but just maybe he could give her something that held greater value than gold.

He planned to pray for her for quite some time, but all of a sudden he was tired. If he'd been home, his father or mother might have sat with him until he slept, but here he was left alone. That very fact caused him to pray all the more for his hostess, but sleep still crept in to claim him. In fact, he was out hard when Pup came to check on him.

She stood quietly by the side of the bed. Even without McKay's eyes on her, her face was unreadable. He would have been surprised to know that she was silently agreeing with Mud. Without a week's worth of growth on his face, McKay Harrington was very good-looking indeed.

Pup stepped from the cabin the next morning and nearly fell over Mud. He was sitting on her front porch, half-lying actually, his head in his hands.

"Another all-nighter, Mud?" she inquired kindly.

"Yeah. Percy always warns me to start home even if it's dark, but I never listen. You got some coffee?"

"Yeah. I'll get you a cup."

Pup brought two and then sank down on the step next to her neighbor. They drank in silence for a time, and Pup refilled their cups. The sun was breaking through the trees when Mud spoke.

"Do you ever ask yourself if there's more, Pup? Do you ever wonder if there's more to this life than panning gold, drinking, and then dying?"

She was silent for a moment and then admitted, "I did when I was a child, but I've seen ugly things since then. It's easier to believe when you're a child."

Mud's mind went back to his own childhood. His father had been a mean man, but his mother, in his mind, had been a saint. The thought of her made him want to weep, so he forced her face from his thoughts.

"How's the patient?"

"Fine. His wound is healing fast. As soon as he gains a little strength, he'll be on his feet."

"I sent word."

"I'll tell him."

Mud turned and looked at her, and Pup returned his stare. Although bloodshot, his eyes still reflected the concern he felt. Why couldn't Pup find someone? She wasn't pretty, but she was kind and smart. Why couldn't McKay see something in her that would make him want to stay?

"Go on home, Mud," Pup said softly, having read the fatherly look in his eyes. "I'll be fine."

"Come and tell me when he leaves," Mud ordered.

"I'll do that," Pup promised, and watched as Mud went on his way.

7

His pants buttoned into place, McKay stood very still at the side of the bed and contemplated his next move. He'd been sitting up in bed and doing a little more in the last few days, but this was the first day he'd even considered moving from the room. He had to try. The days were starting to blur again. Mud had been here on Wednesday, and this was Sunday. At least McKay thought it was Sunday.

"Actually," he said softly, "it might be Monday."

With that he took a step toward the door. The floor was a little gritty, but his mind barely registered this fact in his effort to stay on his feet. Moving slowly, his hand first on the bed and then on the wall for balance, he passed over the threshold and got his first look at the whole room. His eyes skimmed over the small stove and cupboards, table and two chairs, but then centered on a high-backed, faded sofa to his right. He made a beeline for the seat. Working at not jarring his shoulder, he lowered himself onto the cushions, the effort causing his breath to come in uneven gasps. McKay let his head fall against the back, his eyes closed.

I made it, Lord. I actually made it out here. I'm too tired to even look around, but I made it. McKay felt himself dozing off, but no more than a few minutes passed before he heard movement outside. He lifted his head in time to see his hostess come in the door. She stumbled slightly on a raised board that ran across the threshold but didn't lose her balance. In fact, she didn't even seem to notice. She glanced his way but continued on to the table to set down a basket of clothes. She then turned and looked at him.

"You must be feeling stronger."

"Somewhat," his voice sounded a little weary. "I couldn't find a shirt."

"I've got one washed for you. Do you want some help?"

"I would love to refuse, but I can't."

Pup needed no other urging. She went back into his room, opened the closet door and emerged with a denim shirt. It wasn't pressed but it smelled fresh and looked clean. Pup helped him ease it over the bandage on his shoulder and even held the side when he put it on his good arm. She hadn't stared or made any fuss, but she was relieved when he buttoned the front and covered his chest.

"Hungry?" Pup asked; it was nearly lunchtime.

"A little. More thirsty than anything."

Pup walked back to the kitchen area and returned with a mug full of cloudy brown fluid. McKay took it from her hand and sniffed.

"Cider?"

"Yeah," she answered as she went back to her clothes basket. "I've got a press out back."

McKay took a long, satisfying pull. It was tart, but cold and wet.

"By the way, is this Sunday or Monday?"

"This is Tuesday," Pup said as she folded the clean clothing. Her back was to her guest, and she missed the surprised lift of his brows.

McKay sat in silence and watched her work, noticing for the first time how tall and slender she was; so tall that her dress didn't go past her ankles. She wore heavy leather men's boots, thick-soled and mud-brown. He also realized that she could be anywhere from 20 to 30 years of age. He knew better than to ask, but her age was a curiosity. He watched as she carried the basket to the room next to his and knew it must be her bedroom. When she came back, she went again to the table and began to work over a plucked chicken. She was facing him now, but she still didn't feel a need to look at or speak to him.

"You live here all alone, Callie?"

"Most of the time."

"Do you prefer to be alone?"

"Depends."

"On?"

"On if I want to be alone or not."

All of this was said with her head bent over the bird. McKay was fascinated by her economy of words. The women he knew—girls he grew up with, his sister, his mother, all of them—loved to talk. He wouldn't go so far as to call them chatterboxes, but they never seemed to run out of things to say. Thinking of them with fondness, his voice now took on a teasing tone.

"You must certainly want company when you're feeling as talkative as you are now."

A smile pulled at the corners of Pup's mouth, but she didn't comment or look up.

"I tell you, Callie," his tone was still exaggerated, "my recovery is probably going to take weeks longer."

She finally raised her head and looked at him.

"It's all the talking you do. It wears a man out."

A smile spread across her lips, and laughter lit her dark eyes, but she still didn't speak before going back to her work.

Once again McKay let his head fall back against the seat. He took time to carefully study the cabin. It was well laid out, with two bedrooms and one large room set up for the living area. It also appeared to be solidly built, but there was a haphazardness to the contents and placement of furniture. There were no frills—no little lace mats, dried flowers, or pictures.

It wasn't hard to see that domestic life was not overly important to his hostess. The pantry cupboard was in need of painting, and there were several dark, charred smudges on the wall by the stove. His mother would have sanded those off the day after they were burned. With this in mind McKay remembered the meals Callie had served him. They'd been filling and sometimes flavorful, but not fancy by any stretch of the imagination. Sometimes things were rather burnt.

When McKay's eyes slid shut he couldn't remember, but when he awoke he was lying on the sofa, not sitting on it, and there was a pillow under his head and a thin sheet over his body. He shifted his head to look for Callie but found only a plate with some bread, cheese, an apple, and another glass of cider on the little table she'd moved in front of him. He pulled himself into a sitting position and reached for the mug. What had he been thinking about when he fell asleep? He was certain that it had been Callie.

When was he going to have strength enough to keep his thoughts clear and stop nodding off at the drop of a hat? When no answer came to him, he reached for the food, just now realizing how hungry he was. He ate rather absently but felt very full when the food and cider were gone; he was also sleepy all over again. It would have been more comfortable to move back to the bed, but he didn't have the energy. He fell asleep wondering where Callie had gone.

"You're a little way from home." Pup stood in the clearing some yards below the cabin and greeted Travis Buchanan when he walked into view. Pup had heard someone coming and simply waited, her rifle in her hand, to see who it was.

"I am, aren't I?" the tall man agreed with a smile, stopping a few yards off on the other side of Pup's garden. "How are you doing, Pup?"

"Can't complain. Something I can help you with, Travis?"

"I'm looking for a man named McKay Harrington. Have you seen him?"

"He's at my place," she said simply.

"Is he all right?"

"He's getting there."

Travis nodded. He'd not had many conversations with Pup Jennings, but he knew enough about her to know she normally kept to herself.

"I got word from someone in Denver that he might need help."

"He'll be glad to know that his message got through."

"Did you send word?"

Pup shook her head no. "Mud was going to town."

"Mud?"

"Mud Dougan. He and his brother Percy live above me on the creek."

"I guess I have heard of them. Well, do you mind if I go on up?"

"Doesn't make any difference to me."

"All right."

He walked toward the cabin, his horse's reins in his hands. Pup went back to her garden. Things were in good shape now. The weather was finally warmer, and they'd had some rain. With satisfaction she gathered some small beans from the vines. From there she moved to the beets, onions, and tomatoes.

The small of her back was beginning to ache when she heard movement behind her. She straightened to full height and faced Travis.

"He's asleep," he said by way of explanation.

"He does that a lot."

"Can you tell me what happened?"

"Govern shot him."

"Govern Hackett?"

"Yes."

"I didn't realize he lived this far up."

"He doesn't anymore."

Travis stared, taking in her stoic expression. "I don't want to mistake your meaning, Pup," he said slowly. "I take it Govern's dead?"

"Yes."

Pity filled him. Govern Hackett was only a name to him—Travis had never actually laid eyes on the man. But Pup was different. Travis had felt compassion every time he'd seen her in town, and it was worse now knowing she'd been involved with an immoral man like Hackett. He found himself hoping she'd not been left alone with any children. It was a temptation to ask, but he refrained.

"Are you all right?" he finally managed.

"I'm fine." Again the words were simply stated. "The stable's around back," she went on hospitably. "You can feed and water your horse if you've a mind to."

"I think I'll do that," Travis told her and moved off with a brief word of thanks.

Pup finished loading the greens into a basket and headed toward the house. McKay was still sleeping, but she saw that he'd eaten the food she left. Pup was rinsing the vegetables in a pan of water when Travis knocked on the door and stepped in. The knock woke McKay.

"Buchanan," he said with surprise, coming instantly awake. He attempted to sit up, but when he grimaced with pain, Travis came forward to help him.

"Thanks," McKay said on a deep breath. He looked at the other man. "What brings you up the mountain?"

"This telegram." Travis took the paper from the table and handed it to McKay. The treasury man read it.

TRAVIS BUCHANAN
BOULDER, COLO.
HAVE HEARD FROM MCKAY HARRINGTON STOP WAS HEADED INTO HILLS STOP TROUBLE HAS BEEN REPORTED STOP ANY INFORMATION YOU CAN SUPPLY CONCERNING THIS MATTER WOULD BE APPRECIATED STOP
CARLYLE CRAWFORD, DENVER, COLO.

"Did I tell you about Carlyle?" McKay asked.

"I think so. You work for him."

"Yes. One of the men who lives and prospects up here sent word for me. I was hoping to be on my feet by now, but Callie tells me I lost a lot of blood."

"Callie?"

"You must call her Pup."

Both men turned to look at the woman who was working just five yards away, but she never looked up or even appeared to be aware of them.

Travis looked back at McKay. "Do you want me to try to help you ride out of here?"

Regret passed over McKay's face. "I would love to get back to town, but I know I'd never make it. A few more days and I'll try it on my own, but not today."

"In that case, what message do you want sent to Carlyle Crawford?"

"Tell him I'm all right and will send word as soon as I'm back in Boulder."

"All right," Travis agreed, but then looked concerned. "Can you tell me what happened up here?"

McKay nodded and briefly filled him in. He ended by saying, "I woke up in the bedroom right there," McKay pointed to the door. "And until last week I wasn't really aware of anything."

"This happened on what day?"

"The Tuesday after I met you."

Travis nodded again. "I've brought some extra supplies if you can use them. Is there anything else you need?"

"Just your prayers," McKay said softly. "I've never been so weak before, and it's hard to be patient."

"I think I understand. Listen, if you need to see me when you get back to Boulder, don't hesitate to stop in."

"I'm not sure I'll have time, but I won't forget your offer," McKay assured him.

63

"I'm going to head out and hopefully get home tonight," Travis went on. "I'll go for my horse and the supplies, but I'll come back in and say goodbye."

Travis slipped out then, returning with several food items and some wrapped bandages that he laid on the table. He then spoke to his hostess. "I'll just leave these with you, Pup."

"All right," she agreed. "Thank you."

"Is there anything else you need right now?" He was still talking to Pup.

"I'm in good shape for a few weeks. Thank you."

"My pleasure."

Travis turned to the injured man, and McKay put out his hand. They shook and Travis said goodbye. He would have said the same to Pup, but she stopped him.

"Do you know the circle pines, Travis?"

"Yes."

"If it were me, and I didn't hit the pines by dark, I'd stay on the mountain tonight."

"Thanks, Pup. I'll remember that."

"Did your wife have her baby?" she asked unexpectedly.

"Not yet. Another two months or so. She's the reason I want to get back."

"I can understand that," Pup told him and watched as he looked at her. She saw the pity in his eyes but was used to either that or scorn from the people in Boulder. At least with Travis she knew he meant well. A moment later he said his final goodbyes to Pup and McKay and took his leave.

Pup, who had gone on with her work, had nothing to say when he left; McKay was quiet as well. He never dreamed that Carlyle would contact Buchanan, but right now he was very thankful for both men.

8

McKay made himself get up every morning and dress as best he could in the clean clothing Pup always had ready for him. He had yet to make it past the front porch, but he could feel the progress, the slow healing of his body. It had nearly killed him not to return to Boulder with Travis, but he'd been honest when he said he would never have made it. He was walking around the cabin more, but most of his days were spent sitting or lying on the sofa. It was during this time that some light was shed on Mud's cryptic answer about his hostess.

There wasn't a time when Pup came into the cabin that she didn't trip on the threshold. She knocked pans from the stove and bowls from the table. She spilled water and food down the front of herself daily. She continued to dress his wound with tenderness and surprising skill, but when it came to the rest of the cabin, she was an accident waiting to happen. "Clumsy little pup," must have been the phrase that started the nickname, and McKay could see why. But what most fascinated him was that Pup herself seemed completely unaware that anything was amiss.

If he lived to be a hundred, he would never forget the morning she set a kitchen towel on fire. It didn't burst into immediate flames, but did smoke and flame slightly before she noticed it. At first McKay was too stunned to react, and about the time he was ready to open his mouth and warn her, she had spotted it. He was speechless as she made a face that showed the inconvenience of it all and calmly poured some water from the pitcher to douse the fire. The room was a little smoky after that, but she only opened the front door. She didn't turn to him with any type of comment or apology but went back to the meal preparations. She wiped at the mark that it made on the stove top but never referred to it again.

It had been two weeks and four days since he'd been shot, and tonight was the first night McKay was going to join Pup at the dinner table. As he sat in his usual place on the sofa, however, the burned towel incident strongly in his mind, he wondered if this was safe.

"Are you getting hungry?" Pup interrupted his thoughts as she entered the cabin carrying a basket. She tripped but never dropped a thing.

"A little. I thought I would come to the table tonight."

"Suit yourself," she said mildly.

Do things really mean so little to her, Lord? Is she really so disinterested? Or is it because I'm a stranger who has moved into her home? On the heels of these questions McKay remembered the man he shot. She hadn't had much more to say to Travis Buchanan than she did to him, but he must never forget that it was he who shot Govern Hackett. What exactly they had meant to each other McKay could only guess, but he reminded himself that she might never feel overly friendly toward him.

When he saw Pup putting plates and flatware on the table, he rose. He was acutely aware of his bare feet and uncombed hair, but his hostess took no notice. Sitting opposite of where he'd seen her sit, he saw with pleasant surprise that she'd made muffins. McKay spoke when Pup joined him at the table.

"I don't wish to be presumptuous, but would you mind if I returned grace?"

"No."

Her tone didn't indicate any emotion, so taking her at her word, McKay bowed his head.

"Heavenly Father, I thank You for this day. I thank You for Callie's hard work on the meal and for the care she has given me. I thank You for the food she prepared. I ask You to bless us this evening and protect us through the night. Amen."

"Amen," Pup agreed softly, and then passed the bowl of rabbit stew to her guest.

They dished up in silence, but soon McKay commented, "My mother makes rabbit stew. It's my father's favorite."

"It's tastier than squirrel."

"I think so, too."

"Do you want coffee or water?"

"I think water."

Pup rose and brought him a glass.

"Thank you."

She didn't reply to this, and all other attempts at conversation fell flat. She would look at him when he spoke and answer if he asked a direct question, but she offered little if anything of her own. McKay resigned himself to eating in silence just as he bit into his second muffin. With the food still in his mouth, a shudder went all through his body. Pup noticed and stopped eating.

"Are you in pain?"

McKay pulled the muffin away from his lips. Hanging from the muffin was most of an eggshell. Pup scowled at it.

"I wondered where that went," she said blandly before passing him the basket so he could take another.

McKay shook his head no and forced himself to chew what was in his mouth. The crackle of shell was a bit hard to take, but he chased it all down with water. The drink made him feel slightly better, but another little piece in his teeth caused a second shudder.

He wondered when he would stop being surprised by Callie Jennings. While he was still laid up in bed and even resting on the sofa, she had tripped and nearly fallen on him several times. It was not at all unusual for her to stumble and empty half his water or coffee into his plate when she was bringing him a meal. She often bumped him with her arm, hitting him once in the eye and on the nose and several times on the chin: All things his mother would have begged forgiveness for. Callie Jennings never said a word.

He could honestly say he'd never met anyone like her. With this feeling came more pity. Maybe he shouldn't pity her—after all, she did have a friend in Mud, and Govern had obviously cared enough to come back to her once in a while. But her oddities, her solitude, her silence, and the whole situation wrung his heart in pity.

"I've got berries again. Are you interested?"

"That sounds good, thank you."

She brought a small bowl of blackberries to the table and set it between them. She had sweetened them with a bit of sugar, and they were very tasty. Between the two of them they finished the bowl.

"That was delicious."

Pup only nodded and stood to work on the dishes. Having decided to help her, McKay stood as well, but things spun a little when he was on his feet. He gripped the edge of the table for a moment and then looked up to find Pup's eyes on him.

"I can get the dishes. Do you want help to the sofa or bedroom?"

"The sofa."

He tried not to lean too heavily on her as they moved, but he was feeling rather weak. It was a relief when he was able to sink down into the cushions.

"You want your Bible?" Pup surprised him by asking.

"Yes, please," McKay said softly, his heart amazed. He thanked her when she handed it to him and then had a long, silent talk with the Lord. He wouldn't have believed that she even noticed. He'd been looking for an opportunity to talk to her about his faith but had given up on finding one.

I didn't ask believing, Lord. I wanted to, but didn't think there would be a way. You love Callie Jennings as much as You love all of us. If You want me to talk to her, Lord, just open the door.

Three days later, and exactly three weeks since he'd been shot, McKay turned another corner. He could still feel that ache in his shoulder and some stiffness in his limbs, but he knew by bedtime that he was well enough to ride back to Boulder. In fact, when he finally climbed into bed, he didn't immediately fall asleep. Darkness had descended, but he was not that tired. This, too, told him he was ready to go. He had ventured only to the porch and into the front yard on his own, but he knew it was time. He was prepared to take it easy, even sleep a few nights in the hills if need be, but tomorrow he would get a nice early start back to Boulder.

It was during all of these plans that McKay heard the noise. At first he thought it was in the cabin but then quickly realized it was outside. Immediate concern for Pup sprang into his mind and he reached for his pants. He ignored his shirt but swiftly pulled on his boots. The cabin was completely dark, but the moon shining into Pup's bedroom illumined it enough to tell him the bed was empty. He made his way to the door. He was no more than outside when he heard a splash.

Although McKay had never been around the back of the cabin, he swiftly circled the log structure in the direction he'd heard the noise. The moon was nearing full so he was able to move through the trees with some light for his path. He came out in a clear spot that gave him a good view of the lake and stopped. Not 30 seconds later he watched someone, presumably Pup, come from the water. He stared as she reached with one hand toward her face. With the moon at her back he couldn't make out any of her features, but the image of long limbs danced before his eyes. Just a heartbeat later he spun away.

Pup heard the popping of a twig and spoke. "Is that you, McKay?"

"Yes, it's me!" he sounded testy. "What are you doing out here with no clothes on?" he demanded.

"Taking a bath in the lake like I do every night."

"That's ridiculous!" he told her bluntly, his back still turned, his heart pounding. "You don't even know me. I might have attacked you."

There was silence for a moment, and when Pup spoke it was clear that she'd moved closer.

"I don't think you're the type of man to attack a woman, McKay," she said reasonably, and then added with maddening calm, "and if you did, I'd just shoot you."

McKay didn't hear anything after that but chanced a peek over his shoulder. Pup was moving away from him now toward the cabin. She had wrapped some sort of light-colored robe around her and sure enough, her rifle was held in one hand.

McKay turned and followed slowly. The last naked female he'd seen had been his sister. If memory served him correctly, they'd been taking a bath together. He'd been ten and she was five.

He walked into the cabin, moving slowly since it was darker in there. Pup's door was shut, but there was a slight glow coming from underneath. McKay went back to his room and slipped into bed. He felt incapable of normal thought. His mind was blank as to what to think, yet it swarmed with various notions. It was a long time before he actually fell asleep.

McKay's plans to rise early did not go exactly as he'd hoped. The sun was well into the sky by the time he had shaved, dressed, and readied to hit the trail. He found that Pup had left breakfast for him, but she was nowhere in sight. He knew what horrible regret he would feel if he had to leave without seeing her, but he made himself stay calm. If she were gone, he could leave her a note. He wondered if it would be insulting to pay her. The thought had no more formed when he pushed it away. He filled a plate with the food she'd left on the stove and sat down to eat.

He didn't want to gulp his food, but a certain excitement filled him. It was good to be headed out again. Never had he been out of circulation for three weeks, and it would be longer than that by the time he reached Denver, his ultimate destination.

His food gone, McKay made his bed, straightened his room, and gathered his gear. Leaving everything on the front porch, he went in search of Pup. He didn't think she'd left, but he still couldn't find her. His rented horse and saddle were in the small stable. He saddled his mount and led him into the morning sun. It was then that he spotted her. He tied the horse's reins to a post in front of the stable and walked over to where she was hanging clothes.

"Headed out?" She was the first to speak.

"Yes. Thank you for everything."

"You're welcome."

They looked at each other for a moment, and then knowing he had to say something more, McKay said, "I'm sorry about Govern, Callie. I wish it could have been different."

"He made his choices, McKay."

She was so matter-of-fact, so forgiving, but McKay still felt awful. He was glancing around, trying to think of what to say next, when he spotted the cross. Beyond the ropes she hung clothes on and at the base of some thick pines stood a white cross, its paint faded and chipping. Without a word to Pup, McKay walked toward it.

A scant 20 paces took him to the foot of three graves. Two of them had engraved stones: *Davis J. Hackett 1826–1865. Anne M. Hackett 1829–1872.* The third grave was fresh, obviously belonging to Govern.

McKay found his heart asking why it never occurred to him that Callie herself had been forced to bury this man. Why had it also never occurred to him that this was Govern's family home? With all the risks Govern had taken, he could have been gunned down anywhere in Colorado, but he died here and was buried with his parents.

It wasn't until that moment that McKay realized Pup had come to stand beside him. He turned and looked at her. She was tall, only a few inches shorter than he was, and she held her slim frame very straight as she looked down at the graves. As he expected, her face was unreadable.

"I am sorry that you had to go through all of this, Callie."

"I know," she agreed simply, her eyes still on the ground. "But it's good that he's buried here with Mama and Papa."

She looked at him then, and, not surprisingly, found dozens of questions in his eyes.

"He was my brother," she said simply, watching emotions chase across McKay's face. He opened his mouth, but Pup cut him off.

"Take care of yourself, McKay," she said simply, and turned and walked away. She moved past her laundry, then the stable, and disappeared into the trees. McKay could have followed her, but it was obvious that she wanted to be alone. There were so many questions he wanted to ask, so many more things he wanted to say, but she'd walked away.

McKay's eyes dropped to the graves once again.

These people are dead and gone, Lord, but Callie and I are still here. We both need Your comfort and strength. Help us through this time and in the days to come.

McKay turned for his horse. He was back at the porch just a minute later and loading his gear. There was no sign of Callie, and there was nothing else to do but ride away.

9

Denver

"Mr. Crawford is here to see you, Mr. Wallace."

"Send him in, Paine."

"Do you want me to stay, sir?"

Nick Wallace was not put off by the question. His chief aide, Paine Whitter, often stayed to take notes and track down files, but this time Nick shook his head.

"I think we'll be fine, Paine. Thank you."

"Very good, sir. I'll send Mr. Crawford right in."

The heavy oak door closed, and Nick had a moment to think. He hoped that Carlyle was here about McKay. They could have sent a man to gather all the information McKay had compiled, but when he'd discussed it with Carlyle, they had decided to wait for McKay's return. Once they'd heard from Travis Buchanan, they knew it was only a matter of time. Nick now hoped that the time was at hand.

There was a brief knock and the door opened.

"Have a seat, Carlyle," Nick spoke as soon as his coworker was in the room, the door closed behind him. "You have news?"

"Yes. McKay is back. He should be here in about 15 minutes."

"Good. You know that I trust you with this operation, Carlyle, but it might be helpful to me if I can hear McKay's story personally."

"I think that's a good idea. I won't question him on my own. I'll let you know as soon as he arrives."

"You can come in here, or we can meet in your office."

"I think we'll have more privacy in here, Nick."

"Good. I'll expect you within the half hour."

Carlyle left Nick's office, marveling not for the first time over what an excellent manager Nick was. Nick Wallace was Carlyle's superior, but as long as Carlyle got the job done, he was left on his own. Only twice in the last ten years had the older man pulled rank on Carlyle. The result had been so satisfying that Carlyle had never held harsh feelings. In truth, Nick was so good that whenever he got involved, the job would be wrapped up to everyone's satisfaction.

Now was another such case. The investigation involving the Hackett brothers and their possible lead to Duncan Phipps, a man who'd been successfully embezzling funds for years, was near and dear to Nick's heart. He wanted to be in on this one, and the operation could only benefit from his input.

Carlyle was back in his office for just a few minutes when a shadow filled his doorway. He looked up into Harrington's face.

"McKay." Carlyle said the name softly as relief flooded him. He stood and moved to the door, waiting for McKay to enter so he could shut it behind him.

"Are you all right?" the older man asked.

"Yes."

"You're thinner."

"But I'm alive." McKay smiled, and the men shook hands.

Carlyle felt oddly moved. This man was special, and his heart knew it. This agent was the cream of the crop. Loyal, street smart, and hardworking, McKay Harrington's integrity was unbeatable.

"Nick and I want to hear all about it. Are you up to the telling?"

"Certainly."

It came as a surprise to McKay that the top man was going to be so closely involved, but every inch a professional, he nodded and obediently followed Carlyle from the room. The offices were only a few feet apart, so it was literally seconds later that he was shaking Nick Wallace's hand and being motioned to a comfortable chair.

Nick's office was large—large enough to hold his desk and several chairs. A small carpeted area sported a sofa, an overstuffed chair, and a small table. McKay was directed to the upholstered chair, and the two older men sat on the sofa facing him. He knew they wanted to know everything.

"The first thing I want to know, McKay, is if you should be here." Nick wasted no time.

"I'm fine, sir. To tell you the truth, I've been back since late Thursday night. I was too exhausted to move or contact anyone, so I took the whole weekend and yesterday to rest. I'm not back to 100 percent, but I'm feeling stronger all the time."

"Good. If you need to be excused, we understand."

"I should be fine."

"Very well. Can you tell us your story?"

"Yes, sir. I went to Boulder as directed and contacted Travis Buchanan. He came to see me on Saturday the twentieth, but our conversation was brief."

"You wired me about that," Carlyle reminded him.

"Of course, sir. I'd forgotten. Well, I was going to see him again on Monday, but your telegram arrived." McKay was looking at Carlyle as he said this. "When I read that Govern was back in the area, I had to try to find him. I moved swiftly, and it paid off. I picked up his trail right away on Monday and tracked him into the hills for the rest of the day. I lost him just before dark, but it was as you said: He lived much higher up than we expected. At daybreak I picked up his trail again and tracked him right to a cabin tucked into the woods.

"I heard shouting and knew there was someone else inside, so I stepped into the clearing and called to him. A woman was out front and I spoke to her, but only briefly, before the first shots were fired. I shot back and dove for cover but was hit in the upper chest. The shots died down, and I knew if I didn't get help I would die. I figured I had nothing to lose by coming out.

"The next thing I remember is waking up and seeing this woman standing over me. I tried to talk to her, but I'd lost a lot of blood and she kept fading in and out."

"Who was this woman?" Nick wanted to know.

"Her name is Callie Jennings," McKay said, watching Nick's face.

"Callie Jennings?"

"Yes, sir. Have you heard of her?"

"As a matter of fact I have," Nick said quietly. "Can you tell us any more?"

"Well, I was there for three weeks. Much of the first week I didn't have any idea where I'd been, but Callie told me I'd shot and killed Govern, and that I'd been shot myself. She said she took the bullet out and that I'd lost a lot of blood."

"This woman took the bullet out for you?" Carlyle was amazed.

"Yes. I think she thought I was going to die anyway."

"And you're certain Hackett is dead?" This came from Nick.

"Yes, sir. I saw the grave, and if he'd been alive when I stepped back into view, I wouldn't be here."

Nick nodded, his face serious.

"What is it, Nick?" Carlyle wanted to know.

Nick raised his brows for a moment, but he didn't answer the other man. "McKay" he began, "I couldn't be more pleased that you're still with us, but it's ironic." Both of the other men were staring at him, so he continued. "I have a name over on my desk. I was going to give it to you, Carlyle, as soon as McKay came back."

"McKay's contact for Boulder?" Carlyle guessed.

"That's it," Nick told him.

"Let me guess," Carlyle now said, completely missing the way McKay's body was tensing. "Callie Jennings is the contact for McKay."

"You got it. I find it interesting that . . ."

"It's not the same woman." McKay's voice was flat, and the men on the sofa both turned to him.

"She doesn't seem the type," Nick began, even as countless questions came to mind, "but I assure you, McKay, she's—"

"I tell you it's not the same woman." McKay cut him off, his face set in disbelief.

"McKay," Nick's voice grew a bit stern now, "if you'll just let me explain."

"No." he defied a superior for the first time in his career. "It's not that unusual of a name. I tell you it's not the same woman! I tell you you're wrong." McKay had come to his feet now and so had Carlyle.

"*McKay!*" Carlyle's voice was a lash, and the younger man started almost violently.

"Sit down," he said gently now. "You know better than to think Nick and I would play games with you, especially after what you've just been through. Now sit down and listen."

Nick's eyes were compassionate when McKay sat back down, but his voice was all business. He wasted no time in laying down the facts.

"Callie Jennings, who goes by the nickname Pup, is an agent for the treasury department."

The color had drained away from McKay's face, but he remained quiet.

"It's clear to me that Pup didn't tell you anything, McKay. Is that right?"

The younger man shook his head yes, his heart still convinced that they had the wrong woman.

"I need to start by telling you that Carlyle is not privy to this information. Not even Paine is aware of what I'm about to reveal to you." Nick paused, not for drama, but because Pup had been such a well-kept secret; it had become something of a habit not to talk about her. "Pup has worked for me for years, and most often as a man. Carlyle met her one time when she was going by the name Peter Crandall."

"I remember him," Carlyle said with surprise. "Or I guess I should say her."

McKay felt like the conversation was spinning out of control. Nick Wallace, a man he'd always admired and respected, was talking nonsense, and Carlyle Crawford was agreeing with him. Callie Jennings an agent? Ridiculous. Inconceivable.

"She doesn't seem like the type, McKay," Nick continued, "but as you well know, it's the one you least expect."

"She set a towel on fire," McKay said dully.

"I don't doubt it." Nick's voice was still kind, but his voice also took on a note of pride. "McKay, she's the best I've got."

McKay shook his head as if to clear it. "How?" he managed. "How did this all get started? How did you find her?"

"She found me," he said simply. "She was in my regiment during the war."

"The Civil War?" McKay's voice had dropped to a whisper.

"Yes. Posing as a man. She was the best aide I had."

The younger man's eyes closed. The way she'd dressed his wound now came flooding back to him. But the war was 13 years ago!

"How old is she?"

"Twenty-eight."

"But then she must have been—"

"Just 16 when she began working for the treasury," Nick supplied. He fell quiet, giving the younger man time to adjust.

It wasn't hard to guess what the last three weeks must have been like for him. If Pup was told not to reveal something, she would take it to her grave. She must have heard of McKay Harrington but would not have felt free to talk to him.

Nick had to suddenly stop himself from smiling. As surprised as he was to hear McKay report, he realized what the agent had just said about the towel. It was a miracle Pup didn't burn the whole cabin down.

"It's just so unbelievable." McKay was still stunned.

"She's the reason you were told to contact Travis Buchanan," Nick added. "She's lived in the area for years and recommended him for information and a possible safe house."

"She must have known exactly who I was." McKay's voice was filled with wonder.

"I'm certain she did, but as I said, she wouldn't talk without permission."

They fell silent then, and Carlyle, closer to McKay than Nick was, took in the strain around his mouth and his pale complexion. He needed to get McKay out of here if he could.

"Is that about everything, McKay?" Carlyle asked, giving Nick plenty of time to say he had more questions.

The younger man dragged his mind back to the business at hand.

"Just about," he said quietly. Looking into their faces, he saw that they were both serious about Callie, and he needed to take it seriously as well.

"I know we'll both have other questions," Carlyle also added, "but right now you can go and start your report."

"All right." McKay stood slowly, his mind busy. "She really works for you?" He couldn't help but ask Nick one more time.

"Yes, she does."

McKay took a deep breath. "You haven't asked me why Callie was at that cabin with Govern, but I think I'd better tell you one more thing."

"What's that?"

"Callie Jennings is Govern Hackett's sister."

The shoe was suddenly on the other foot. McKay had not planned to get the upper hand, but he now knew what his own face must have looked like just a few minutes past. McKay had been on his feet to leave, but as it was he didn't get out of Nick's office for another hour.

79

10

"Do I start my speech now or later?" Camille Wallace asked Pup as she ushered her into a bedroom upstairs in the home she shared with Nick.

"I take it we're in a hurry?"

"I'm not," Camille stated firmly. "It's Nick."

"I wouldn't have even gotten word, Camille, if a neighbor hadn't brought my mail from town," Pup said after she'd taken a seat before a large mirror. "I wasn't planning to head into Boulder for another week."

"Then Nick probably would have come after you himself. As he likes to put it, he's got *a live one*."

"What am I going to be doing?"

Nick's wife didn't answer until she'd put a sheet around Pup's slim form and had her positioned in front of the mirror the way she wanted.

"I believe you're going to be a clerk. I don't know why you can't go as a woman," she muttered at the end.

"Yes, you do." Pup had heard her. "The last time I tried that the padding kept slipping down the front of my dress. It's hard to remember you're supposed to have a British accent and answer to the name Lottie, when your breasts keep falling down around your stomach."

Camille couldn't keep from smiling, but it wasn't long before she was frowning again.

Pup caught her eye in the mirror. "Putting it off isn't going to make it go away," she said logically.

"Oh, Callie." She never called her Pup. "Most women would kill for the black curls I'm about to chop off your head. I hate doing this."

"It's just part of the job, Camille." This was Pup's standard line, but as usual her logic brought a grimace to Camille's face. Still, the older woman began to cut.

Pup hadn't been on a job for many months, so her curls were longer than they had been in quite a while. It would have taken many years of growth before they hung to her shoulders, but Camille thought the way they curled around her temples and jawline was so pretty. She'd never had a daughter of her own, and so she longed to put some finishing touches on Pup. The fact that she'd never been allowed to was always a frustration to her. The few times that Pup had gone out as a woman she'd been a saloon girl. It had been more fun to see her in a dress, but red cheeks and fake beauty marks were not the touches Camille had in mind.

"Do you expect Nick soon?" Pup asked as snips of hair dropped into her lap.

"No. If you'd gotten in this morning I'd have sent word. He'll probably be home at the usual time."

Pup's mind went to McKay. It was a temptation to ask Camille if he'd gotten back safely, but the older woman probably wouldn't know. Pup had also come to learn that she mustn't show too much interest in any one man. Camille was always on the lookout for a match.

"How short should I go?"

"I don't know. Just about the time you shear me, the job will wrap up in a few weeks."

"Are you saying I should leave it longer?" Camille asked in surprise.

"No." Pup was still logical. "I have to look like a man even if I only pose as one for a day."

Pup heard Camille sigh but didn't comment. Her mind had slid to McKay, then to her brother, and back to McKay. She was once again lost in thought when she heard a man's voice on the floor below.

"Camie!" Nick's voice boomed.

"Upstairs." She'd stepped to the door, called down the hall, and then come back to Pup's hair. She was trimming Pup's neckline, her face intent on her task, when her husband walked into the room. Nick stood beside her, his serious eyes catching Pup's in the mirror.

"I would say hello, Callie," his voice had an edge to it, "but that's probably not the right name, is it?"

Pup met his look straight on and said softly, "Games, Nick? I'd have thought better of you." With that she dropped her eyes back to the mirror and did not look up again. It was good to know that McKay must have made it back safely, but with the way Nick had just treated her, it was little comfort.

Pup could hear Nick moving around now. Camille wisely remained silent. Pup's peripheral vision caught the way he pulled a chair close to the side of the mirrored dresser and sat looking at her, but she kept her eyes locked on Camille's hands.

"I'm sorry, Pup." Nick's voice was soft and contrite.

She glanced over at him and couldn't look away.

"I think I can guess why you kept your true identity from me, but I'd like to hear it from you."

It was not a request she could deny, and in truth she had no desire to do so. While Camille worked, she began.

"When I came back to you that day, Nick, my mother was still alive. My father had been dead only a few months and she was still in deep grief. The name Peter Crandall couldn't hurt her, and neither could the name Callie Jennings. Those names had no tie to her. Young as he was, Govern had taken off by then, wounding her even more. Jubal was still at home but starting to turn wild. I had to think of my mother. I had to keep my privacy."

"But you had to have known that I've been tracking the Hackett brothers for years, Pup. Do you know some of the things they've done?" Nick's eyes pleaded with her to help him understand.

"Yes, I do know," Pup said sadly. "And I certainly did know that you were after them. But family is family. If knowing who I am means you expect help in finding Jubal, then I haven't made myself clear."

"But you know where he is?"

"As a matter of fact, I don't," she told him honestly. "But even if I did, I wouldn't tell you. If that's what you now expect of me, I'll tender my resignation, effective immediately."

Nick swiftly shook his head no. "I don't expect that, Pup. Please believe me. The last thing I want is for you to leave. I'm just coming to terms with your tie-in to the Hackett brothers. That's all this is about—my trying to understand."

"All right," she said with relief.

Nick glanced up at Camille just then, and his eyes filled with concern. Pup followed his gaze and found Camille's tragic eyes on her.

"Your brother is dead, Callie?" she whispered.

"Yeah." Pup's voice was soft as well. "I didn't know how to tell you."

Tears filled Camille's eyes, and as Pup turned to her, she wrapped her arms around the younger woman. For the first time since Govern showed up at the cabin, Pup felt free to cry. She hadn't cried as she cleaned his blood from the floor and the rug or when she'd had little choice but to drag his wrapped body to the hole she'd dug. She hadn't cried as she looked down at his fresh grave or thought about the awful life he had led and how he'd broken their mother's heart. She didn't cry as she cared for McKay, thinking many times that Govern had taken yet one more life just minutes before his own had ended. But here, with the only woman she'd been close to since her mother died, she was able to let down.

Nick did not shy away from this show of emotion. He adored his opinionated wife, and Pup was utterly dear to him. He waited until the worst of it was over and then offered his handkerchief. Camille had one, so Pup took his and blew her small, straight nose.

"Better?" he asked both of them. They nodded.

"Your name's not Callie Jennings?" Camille asked, her handkerchief still near her wet eyes.

Pup shook her head no.

"What is your name?" Nick asked, his voice so dry that Pup wanted to laugh.

"Andrea May Hackett."

"Are there any more of you?"

"Hacketts? No. I'm the oldest and Jubal is the youngest. It was just the three of us."

Nick didn't think twice about not believing her. Her name was the only thing she hadn't come clean about in all these years.

"Andrea May." He rolled the name off his tongue.

"Yeah."

"Do you want to be called that now?"

Pup thought about it. "I don't think so, Nick. My mother called me that name. She was the only one since I was Pup to Papa and the boys." Her voice turned very soft now. "I think I'll save Andrea for my mother."

Camille's eyes filled all over again, and even Nick's throat went tight. He cleared it several times before he spoke.

"Are you about finished, Camie?"

"Almost," she answered, seeming relieved to get back to normal footing.

"Good. I want to talk things over during dinner."

"Very well."

"Am I headed out in the morning?" Pup wanted to know as the curls began to fall again.

"If we can finish your briefing tonight. You can show up any time this week and still have the job."

"Camille said it was a clerk's job."

"Yes, but it's special. You'll be in Duncan Phipps' bank."

Pup smiled. She knew the name well. Nick had wanted to get a handle on this successful but shady bank owner for a long time.

"Am I gathering information or going for broke?"

"I'm not sending you in there to make an arrest if that's what you mean, but if it comes to that I'll welcome it. As you know, the evidence has got to stick."

Pup didn't do anything more than nod, but her eyes were still on her boss. There was a gleam in Nick's eyes that Pup had seen before. It was as Camille had said; he believed he had a live one.

"You'll be in a boardinghouse this time," Nick said between bites of food.

An unreadable look came over Pup's face upon this announcement, and Nick, who was drinking water from a crystal goblet, knew from experience that she was thinking. She had seemed herself through the meal, spilling her own water once and dropping her knife a few times, but now the mask had dropped over her face. It was all too easy to imagine this was the only face McKay Harrington had seen. Pup would not have felt free to be herself with McKay. The fact that she'd lit a towel on fire told Nick that she'd been partially herself, but her silence could unnerve a man. Nick knew this firsthand.

"Talk to me, Pup," he said at last.

"I'm sure you're not asking me to share a room, Nick, but when do I let down? If I can't even eat my meals alone, when do I get to relax?"

Nick knew in that instant that he'd taken her for granted. She was so good at what she did—so good at stepping into a role and never slipping, at looking innocent or even dull-witted when things got hot or she was questioned—that sometimes he forgot that it was all pretense. She did need time on her own. People couldn't pretend forever. If they could, the treasury department would never catch anyone.

"I'm sorry about this, Pup. I had Paine set it up," Nick said thoughtfully. "I was busy with something else and just told him we needed a place for a new man. It's my fault for not handling it and, again, I'm sorry. However, I don't think it will be too bad. If my memory serves me correctly, you're boarding with a mature woman who rents five rooms; she stays in the sixth. I think you're on your own for breakfast and at noon, but you eat dinner together. It's all men, so you don't need to worry about anyone proposing to you again."

Pup's shoulders shook with silent laughter. It was funny now that it was two years past, but it had been no laughing matter when a woman who was employed next door to the bank where she was working as a male clerk fell for her and proposed. The woman had been heartbroken, and Pup had been ready to give up spying forever.

"What about the proprietress herself?"

"I think everything is aboveboard, but until I find out, you'll stay put. Are you clear on the job itself?"

"Yes. Did you say that you'd told Paine it was for a new man?"

"Yes."

"Good. I don't want to go in as Peter Crandall this time."

This got Camille's attention. As much as she hated to see Pup's hair cut, she was intrigued by what the younger woman did. She leaned across the table slightly and said, "Whom are you going as?"

Pup thought for a moment. "What do you think of the name Daniels—Bryan Daniels?"

"I like it," Camille said firmly, looking at her spouse, her eyes almost daring him to disagree.

Nick grinned at her before saying to Pup, "Where did you come up with that one?"

87

"I don't know, but if I have to share even partial lodgings with someone else, I can't go as Peter Crandall."

"Why not?" Nick was still not catching on.

"Because Peter's lived in this town before. I need to act differently this time. If I come across someone who recognizes the name Peter Crandall, I'll fall under scrutiny. Bryan Daniels is new in town, he's from the East, and no one's ever heard of him or seen him before."

"What are you going to do to make yourself look different?" This came from Camille.

"Those thick-rimmed glasses should do it, and I found some flashier vests the last time I was out; Peter always dresses in such dull colors."

Sitting quietly now, Nick knew this was one of the reasons he took her for granted. It had never been necessary to tell Pup what angle to take. She had been play-acting when he met her, so any advice he might try to give would have been pure foolishness.

"Any problems?" Pup had been watching Nick's face.

"No," he said honestly, "I'll let you go to it. Plan to visit here at least twice a week, preferably in the evening. You know which door to use."

Pup nodded and smiled at Miranda, the Wallace's cook and housekeeper, as she set a piece of pie in front of her.

"It's nice to see you again, Mr. Crandall."

"Thank you, Miranda, it's nice to be here."

There was no way the loyal Miranda couldn't have known who she was. She'd been cleaning Pup's room upstairs for years, the room that held her regular dresses along with a dozen costumes, some of which included beards and wigs. But she never greeted her as anyone except who she looked like. And since her hair was already cut, Pup had been forced to dress as Peter Crandall before coming downstairs. It wasn't a problem for her really, since mentally she was already starting to fall into the role of Bryan Daniels.

Andrea Hackett, alias Peter Crandall, alias Callie Jennings, alias Bryan Daniels, could have probably enjoyed a successful life on the stage. Instead she was an agent for the treasury department of the United States of America. She could honestly say that there was very little about it that she didn't enjoy. In fact as she was finishing a wonderful meal and contemplating sleeping in a comfortable bed tonight, she couldn't name a thing.

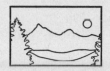

11

You can talk to McKay had been some of Nick's last words to her that afternoon. She hadn't known exactly what he meant and hadn't taken time to question him, but now it was all too clear. Standing in the foyer area of Mrs. Meyer's Boarding Home for Gentlemen, Pup could see McKay at the dining table. Hoping he wouldn't notice her, she turned slightly away and waited for Mrs. Meyer to return with the key.

"Now then, Mr. Daniels," she said as she suddenly appeared. "We've just sat down to dinner. Would you care to join us?"

"N-no th-thank you, ma'am," Pup stuttered. "I'll j-just go to m-my r-room."

"Of course," she smiled kindly. "You must be tired after your train trip. You can meet the other gentlemen tomorrow night."

"Th-thank you," Pup said with a smile, and followed her a short way down the hall and up the stairs. She was careful to keep her face averted as she passed out of view of the dining room. McKay was going to see her—it was only a matter of time—but she wasn't prepared. There was no way she could hope to go unrecognized—after all, he'd spent three weeks in her home. But this was her first day out as Bryan Daniels, and Pup thought it might be easier for her if it could wait even one day. She started at the bank in the morning; she would be ready by tomorrow night.

"Here we are," Mrs. Meyer said as they stopped before a door at the far end of the upstairs hall. Pup snapped her mind back to attention as Mrs. Meyer used the key and showed her into a nicely furnished bedroom. Pup took a swift glance back out to the hall and saw a closed door across from hers before turning her attention to her own room. The room had two windows with simple blue curtains, a full bed with a wooden headboard and a thick quilt, a washstand, a tiny stove that vented out the roof, an oak dresser, and a small writing desk and chair. Pup was pleased with the overall effect.

"Now, Mr. Daniels," Mrs. Meyer was saying, "this room is 25 cents more a week because of the stove. Did you understand that when you read the advertisement?"

Pup nodded.

"I collect the rent every Monday evening. You can leave it on your dresser if you're out. I clean this room on Wednesdays. I *never* go through my boarders' possessions. Your things are always safe here. Does that meet with your approval, Mr. Daniels?"

"Yes, m-ma'am. Th-thank you."

"Very well," she beamed at him. She wasn't a large woman—on the round side, but not what anyone would call heavy. Her face was unlined and there wasn't so much as a strand of gray in her hair. Her smile encompassed her whole face, and she seemed genuinely pleased that Bryan Daniels was moving in. "I'll leave you to settle," she turned toward the door, "and expect you tomorrow night for dinner."

"Yes, m-ma'am. Th-thank you, m-ma'am."

"Good night," she said cheerfully, going out the door and closing it behind her.

Pup turned in a full circle to see if she'd missed anything on the first look. It was a temptation to remove the glasses and *really* look around, but she had to get used to seeing through the clear glass in the frames.

The rug she was standing on was an even weave of blues, rust, and gold. It was clean and covered most of the floor. Pup walked toward one of the windows, her footsteps nicely muffled, and was relieved to see shades that could be pulled down on both windows. The windows looked out at another home much like Mrs. Meyer's. Pup opened the closet door and found it clean and empty, save for a dozen or so hangers. Her chest rose and fell with a satisfied sigh. The room was very nice, and so was Mrs. Meyer. The close proximity of the other rooms in the hall and the community dining table in the evening, however, were going to make for some adjustments. Ah, well—her heart was pragmatic as she began to unpack her bag. Another job had begun.

Mr. David Carrie jumped up the moment Mrs. Meyer came back into the room. The other four men watched as he helped her into her chair at the head of the table. It was plain to see that he was sweet on her, and that Mrs. Meyer enjoyed the attention in return.

"The new boarder's not joining us?" Mr. Ramsey, who also had a room upstairs, asked.

"Not tonight," Mrs. Meyer explained. "He wants to get settled in. I'm sure the train ride was tiring." She paused to take a sip of coffee. "He has the most dreadful stutter, poor dear. And not very old," she added as if this should make a difference.

Mrs. Meyer did not allow smoking or gossip in her dining room or parlor, but she felt so badly for the poor man upstairs that she had to mention his stutter. The men did not comment on this but continued with their meal. Not all of Mrs. Meyer's rules were easy to live by, such as no noise after 9 P.M. and no kitchen rights, but the cleanliness and the meal each evening were worth the rent and inconvenience.

"I've got chocolate cake," she announced a moment later. "Anyone interested?"

They all were, of course, and with pride she cut large slices and passed them around. McKay's was larger than the others.

"You're still a little thin, Mr. Harrington," she explained to him.

"Thank you," he said with a charming smile as he took the offered plate. "Considering the flavor of all your cakes, Mrs. Meyer, I won't refuse."

She dimpled at him, wishing not for the first time that he was 20 years older. In her opinion he was the best-looking of her boarders with his dark wavy hair; square, masculine jawline; and broad shoulders. She suspected he had a girl back home in Longmont, but he never spoke of it.

Several weeks back he'd paid her double, explaining that he might be on a trip. When he'd been gone three weeks she began to worry, but someone from his office with the treasury department had come by and explained that he would be returning. The man had even paid Mr. Harrington's rent for the following two weeks. When he finally returned late last Thursday night, he'd been so thin and weak that she'd broken her rule about kitchen privileges, allowing him to come down on Friday and through the weekend to fix meals as he needed. Now he was filling out fast and had even gone back to work Tuesday. He was one of her quieter, cleaner boarders— *religious* is what Mr. Ramsey had called him. Mrs. Meyer didn't care what the reason was; she knew only she had no desire to lose him.

Ten minutes after Pup arrived at the First National Bank of Denver, she thought she had cut her hair for nothing. The head cashier, a Mr. Conway, had heard her stutter and looked at her with something akin to horror, but that was before she stuttered through an explanation of having applied for a job as a book clerk and not a teller. The relief on his face had been comical. By noon, however, he was singing the praises of Bryan Daniels.

With an amazing head for figures, Pup had worked over four different account books in the time it had taken their last clerk to do two. She stuttered painfully and acted rather shy when the big boss, Duncan Phipps, came near, but there was no criticizing the work she did.

She left the bank that evening wanting to give in to her fatigue, but she reminded herself that she had a role to play all the way through dinner. Not only that, she would see McKay—and not just see him but have to face his reaction to her as a man. That had never bothered her in the past, but then she'd never had the roles reversed this way. In the past she had been a man, telling someone she was really a woman. How would McKay react?

Pup remembered something so suddenly that she stopped in the street. How foolish of her! The department had set all of this up. Nick certainly would have told McKay that for a time she was going to be living in the same boardinghouse with him. He might even be assigned to the same bank. Pup's step was much lighter as she finished the walk to Meyer's. The other men were not a worry to her. Now McKay was put to rest as well.

$\backsim$

Boulder

The cabin looked the same. McKay didn't know why he thought it wouldn't, except that everything had changed in his mind—and that also meant the cabin. The second thing he noticed was that things were quiet, and he wondered if she were even around. He tied the horse's reins to a branch and started toward the steps. He'd gained only the first tier when the door opened.

"Mud!" McKay looked up with surprise. His mind briefly wondered if there might be more between Mud and Callie than it appeared.

"Hello, McKay."

"Hello." It was a temptation to ask what he was doing here, but McKay knew it was none of his business. "I'm looking for Callie. Is she around?"

"No. Rode out after I brought her the mail on Monday. She does that sometimes," he added absently.

McKay's disappointment knew no bounds. He had some things he wanted to say to Callie Jennings; he also had some questions.

"Will you be here when she gets back?"

"Only if Percy's still driving me crazy."

McKay nodded. "When you see her, tell her I stopped by, will you?"

"Sure. Sorry you missed her."

"Thanks, Mud."

McKay turned away. There was no reason to stay. He had asked Carlyle for an extra day on the weekend to visit his family, but on the train back to Boulder where he would catch his connection to Longmont, he realized he had to see Pup again. It had all been a waste of time. She wasn't there, and in his mind nothing was resolved. He realized that he was going to have to put the last month behind him. He couldn't keep chasing up this mountain, not even mentally, in search of a woman he hardly knew. McKay urged his mount down the mountain as swiftly as he dared. Suddenly he was eager to be home, eager to be with his family and off the job, at least for a couple of days.

~

Denver

"Welcome, Mr. Daniels," Mrs. Meyer beamed happily as Pup gained the dining room. "We're so glad you could join us."

"Th-thank you, m-ma'am." Pup's head bobbed as she got the words out, standing still in feigned awkwardness while waiting to be directed to a chair. Mrs. Meyer was standing behind her own chair as she began.

"You'll sit second down on my right, Mr. Daniels, but first I want you to meet the other boarders."

There had only been one man present, but as if by magic, two other men appeared at the door. They came to their seats as Pup stepped behind her own.

"Good evening, gentlemen," Mrs. Meyer greeted them warmly. "Now, Mr. Daniels, at the foot of the table is Mr. Paul Ramsey. His room is at the top of the stairs. Next to you is Mr. David Carrie, whose room is also upstairs. Across from you, second on my left is Mr. Claude Becker. His bedroom is on this level. The empty place first on my left is Mr. McKay Harrington. His room is directly across from yours. Mr. Harrington has gone home to see his family this weekend." The men all had brief nods or words of greeting for her, and Pup nodded to each one in turn.

The amenities out of the way, Mrs. Meyer moved to sit down. Mr. Carrie jumped over to assist her, and the meal was underway. It was a quiet group to start, but that was because everyone now concentrated on his plate. And Pup didn't blame them. The food was delicious.

Mrs. Meyer served fried chicken, golden and lightly breaded, muffins, and fresh butter. A large bowl of whipped potatoes adorned the table, along with bowls of applesauce, green beans, baby carrots, and sugared beets. Both coffee and water were already poured and waiting at each plate. Not until dessert was set on the table did conversation begin again. Pup had never in her life coaxed a cake to rise so high, but then Mrs. Meyer cut it and she saw that it had three layers. For a moment Pup forgot where she was. Mentally she was going over her own cake recipe in the cabin in the hills. She remembered to take her eyes from the cake and fall back into her role just in time to hear Claude Becker say, "Where'd you say you work, Mr. Daniels?"

"I w-work at th-the b-bank," Pup got out. "J-just s-started t-today," she added almost shyly, ducking her head afterward.

Not surprisingly, "Oh" was all she heard. Conversation picked up as Mrs. Meyer replenished the coffee cups, but nothing more was directed at Pup. This was exactly what she'd been hoping for, and she knew a sense of satisfaction that her plan was working so well. Tomorrow she would take some time for herself. She would head to the Wallaces' home and pamper herself with a long, hot bath.

"I don't know how I'm supposed to come in the evening, Nick," Pup said from behind the screen. "I have to eat with these people, and if I disappear two nights a week, I'm going to draw questions."

"All right," he conceded, "come when you can. Now what did you see at the bank?"

"Can't this wait until she's out of the tub, Nick?" Camille asked pointedly, staring at her husband.

"No." He stared right back and sat down on the edge of Pup's bed. "I need to know if other men are needed."

"She's not a man—" Camille began, but Pup jumped in to avoid an argument.

"It's a little early to tell, Nick, but all the books I checked yesterday were spotless."

"It's going to take some time for him to trust you."

"Do you want me to suggest anything or hint around?"

"No, last time one of my men did that, he got the case dismissed. I might have one of the men do a spot check. That would take all suspicion off you. I want you to hold off for right now. If he has another set of books, one that isn't readily available to the public, he'll eventually bring them out and pay you to stay quiet about them."

"And if he doesn't?"

Nick didn't reply. All his other undercover agents were men. He would leave any one of them on the job for months, sometimes close to a year, in order to gather the needed information. But Pup was different. He would never do anything to put her into immediate danger.

"Are you out there?" she asked when he remained so quiet.

"Yes, but I don't have an answer for you."

Pup wasn't certain how to reply, so she remained quiet. Camille had no such qualms.

"This girl is going to be water-logged if you don't get out of here, Nick."

"I'm going," he replied as he rose tiredly. "I still want to talk to you, Pup. Come down to the study when you're ready."

"All right."

Nick left the bedroom, and Camille poured another bucket of steaming water into Pup's tub. Pup sank a little deeper and thanked her hostess with a sigh. Nick wanted her in a hurry, she could tell by his voice, but she wouldn't know this luxury for at least another week. Pup picked up the soap. It wasn't as good as bathing in the lake at home, but right now Pup refused to be rushed.

12

McKay left the treasury office building on Monday morning and headed for a spot check at the First National Bank of Denver, but his mind was not on his work; it was on Brita Stuart. Her family had been invited to join his for a special outing on Saturday, and if eyes could be trusted, especially Brita's eyes, she was interested in him. Seeing interest in a woman's eyes was not unfamiliar to McKay, but not often did he feel interest in return.

In his mind the problem with getting involved with a woman was his job. He was on the road so much. Although based in Denver, his job took him elsewhere for a good part of every year. And there was always the possibility of danger; his shoulder was a good reminder of that. Could he really ask a woman to sit at home and wait for him, given the chance that he might not come home at all? The bank was looming before him, and he still had no answers. For now, he acknowledged to himself, maybe it was best he didn't. After all, he had a job to do that could possibly include days of pouring over account books—none of which had anything to do with the sweet and lovely Miss Stuart.

"Spot check!" Duncan Phipps growled in McKay's direction, but the treasury man only shrugged.

"Just doing my job, Mr. Phipps."

"I thought we put all this to rest two years ago."

"If you're referring to another check, Mr. Phipps, I wasn't involved in that. I assure you, this is strictly routine."

Duncan scowled at him, but McKay took little notice. Coming toward them was Callie Jennings. McKay's mind registered disbelief, but it was all too true. He'd gone up the mountain to find her, and here she was in Denver!

"M-Mr. Ph-Phipps, " McKay watched as she stopped beside the older man and stuttered painfully. "I c-can't f-find the b-books that g-go t-to those s-special r-reports. I've l-looked, b-but they're n-not th-there. D-do you w-want-" Pup went on, but McKay had shut down.

Nick had said she most often went out as a man, but nothing could have prepared him for what he saw. There were no curves anywhere. The rather fancy vest she wore in blue and red fell straight down the front of her chest. There was no definition of hips and McKay struggled to remember if she'd been this straight up and down in a dress. As she turned slightly he noticed a slight roundness to her seat, but even that wasn't feminine with the rest of her covered in men's clothing.

McKay suddenly caught the direction of his thoughts and dug his nails into the palm of his hand in order to snap his mind back.

Think of her as a man, McKay. She's a man right now. Wait for an introduction, and pull this off. There's no room for emotion here. You're a professional. Now act like one!

"Have you checked with Mr. Conway?"

"Y-yes, s-sir, b-but he w-was b-busy."

"All right. I'll look into it. Actually I'm glad you came by my office, Bryan," Duncan now said with an odd gleam in his eyes. "This is McKay Harrington from the treasury department. He'll be doing a spot check on our ledgers. Make yourself available to him for any questions he might have. I'll get back to you on the missing books. By the way, McKay," he now turned, his smile triumphant, "this is Bryan Daniels. You can ask him anything. He's new, but he knows all about our records."

Duncan turned back to Pup.

"Do *lots* of talking to McKay, here, Bryan. Tell him *everything* he'll need to know."

Duncan turned away, feeling he had scored a victory. He hated those arrogant auditors the treasury sent over. It was getting more and more difficult to gain the upper hand, but this time he'd done it. He thought as he walked away, *Spend a few hours with that stuttering Daniels fellow, McKay, and you'll be begging your boss to close this job fast.*

"It's n-nice t-to m-meet you, M-Mr. McK-Kay." Pup turned to McKay and held out her hand the moment Duncan moved around her to leave.

"It's Harrington," McKay corrected her automatically, his own professional cloak falling over him. "McKay Harrington."

"H-Harrington," she repeated, as though needing to memorize it. "I'm s-sorry, M-Mr. H-Harrington." She stared through the lenses, her gaze a bit vague. "Th-the b-books are th-this way, if you'll f-follow m-me."

McKay did as he was asked, his mind still telling him to treat her like a man. To him she was every inch a female, but he realized that none of these people—neither the bank employees nor the customers—had seen her as he had. She was not a woman just dripping with feminine curves and charm, but she *was* a woman, and he'd watched her work and live in rather familiar surroundings for three weeks. The sudden image of her coming from the water, a tall, black silhouette with slender limbs, flashed into his mind. He began to pray.

Help me, heavenly Father. I can't think of her that way, Lord, not now and not ever. We've got a job to do here. I have to treat her as I would Carlyle or Nick. No special treatment or eye contact.

"W-where d-did you w-want t-to s-start?" he suddenly heard Pup ask him.

"January 1875, I think," he answered quickly, naming a date over three years back. "I'll start there and let you know if I need anything else."

Pup found the account books for him, not hesitating to speak and explain things as she went. McKay had to force his eyes away from her mouth. He couldn't believe she could pull this off so well, and it was fascinating to watch her lips push the words out.

"Thank you," he spoke briefly, as he sat across the large table from her. They were in a partially secluded area, but Pup never gave him a moment of recognition. She immediately went back to the ledger she was working over, her eyes intent, her fingers moving fast as she checked column after column of figures. McKay did in fact have questions, and she answered them to the best of her ability, but several times she directed him to Duncan or Mr. Conway.

As lunchtime neared she told him she was going to the Brown Palace for lunch and asked if he would like to join her. McKay accepted without hesitation, but if he thought she invited him so they could be themselves, he was wrong. She was Bryan Daniels through the entire carriage ride over and all through the meal.

"Th-the c-coffee is g-good here" was the first thing she said. "M-Mr. Ph-Phipps and M-Mr. C-Conway eat here s-sometimes t-too."

McKay knew in an instant that he was going to have to go along with her.

"Do you think you're going to enjoy working at First National?" he asked.

"Y-yes. I l-like a-accounting. It's m-my b-best w-work."

McKay smiled a genuine smile, and Bryan Daniels smiled back at him. She was still in character, but McKay was not. She might be good with numbers, but math wasn't her best work. Never would he believe that after watching her all morning. As their food arrived he thought, as he often had in the cabin, that he'd never met anyone like her.

He was also aware of the fact that her manners were perfect. Not one drop of food went onto the front of her vest. Her water glass remained upright, and she didn't so much as brush against his feet with her own, although they nearly touched under the table. Nick had said with a great deal of pride that she was the best he had. McKay could see that it was all too true.

From inside his bedroom, McKay heard a man stutter in the hall that morning. Mrs. Meyer had come down after the new boarder arrived and said the man had a terrible stutter, but McKay had not caught on. Callie Jennings was standing behind a chair in Mrs. Meyer's dining room as if she'd been doing it all her life. McKay thought if he had one more surprise today he would go mad. Did she know that he lived here? When could she have moved in? He'd only been gone over the weekend. Was that enough time?

Of course it was, you fool, McKay castigated himself. *Now pay attention or all the work you did today will be destroyed.*

"It's nice to see you back, Mr. Harrington," Mrs. Meyer said sincerely. "How is your family?"

"Doing well, thank you, Mrs. Meyer."

"You haven't met our new boarder, Mr. Harrington—" the landlady began, but McKay cut in.

"Actually we have. My job took me to do a spot check at the First National today. I met Mr. Daniels when I was there."

McKay and Pup exchanged pleasant nods.

"How nice. Oh, there you are, Mr. Ramsey," she spoke as the last diner joined them. "Shall we begin?"

They sat down, and the dishes were passed. McKay ate and enjoyed the food, but his mind was clearly elsewhere. He didn't know when anyone so distracted him. He was aware of every move Pup made. Little conversation was directed toward her, but that was something she'd clearly orchestrated herself. The awful stutter and the shy way she ducked her head did not invite conversation.

The meal passed in something of a haze for McKay. He did join one conversation about a local minister, but for the most part he was content to listen and watch. Normally he went for a walk after dinner or headed up to his room to read or study his Bible. Tonight, however, as he watched Pup move toward the parlor with Mrs. Meyer and the other men, he joined them. Coffee was served and two of the men, Ramsey and Becker, went right to the chessboard that was set up on a table by the window.

Mrs. Meyer and Mr. Carrie began to discuss a book they had both read and enjoyed. McKay had heard about the book and asked a few questions, but he noticed Pup went for the newspaper and began to read. Conversation flowed around her, but she kept her eyes on the print. He saw a few compassionate glances from Mrs. Meyer, but she clearly understood that her newest boarder did not wish to talk.

It was just before nine o'clock when the chess game broke up. Paul Ramsey announced that he was off to bed, and everyone bid him goodnight. Not three minutes passed before Pup laid her paper aside and stood as well.

"Th-thank you f-for a p-pleasant evening, M-Mrs. M-Meyer."

"You're welcome, Mr. Daniels. Are you turning in?"

"Yes, m-ma'am. G-goodn-night, everyone."

"Goodnight," the room chorused, and McKay made himself sit still for a few more minutes. The temptation to bolt after his coworker was torture. Struggling for a picture of nonchalance, McKay eventually rose and said his own goodnights. He made himself take the stairs slowly, but there was no need. Pup was in the hall having a few words with Paul Ramsey. He forced himself to walk by them without a word and move to his own door. Once there he used the key, entered, and lit a lantern, but he left the door wide open.

He heard Pup tell Mr. Ramsey goodnight, but he was standing far enough back in the room so that Paul could not see him. He watched as Pup came to her door and reached to remove the key from her pocket. She never even looked in his direction. With a swift move he poked his head out and found the hall empty, save for Callie. Before Pup could even get her key to the lock, she was pulled backward into his room, the door was shut, and she found herself up against the wall. McKay Harrington leaned slightly over her, his hand still on her arm.

It occurred to Pup that the large, firm hand holding her no longer belonged to a weak, ill man, but she still looked unflinchingly into his eyes. A moment later the hand dropped, and she watched as he reached up and removed her glasses. She made no protest when he lobbed them carefully onto the bed and then turned back to her, his hand now on the wall near her head.

"Do you have any idea how sorry I was for you?" he asked softly when he was able to really see her dark eyes.

Pup shook her head no, and McKay continued in a hushed tone.

"I thought you were the most pitiful creature I'd ever seen—cut off from society, slow-witted, pathetic, and dreary. My heart ached with sadness for you."

Pup compressed her lips, but the sparkle in her eyes gave her away.

"Don't you dare laugh at this," he warned softly. "I'm angry with you."

He sounded so *un*angry that a full smile spread across Pup's mouth. Her eyes were still on him, and she watched as he took in her hair.

"Who cut your hair?"

"Camille Wallace always does."

He continued to study her, his eyes moving all over her features and then back to her eyes.

"Did you know I was going to be at the bank today?"

"No."

"And here, did you know I lived here?"

"Not until I walked through the front door last Thursday night."

McKay shook his head in amazement. "You were incredible today."

Pup shrugged, but she was pleased. "It's all part of the job."

"Nick says you're the best he's got."

Again she shrugged, but didn't look shy or deny the compliment.

"Were you really involved in the war?" He had to ask.

Nick had done more talking than Pup thought he ever would, but she still answered.

"Yes, I was very young and saw awful things. I don't think I would ever do it again."

"And that's how you met Nick?"

"I was his aide. It was fascinating, but like I said, not something I want to repeat."

"Why as a man, Callie?"

"You can't call me that, McKay. You can't think of me as a woman."

"But why as a man?" he persisted.

"You can look at me and ask me that?" she challenged softly.

McKay nodded his head. "Yes, I can. I don't think you look like a man."

"But everyone else does, and that's my job," she explained simply. "I'll tell you, McKay, people see what they want to see. Camille has been saying that for years. I don't look like a man. But people see the clothing and they don't really look any further. I don't have any facial hair, but many men don't have heavy beards." In a bold move she brushed a finger across the day-long stubble on his jaw. "You could never pass for a woman."

"Thank you," he said dryly, "I think."

Pup smiled cheekily at him, but his eyes were serious.

"I won't continue to bring this up, Callie, but I have to say it one more time. I'm sorry about your brother."

"Thank you, McKay. I know it wasn't malicious. You were doing your job."

He nodded and continued to study her.

"Speaking of jobs," he now asked, "how long will this one be?"

"I don't know. Nick wants Duncan. He wants him badly. I'll probably be here for a while. How about your end of it?"

"Just a few weeks. I went all the way back up the mountain looking for you," he said suddenly.

"You did? Why?"

"I had some things to say and some questions to ask. I still do."

Pup smiled, feeling completely in control of the situation.

"They'll have to wait," she said simply. "I'm tired and headed to bed."

"But you do understand that we're not done, don't you, Mr. Daniels?"

Pup ducked under his arm and went for her spectacles on the bed. When they were in place she glanced around the room.

"Did you hear what I said to you?" McKay tried again, but he was ignored. He watched as she grabbed the bar of soap from his washstand. Without warning she opened the door.

"Th-thank you f-for the s-soap, M-Mr. H-Harrington," she stammered, her voice back to normal level.

"That's my last bar," McKay hissed at her.

Pup took a swift peek into the hall. It was empty. She leaned toward him long enough to hiss back, "You should have thought of that before you dragged me in here."

With that she was gone. McKay stood in his room and watched her use her key in her lock and then slip inside. She glanced up at him just before the door shut, and he thought he caught a smile on her face.

McKay swung his own door closed. He stood for a long time thinking about their conversation. His head shook and a smile slowly formed. He didn't know what was going to happen next, but it was certainly going to be fun.

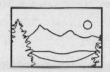

13

Pup worked hard the next two weeks, often with McKay directly across the table from her. On Friday of the second week, she was asked to lunch with Mr. Conway, something rather unusual if bank gossip could be believed. She went along and thought she caught some additional interest on his part. He questioned her extensively as to her background, in a very polite way of course, but Pup had seen this type of operation before and was not easily fooled. He was working up to ask her a favor—maybe not today, but soon.

She caught momentary looks of frustration over the way she struggled to express herself, but he was swift to recover his composure. This, more than anything else, told Pup he was after something. Indeed, by the time they left to return to the bank, he gave her a compliment she was supposed to take as high praise.

"I can see you're a real bank man, Daniels. There's a great future in this company if you know what I mean."

Pup stuttered out a thank-you as they exited the restaurant, and she looked shyly pleased as they drove back to work in the small carriage Mr. Conway had hired to take them across town. McKay was back at the table ahead of her, and she broke character for the first time in ten days of working together.

"Are you headed back to the office tonight?" she whispered, her eyes still on the figures in the book.

McKay was so surprised that he almost looked up.

"Yes," he whispered back, careful to keep his eyes on his own accounts.

"Get word to Nick that I'll be at the house tomorrow."

McKay opened his mouth to say something, but they were interrupted.

"Mr. Phipps would like to see you, Mr. Harrington."

"All right," McKay spoke and pushed his chair back. The clerk was waiting for him, so with only a glance at Pup's bent head he was forced to leave her alone.

~

"Nick is looking for you," Camille commented as she came into the bedroom the next morning.

"This water feels too good, Camille. Besides, I thought we were going to talk after lunch."

"I thought that was the plan, too, but now he's got a man down there."

"Oh," Pup had to think about this. "So do I go down as Peter Crandall or Bryan Daniels?"

"Why don't you go as Callie Jennings?" Mrs. Wallace asked with innocent eyes.

The sponge froze in Pup's hand. "Camille," she asked with great patience, "who is this man?"

"McKay Harrington." She became suddenly eager. "He's very good-looking."

"And he's already seen me in a dress, so there's no need to bother." She went back to soaping.

Camille dropped onto the edge of the bed as though a prize fish had just gotten away.

"When was this?" she demanded in a disappointed tone.

"When he got shot and had to live at my place in the hills for three weeks."

"That was McKay?"

"Um-hmm—" Pup said absently while lathering the length of one long leg. "I can't believe Nick didn't tell you."

"He told me it had happened, but not who it was. Are you sure you won't come as Callie?"

"I'm sure, but I am tired of the glasses, so warn Nick to call me Peter."

Camille sighed. It was no use. Pup's mind was always on the job. Her husband's top undercover agent simply had no desire to be attractive to men. McKay Harrington was so polite and handsome. And what could be more convenient than the two of them working for the treasury department? Again she sighed but decided to let the matter drop. If she didn't go now, she'd forget to tell Nick that Peter was arriving. She let herself out into the hallway, passing Miranda who was bringing more towels to Pup. Camille Wallace asked herself if there was another woman in all the state of Colorado whose life was quite like her own.

"Peter," Nick spoke the minute he saw Pup, "it's good to see you. Come on in. I think you met Carlyle Crawford a number of years ago." Nick paused while the two shook hands.

"It's good to see you, Mr. Crawford," Pup said.

"The pleasure is all mine, and please call me Carlyle," he said graciously, silently awed by her appearance. She looked like a finely dressed young man, tall and slim, ready for a day in the city. There was a smooth confidence about her that never even made him suspect it was a disguise.

"And this is McKay Harrington," Nick went on, a twinkle in his eye.

McKay was smiling as well. "I tried to tell Bryan yesterday that I would be here, but we were interrupted." He paused in order to give up the pretense. "And then you weren't at dinner last night."

Before answering McKay, Pup glanced at Carlyle to see if he had been informed. "No, I wasn't," she said. Then she readily admitted, "If I keep eating Mrs. Meyer's cooking, I'm not going to fit into any of my pants."

McKay smiled a little more, but then asked out of frank curiosity, "Where do you get your clothes?"

"Camille gets most of them for me, but I do shop for accessories."

"Something to drink, Pup?"

"No thank you, Nick," she said, taking a seat on the sofa. McKay declined a drink as well and sat opposite her. Carlyle and Nick took the chairs.

"Camie's planning to put a meal on the table in about 30 minutes, but I want to know what you've got," Nick began. "McKay mentioned that you'd gone to lunch with Conway. Any news?"

"He told me that I had a promising future if I could catch his meaning," Pup explained briefly. "I did, but all I said was thank you."

"He wasn't more specific?"

"No, but McKay was called into the office right after I got back. My guess is that they won't move on me until he's out of the way."

McKay's admiration for her grew. That was exactly why Duncan had called him into the office yesterday—to inquire in a not-so-sweet tone as to when the bank would be seeing the last of McKay Harrington.

"When can you finish up, McKay?"

"Two days, three at the most."

"Good." Nick looked satisfied. "Can you manage the boardinghouse a bit longer, Pup?"

"I think so. It would help if the man across the hall didn't snore."

"How do you know it's me?" McKay wished to know, his head turned to look at her.

"Because it didn't start until you returned from your weekend out of town."

McKay shook his head as though addressing a simple child, "I'll have you know, Miss Jennings, I never—"

"That's Mr. Crandall to you," Pup corrected him pertly, and back and forth they went.

Nick and Carlyle sat and stared in wonder at the two of them. At one point Nick looked up to see that Camille had come into the room. One look at her and he knew that she was observing the sparring couple as well.

"Lunch is ready," she announced, and although Nick was certain no one else noticed, he couldn't help but hear the smug tone in her voice. She would wait until everyone was gone before she would bring it up, but Camille definitely had something on her mind.

"Why didn't you tell me McKay was the one who got shot?" Camille had waited only until Nick was in the bedroom door. Their guests had been gone for hours, but still she waited for the end of the day. Now she was sitting in bed brushing her hair, clearly anticipating her husband's arrival.

"I thought I did," Nick said honestly, shutting the door and reaching for his tie.

"Well, you didn't. I had to find out from Callie. I tell you, they're ideal for each other."

A romance between Pup and McKay had never entered Nick's mind, so there was no feigning the confusion on his face.

"Ideal for what?"

"Marriage," Camille said simply, her face alight with pleasure. "What could be more perfect?"

Nick shook his head and scrubbed at his ear. He couldn't have heard her right.

"You mean Pup and McKay?"

115

"Of course."

"Camie," he began patiently, "that's not going to happen."

"How do you know?"

"Because I know," he retorted with complete conviction. "McKay is a dedicated treasury man, and Pup is the best undercover agent I've got."

"And those things mean they can't fall in love?" Camille's voice rang with skepticism. However, Nick was not swayed.

"It doesn't mean they can't; it just means they won't."

Camille was reminded for the thousandth time in their marriage that men and women simply didn't think alike. And to Camille's way of thinking, it was too bad. There would be so much more they could all get done if husbands would just go along with their wives' plans. Settling back against the pillow, Camille let the matter drop. She would have been outraged, however, if she could have heard her husband's thoughts.

Standing in the closet, he pulled the belt from his waistband and reached to unbutton his shoes. He wanted to laugh but refrained. *Pup and McKay! What a joke. I love you Camie, but sometimes you definitely have more beauty than brains.*

True to his word, McKay finished up at the First National Bank of Denver early the next week. Pleased to see him go, Duncan Phipps was in a rather expansive mood and asked Bryan Daniels to join him and Mr. Conway for dinner that evening. There was no time to warn Mrs. Meyer, but Pup couldn't let this opportunity slip away.

The gentlemen escorted Pup to a fine Denver establishment. It was much smaller than the Brown Palace or The Mills House, and also had a much more secretive air. The waiters' faces were open and friendly, but the tables were all set back in booths, some surrounded by curtains. Pup found herself in the middle of a booth—Phipps and Conway on either side of her.

No talk of business came up during the meal, but Pup could almost feel the tension in Conway. Phipps, though not an old man, had been a liar and a cheat from long years past. He ate his meal with relish and downed several glasses of wine, and then looked very pleased with himself as the plates were finally cleared. Pup watched in silence as he lit a cigar.

"Conway here tells me you've got quite a head for figures, Daniels."

"Th-thank y-you, s-sir." Pup's whole body shook with the effort, and then she ducked her head.

"In fact," Phipps went on expansively, "Conway is so impressed with you that I've decided to let you do a little work for me."

Pup forced herself to think of the most embarrassing thing that had ever happened to her and actually managed to blush.

"M-me, s-sir?" she looked shyly delighted. "Th-thank you, s-sir."

The look of strained patience that she'd seen in Conway's face many times crossed Phipps' features, but he managed to keep smiling.

"I've got some special accounts," he began.

"S-special, s-sir?"

"Yes," his voice dropped to a confidential tone. "You see, Daniels, every bank has special customers. You know of course that all our customers are special to us, but we also have a few *extra*-special accounts."

Awe filled Pup's eyes, and Duncan Phipps' chest swelled with success. He went on to explain that he would want her to come in at regular times, but in the afternoon she would go to work in their special office. Pup took it all in—presumably hook, line, and sinker. By the time the men parted for the evening, the bankers thought they had found a bookkeeper worth his weight in gold.

Pup eased the door to McKay's room open and hoped he wasn't asleep. The lock had been child's play to flip, but the door hinges had a low groan to them. Pup had just closed the door behind her and leaned against it when she felt cold steel against her neck.

"I'd rather you didn't shoot," she whispered and heard McKay's breath leave him in a rush.

"What are you—" he began, but Pup cut him off in an equally soft whisper.

"Get word to Nick. There's another office. They call it the 'special office,' and it's not on the premises of the regular bank. I'll be headed there tomorrow afternoon to work on some special accounts. Tell Nick I'll be by early Thursday morning to tell him where it is."

With that she turned to reach for the door handle, but McKay caught her arm.

"What's the matter?" she asked.

"Nothing, I just wondered how you're doing."

"I'm all right."

"Good" was all McKay said, but he continued to hold her arm in indecision. Was he allowed to tell her that he had a lead on Jubal? Or even that Jubal had been spotted in the city? Not knowing for certain, he realized he had to let the matter drop.

"Are you all right?" Pup finally asked in the silent darkness.

"Yes."

His voice was not convincing to Pup. She wished she could see his face, but now was not the time to get into this.

"Thanks for taking the message."

"You're welcome. Take care."

She didn't answer but slipped quietly back out of the room and into her own. Not bothering with a lamp, Pup readied for bed in the dark and crawled between the sheets. As always, her first thoughts went to Boulder and how she missed her bath in the lake, her own bed, and her favorite flannel nightgown. Tonight her second thoughts were on McKay. Something was wrong. She didn't know what or why, but something was clearly amiss. Pup fell asleep wondering if it had anything to do with her.

14

"Nick not up yet?" Pup walked into the kitchen at the Wallaces' early Thursday morning and spoke to Miranda, who was working over the stove.

"He was here a moment ago," she said calmly, "but then left. He looked a little sleepy. You want coffee?" Miranda asked as she set a steaming mug in front of Peter Crandall.

"Thank you," Pup spoke as she took a long satisfying pull at the hot liquid. She sat drinking in silence, her mind on what she must report to Nick concerning the special accounts. Just before he came in her thoughts had swung to McKay, so when Nick arrived she only stared at him.

"Are you awake?" Nick asked when she looked at him.

"Yes," Pup gave a little shake of her head to dispel McKay's image. "Are you?"

"Barely. Just how early do you have to be at this office?"

"Not early at all, but I can't be seen coming from here and then going right to the bank. I'd find myself at the wrong end of a gun."

The cup headed on the way to Nick's mouth paused in mid-air.

"Have you been threatened?"

"No, I haven't, Nick," her voice was logical, "but Duncan Phipps is not going to be pleased when he finds out he's been duped."

"He's not going to find out," Nick said, and then drank from his suspended cup.

Pup's brows rose.

"The location of this special office is all I need," Nick explained. "I'm not going to move on it anytime soon, but knowing where it is, I can watch it and catch Phipps and Conway in the act."

"So how long will you want me to stay on?"

"For a time, if possible, so they won't suspect. I'd actually like to throw you in jail with the rest of them, and then your cover would be completely masked."

Pup was impressed. She didn't relish staying on the job much longer, but it was an excellent plan.

Miranda put food on the table now, and between bites Pup told Nick all she'd seen and been expected to do. None of the account names were a surprise to her superior, but she knew he was pleased to have his suspicions confirmed. Thirty minutes later Pup went on her way. She deliberately walked back to the boardinghouse before starting toward the bank. She had no sense that she was being followed but wasn't willing to take a chance.

Little more than 24 hours later, Pup stood by the work table at the bank and told herself to breathe. It was almost time for her to head to the special office, but she felt frozen to the floor. She'd been on her way to Duncan Phipps' office to deliver some paperwork when her brother Jubal came from the office, Duncan on his heels. He didn't see her—he'd been too busy taking instructions from the banker—but Pup felt her world rock.

She had known for years that her brothers had been up to no good, but never had she heard of a tie-in to Duncan Phipps and the First National. Now, having seen the special accounts and the hundreds of thousands of dollars that were unaccounted for and thus untaxed, she wanted to be sick. How could they have sunk so low? How could they have chosen to work for a swindler like Duncan Phipps? Oh, he was classy with his fine suits and smooth manners, but the man was a thief, avoiding taxes through whatever means possible—phony mine stocks, out-and-out theft, or something he termed "special accounts." The man wasn't picky

Nick's face suddenly flashed into her mind, and Pup found she could hardly stay on her feet. The direction of her thoughts was suddenly too much for her. One of the tellers was saying something to her, but she couldn't attend. A few minutes later Conway was standing before her, finally arresting her attention. Not realizing how pale her face had become, she saw that his eyes were concerned as he stared at her.

"What is it, Bryan?"

"S-sick," Pup barely remembered to stutter.

Conway took a step backward. The last thing he wanted was to be ill. Bryan Daniels had turned out to be the perfect bank employee, but right now he looked awful.

"Go home," he urged the younger man. "Maybe you'll feel better by Monday. Go home, Bryan."

Pup only nodded and started toward the door. Her brother was long gone, but she could almost feel his presence. Would he have recognized her? Would he have even looked in her direction? And the biggest question of all: Would Nick really do this to her?

"Callie?" Camille said with surprise when Pup stood in the doorway of her dining room. She had come in through the kitchen and passed Miranda, not answering any of her questions.

"Is Nick here?"

"No, of course not. He's at the office. Callie," she tried again while taking in Pup's white features. "What is it? Are you ill?"

"Tell Nick when he comes home that I'm waiting for him in his office."

"But it's early, Callie, he won't be home for hours."

"I'll wait for him."

With that, Pup moved through the room. Camille's mouth opened and closed but no sound came forth. Pup looked horrible. What in the world had happened? She looked back to see that Miranda had come to the edge of the room and witnessed the scene. The two exchanged a look. Camille knew then that she had to get word to Nick. Even if she had to go herself, she had to let Nick know.

The dull, lifeless eyes that Camille had seen were long gone by the time Nick arrived. After his wife's summons, he let himself quietly into the study to find Pup pacing with irritation before the desk.

"Did you know?" she shot at him even before the door could completely close.

"Did I know what?" Nick asked cautiously as he went to stand behind his desk.

"Did you know he would be at the bank?"

"Who, Pup?"

"Don't play games with me, Nick!" her voice was a lash as her hand slammed down on the wood surface. "I saw Jubal! I saw him with my own eyes. *How could you set me up?"*

The room was utterly still. Nick had never seen her this way. Carlyle had reported to him that Jubal had been spotted, but with Duncan Phipps nearly on the hook, he had given it little thought.

"I wouldn't do that," Nick finally said softly. "I can see how it would look that way, Pup, but I swear to you, I would never set you up."

"I don't believe it, Nick. Even McKay was acting oddly the other night. How could you do this?"

"I didn't," he spoke firmly now. "With Duncan Phipps so close, I hadn't given Jubal Hackett any thought."

"You didn't know that Jubal would be at the bank today?" she questioned softly.

"No."

Pup saw the truth in his eyes, and her own slid shut.

"I just gave him away," she whispered. "I just gave my brother away to you."

Pup's hands went to her mouth, and tears slipped out from between her lids. Harsh sobs broke from her throat, and she was barely aware of Nick's hands and the way they gently led her to a chair. The pain was more than she could take. First Govern and now Jubal. They were awful men, but they were her brothers.

She tried to calm down, but it took some time. Nick had not set her up, but the pain of believing that he had had been too much to bear. And then her own stupidity. How could she have barreled in here and given her brother away? She knew that Jubal would be caught someday and probably killed just like Govern, but she could not be the one to do it.

She opened her eyes now and found both Nick and Camille bending over her. She looked into their concerned faces and felt shame. How could she have thought they would ever do anything to hurt her?

"How are you, dear?" Camille whispered.

"I'm okay."

"I want you to go home, Pup," Nick said.

"Home?"

"Yes, to Boulder. This assignment is over for you."

"But we're so close," she began.

Nick was shaking his head. "It doesn't make any difference. I don't want you this upset, and I don't want to use you to get Jubal. You know I will nail him if ever I have the chance—I'll nail everyone involved in this. Go home, Pup."

"You'd do that, Nick? You'd let me go in the middle of an assignment that means this much?"

Nick nodded without hesitation. "The work you've already done has been invaluable. No one else could have pulled it off. You've earned a rest. Go home."

It took a little more talking, but Nick's mind was made up. Pup didn't know what she wanted right now, but she did as she was told. She pitied the people at the bank and at Mrs. Meyer's since they would all be told that Bryan Daniels had met with an unfortunate accident. His things were collected at Mrs. Meyer's that afternoon, but the man who took them could not tell a stunned Mrs. Meyer when the funeral service would be.

As for Pup, she put a hat on her head and lost the flashy vests and stutter. She stayed at the Wallaces' until it was time to leave for the station. Peter Crandall boarded a northbound train for Boulder that very afternoon, having not seen McKay Harrington or anyone else.

That night the men gathered around Mrs. Meyer's dining table were very subdued. Mrs. Meyer had tearfully filled in the other boarders concerning Mr. Daniels, and then tried to make the meal as normal as possible. The men were naturally quiet, but only one tenant was broiling inside. His appetite was affected just like everyone else's, but for an entirely different reason. He knew very well that no one had died, but that was not good enough. He wanted to know where Callie Jennings was, and he wanted to know now. It took great restraint on his part to finish the meal, but he didn't attempt to pretend over dessert. He excused himself as soon as it was possible and headed to Nick Wallace's home.

"Where is she?"

Nick and Camille had dined late that evening, so McKay caught them at the table.

"On her way home," Nick answered, not worrying about Camille's presence in the room.

"Why?"

"She spotted Jubal at the bank today and thought I set her up. When she realized I hadn't, she fell apart, sure that she'd given him away. I sent her home."

"All by herself?"

Nick sighed, but he answered patiently.

"Much as it's hard to believe, McKay, Pup is used to taking care of herself. I could have offered to go with her, but she would have refused."

McKay was clearly not happy with this answer, but Nick felt no guilt. This was not the first time he'd put his love and concern for Pup ahead of a work issue. But holding her hand all the way home was simply not necessary. He would wire her in a few days, and if she didn't answer within several weeks, he'd go and check on her. They'd been doing business this way for over 13 years.

"Did she want to leave?"

"I didn't ask her, but I could tell it was time. It would have given me a stronger case to have more from her, but what she's already supplied will be sufficient. As upset as she was, I felt the only wise thing was to send her home."

Not accustomed to explaining himself to underlings, Nick wondered at his own words, but something in McKay's face wrung his heart with pity. For the first time he thought about his wife's words. *Could McKay be falling for Pup?*

He certainly hoped not. Romance did not mix well with business.

"I'm sorry to have disturbed you, sir," McKay was now saying, effectively breaking back into Nick's thoughts, "and you, Mrs. Wallace. Goodnight."

Both husband and wife bid the young treasury agent goodnight and even spent some time talking about Pup and the case. Nick didn't tell Camille everything that was on his mind, but he was not the least bit surprised to learn from Carlyle the next day that McKay had been to see him. Nick wondered if the recently wounded agent had come back on the job too soon; he had requested a few weeks off as soon as he finished his present assignment.

15

Boulder

Nothing ever felt so good to Pup as returning to her cabin. Compared to the elegance at Nick and Camille's, it was like a sod hut. But for Pup it was home. She loved the feel of her own bed and the smell of her own sheets. She arrived home from Denver too late to make the trek all the way up the mountain, and since she'd camped in the woods, she climbed into her bed as soon as she could change into her comfortable nightgown.

She woke sometime early Sunday morning, knowing she'd slept for over 18 hours. Even at that she was in no hurry to get out of bed. She lay there, her eyes on the trees out the window, and thought about Jubal and her own guilt of seeing only what she wanted to see. Her brother was six years younger than she was, which would make him 22 right now. From what she could see of him in the bank, he didn't look that young. It was probably the life he'd lived. They'd had very little contact for years, but word about his activities had come to her from time to time.

Govern had come up the mountain more often. He was always out of money and running from someone. Pup found herself wishing that Jubal had come home a little more. He'd never been as hard as Govern; maybe she could have reasoned with him. It now looked as though it was too late. Even if he completely changed his ways, he was wanted for past crimes.

Govern had clearly thought nothing of starting a gunfight with a treasury man in order to escape. Was Jubal as desperate?

Pup knew that such a line of questioning was pointless. She had no answers and each thought only raised more anxiety. However, before she could push Jubal completely from her mind, she wondered what she would do if she were ever expected to aid in his arrest. Such action could save his life, but she wasn't sure she could live with herself when it was all over and her brother was behind bars. But could she live with herself knowing that he was running loose and causing no end of pain for the people he helped to rob and cheat?

Enough! Pup suddenly thought. Determined to put Jubal from her mind, she threw back the covers. Her garden was probably a mass of dried stalks, but she'd never find out just laying in bed. She was also in the mood for trout. The chances of her finding a fresh one to jump into her pan were slim to none; she'd have to get out her pole. It was time to go back to work, but Pup didn't dread it—she was home and that was all that mattered.

Thirteen days after McKay was told that Bryan Daniels was dead, he rode up the mountain on a rented horse yet again. Things had cooled slightly with Duncan Phipps. McKay had been assigned to two other banks for spot checks. The last one was a job that had not required many days' work, and from there he'd packed his things, paid Mrs. Meyer a few weeks' rent, and headed for the train station. His last conversation with Carlyle played on his mind with every rocking sway of the passenger car.

"What's really going on here, McKay?" the older man wanted to know.

"I'm not sure I know what you mean."

"Only that this is all rather sudden."

McKay had been quiet for a moment. "I don't mean any disrespect, Carlyle, but it's easy for the men who work in the home office to look at agents as work animals." Carlyle had looked so surprised that McKay had stopped and tried again.

"Do you know how many years it's been since I took a vacation, Carlyle?"

The other man paused to think and then shook his head no.

"It's been at least two years, if not longer. I go home for the weekend from time to time, and even take an extra day now and again, but it's not the same."

"So this doesn't have anything to do with Callie Jennings?"

"Yes, it does," McKay admitted, surprising the older man, "but not the way you think."

Carlyle still looked confused, so McKay tried again.

"I always go home through Boulder, and on the way I'm planning to stop and see how she's doing. She's accustomed to being on her own, but where I come from a woman gets tender care and nurturing. The first time I met Callie she was a woman, not a man. I can't get that image from my mind. Nick Wallace had no problem sending her away on her own. I'm not comfortable with that. I don't know if she needs anything or not, but the last few months have been rather rough on her. I was the cause of some of her problems, and since I care about her well-being I'm going to check on her. If my sister had had a rough time and had no close family, I would hope someone would check on her.

"From there I'm headed home to be surrounded by my family. I'd like to visit with them knowing I don't have to leave in two days. I don't get much of that anymore and usually that's fine, but right now I'm tired and need a break. I'm also going to ask Callie Jennings if she wants to join me in Longmont. She doesn't have much family left, and I know she'd enjoy mine. I think she needs to be nurtured even more than I do."

McKay could see that he'd surprised Carlyle with this admission, but also that he appreciated the younger man's honesty. The older man's hand had come out in genuine friendship.

"Have a good trip, McKay. I'll miss the hard work you put in, but more than that I hope you find everything you're looking for."

It was this last statement that lingered in McKay's mind. *What am I looking for?* He didn't really know, but that didn't stop his climb up the mountain. He'd been this way twice before, but the foliage was thicker this time, and twice he had to backtrack. It was much later than he'd planned by the time he rode into the clearing in front of Pup's cabin.

Pup sat down at the kitchen table and pulled the boots from her feet. She was tired and achy and couldn't wait for sundown so she could bathe in the lake. She'd carried water for days to revive her plants, and they now looked like they were going to make it. It looked as if Mud or someone else had given them a little water, and most of them were going to survive. The potatoes were sure to be on the small side, but she would take what she got.

The boots finally off, it was time for dinner. Pup had just picked up the coffeepot when she heard the horse. Her gun, always handy, was in her grasp when someone called from outside. Pup opened the door and stared in disbelief at McKay as he stood in the clearing beyond her porch—tall and handsome—his saddlebags hanging from his hand, his rifle in the other.

"Bad time?" McKay asked quietly.

"No." Pup remembered her manners and watched as he started forward. "Come in." She backed up so he could enter. "I was just about to fix something to eat. Are you hungry?"

"Actually I am," he said as he recognized the gnawing in his stomach.

He watched her turn away, and as she did, she tripped over a boot lying on the floor. It was then that McKay remembered what he might be letting himself in for.

"Can I help?" he offered out of self-preservation as well as a need to do something besides stand there.

"Sure," she said with her back still to him. "I'll start the coffee if you want to peel some potatoes."

"Okay. I've got some salt pork in my saddlebags if you want that."

"You should hold onto it. I have a rabbit that has to be eaten today."

Her voice was completely normal, and McKay said only, "All right."

He began to peel potatoes and for some reason felt oddly tongue-tied. She was so much the same, her dress was faded and stained, and other than her hair, still cut very short, she looked the same. Still McKay did not know what to say. He had not known who she was the last time they were in this cabin. Why that made a difference now he couldn't say, but it did.

"What is this, a stew?"

"Yeah, I've got the meat ready, but the carrots need to be washed."

"I'll clean them up."

McKay did this and silence again prevailed, causing McKay to be slightly uncomfortable. A glance out the side of his eyes told him Pup was busy and not noticing. They worked with little conversation for the next 30 minutes until the pot was boiling on the stove. Knowing it would need some time to cook, Pup put the lid on and finally turned to look at McKay.

"How have you been?" he asked her.

"All right. How about you?"

"Fine. I'm tired and headed home for some time off. You headed out on another job soon?"

"Not that I know of."

"Good."

Pup cocked her head. "Why is that good?"

"Because I want you to go to Longmont with me."

Pup blinked at him. McKay had been planning to wait at least until they'd sat down to dinner, but suddenly saw that now was the time.

"Why?"

"Because I think you need a rest, too."

"I can rest here."

"I want you to come with me."

Pup shook her head. "Thanks, McKay, but I'll stay here." As usual, she thought this was the end of it.

"You'd enjoy it."

Pup, who had been on the verge of setting the table, stopped and looked at him.

"My family's home is not right in town." His voice was persuasive. "It's out a ways, at the base of the peaks. The setting is perfect."

Pup never even blinked.

"There's a lake."

Still no response.

"Come on, Callie. Just say yes."

"You're a nag—do you know that, McKay?"

"I am not!" He was as indignant as the first time she had accused him, but Pup ignored him. Having heard enough, she moved toward the door, headed outside, and walked right past her boots. Not so easily put off, McKay was right on her trail.

"I wouldn't ask you if I didn't think you would have a good time," he said as he followed her. "You'd love my parents. My sister lives close by with her husband, and they have a baby. The baby's name is Marcus. Are you listening to me, Callie?" he now asked as he trailed her to the lake.

"No."

"Well, at least I got an answer," he went on. "Ask me anything; I'll tell you all about it."

"About what?" She now stopped by the water and looked at him, her brow creased in confusion.

"About Longmont," McKay said simply.

Pup growled low in her throat and turned away from him.

"I know you'll love it." He continued to badger her.

"I won't love it, McKay, because I'm not going."

"My mother loves to cook, and you could sleep in my sister's old room. It looks out over the mountains."

"No, McKay."

"Why not?"

"Because I don't want to."

"Yes, you do; you just don't know it."

"No, McKay," she said again, wondering why she even bothered. She moved closer to the lake, hoping he wouldn't follow.

"Come on, Callie," he tried again, still staying very close. "What are you afraid of?"

McKay watched her start suddenly and wondered if he'd finally gotten through. He was still talking when she sat on a fallen log by the lakeshore and stared across the water. McKay's tirade had gone on for at least a minute straight when Pup quietly said, "All right, I'll go with you."

McKay blinked.

"Just like that?" he asked, but she didn't answer. "Well," he said slowly, some of the enthusiasm leaving him in the midst of his surprise, "I know you'll have a wonderful time." But when she still didn't look at him, he moved close enough to really see her face. She looked pale, and there was a small strip of moisture over her upper lip.

"What is it, Callie?" he whispered softly. "What have I done?"

She finally looked at him. "I've stepped on something, McKay." Her voice was breathless. "It's in my foot."

"Which foot?" he asked, but she couldn't answer.

McKay looked down and noticed for the first time that she was in stocking feet. Grasping her ankle he lifted her right foot carefully and checked the bottom. Seeing nothing, he reached for the left. Protruding from the tender flesh of her arch was a fishhook. Her stocking was already stained with blood. McKay felt a chill go over him at the thought of her pain.

135

"Okay, Callie," he said quietly, carefully letting go of her ankle. "I'm going to lift you now and carry you back to the cabin."

She didn't answer or protest once she was in his arms, and McKay, a rush of protection filling him, thought she weighed little more than a child. It wasn't two minutes before he was placing her on the well-worn sofa, careful not to bump her foot against anything. Pup rested her head back the moment he laid her down, so she missed the appearance of his pocket-knife. She felt a pull at the stocking around her ankle and then the cool air as he cut it free and tried to bare her foot.

"I've got to take it out, Callie. I can't remove the stocking unless I do," she heard him say, but the pain was making her sick. Her hand went over her mouth as he grasped the hook and removed it. She felt the pressure of a dry cloth against her sole, but she was too busy gasping for air to move or speak. Her whole frame trembled with the intensity of the pain, but she never spoke or cried out. She felt more movement down at her foot just before a cold wet cloth was placed against her face. McKay tenderly wiped her face and then folded the cloth to place across her brow. Pup opened her eyes to find his face close above her.

"Hi," he said softly.

"I lost that hook," she said in a small voice, "but I was certain it was in the lake."

McKay nodded and adjusted the cloth on her face. "It's out now, but it tore quite a bit."

Pup took a shuddery breath. "It hurts."

"Yeah."

There didn't seem to be anything else to say. McKay pulled a kitchen chair close to sit by her. Her foot throbbed, but in time she fell into a light sleep. He then took the stew from the stove and ate a little, barely tasting it. He lit the lanterns and went back to the chair next to the sofa, sitting down again until she woke up. When she didn't want anything to eat, he carried her to her bedroom.

"Can you manage?"

"Yes."

"I'll be in the stable tonight. Just tap on the window if you need me."

"You can sleep in the spare room, McKay. The bed's made up."

"No," he answered, even as he was reminded that they came from different worlds. "I'll be outside. Just holler if you need me."

McKay moved toward the door.

"Goodnight."

"Goodnight, Callie. I'm sorry about your foot."

"It's all right."

"Don't try to do anything in the morning. I'll be in and make you some breakfast."

McKay watched her nod. He carried the other lantern out with him and settled in the stable for a long, cold night.

Denver

"He's gone where?" Nick asked Carlyle, his face showing frank disbelief.

"Longmont."

Nick licked his lips. The two men stared at each other.

"I can't believe it," Nick finally whispered. "What made you—" but he couldn't go on.

"Have him checked out?" Carlyle finished.

"Yes."

The younger man shrugged, his face filled with concern. "I just didn't like what I was seeing. It was all just a bunch of little things, but then I thought he might be a little too close to the situation, you know, emotionally. Now reports have come back."

"From someone you trust?"

"Yes." Carlyle's voice told of his regret. "I checked him out myself."

Nick's eyes closed before his hand scrubbed over his face. He looked weary and hurt, and then angry.

"We can't take usual channels with this; he would recognize anyone we sent."

Carlyle didn't interrupt; his boss was clearly thinking.

"I need Pup," he finally stated. "Send word for me."

"I'm not certain she's in Boulder."

Nick looked at him.

"McKay's plans were to ask her to go with him to Longmont."

Nick was thunderstruck. Then a steely glint entered his eyes.

"Who's our contact in Longmont?" his voice was hard.

"Barnes. Charlie Barnes."

"Of course. Get word to him. Don't go so far as to say one of our men has turned, but stress the importance of standing by."

"So you don't want to move right away?"

"No, but he *must* be ready. Duncan Phipps and Jubal Hackett may be on hold for the moment, but I won't let this one get away."

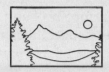

16

McKay pressed a mug of coffee into Pup's hand and then went back to the kitchen. Pup eyed him from the sofa, her look wary; he was a little too quiet.

"So, when can we leave?" he asked a moment later.

It was just what she dreaded. Her sigh could be heard across the room.

"I know I said yes, but I don't want to do this, McKay."

"Why not?"

Pup remained silent.

"Give me a reason."

"You're not going to start that again, are you, McKay?"

"Yes, I am," he said calmly. "Why don't you want to come with me?"

Pup took a deep breath. Yesterday he hadn't said a word about the trip until he was leaving to go back out to the stable for the second night. She'd been in pain all day, and he'd waited on her hand and foot, not nagging her once. But right before he left he'd turned and said, "I still want you to come with me."

It would have been easy to pretend she didn't know what he was talking about, but she didn't do that. Instead she didn't answer, and he'd had no choice but to let the matter drop.

Now, first thing this morning, he was back on the trail. Pup was strongly tempted to throw her coffee mug at him. Without even looking at her, he cracked eggs into a pan and spoke. His whole manner was relaxed.

"I want to head down the mountain within the hour and catch the train for Longmont this afternoon."

"Have you forgotten my foot?"

"No. You'll be on horseback, then on the train, and finally in a wagon to my folks' place." He now turned to look at her, his eyes amused because it wasn't like her to complain. "No walking at all."

Pup shook her head no again, her look remaining stubborn.

"Give me a reason."

He heard her sigh. "I don't want to dress as a man again, McKay. I'm tired of that."

"You don't have to dress like a man." He was still so calm.

"McKay," now Pup's voice was patient. "With my hair this short I can't go anywhere in a dress. I wear a hat every time I even walk outside." She would have gone on, but McKay cut in with one quiet statement.

"Camille sent you something."

If Pup had been wary before, she was now downright tense.

"Camille can be rather busy," she said cautiously, watching as he walked toward the saddlebags. A moment later he lifted a curly, black-haired wig and positioned it on his hand. He held it carefully, looking at it and then at her.

"It even looks like your hair."

"It is my hair," she admitted quietly. "Camille had it made up for emergencies."

McKay nodded. "She also sent a few dresses; she said the things you wear at home are all too short."

"So you've talked this over with Camille."

McKay shrugged. "I hadn't planned to, but I had some papers to drop off the day before I left. Carlyle wanted them given to Nick, and he was at home. Mrs. Wallace and I got to talking. When I told her of my plans, she got rather excited."

Pup stared at him. Why had she thought this had all been on the spur of the moment?

"Why, McKay?" she had to ask. "Why must I do this? If you're trying to make up for the loss of my brother, it's not going to work."

"I'm not, Callie, but I'm glad you said something. My motives are pure. My family is wonderful, and Longmont is beautiful. You never have a break here. You're either working or on some job for Nick. At my parents' home, you can relax."

He saw her vacillate.

"There's a lake," he coaxed her.

She wouldn't look at him.

"The windows in your room overlook the mountains, and my sister says the bed is soft."

Pup could not believe she was being swayed by his sell-job. She looked over at him and asked herself how anyone could be so charming and good-looking.

"Right after breakfast I'll go saddle the horses," he responded as if she'd agreed, his eyes on her face. "You can take time to pack then. Oh," he stopped before turning back to the stove, "that's the package Camille sent." He gestured to a parcel on the small table in the corner. Pup hadn't even noticed it.

When McKay turned away, Pup reached for the bundle. She left the string in place and tore the paper back just enough to see which dresses were there. Two of them were her best, and the third was a simple day dress. Pup sat for a moment longer, her eyes at first seeing nothing and then focusing on her wig; it still lay on top of McKay's saddlebags on the chair. She couldn't believe she was actually going to do this.

From the moment he put her on the horse to the moment they took their seats on the train, McKay's treatment of her could not be faulted. Pup was still not certain his concern wasn't over her brother, but she realized that even if it was, she would have to let this man get it out of his system. She didn't think he was being untruthful in any way, but not everyone saw things as they really were. He wanted her to meet his family because they were kind and wonderful. She was glad he thought so, but a family as loving as McKay spoke of was just too good to be true.

"You have just one sister?" Pup asked as the train picked up speed. They had done nothing but talk about the Harringtons since leaving home, but Pup hadn't always been listening.

"Yes, but lots of cousins. In fact, one of my cousins is getting married next week."

"Will you go all the way back for the wedding?"

"I won't need to; I'll still be there."

Pup's head whipped around to look at him.

"Don't you have to go back to work?"

"Not for almost two weeks."

Pup stared at him.

"Your hair looks nice," he said simply, but Pup barely heard him.

"Why don't you have to work?"

"Because I needed some time off."

"You weren't planning on my staying for two weeks, were you, McKay?"

"No. I think it'll be just over a week."

"I can't even stay that long. My garden will be a dried-out mess."

"Mud will see to it."

"Why would he do that?"

"Because I went up and asked him."

It was then that Pup understood how accustomed she was to being in control. She didn't even go on the jobs Nick had for her if she still needed time off. McKay had come in and practically dragged her from the mountain—all the while smiling kindly and making her think it was just what she wanted.

"You're not going to renege on me, are you, Pup?" He surprised her by using her nickname.

"I don't know how my leaving early is reneging."

"Because you'll miss all the fun if you don't stay the week."

Again he found himself under her scrutiny. He wondered if she knew how often she just sat and studied him. She was so good at covering all emotion in her face. He'd have given much to read her mind or even her mood. He was tempted to rattle off the activities he had planned but refrained. If she wanted to know, she could ask. She didn't ask.

After a few more moments, she turned her head and looked at the people seated in front of them. He was certain she didn't really see them, but McKay remained quiet and let her be.

The train had a rocking motion to it that tended to soothe, and it wasn't long before both of them were nearly asleep. McKay eventually laid his head back, and Pup's went against the window.

"Wake up, McKay" was the next thing he heard. "You're crushing me."

There was laughter in her voice, but having gone out hard, McKay moved only slightly and blinked at his seat-mate in confusion.

"What did you say?"

"You fell asleep on me, and I couldn't breathe. What do you weigh, for mercy's sake?"

McKay smiled then, just before reaching up and adjusting her curls.

"Was it crooked?" she whispered furiously.

"Just a little."

Pup snorted with anger and disgust. "You think it's so simple," she hissed at him. "Just put the wig on and wear a dress. Well, I'll tell you, McKay Harrington, the most embarrassing thing that ever happened to me happened in this wig."

"It looks fine now," he assured her, no longer smiling.

"Yeah? Well, who's going to shadow me this week and tell me if my hair's on straight?"

"It won't be that bad."

"Won't it?" She was still whispering furiously. "This thing is not made for sleeping in."

"So you can take it off at night."

"At the Wallace's," her eyes were glaring now, "Miranda comes in every morning unannounced; she doesn't even knock. Who can I expect in my room, finding me in a woman's nightgown and no hair?"

Her voice must have gone up because the man in front of them turned and glanced behind him. Pup turned away to the window, and McKay stared at the back of her head. He'd been completely honest. Her hair looked fine, but she was right. He really had no idea how difficult it could be.

"I'm sorry, Callie. I didn't think about anything but wanting you to come."

She turned and looked into his eyes, her head shaking in confusion. "I still don't understand what that's about either, McKay."

"It's not complicated. By the end of the week, I hope you'll see my parents' place as a second home. I hope you'll be as relaxed with them as you are with the Wallaces. And the church family, too, if you want to come," he added, having just thought of it.

Pup cocked her head to one side, her hair forgotten. "What church do you attend?"

"Longs Peak Bible Church."

Pup nodded and looked off at nothing. "I don't get to church much."

"Why is that, Callie?" McKay asked with genuine interest.

"A couple of reasons, the first being that I don't like town much, and the second that I'd have to leave the cabin in the middle of the night to be there when the service started."

"Couldn't you stay with someone in town?"

She shook her head no. "I don't know who it would be."

McKay wanted to say, *What if I found someone for you? What if I worked out a place for you?* But he couldn't do it. Just attending church was not what was needed here. It might help. It might be a start, but Pup needed to understand more about God and His Son. That was the place she needed to begin. They had both fallen quiet again and remained so for the rest of the ride, but McKay's mind was on Pup. He wondered if there would be an opportunity to talk to her about his faith before the week was out.

Longmont

Laid out symmetrically with a splendid view of Longs Peak, Longmont, Colorado, was a beautiful town. Streets ran parallel to each other and bustled with activity. Pup tried to take in as much as possible from the train station, and from her vantage point she liked what she saw. Her foot brought some pain as she moved with McKay along the platform, but the boards were level and he kept a hand under her arm at all times.

No one had ever treated her as McKay Harrington did. Camille had never done anything but respect and treat her as a woman, but it wasn't the same as McKay's care.

"How's that foot?"

"Just a little tender."

"Well, sit here." He led her to a bench that sat against the station office wall. "I'll get some transportation, and then we'll head for home."

"I can come with you, McKay. It's no trouble."

"No." He spoke with a hand to her shoulder, effectively holding her in the seat. "I'll have the porter bring the bags over to you, and I'll be back as soon as I can."

He was gone before she could protest. She didn't want infection to set into her foot, so she chose not to ignore his orders and follow him as she would have liked to have done. But the longer she sat, her neck craning slightly to see the town, the more she felt amazed by his kindness. The livery, from what she could see of things, was quite a ways down the street.

Yesterday, the day after she'd stepped on the hook, came rushing to her mind. McKay had risen early to chop wood for hours. The supply ended up overflowing her box and was stacked against the side of the cabin. After lunch he removed a strip of wood from her doorway and inlaid a piece in its place, telling her that this one wouldn't trip her. He'd prepared three meals, one of which included fresh fish, and cleaned the kitchen until it shone. And again he'd slept out with the horses.

It's because you dress as a man so often, Pup, she reasoned with herself. *You're not used to being treated this way because you don't usually look like a woman.* For some reason the thought comforted her. Was it because she didn't want a relationship with McKay that went beyond work and friendship, or because she didn't quite trust her own heart in the matter? Pup decided it was the latter. Her heart did funny things when McKay was around. For all she knew he was engaged to be married, but that didn't change the attraction she felt. He didn't do anything that led her on, but he was a very fascinating, attractive man. The only thing that wasn't clear for her were McKay's feelings toward her. Were they only friends, or did he want something more? As the porter delivered the bags and she continued to wait for McKay to appear, Pup couldn't help but wonder if she'd have any more answers a week down the road.

17

Pup didn't say anything to McKay, but the sight of the Harrington home was a wonderful surprise. Set apart from town, it was large and rambling on the outside. Once in the front door, Pup fell in love with the painted wood and simple touches that made it a home. From where she stood at the front door, the stairs that rose to the upper level were before her. To her left was a large living room, and a dining area lay to her right. The colors—and even the smells—were immediately comfortable to her. She would have enjoyed easing into the warmth of this home, but she wasn't in the door five seconds before she was meeting McKay's parents.

"Mickey," his father called as he approached and embraced his son immediately. "Welcome home. Was it boiling hot?"

"Not too bad."

"McKay," his mother called warmly, moving to hug him as well. "How long can you stay?"

"All week."

"All week?" she said with obvious delight. "That's marvelous!"

"You brought a friend." His father was speaking again, his voice very pleased.

"Yes." McKay brought Pup forward with a hand to her back. "This is Callie Jennings. Callie, this is my mother, Elizabeth Harrington, and my father, Bernard Harrington."

"Just Harry," he corrected. "Everyone calls me Harry."

"And I'm Liz," the older woman spoke, taking Pup's hand. "I'm so glad you could come with McKay. You'll stay the week, I hope."

"Well, I'm not entirely certain," she tried to explain, but there was no need.

"It doesn't matter how long you can stay," Liz was smiling, "just so you know you're welcome."

"Thank you," she said quietly, feeling slightly overwhelmed.

"Have you eaten?" Harry wished to know.

"No, and I'm hungry," McKay proclaimed. "How about you, Callie?"

"Sure," she said and tried to smile, but it was so unlike anything she'd imagined. After learning that he'd planned to ask her to Longmont before even coming to Boulder, she assumed that he'd informed his family. But clearly they hadn't even known he was coming, let alone coming and bringing a stranger into their home. Pup was more fascinated than ever.

"I just baked bread," Liz said as she headed off through the dining room. "And I have plenty of cheese and ham. How does that sound?"

"Like a feast," McKay said as he brought up the rear. Pup would have been left standing by the front door if he hadn't once again propelled her with a hand to her back. Harry had followed his wife, and McKay had started after them but then came back for Pup.

"They're not going to bite you," he whispered softly from behind her, thinking he'd read her look as fear, but Pup didn't respond. Indeed, she was so intent on the large room at the rear of the house that she barely heard him. Past the dining room was a huge kitchen. It was hot from the day's baking, but Pup loved it on sight. The walls were painted white, and the curtains at the windows were a dark blue.

"Here, Callie." Liz was speaking again. "Sit here and make yourself comfortable. Trains can be so tiring."

Pup sat down, her eyes still watching, her mouth quiet. She heard McKay and his father start to talk, but it was some minutes before she paid attention.

"So you just told Carlyle you needed some time off?"

"Yes. He was very understanding. I was only going to take the days around Stan's wedding, but I realized I needed more."

"Well, good. It's been a long time since you have."

"That's what I thought."

Harry smiled at his son and then turned a kind eye to Pup. "Do you live in Denver, Callie?"

"No, sir. Actually I live in Boulder, up in the hills."

"That's pretty country down there."

"Yes it is."

"How did you meet?" Liz asked as she worked over the breadboard.

Pup was searching for a way to answer when McKay spoke up.

"Callie is the woman who nursed me back to health when I was shot."

"Oh, Callie." Liz had stopped what she was doing to look at her. Her voice was soft and sincere. "Thank you for taking care of McKay, but we're so sorry about your brother."

"Thank you." Pup barely choked the words out, not because she was feeling emotional, but because she was amazed that McKay had told them about it. Her next thought made her smile.

What's so amazing, Pup? You know firsthand that he's a chatterbox. She looked over to see McKay staring at her, his eyes frankly curious.

"Should I be worried about that smile?"

The smile grew, but Pup didn't answer.

"Here, McKay," his mother now commanded him, "take Callie upstairs and show her her room. Lunch won't be ready for a minute, and I completely forgot my manners."

Liz threw a beaming smile at Pup, and she couldn't help but smile in return. Rising to follow McKay, she realized they were retracing their steps back through the dining room, toward the front door, and then up the stairs. He had picked up her bag at some point, and Pup realized she hadn't even remembered setting it down.

You'd better start paying attention, girl, or you're going to forget where you are and do or say something you can't take back.

"Are you all right?" McKay was asking.

"Yes. Why wouldn't I be?"

"You're just very quiet—even for you."

McKay had led Pup into a lovely bedroom and turned to look at her. Pup stared back at him, the fog lifting quickly. She moved silently, shut the door, and leaned against it. When she began to speak her voice was quiet but firm.

"You and I don't have the same type of job, McKay. I'm not certain you can really understand how it is for me. I like my solitude, but that wouldn't have kept me from talking to you when we first met had my situation been different."

McKay frowned at her in confusion, and Pup knew she was going to have to spell it out.

"I can't be too friendly to your parents, McKay, and talk their ears off. I can't do that with anyone if I don't have Nick's permission."

McKay saw very swiftly that he hadn't considered this, but a sudden question came to mind that he could not push away.

"Would it really be so bad, Pup, if you blew your cover and lost your job?"

"My job, no," she stated plainly. "My life is another story."

"Your life? I don't know what you mean."

"I mean that if Duncan Phipps or any number of other men ever found out the way I duped them, my life wouldn't be worth the shoes I'm standing in."

"Longmont is not Denver, Pup," he felt the need to remind her, his voice a bit tolerant.

"Can you really be so naive, McKay?" Her voice was still soft, but she was making her point. "With train travel and telegraph lines, the territory's not that big anymore. I can't *ever* let my guard down. Not with strangers on the street and not with kind people like your parents."

"My parents would never talk."

"McKay, think about what you just said. Why would you ever want to put them in that position?"

He had no answers for that. They stood for a long time and just stared at each other. McKay was not sorry he'd brought Pup—not even slightly—but she was right, there were aspects to her life that had never even crossed his mind.

"They didn't come down with you," Liz asked as soon as Harry appeared back in the kitchen.

"No," his voice was thoughtful. "They're in Maureen's room."

"They didn't see you come up?"

"The door is closed."

This widened Liz Harrington's eyes a little, but she didn't immediately comment.

"She's so quiet," Harry commented.

"Yes, she is," Liz couldn't help but agree. "Do you think it's us, Harry?"

"No, Liz, I honestly don't. I think Mickey must have thought this would be best for her, but not everything works the way we think it should."

"You don't think she'll stay?"

"I can't honestly say, but I wouldn't be too surprised if she didn't."

They both heard steps on the stairs, so conversation ceased. There was no need for their silence; McKay came back into the kitchen on his own.

"I came upstairs to check on you, Mickey," his father began right away. "Is everything all right?"

"Yes," he said slowly. "I think things are fine. Don't worry if she's on the quiet side. She's like that." There was something in McKay's face and voice that told them he was disturbed, but neither one of his parents questioned him. Pup joined them a few minutes later, and the meal was eaten with light conversation. Pup enjoyed it immensely but caught McKay's eyes on her a number of times. She kept her sigh very quiet, but she knew it was going to be a long week.

I told her I didn't have an agenda, Lord, but maybe that's not true. I just thought it would do her such good to get away. I thought she could relax and feel at home. I don't love to be alone all the time, so I have a hard time believing that she does.

McKay was in bed, his eyes on the ceiling. He'd been lying there for more than an hour, but sleep was miles away. He had to give Pup over to the Lord, but it was not going very well.

Why am I so disappointed that she can't just toss the past away and be Callie Jennings here, Lord? McKay sighed.

It had all seemed so easy. She hadn't jumped at the chance to come, but he had managed to bring her. After that, everything else was supposed to fall into place. She was going to laugh and joke with his parents as she did with Nick and Camille Wallace, and they were all going to have a splendid time. Like so many other lonely people in the Longmont area, she was going to see the Harrington home as a safe and wonderful haven.

I have to give this to You, Lord. I have to surrender my will to Yours. I may change my mind later, Father, but don't listen to me. Take Pup, take me, and take the whole situation. Have it be what You want it to be. I'm trying to play God, and You don't need my help. Cleanse me, Lord, from pride and stubbornness, and help me trust again.

McKay was finally able to relax. It helped that he was home in his own bed and bedroom. And it also helped that his favorite hymn came to mind. He sang it to himself as he drifted off to sleep.

McKay didn't have to ask Pup to join them for church in the morning. She was up, dressed in one of her good dresses, and ready to go before he was. She sat at the kitchen table, coffee in front of her, and turned from gazing out the window when he arrived.

"Hi," he said softly. "You're up early."

Pup smiled. "I hope it was all right for me to put coffee on."

"Certainly. In this house the first one up docs it anyhow."

McKay poured himself a cup and joined her.

"What time do we leave for church?"

"Not for a few hours yet. It starts at 10:30."

"Is it far?"

"Back into town, but it's on this side."

"I don't have a Bible," she told him.

"You can use mine," he offered.

Pup nodded and drank some more of her coffee. She surprised him by saying quietly, "I had a job one time with a man who was religious. He always kept a Bible on his desk. I read some of it the summer I was there."

"What did you think?"

"I thought it was wonderful," she shocked him by saying. "It's my own stupid fault that I never bought a Bible of my own."

McKay's heart was pounding, but he managed to keep his voice normal. "What part of the Bible did you enjoy the most?"

Pup really smiled now. "The stories about Jesus Christ." She shook her head in wonder. "I was always a little amazed at how many people didn't think He was God. It was so clear to me."

Not in a hundred years would McKay have dreamed that things would go this way, but he was not going to let this opportunity pass.

"Was it also clear to you, Pup, that you can have a personal relationship with God through His Son?"

Her face was very thoughtful now. She looked at him with sincere eyes and then at some distant spot on the wall. "I had a religious experience once, McKay. I was with my mother, and we'd gone down to Boulder. This was all long before the war. I don't even think there was a church in town. A traveling preacher had come, and he stood on the corner and preached, a Bible in his hand. There were a few people gathered when my mother and I moved close, and to my surprise, my mother stayed. She'd been in a hurry that day, but she took time to hear that man. In fact, when the crowd cleared she held my hand and we went up even closer, right in front of him. I hadn't been paying too much attention up to that point, but then we were face-to-face with this man.

"My mother began to question him, and I'll never forget it," she stopped and looked at McKay in wonder. "He had tears in his eyes. He said that Jesus loved us so much that He didn't care who we were or what we'd done; He died for our sins. He looked at my mother and asked her if she wanted to believe. I remember thinking, 'Ask me, ask me,' but I couldn't say a word. And then it happened." She paused then, her voice so filled with wonder that she might have been that child again.

"He turned to me and said, 'And how about you, little one? Jesus is waiting for your prayer too.' I'll never forget it. And I did it, McKay. I told Jesus I was a sinner and asked Him to save me." Pup's eyes grew distant again and a little sad. "But I don't know how to pray. I haven't been to church much, and I only read the Bible that one summer so many years ago. I don't suppose it really took."

"Callie," McKay spoke, his voice hoarse. She turned to find him staring at her. "I've been a follower of Jesus Christ for many years, and I've also spent many years studying the Bible. You can believe what I'm about to tell you."

Pup nodded and watched him, utterly captivated by what she saw in his face.

"That day, if you sincerely believed Jesus Christ died for you and that you needed Him to save you from your sins, then it took, Callie; it took. You're a born-again child of the King, and nothing will ever take that away. I won't tell you that once you're saved it doesn't matter what you do, but if you reached out in childlike faith, Callie, then God made you His for all of eternity."

"Do you think so, McKay?"

"Yes, I do. I believe it with all my heart. If there's any doubt in your mind, Callie, and you want to pray again, I'd be happy to help you, but I do believe that nothing can take us from God's hand."

Her eyes were intent on him, but McKay didn't think she was really focusing. "There was a verse I remember, McKay. I think it was in John. Something about no one snatching us from the Father's hand."

"I know the one. It's in John 10. Shall I get my Bible and show you?"

"No," Pup told him, but her voice was not defiant. "I remember it now, it says that God's hand is even greater than His Son's. I read the book of John several times that summer. I know the one I'm thinking of." She surprised him by standing. "I might want to see that verse later, McKay, but right now I need to take a little walk."

"All right. If you need me, Callie, don't hesitate."

"Thanks, McKay," she said sincerely. She paused. "Thanks for everything."

With that she was gone. McKay heard the front door open and shut, but he didn't move. Indeed, he was still sitting in the same place when his father entered the room many minutes later looking for hot coffee.

18

"I haven't done enough of this," Pup whispered quietly to God. She walked until she reached the lake and then stood very still, her eyes on the mirrorlike surface. "I remember talking to You as a child, but I just stopped. I didn't know it could be like this. I didn't know I could be so certain. I remember now. I remember so much of what I read that summer in Denver."

She stopped, too full of emotion to go on. Verses and stories came flooding back to her: The lame man who wanted to get into the water, but no one would lift him; the woman who had had five husbands and was living with yet another man; the small man who climbed a tree just to gain a glimpse of Christ. She had gobbled up those stories, but the man she'd been working with had not been like McKay Harrington. He'd been cold and unapproachable. McKay's faith was sincere. And now wasn't her faith, too?

"I've had You all along and not really understood. It was suddenly so clear when McKay talked to me. At times I think I had a grasp, but then I was too busy to pay attention. I want to pay attention now, God. I want to be as sincere as McKay is. I want it to be real this time. I want to tell Nick and Camille. The church at Boulder," she suddenly said, "I could go there. The one that Travis Buchanan attends. I could start down on Saturday nights and sleep in the woods until morning. I wouldn't look fancy, but that doesn't matter."

Pup stopped, her eyes closing. Her mind was going so fast she felt she would burst. Suddenly it was wonderful that she wasn't at home or on a job. She had been disappointed that McKay hadn't been more aware of her situation, but now she really had time to think about this. Suddenly she had to see him. She turned from the bank toward the lake, tripping on a branch as she went. As usual she never noticed. Something else was on her mind.

McKay had become concerned, so he was in the backyard when he spotted Pup coming from the direction of the lake. She didn't seem to notice him and would have walked right past, but he called to her.

"Oh, I didn't see you," she spoke as she approached, tripping again as she came. She stopped so close in front of McKay that they were nearly touching. "McKay, may I see that verse in John—the one we were talking about?"

"Of course. Come on in. Did you go to the lake?" he asked as he led the way, but Pup didn't answer. Her head was bent, her mind busy with the verse. She preceded McKay into the house as he held the door and then followed him to the kitchen, running right into the back of him when he stopped by the table. A smile lit his face before he turned to her. This was the Pup he knew best.

"Why don't you have something to eat, and I'll get my Bible."

Pup then noticed that they were alone.

"Do your folks sleep late?"

"No. They've been down to eat, and now they're getting ready for church."

"Oh."

"Here, sit down." He got her to the table and put more coffee and a plateful of eggs and potatoes in front of her. He slipped upstairs for his Bible, but she still hadn't eaten when he returned.

"Eat up, Callie. I'll find the verse."

She began by picking up the fork, but it didn't go to her plate. She stirred her coffee with it and then set it back down, all the while staring at McKay.

"It's right here in chapter 10, verses 28 and 29. I'll read them to you. 'And I give unto them eternal life; and they shall never perish, neither shall any man pluck them out of my hand. My Father, who gave them to me, is greater than all; and no man is able to pluck them out of my Father's hand.' And then, just as you talked about, Callie, we can know that Jesus is God's Son because the next verse is Christ's own words. It says, 'I and my Father are one.' "

He looked up to find her absentmindedly taking a drink of coffee and dripping some on the dark fabric of her dress. McKay came to earth with a thud. He desperately wanted to discuss these verses with her, but this was important too. With one hand he took her coffee mug from her and set it on the table. With the other hand he gently captured her jaw. When her face was turned and her eyes met his, he spoke.

"You're going to ruin your dress for church if you don't watch what you're doing."

"Oh," Pup's eyes widened, and she gave herself a shake. "I completely forgot to act."

McKay's heart clenched with pain. Pup, who was still looking at him, read it in his eyes.

"It's like that, you know," she stated quietly but without apology. "I'm clumsy if I'm not playing a role."

McKay looked at her a moment longer and then stood. He went to a drawer in the kitchen and brought out a tablecloth. A moment later he was draping Pup, loosely tying the ends of the cloth around her neck. He sat back down at the table to find her looking at him in surprise.

"My mother never wears her Sunday dress to eat," he said conversationally. "She always eats and then changes for church. You go ahead and eat, and I'll keep your coffee warmed up."

Pup picked up her fork and began, but she didn't taste much. She kept looking up at McKay. Finally she said, "You're very kind, McKay. I've known that for some time now, but I never told you."

"I'm glad you find me kind. I wouldn't want to treat you any other way."

Pup's heart was too full to say anything more. McKay was very attractive to her right then, and with just a glimpse of insight into what had happened to her all those years ago on the streets of Boulder, she was overwhelmed.

"How's the coffee? Want more?"

"No, it's fine. Did you make the eggs?"

"No, my father did the honors this morning."

She continued to eat but felt suddenly tired. She didn't want to miss anything, but she would be tripping and spilling things the rest of the day unless she concentrated on her movements. However, she wasn't given any more time to speculate on the matter or to give in to her fatigue. McKay's parents were coming downstairs; it was time to go to church.

The Longs Peak Bible Church was larger than Pup had been expecting. It was high-steepled, long, and unusually wide. There was a bell tower below the steeple, and the entire building was painted a soft dove gray. Because she pulled herself into a role the moment she finished eating breakfast, she was able to walk up the stairs and through the double doors without mishap.

She was aware of McKay's eyes on her but didn't look at him. She couldn't help play-acting right now; it was the only way she would not make a spectacle of herself. This lasted only until the sermon started and McKay, seated to her left, opened his Bible and held it out between them. With that Pup was lost. She had heard the opening words the pastor shared, but as soon as she noticed that McKay's Bible was open to the book of John, she began to read and never looked up.

McKay heard little of the sermon himself. His head was turned just enough so that his eyes were intent on Pup's profile. It looked as if she read quickly and then at times would sit back slightly, her eyes focused straight ahead but not seeing the person in front of her.

McKay glanced over at one time to find Brita Stuart's gaze on him from the pew behind them. He smiled at her, and she smiled back, but there was little warmth in it. It was then that McKay realized how intently he'd been watching Pup. Things weren't as Brita thought, but there was no way to explain. McKay continued to keep a close eye on his guest. His parents seemed sensitive as well, and from time to time he saw them glance over. He'd had a few minutes to tell them what had gone on at the table that morning so they could pray, but he knew that Callie Jennings was a complete mystery to them. He had to conclude that she was something of a mystery to him as well.

He was somewhere in the middle of this thought when the organ sprang to life and everyone stood for the closing hymn. Pup shared a hymnal with Harry, who was on her right, and the moment they stopped singing she asked about a particular verse. Harry was so like McKay that she felt immediately comfortable with him.

"That's right out of Scripture," he explained when he'd heard her out. "Would you like to see it?"

"Yes, please."

Harry opened to the book of 2 Chronicles, and Pup, nearly his height, leaned close to follow his finger as he read one verse. "This is referring to sin and forgiveness. It shows God's great love for His people," he said.

"By His people, you mean followers of Christ."

"Not in this verse. This verse is talking about Israel—the Jews—God's chosen people all through history."

"But they rejected Him, didn't they? I mean, wasn't He crucified by the Jews?"

"Yes, He was, Callie, but that's an amazing thing about God's love. It never changes. Because God is God, He knew His Son would be killed by the people who filled His heart, but He chose them and they remain His forever."

"Just like we do. No one can pluck us from the Father's hand."

"That's right."

McKay, who had been standing quietly to the side of them, watched the smile in his father's eyes and knew just how he felt.

"It wasn't clear to me until this morning."

Harry nodded as he looked into her dark, intelligent eyes and saw how serious she was. "What was the turning point for you?"

"Something McKay told me—that the decision I'd made as a child was still valid in God's eyes. I haven't been to church regularly. At first I had no choice because I was so young, but lately I've just gotten accustomed to doing things on my own. That's a sin, isn't it?"

"Yes, Callie," he said gently. "Anytime we omit God from our world, we sin against Him."

"That's just what I did," she confessed plainly. "I left Him out of my life, but I realized today that He never forgot me. I think that's a miracle."

Harry smiled. "It's pretty wondrous."

Pup stepped back and bumped into McKay, stepping on the toe of his boot and putting her elbow into his stomach. She never even noticed he was there. McKay still felt the pressure on his toe and the blow to his stomach, but in a way they felt good. It meant that all pretense had dropped away. She was Pup once again.

"How about a walk?" McKay asked Pup when Sunday dinner was over.

"Sure," Pup accepted, "just as soon as I help your mother with the dishes."

McKay's look at the front of her dress caused her brow to lower.

"I'll pay attention," she told him.

"I'll believe that when I see it," he said good-naturedly.

She wanted to feel angry with him, but in truth he had reason to doubt. All conversation during the meal had been about Scripture. Pup had spilled and upset her way through the entire meal. She had laughed when McKay got the tablecloth out for her again, but it was the only reason she didn't look worse.

"I will pay attention," she said again. "I want to help."

"Why don't I help?" Harry suggested. "You two go walk, and Liz and I will do the honors."

"Of course," Liz put in. "Harry and I work very well together."

Pup didn't answer, but McKay took her arm and led her toward the door. They were no more on the porch when she said, "I wouldn't have broken anything, McKay."

"You didn't come here to work, Callie."

"Well, I certainly didn't come here to be waited on by your poor mother."

She had stopped on the porch, and he could see that she was not going to budge.

"Be honest with yourself, Callie; you're rather preoccupied today." He couldn't stop his eyes from dropping to the small spot on her front.

Pup might have forgiven him this if he hadn't looked so amused. She crossed her arms over her chest.

"I've done it now," McKay mumbled.

"I was not going to think about the Bible at all," she declared, seeing in McKay's eyes that he was barely holding his laughter.

"Don't you laugh," she told him, but by now she was smiling.

"Oh, Pup, what am I going to do with you?"

"Not the dishes," she managed to sound affronted, "that's for certain."

She walked off the porch to the sound of his laughter. He followed her and caught up to walk by her side, but it was some time before either spoke. McKay had never known anyone like her. He was fairly certain that she was brilliant. Her social skills were excellent when she was acting, but when she was herself, such things like spilling coffee on her dress or mixing eggshell into her muffins were not a concern. Did any of that matter? McKay honestly didn't know. It would have helped him to know that his parents were in the same quandary. They were discussing the issue right now.

"Do you know what's going on, Harry?" The young people had been gone for barely five minutes.

"Not exactly," he admitted.

"Does McKay?"

"I don't know."

Husband and wife looked at each other.

"She's absolutely fascinating," Liz said not unkindly.

"She is that."

"All she wants to do is talk about Scripture, Harry. We don't know anything about her personally."

"No, and I think it's going to have to be that way, Liz."

Liz Harrington turned away from the cupboard and stared at her mate. Harry went on quietly.

"Mickey always tells us everything he can. He never tells us things that have to remain confidential because that's his job. I think it's the same with Callie."

Liz stared at him. "You don't mean you think she works for the treasury department?"

Harry just looked at her. Liz couldn't take it right then. She picked up another plate to dry, and Harry went back to scrubbing the large kettle.

"Do you think she has any family left?"

"I would guess not," Harry answered. "But none of that matters. She's here now and we'll do all we can to show her love."

"Do you think McKay will become serious about her?"

"There's something special about that girl, Liz, I'll give you that. But as to McKay's feelings, I don't know if he knows himself."

They finished the dishes in silence. Harry and Liz deeply loved their only son, and now God had brought this unusual woman into their midst. They both felt a sudden urge to pray.

19

Although they hadn't discussed where to go, McKay and Callie walked to the lake. The lake reminded Pup of her home, and McKay had let her lead the way. They sat on a log, a fat one that had fallen years before, the sun at their backs, their eyes out over the surface of the water. It was then that McKay noticed the drops of perspiration on Pup's brow. He was very comfortable in shirtsleeves, his tie and collar gone and the top button undone, but although Pup didn't say anything, he could tell she was very warm. It suddenly occurred to him: The wig. It would have been like wearing a tight hat, one that didn't let your head breathe.

"Would you be cooler if you took the wig off?"

Lost in thought, Pup looked over at him.

"What's that?"

"I just noticed that you look hot. It's pretty private here. You could take off the wig." He was thinking of her and not of his own embarrassment.

Pup glanced at the trees around them and then along the open spaces before looking at McKay.

"It would be cooler, wouldn't it?"

McKay nodded. "I would think so."

With that Pup reached up and pulled the curls from her head. Her eyes closed with relief as soon as the breeze blew against her damp head.

Watching her, McKay asked, "Better?"

"Yes. Thank you."

"You have the curliest hair I've ever seen," he commented as he looked at the dark ringlets all over her head. "What is it like when it gets very long?"

"It takes awhile for it to get heavy enough to hang down; it's only happened once in the last 13 years. When it gets to that point, I just keep cutting it away from my face." She ran a gentle hand over her scalp, slightly fluffing the black curls. "One time I pulled a hair straight out from the crown of my head. It was two feet long, but with the curls it only hung to my shoulders."

McKay shook his head in amazement.

"My mother's hair was light brown and straight—Jubal got that," she informed him, "but Govern and I got Papa's black curls."

"Govern did look a little like you. I'd have never made the connection without seeing you standing side-by-side, but there was a resemblance."

"Yeah," Pup said softly, her eyes shifting back to the water. McKay wondered if he'd upset her.

"Do you think about your folks much, Callie?"

"I have this morning," she admitted with a soft sigh. "I know Mama's decision for Christ was as real as my own, but I don't know what Papa believed. He was a fair man and an honest one, but he never had much time for church." She paused for a moment. "Hell is a real place, isn't it, McKay?"

"Yes, it is."

Pup sighed.

"Does that upset you?"

"I've always considered myself a realist, McKay, but I've been in some sort of dreamland concerning my brothers. I've wanted better for them, and unless they were staring me in the face, I imagined it to be so. When I saw Jubal at the bank in Denver, I thought I would die. Before then I think I had

168

myself convinced that it was all a case of mistaken identity or some other nonsense."

"That night you came to my room and asked me to get word to Nick," McKay suddenly remembered, "I had seen Jubal in Denver and didn't know whether or not I could tell you."

"I knew something wasn't right," Pup said, turning her head to look at him. "I thought Nick had set me up."

"He wouldn't do that."

"No, he wouldn't. It was wrong of me even to think it."

They fell quiet again. Having told McKay how she felt about her brothers, Pup felt better, but as it had in the morning, her mind swiftly turned back to all she had remembered about her conversion.

"Tell me some more about Jesus Christ, McKay, will you?"

"Sure." He was more than happy to oblige. He began with Christ's birth and was sharing with her about Jesus' visit to the temple when she surprised him with a question.

"He'd actually gone off and not told His mother where He was?"

"That's right."

"But isn't that a sin?"

McKay shook his head no. "Be careful not to lay the sin of Joseph and Mary on Jesus."

"I don't follow you."

"They were both told by an angel that this child was the Christ, right?"

"Yes."

"They knew before He was born that He was God."

"Okay."

"So this was something they needed to believe, *truly* believe. It was their choice, but they forgot that. The Bible says they searched for three days before checking in the temple. It was the last place they looked. And what did Jesus say to them? He said, 'Why were you searching for me? Didn't you know I would be in my Father's house?' If they had remembered who He was, they'd have looked there right away. Do you see what I'm saying? And don't forget—this is God we're talking about here, Callie; there was no sin involved."

She nodded with understanding, her face intent on his as she hung on every word. They talked on this way for several hours. A few times Pup asked questions of McKay that caused him to consider why he believed as he did, and he loved being challenged. She was like a thirsty cloth where Jesus was concerned, and a few times McKay mentally gasped at the depth and insight of her comments and inquiries. Before today he would not have considered her a seeking individual, but now he was seeing another side of her.

"I'm getting thirsty," McKay said when there was a lull. "How about we continue this on the porch with some tea or lemonade?"

"All right."

Pup pulled her wig back into place, and not for the first time McKay was amazed at how it changed her appearance back to that of the woman he'd first met. They stood and had begun walking toward the house when McKay said casually, "I'm going to change into denim pants for the hayride tonight. You might want to change into something less dressy yourself."

"Hayride?"

"Yes . . ." McKay's voice remained calm, "the hayride and bonfire with the church family tonight."

Pup came to a complete stop and looked at McKay.

"I didn't tell you," he stated, having just realized. "I'm sorry, Callie. We talked about so much on the way here that I thought I'd mentioned it."

"You didn't." She was not upset, but neither was she thrilled.

"You don't have to attend."

"What do you do?"

"It's just a regular hayride," McKay began, not realizing that Pup had never been on one in her life. "And afterward we'll have a bonfire and cookout. It's for Stan and Lisa. Stan's my cousin. Remember—I told you he's getting married. You might have seen him this morning. He plays the organ at church. Lisa Giss grew up around here; in fact, her family is our closest neighbor."

"And how do you know I'm invited to this?"

"Because everyone is—the whole church. The more the merrier and all that."

"I don't have a gift, McKay."

"No gifts are expected. The wedding isn't until Saturday."

Pup started to walk again, but not out of anger; she thought better when she was moving. It was hard enough not to respond to Liz and Harry's kindness; how would she keep an entire church family at arm's length? For the first time in 13 years, Pup wondered if her job was worth the pain of trusting no one. She was used to being alone but not lonely. Now she'd come home with McKay, not believing all he'd said of his family but finding it to be true. They didn't do anything but welcome her and treat her like a woman. She knew they must be curious—who wouldn't be? But they couldn't have been more gracious if they'd tried.

"I am sorry," McKay now repeated, and Pup knew she had to explain. But how to start?

"It's all right, McKay. I'm just trying to figure out what to do."

"Why wouldn't you want to go?"

"There are many reasons, but the main one is what an oddity I'll be if I come and don't talk to anyone."

"You can talk to people, Callie—at least to some," McKay said sincerely. "You can ask questions and show an interest in them while simply sidestepping questions that grow too personal. My parents are the only ones who know how you and I met. When the pastor asked about you this morning, I told him we have mutual friends and acquaintances in both Boulder and Denver. The people here are not naturally suspicious. I was able to be completely honest, and my explanation was taken at face value."

They were almost back to the house. Both had slowed their steps, and with a hand to her arm, McKay brought Pup to a slow halt. She faced him.

"It really is fine, Callie, if you don't want to come. But I know you'll have a good time if you do."

She looked into his eyes, which were almost on the same level as her own. He was utterly sincere, and if Pup was honest with herself, she wanted to go.

"All right, McKay. I'll go."

"Great," he said with warm sincerity. "As I said, I think you'll have a good time."

Once more Pup started toward the house, but McKay caught her arm again. He reached up and carefully adjusted Pup's wig so it sat straight on her head.

"Mickey." Harry chose that moment to call from an upstairs window. McKay's head turned so he missed the way Pup's eyes closed in despair. How would she ever make it through the evening?

"Callie Jennings, this is my sister, Maureen Pile." McKay introduced Pup the moment they arrived at the church.

"Hello, Callie," Maureen said kindly, shifting the baby on her hip so she could hold out her hand.

"Hello," Pup said in return, shaking her hand and thinking how much she looked like her mother.

"And this," McKay went on, tickling the baby's exposed bare foot, "is Marcus. Are you going to come and see me, Mark?" he asked of his nephew, but was only watched suspiciously from his mother's hold.

"Not today, Mickey," Maureen explained. "I think he's cutting teeth, and he wants only Luke or me. He wouldn't even go to Grandpa."

"Now that *is* serious," McKay said as he tried again to wring a smile from his nephew.

"Are you going to ride or stay here?" McKay asked his sister.

"I'll stay here, but Luke is driving one of the wagons."

Maureen's eyes shifted to Pup. Although uncomfortable, Pup tried to think fast.

"How old is your baby?" she asked, and almost smiled at her own genius.

"Almost a year," Maureen said proudly. "He was born June 29." She looked down at her son now, and he managed a small smile for his mother before laying his head against her shoulder.

"How long are you here, Mickey?"

"All week—at least that's the plan right now."

"A week—good. You've needed some time off. Oh, there's Luke waving at us. Come and meet my husband, Callie."

McKay and Pup trailed after Maureen, and it was decided that they would ride on Luke's wagon. It was all done with little ceremony. The pastor and his two children were on the same wagon, so Pup met them, but so were a dozen other people whose names she couldn't have remembered if she'd been held at knifepoint. As she climbed aboard, she felt some concern that she would be jostled and lose her hair, but other than a few wiggly children, everyone sat still and enjoyed the ride. The area was beautiful, and Pup was content to sit and listen to the talk and singing around her.

It was a long ride—almost two hours—but the peaks of the mountains were even more beautiful when the wagons moved out of town. With McKay sitting nearby, his presence rather comforting, and no one trying to talk to her, the time flew. When they arrived back at the church she found that tables, some laden with food, had been set up for the meal.

A plate was pressed into her hand, and for the first time all evening she and McKay were separated. She felt a tickle at her neck and reached up to remove a piece of hay, but otherwise stood still. There were people before and after her in line, but no one spoke to her. Pup wasn't wounded by this. She was content to stand quietly and try not to scratch the back of her legs where she'd sat on the piles of hay. The line moved slowly, but all at once the food was before her. She filled her plate and, still not seeing anyone from McKay's family, found a seat at a long table and tucked into her plate, remembering just in time to drop into a role and keep the food on her plate and not on her dress. A young couple sat across from her as she was finishing, and although they both said hello, they started a private conversation.

It was swiftly growing dark when Pup rose, put her plate on a side table, and moved toward the bonfire that was well underway. People couldn't stand too close to the blaze, but it wasn't long before a huge circle surrounded the fire. From time to time Pup glanced around for a glimpse of McKay, but not until she changed sides did she find him standing with his mother.

"Here you are," he said kindly when she approached. "Did you get something to eat?"

"Yes. I just finished."

"Good."

"Oh, Callie," Liz spoke. "You got some straw in your hair."

Pup bent her head a little, and Liz innocently reached up and pulled at the straw at the top of Pup's wig. She visibly started when one piece stuck and Pup's entire head of hair moved down her forehead almost an inch.

A moment later Pup found herself hauled into McKay's arms. He set his cheek against hers as if they were embracing, and with a quick hand to the back of her hair, righted the wig. The next moment he let go of her. It was all done in a matter of seconds, but time seemed to stand still for Pup. McKay's arms felt wonderful. Pup looked up at him in something akin to wonder. She could have stared all night, but a small noise made her glance over at Liz. There was no mistaking her expression of alarm.

"I'm sorry, Callie," the older woman whispered. "I'm so sorry."

"It's all right, Liz," she said, and she meant it. All she could feel was McKay's arms. But then the reality of the situation—where she was, how the wig had moved, the reason for McKay's hug—hit her like a fist. She put up a front so quickly that McKay blinked.

"I'm sorry," Liz was saying again.

Pup beamed at her and laughed a little. "It's fine, Liz." Even her voice was different. "Did you get some coffee?"

"No," Liz answered without hearing herself.

"I'll get you some, shall I?" With that Pup moved off.

Liz couldn't bring herself to look at McKay. She could feel her son's eyes on her profile, but she made herself stare into the flames. She didn't blink, not even when smoke drifted her way. She was glad for it. If someone asked, it would be easier to explain why her eyes were wet with tears.

20

McKay's light was out, but he was not asleep when his mother opened his bedroom door. She held a lantern in one hand and the front of her robe with the other. McKay immediately scooted up against the headboard and reached for the lantern in order to set it on the night table. Liz sat on the edge of the mattress. Not until he turned the flame higher however, did he see his mother's tears.

"Oh, Mom," he said compassionately, his voice low.

"Has she been ill, McKay? Just tell me that," she whispered.

"No, Mom. It's nothing like that."

She drew in a shuddering breath.

"Please tell me you're taking good care of her, McKay, please."

"I'm trying to, Mom, but it's not as easy as you might think."

She was shaking her head. "I don't know why I said that. I can see it's not a simple thing, and I've tried never to intrude, but there's something about that girl that just wrings my heart dry."

McKay could well understand. He remembered the way he felt when he left her cabin that first time. He'd been sick with pity for her. He had thought her the most pathetic creature he'd ever encountered. But to explain all of that to his mother would entail a huge breach of confidence; he had to find some words to help her.

"Mom, this is going to sound cold, but you mustn't pity Callie. I did at one time, but the truth is—" Here he stopped. What was the truth? That she was the most intelligent and capable person he'd ever met? That she was a brilliant spy for the U.S. Treasury Office?

As a matter of fact, Pup had been very upset by the wig incident. She'd maintained the facade of a polite stranger until she retired for the night, but she was not someone to be pitied. McKay took his mother's hand.

"I simply can't go into it, Mom, but I will see to it that she's all right. Don't be upset about this the rest of the week. Pu—." McKay stopped and began again. "Callie is a very private person, but get to know her as much as you can. I know you'll enjoy her."

Liz nodded. She knew she couldn't expect any more, but it was so unsettling. She stood, and McKay handed her the light.

"I'm sorry, Mom."

"It's all right, McKay. I'll just take your advice and be myself tomorrow. Goodnight."

"Goodnight."

She exited on that note, and returned to her own bedroom. She blew the lantern out, but when Harry felt the bed move as she climbed in, he came up on one elbow.

"You just coming to bed?" He didn't remember falling asleep without her.

"Yes. I had to talk to McKay."

Harry heard the tears in her voice.

"Are you all right?"

"No." There was a distinct quiver now.

"Well, come here and tell me about it."

Harry's offer was sincere, but once in her husband's arms, all Liz could do was cry. It wasn't long before she was asleep. They had a chance to talk about it briefly the next morning, but since Harry had no more answers than Liz did, they knew they would have to take McKay at his word and act as normal as possible.

"You're going to drop the act, Pup," McKay said firmly, his face close to Pup's. "And you're going to drop it now."

McKay could have howled with frustration when her brows rose in question and she only looked at him. Breakfast, eaten an hour past, had been without a spill or upset. Liz and Harry acted as normal as ever, and even though Harry was headed into town where he was a druggist and ran a small office, Liz had given McKay her list and asked him to go to town for a few things. McKay had *told* Pup, not asked her, to join him, and even though they were now alone in the barn, the perfect mask of composure was still in place.

Praying for calm, he turned away and finished hitching the horse to the wagon. Without so much as a missed step, Pup took McKay's offered hand and climbed aboard the wagon. McKay swung into the seat, his whole being praying for wisdom in this situation.

They had just moved onto the road from the drive that led to the house, when he said, "I was reading in chapter ten in the book of Mark this morning, where the children ran to see Jesus but the disciples wouldn't allow them to get close."

McKay forced himself not to look at Pup.

"Jesus rebuked the men and told them to let the children in. And the little ones ran to Him and were blessed by Him."

"Jesus actually said that—that the children should come close?"

McKay had to stop from closing his eyes in relief. She was back. She was even leaning forward in the seat to better see his face, bumping his arm in the process. McKay now allowed himself to look over. Her eyes were soft with question. A tenderness so strong and poignant that he could hardly speak filled him.

"I didn't know that," Pup said when he didn't answer her. She sat back on the seat. "I wonder if Jesus ever wanted children of His own? I mean, He never married, did He, McKay?"

"No, He didn't." It was a nice, normal question, and McKay was able to get his reply out. He thought fast and went on. "Jesus was very single-minded in His purpose for being on the earth, and He knew He was going to die. I think His compassion and tenderness toward women was evident every time He dealt with them, but clearly a wife and family of His own did not figure into the picture."

"I can't believe how much there is to learn. I read a lot that one summer, and snatches are coming back, but it's all so huge. Did you say you read your Bible in the morning, McKay?"

"Yes."

"Could I possibly borrow it tonight?"

"Certainly. I'm sorry I didn't offer it to you. Was there something in particular you wanted?"

"Just more," she said quietly, and McKay let it be. Five minutes later they were outside Longmont's general store.

"Well, Brita," McKay said as he turned down an aisle looking for the cornmeal. Pup had spotted some used books up front, and he'd left her there.

"Hello, McKay." Her voice was soft, and McKay knew she was hurt.

"How are you?" he asked sincerely, his voice kind.

"All right," she told him, but clearly she wasn't. It looked to him like she might have been crying.

McKay didn't know what to say. There was no way he could explain his situation, but not explaining was going to make things impossible between them. Surprisingly, Brita took the decision out of his hand.

"That weekend our families were together, McKay—was that all in my imagination, or did I see interest in your eyes?"

To be put on the spot in such a way was beyond discomfort; it was dreadful.

"No answer?" her tone was a little hard now. "Well, it's no surprise. You're obviously looking for a woman who doesn't care if you hug and kiss her in public."

McKay looked so shocked that she let him have it again.

"And don't you deny it, McKay Harrington. I saw you at the fire."

"I did not kiss her," he stated quietly.

"But you did hug her; don't deny that!"

McKay's heart squeezed in pain. What a horrible mess. He had wanted everything to be so special. He had wanted Pup to feel loved and welcomed and a part of the family, both at church and at home, but he hadn't foreseen anything like Brita Stuart standing there glaring at him. He couldn't say she was being petty; after all, it looked terrible, but McKay suddenly wondered what he'd seen in her.

"Callie Jennings is my friend, and I'm sorry that's a problem for you," he said softly. Some of Brita's fire left her. "I never meant to hurt you or play games with you, and I'm sorry that it's come across that way. I'm also sorry that you believe we've made so much of a commitment to each other that I have to explain my actions to you."

The pain that crossed her face was almost more than he could take, but he kept on.

"Again, Brita, I'm sorry. But I think if we're honest, we both know it's probably for the best."

Wanting to be brave she nodded, but inside she was miserable. She made herself go back to her perusal of the shelves and managed to say goodbye when McKay moved on his way. Her eyes didn't see the well-stocked shelves; they only saw the woman who was with McKay. What he saw in such a plain woman whose figure resembled a broom handle she couldn't possibly understand. But even the knowledge that she was much prettier, in both face and figure, didn't stop the pain. She could have been kind to McKay when he'd come up, but instead she was mean and accusatory. Her young heart told her it was time to face facts. She let McKay Harrington get away, and she was probably going to regret it for the rest of her life.

"I can walk home, McKay," Pup surprised him by saying. She had just tripped on the boardwalk, and he'd caught her. He now looked into her eyes and saw that she was serious.

"What are you talking about?"

"The girl inside. If you want to see her home, I can get back to your folks on my own."

"It's all right, Callie; she's just a friend."

"Then why didn't you bring her over and introduce me?"

She had him, and they both knew it.

"It's rather complicated."

Pup looked at him. She was not the type to mother people and question everything they said. She'd already questioned him once, so she let the matter drop and allowed him to help her into the wagon. As they pulled away, Pup wondered if the problem stemmed from the hug at the campfire. Again her heart squeezed in pain. Much as she would have hated to admit it, she could have put the other woman's heart at ease in a moment. The hug hadn't meant a thing to McKay.

"Don't you like it?" Liz asked Pup later that day as she carefully watched her face. The younger woman had just tasted a piece of berry pie.

"It's wonderful, but how do you get your crust to taste like this? Mine is always a little, oh, I don't know, off, I guess."

"Do you beat your eggs?"

"You put eggs in this?"

Pup's look was so comical that Liz couldn't stop the small laugh that escaped her throat. Pup's look turned to one of chagrin, and then she laughed a little too.

"I suppose McKay has told you that cooking is not my strong point."

"He never mentioned it," she said honestly.

Pup shrugged, her look still comical. "When you live alone, you're just not that fussy. At least I'm not."

"Do you enjoy living alone?" Liz asked, hoping it was a safe enough question.

"Most of the time, but it's been nice here, having someone to visit with over meals and in the evening."

"I hope you won't let this be your last visit," Liz commented, topping off their coffee cups. "Summer can be hot, but spring around here is lovely."

"Come spring I'm usually stuck in the cabin a little longer than most."

"Do you live that far up in the hills?"

"Not all the way up, but pretty far."

Liz opened her mouth to comment on how far McKay must have had to track Govern Hackett, but she remembered just in time that the man was Callie's brother. *Hackett and Jennings.* The names came together in Liz's mind for the first time. Had Callie been married before? Or had Govern Hackett only been a half-brother to her? It was yet one more curiosity over their house guest.

"Do you have any neighbors?" Liz tried another safe tack.

Pup couldn't stop her smile. "The closest ones are Percy and Mud Dougan."

"Percy and Mud?"

Pup now laughed. "They're brothers who mine Boulder Creek. Percy keeps to himself, but Mud goes to town whenever he can get away."

"They sound fascinating."

"They are that," she couldn't help but agree, a fond smile lighting her face. But that smile wasn't just for Mud.

Pup knew what Liz was doing, and had she been a more demonstrative person she'd have hugged the older woman. They'd been in the kitchen for more than an hour and managed to talk only of generalities. It did Pup's heart a great deal of good to know that Liz Harrington cared enough to treat her so graciously, but something was niggling at the back of her mind.

I can never get close to people, she told herself. *I'm forever keeping folks at arm's length. McKay tells his family everything, and I tell Camille and Nick some things, but I know whose life is richer.* Pup wondered if Christ was the difference, or if McKay was just a more open individual. She strongly suspected that his relationship with God had much to do with it.

The afternoon moved into evening, and the four of them played whist until rather late. It had been a pleasant day and evening, but Pup couldn't get a few questions from her mind: Was her job worth her having to live the way she did? Would God want her to continue living a life of subterfuge and privacy? Pup simply didn't have a clue, and it was hours after she climbed into bed before she fell asleep.

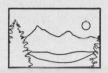

21

The week was moving along in splendid form. Pup began reading McKay's Bible, and dozens of questions surfaced. He and his parents willingly answered them, and Pup's knowledge and awareness increased daily. Time took on a new quality. The days didn't rush by; they were spent visiting, walking, and reading. There was no reason to hurry. It seemed that the week with this family would joyfully last forever—until McKay's father came home on Wednesday evening with a sealed telegram for his guest. Harry and the two others who witnessed this exchange were filled with curiosity, but no one asked about the contents. Pup only thanked him and put the letter in her pocket. She did not mean to be overly private, but she was intent on something McKay had just said about creation and hardly even noticed the piece of paper.

It was not until she was readying for bed, and after she'd upset her night table and glass of water, that she found the note in her pocket. What she read made her sit down on the side of the bed rather hard. Having come quickly back to earth, she stared into space, her mind trying to deal with the transition. To be called back to work so abruptly was something of a shock. She once again read the missive in her hand.

CJ: Report to Charlie Barnes, Longmont, Colo. Status: Immediate. NW.

Only one other time had Pup been summoned to a job while not at home. It was years ago now, but she would never forget it: A treasury man had been suspected of betrayal. Was this the same situation? Had information been leaked? Pup felt chilled to the bone. She had to leave; there was no other choice. She had to contact this man—this Charlie Barnes—and learn what was expected of her. Nick was probably losing his mind as it was. Determined to leave on the spot, Pup stood and then realized the hour. She couldn't wander around Longmont in the dark, not to mention disturb her host and hostess. Pup mulled over the various options and found none satisfactory.

She had tried telling McKay that it didn't work to get close to people, but he hadn't understood. Now she would have to leave Liz and Harry with no explanation. They were bound to be hurt. It then occurred to her that she could not face them. It wasn't that she felt ashamed, but she knew how awkward it would be for all of them if she told them in person.

A moment later Pup sat at the small writing desk that sat under the window in her room. She found paper in a drawer, and opening the ink pot, found it fresh. Not given to flowery phrases, she dipped the quill and wrote what was in her heart.

Dear Harry and Liz,

To say thank you for this time seems woefully inadequate. I can't begin to tell you how wonderful it has been. I have responsibilities, however, and my time is not always my own. Now is such a time. I hate to leave without seeing you, but I feel it is best for all. I would like to say that I will see you again, but I can't predict this either. Thank you for the caring you've shown me. McKay said you were wonderful, and I thought you sounded too good to be true. God has shown me much this week, including the fact that there are two people in this world whose hearts are as big as the mountains.

Sincerely,
Callie Jennings

Pup felt indescribably tired after she finished. She wanted desperately to lay her head down and weep, but she forced such feelings aside. Knowing she would need to walk from the Harringtons, she kept out the most casual of her dresses and only a few other things for the morning. When at last she put her head on her pillow, she wondered if she would sleep at all. She must be away before daybreak, before anyone else was up. It was the only way her plan was going to work.

McKay didn't try to analyze his decision, but he decided to sleep with his door open. He didn't know if it had to do with the telegram Pup received or with the look on his mother's face. She was worried; he could see it in her eyes. His father looked uncertain as well. He could tell they wanted to ask questions but were restraining themselves. He knew their motives were driven by concern and not merely curiosity. McKay didn't have a chance to tell them that he had the same concerns for Pup's well-being, but there was little he could do about it at the time.

He fell asleep with his guest heavy on his mind, and while the night was still very black, woke suddenly and stared into the darkness. He didn't think he'd heard a noise, but he was certainly wide awake and alert. Lying very still, he waited a few minutes, and when he heard nothing, rolled onto his stomach to go back to sleep. He got as comfortable as possible, but sleep would not return. He made himself lie still: Tossing and turning never helped. Still he did not sleep. After only 20 minutes, he rose, pulled on his robe, went downstairs to the living room, and lit a lantern. He'd only been settled into a chair with a book for ten minutes when he heard steps on the stairs. A moment later he saw Pup come into the shadows of the room.

He was on the verge of asking her if she was having trouble sleeping when he saw that she was dressed. Turning the lantern brighter, he came out of his chair and went to stand before her. His eyes took in the bag in her hand and the shawl over her arm.

"I can't believe you would leave like this."

"I have no choice."

"Without word to anyone?"

"I left a note for your parents."

"What was in that telegram, Callie?"

She shook her head. "You know better than to ask, McKay."

Now he was shaking his own head. "This is foolishness, Callie; you can't get a train to Boulder at this time of the night."

"I'm not going to Boulder."

Pup very suddenly found herself nearly hauled up against McKay's chest. He'd taken her by the upper arms and moved her close so he could look down into her face. His own features were taut with severity.

"If there's an operation going down right here in Longmont, Pup, I want to know about it."

"Then you'll have to ask Nick," she said with more calm than she felt.

Suddenly he was angry. His heart told him to let her go, but he didn't listen.

"I don't know how you can stand to live like this."

Pup didn't answer, and turning slightly away from her, he let go.

"Who will you be next time we meet? Bryan Daniels? Peter Crandall? Or maybe someone I haven't met yet?" His voice had taken on a measure of scorn, but Pup stood unflinching and silent. After a moment she heard him sigh. He turned back to face her.

"In all honesty, Callie," he continued, his voice sounding slightly warmer, but also mirroring his genuine confusion and concern, "I don't know how you keep up the pretense."

"I've thought a lot about that the last few days, McKay, but I still haven't come to any solid conclusions. With that in mind, I'm going to go back to work and keep thinking on it. It's tempting to up and quit right now, but Nick took the trouble of tracking me down here, so I know he needs me. It's for Nick that I'm doing this, McKay. I'm sorry you don't understand."

She turned away, and just as McKay was opening his mouth to tell her he did understand, his father's voice called from the top of the stairs.

"Are you up, McKay?"

The younger man went to the stairway.

"Yes. I'm sorry we disturbed you."

"Callie up, too?"

"Yes. In fact she has to leave. I need to take her into town."

"Can't it wait until morning?"

"No." His voice was soft and regretful. He turned back to Pup. "Wait here. I'll get dressed and take you."

"No," she said quietly. "The sky will be getting light soon. I have to leave now."

"Callie," McKay began, but she was already at the door. "I want you to wait."

She didn't answer him this time, but opened the door and slipped quietly out. McKay dashed up the stairs and grabbed some pants, his boots, and a shirt, and then ran for the barn. He couldn't have been more than ten minutes behind her, but there was no sign of her. He hadn't even taken time to saddle the horse before he rode toward town, but she was gone. He wondered if there had been a ride waiting for her. It made sense, but who knew she was here? And wouldn't they have heard the horse? The sky was growing very light before he turned his mount around. Instead of finding Pup and answers to his questions, he was forced to return to the house with a dozen more riddles swarming through his mind.

While still sheltered by a large barn at the edge of town, Pup took the shawl and put it over her head and shoulders. She hunched her shoulders slightly and walked with a stoop. She knew her back would never be the same if she didn't find the house soon, but she had no choice. It was fully light now, and too many people had met Callie Jennings.

She hobbled along in this fashion until she came to a row of homes. Longmont was a fairly widespread town, and she had no choice but to start where she was. She had stopped for a moment to survey the line of homes before her when the sight of a small boy made her blink. He was crawling from the window of the end house. Shoeless, he was looking from side to side as he climbed, guilt written all over him. Where he didn't bother to look was directly behind him. He spotted Pup as soon as he turned around. Pup had to fight laughter when he looked completely deflated.

"You gonna tell my mom?"

"Not if you help me." She made her voice sound old and rough.

"Help you with what"

"Charlie Barnes. Where does he live?"

"The shoe man?"

"Yeah," Pup guessed, asking herself how many Charlie Barneses there could be.

"You need shoes made?"

She ignored the question. "Where does he live?"

"A block over in a white house. You gonna tell my mom?"

"Where you headed?"

"Fishin'. It's my gramps' birthday, and I want to catch him a fish for breakfast."

"Where's your pole?"

The boy bent and retrieved a fishing pole from the ground. Pup's eyes had been so intent on his adorable, freckled face that she hadn't even seen it.

"Go on now," she said, her voice still rough. "Catch a big one."

She was rewarded with a face-splitting grin, and a moment later he was on his way. Pup continued her odd gait to the next block, and by the time she spotted the house with the shoe-shaped sign out front, the painful hobble was no longer a pretense—her back was screaming at her.

She moved slowly up the front steps and rapped on the door. It opened. A man stood just inside, but Pup only looked at him.

"Good morning," he said quietly.

Pup didn't respond.

"May I help you?"

"I'm not sure," she finally said, her voice now quavering a little, as though she were afraid.

"Well, what did you need?"

"To see Charlie Barnes."

"I'm Charlie Barnes."

"Are you a friend of Nick's?"

His demeanor changed in an instant. "Are you Jennings?" His voice was low.

"Yes, I am," she spoke in her own voice, and a moment later Charlie Barnes stepped back so she could enter. The shawl came off her head as soon as the door closed, and she turned to face her contact.

The man facing her was Nick's age. His eyes were shrewd and yet kind. Shoes were stacked on shelves along two walls of the living room, but there was clearly more to this man than new leather. Looking at him, she could well imagine the work he must have done for Nick over the years.

"I thought you would be a man," he admitted, his eyes watchful.

Pup's heart sank, but she didn't show it.

"So you don't have any supplies for me? Nothing has been delivered?"

A look crossed his face that told Pup she had just passed a test, but his voice was casual as he answered. "I do have some things."

"May I see them?"

Still not sure this was the person he'd been informed of, Charlie moved to a door off the living room and stepped within. He returned with a parcel that he'd already untied. He now stopped in front of Pup and opened the paper so she could see.

Pup reached out and fingered the rough cloth and old felt hat.

"Anything else?" she wished to know.

Charlie's estimation of her grew as he brought forth a smaller parcel he had hidden beneath the larger, unwrapped one. The small package had not been touched.

"I thought after seeing what was in this one," he admitted, indicating the larger of the two parcels, "I ought to leave the other intact."

Pup took it in her hand. She knew without unwrapping it what it was.

"Tell me, Mr. Barnes, do you have any distant cousins you don't like and who would never visit you here in Longmont?"

A small smile came to Charlie Barnes' face. What a fascination. She was the strangest woman he'd ever encountered.

"Morton. Morton Barnes. Lives in Texas. Says Colorado is nothing but hills and should never have been made into a state."

Pup nodded and asked, "Do you have a room I can use?"

"Certainly. Right here," he pointed to the room from which he had just emerged.

Pup thanked him, picked up her bag, and disappeared inside with the parcels. She was gone for quite some time, but Charlie never moved from the room. He hadn't had breakfast and had things to do, but he wasn't moving until Jennings came from the room. When she did he was speechless. He wouldn't have believed it if he hadn't seen it with his own eyes. He'd been doing small jobs for the U.S. Treasury Department for more than 20 years now, but this amazed him.

"The name's Barnes," Pup said, approaching him and sticking her hand out. "Morton Barnes."

Charlie shook the outstretched hand without thought and then watched a smile light Pup's eyes. He had one to match.

"You had breakfast?" he asked.

"No, sir, I haven't."

"Come on in," he said warmly and started toward the kitchen. "I'll put some food into you and tell you what I know."

22

Harry and Liz said nothing to their son when he came down for breakfast. Upon returning to the house, he'd gone to his room to clean up. He'd also taken some time for prayer, but his parents didn't know this, having left him alone until the meal was ending.

"Callie left us a note," Harry told him.

"She told me she had."

"So you knew she was leaving, McKay?" his mother wished to know.

"Not until she came downstairs before daybreak." He'd been looking into his coffee cup but now looked up. "What did the note say?"

"Just how much she enjoyed her stay and how thankful she was to God that we'd had this time."

McKay looked into the confused faces of his parents and sighed. He had to tell them something.

"Callie doesn't just live in the mountains; she has a job," he said quietly. "The job takes her to different locations. She had to leave because she was called back to work. It's not anything she would ever discuss with you, and I'm not at liberty to say more, but that's why she left. It wasn't because she wasn't enjoying herself."

His mother looked so relieved that McKay said a word of thanks that he'd been able to give her that much. His father, however, was looking at him intently. Harry didn't say anything at the moment, but McKay was not at all surprised when he spoke to him privately before he left for town.

"It's not that simple, is it?" Harry said without preamble after he'd asked McKay to walk him to the barn.

"What's that?"

"This thing with Callie. You wanted your mother and me to feel at ease, but *you're* not at ease yourself. I could hear it in your voice this morning while Callie was still here and again at the kitchen table. I don't suppose you can tell me, Mickey, but I know you're not happy about this."

"No, I'm not," he admitted, "but there's little I can do about it."

Harry looked at him. "I've never had to know what you were doing, Mickey. It's never bothered me too much not knowing every aspect of your job, but this is personal. I know Callie must be tied into your work, or you'd be saying more, but I'm putting all of that aside. You're hurting over this woman in a way that has nothing to do with the U.S. Treasury Department."

Harry had always been plainspoken with his son, but never had McKay felt he'd been robbed of air. This *was* personal. Yes, he was worried that an operation was underway right here in Longmont, but mostly he was concerned for a dark-haired woman who'd been playing havoc with his heart since he'd met her. Romance was not on his mind, not as romances went, but Pup was. Such a thought didn't make sense even to McKay, but it was true. She was the most fascinating woman he'd ever encountered. The realization was stunning; it was also very sobering.

Only days ago Pup had realized she'd accepted Christ when she was a child. McKay shuddered at the thought that he might have been this fascinated with a woman who was not a believer.

It wouldn't have made any difference, McKay was able to tell the Lord immediately after the thought formed. *I would still honor You, Father. I would walk away and never see her again before I would ignore Your command about both husbands and wives believing in You. Thank You, Father, that it wasn't a problem. I don't know what you have for Pup and me, but thank You that no matter what, she has You.*

"Mickey?" Harry called his name softly. He'd been watching his son very closely.

"I'm sorry, Dad," McKay came back abruptly. "Some things just came to mind, and I'm not sure what to do about them."

"Are you in love with Callie?"

"I don't know," McKay answered honestly. "I'm fascinated, that's for sure, but I don't know about love."

Harry put his arm around McKay. "Your mother and I think a lot of Callie, but your heart must be sure. I want to say, '*Don't let this one get away, Mickey. Hold on to this one.*' But that's not right, even though of all the girls you've grown up with, she's the one who makes me think that it would work."

McKay could only stare at his father. He went on gently.

"She isn't the type to sit and pine for you if you don't come home on time, Mickey. In your line of work, your wife would have to understand the hours. I don't think Callie would struggle with the fact that your job took you away. You might not want to travel forever; in fact, I think family is more important, but she's the type of woman who could rise to the challenge if she had to."

At that moment Harry saw that he was overwhelming his son. "Have I said too much?"

"No," McKay answered, but he didn't sound too certain.

Harry knew it was time to let the matter drop.

"I've got to get into town."

"Right." McKay wasn't relieved exactly; he sounded somewhat stunned. He barely managed, "I'll see you later, Dad."

"I won't bring it up again, Mickey, unless you want me to."

"Okay. Thanks, Dad."

McKay stood in the barn for quite some time after his father left, his mind on Pup and then on his father's words. *She isn't the type to sit and pine for you if you don't come home on time.*

"No, she isn't," McKay said softly in the quiet barn. "Since she'll probably be out on a job of her own." No one but the cow and Peter, the extra horse, heard McKay's sigh, but it was deep and heartfelt.

As early evening fell into darkness, Pup made her way from Barnes' home dressed as an old bearded man. The wig, hat, and rumpled set of clothes for this costume made her look like a miner down on his luck. She and the shoemaker had spent the day together, and Pup had even gone so far as to "practice" on a few of Charlie's customers. To a person they were delighted that Charlie had a cousin named Morton who had decided to visit from down south. She made her way slowly toward the evening sounds of Longmont's downtown area.

The area contact had told her he would fill her in on what he had, and Pup had been surprised by how much he knew. As she had expected, an agent was under suspicion. Charlie had a name for her and a number of details, but Pup had had to work hard not to openly stare at him. Could it be true? she had asked herself, but the more Charlie talked, the more she understood: She had been totally blind. It had taken all of her will not to gasp from the emotions flooding through her or to show personal interest in the case. Contact or not, she was not about to let Charlie Barnes know more than he needed or how much his words had affected her.

Now she came to the first bar, lights streaming from the windows and open door. She stepped up to the threshold, the smell of smoke and whiskey assaulting her. Hers was not a huge task. "Gather information and keep your eyes open" had been the command from Nick. Simple as the assignment seemed, Pup knew it was going to be a long night with probably several other long nights to follow. Then again, if she was in luck, something might come up right away and she could relax again.

Pup was lost in thought about whether or not she really believed in luck when a gruff voice behind her inquired, "You going in?"

Pup mentally started but didn't turn. As she stepped inside she reminded herself that her name was Morton Barnes.

McKay knocked a pan over in the kitchen and froze at the noise it made. He was up very early and intended to be as quiet as possible, but the pan had been hot and his hand had brushed against it. Using a thick towel, he retrieved the pan silently and went on with his breakfast preparations, thankful that it was at least light in the sky.

McKay had woken early, very early, upon remembering that Longmont had a contact. Not in all these years had the young treasury man talked to Charlie Barnes concerning official business, but McKay had known he was there. Why Charlie's presence had not occurred to him before now he didn't know. Or did he? McKay pushed the thought away and cracked two eggs into the hot skillet.

"Mickey?" his father asked softly from the edge of the room.

"Did I wake you?"

"I heard a noise." Harry came forward now. He stopped next to the small baking table and watched his son work over the huge black stove.

"I dropped a pan. I'm sorry, Dad."

"It's all right. What time is it?"

"I think just past five."

"Are you leaving?"

"I have to go into town."

"You actually have someone who wants to meet with you at this time of the day?"

The question stopped McKay in his tracks. He didn't turn, but his hands stilled and then moved very slowly. What in the world was he doing? Charlie Barnes was not going to welcome a visit at this time of the day!

McKay sighed. He thought he had put his emotions aside, but it wasn't true. He was still consumed with thoughts of Callie Jennings.

"You're going to burn them." Harry's voice was calm.

McKay started this time and grabbed for the wooden spoon. He worked silently for a few minutes, aware that his father had poured himself a cup of coffee and gone to the table. His scrambled eggs and ham steak done, McKay took the bread and butter to the table along with his plate, joined his father, and settled down to pray and eat. All of this was done in silence. Not until McKay pushed his plate away did the men speak.

"You must still be thinking about Callie."

"Yeah," McKay admitted. "I thought I had it under control, but as you can see, I don't." McKay passed a weary hand over his face. "I've been awake for hours, and without even considering the other person, I'm headed out to pay a call as if it were noon." McKay took a drink of his coffee and fell silent. Harry regarded him. It would be so easy right now to start a speech or quote Bible verses that his son already knew. But Harry knew that wasn't what was needed.

"Do you suppose Callie will be back to visit?" Harry asked suddenly.

"No." McKay's voice was soft.

"You sound quite certain. Did you two have words?"

"As a matter of fact we did, but that's not why she won't be back. I certainly don't know for sure, but something tells me her responsibilities will take her awhile."

Harry knew he couldn't ask for an explanation, so he drank a little more of his coffee.

"I take it you've decided to leave for town a little later."

"Yes. There's probably no need to hurry."

Harry eyed him, wondering if he should remind his son that he'd come home for a rest. He opted against it.

"I wonder if Stan and Lisa are nervous," Harry commented casually.

McKay knew what his father was doing and smiled. "Probably," he answered and then admitted, "I think I would be."

"Well, it'll all be over tomorrow," Harry went on. Thankfully the conversation moved to how many out-of-town family members would be at the wedding.

McKay was pleased over whom he was going to see, but mostly for the way his father managed to take his mind off Pup. It was close to nine o'clock before he headed toward town. Charlie Barnes' house and shoe shop were on the way, but he felt compelled to bypass it for the moment. He picked up the mail and to his surprise found a telegram from Carlyle. From that point on the day did not go as he'd planned.

"You want what?"

"A gin or whiskey bottle. Either one will do," Pup answered Charlie calmly, her eyes slightly preoccupied.

"I don't drink."

"What about a neighbor?"

"They're not going to hand me their liquor without a lot of questions."

"I don't want the booze, Charlie, just the bottle. There's got to be one lying around somewhere."

He was catching on now and suddenly remembered he had what she needed. It was late Friday afternoon. Pup sat quietly at his kitchen table and watched while he dug into the back of a cupboard. She smiled broadly when he presented with flourish a clear bottle, label still intact.

"Will this do, Morton?" Charlie asked with a grin of his own.

"Perfectly. Boil some water, Charlie. It's time to make tea so I can get to work."

The last thing McKay expected to be doing on Friday night was searching Longmont bars for Jubal Hackett, but that's what he was doing. The telegram from Carlyle had left little choice. He'd been called back to duty and without hesitation had responded. Guilt assailed him at the hard time he'd given Pup. She had obeyed her summons exactly as he had, but at the time he didn't realize how closely their loyalty and commitment matched. He asked himself where she was and indeed wanted to look for her, but he pushed the distracting thoughts away and made himself move on to the next saloon.

Unlike some of the other bars in town, the Brass Cup had no stage, only a long bar and two dozen tables with chairs. As saloons go, it was one of the classier establishments, but the smoke and smell of strong ale was always hard to take. Added to this McKay didn't drink, making it a challenge not to be noticed. McKay now moved along the edge of the room and chose a table away from the windows. He sat down, tilted his hat rather low over his brow, and slowly scanned the room.

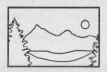

23

From a corner table in the Brass Cup saloon, Morton Barnes watched McKay Harrington. It had taken a little work to get in the door and keep the bottle concealed, but the whiskey container filled with tea was now on the table. Pup was slumped over the wooden surface as if she'd drunk most of the bottle's contents. She was a quiet drunk this evening, whereas last night, in order to get close to a rowdy group, she had been quite boisterous. It hadn't done her any good: The group did not have the information she was looking for, so she was out again tonight. She had gotten one lead early in the evening and was now waiting patiently.

At the moment she pretended to be half-asleep in order to watch her coworker as well as the other occupants of the room. A swift glance around told her that no one was taking any notice of McKay, but the treasury agent's eyes were covering plenty. It didn't take her long to figure out that he'd gotten word from Denver. For just an instant she entertained thoughts that McKay might be looking for her, but someone came in the door, and her attention was instantly diverted. She glanced at McKay, but other than a swift perusal of the newcomer, he took little notice. However, Pup was more informed. This was exactly the man she was looking for. She shifted and sighed audibly as if trying to get more comfortable, but in actuality her movements were deliberate in order to see the man headed into a door at the back wall of the room.

Completely forgetting McKay or anyone else, she rose and acted as if she needed to be excused. A genuine drunk wandered by at that point, and she was forced to speak.

"You done with that?" his voice was slurred, but his eyes were fastened on the bottle.

"No," Pup's voice was ornery and low, her beard and mustache moving as her lips formed a snarl. Her eyes were so fierce that the other man moved off. Pup stood for a moment then, as if in drunken indecision. She stood for so long that six cowboys, whom she would have liked to thank, came noisily through the swing doors. Nearly all eyes were drawn to them and she grabbed the opportunity. A moment later she slipped inside the door her prey had used and found herself in a dark hallway.

For a time she froze. Not just to adjust her eyes, but also to listen. This was no easy task with the saloon on the other side of the portal. She was just about to take a step further into the darkness when the door opened halfway. Again she went completely still.

"It's not up there," an irate voice called from without. "The other door."

Pup had no idea what they were speaking about, but the partially open door cast just enough light to show her there was a stairway at the end of the hall. Determined not to waste any time, she waited for the door to close completely and quickly moved toward the steps. There was a dim light coming from under a door at the top, but it was enough illumination for Pup. Miraculously the noise from the bar cut off sounds of her movement as she started up the stairs. She was only three-quarters of the way up when she was able to hear every word.

"Why Longmont?" a curious voice asked.

"Because no one suspects," the second voice replied in an amused tone. "Boulder is such a den of iniquity these days that we look like the first rose of spring."

"And what about our new friend here?" the curious man questioned.

"I have an influential family member," a third man responded in a voice that Pup recognized immediately.

The curious man must not have been satisfied, since he said sarcastically, "By *family member*, just how close do you mean?"

"My uncle," the familiar voice stated. Pup thought he sounded uncertain.

"Your uncle?" Curious was clearly not convinced. "Who is this man?"

Silence fell. Pup strained to hear, but it took a moment. Finally the amused voice encouraged the third party.

"Go ahead, Mr. Whitter. You can tell Mr. Stuart—he's one of our biggest investors."

"Duncan Phipps." The words were said a bit breathlessly, and Pup imagined that he'd pushed the words out. As it was she felt a little breathless herself. Had Nick known about their relationship?

"Why has it taken you so long to come forward?"

"I've never wanted to get involved before." Mr. Whitter's voice sounded instantly angry. "I used to be appreciated where I was, but no longer. If they're not going to take care of me, I'll go where someone will."

"And the other gentleman?" Mr. Stuart inquired, and Pup realized for the first time that a fourth person was in the room.

Mr. Whitter answered in the firmest voice yet. "Mr. Hackett works for my uncle. He stays with me."

Pup was so surprised by the name that she moved on the step. It squeaked loudly. She heard, "*What was that?*" just before she made a beeline out of there. The door was already opening as she hit the bottom stair, and with a swift decision she let herself slip to her knees. She was groping for the wall when she was grabbed from behind.

"What? What is it?" she managed in a drunken slur.

"What're you doing back here?" It was her brother's voice.

"I gotta get out," she mumbled. "I gotta go."

"It's just an old drunk!" Jubal snapped toward someone back up the stairs. A moment later Pup found herself lifted by the coat and propelled to a door she hadn't seen—a moment after that she was lying face down in the alley. Jubal slammed the door without another word, and what little light she'd had was cut off completely.

The groan that escaped her lips was very real. The wet spot on her side as well as the pain in her hip told her she'd fallen on and broken her bottle. She was coming to her hands and knees when she felt other hands helping her. She finally rose to her feet.

"Okay, old-timer. You're going to be all right." It was McKay's voice. Pup thought she would quit if she had one more surprise tonight. She was on the verge of speaking in her normal voice and giving herself away to him when Charlie Barnes spoke from behind them.

"That you, McKay?"

"Yeah." He spun swiftly, dismissing the old drunk from his mind.

"It's Charlie Barnes. Someone would like to see you."

Without question McKay followed him. Pup stood very still and heard Charlie softly say the name Crawford. So Carlyle had come. Pup stood for a moment, gripped with indecision. She watched as the men disappeared into the darkness and then swung her eyes to the back of the saloon.

My brother just threw me to the ground as if I were no more than a pesky moth. Pup told herself it was foolish to cry and concluded that she must be a fool because the tears would not be stemmed. There was a box pushed against the building, and she went over and sat on it. It creaked as though it would break under her, but she didn't care. She didn't know if it was the wig or her tears, but a horrible headache was starting. It made her all the more miserable. Indeed, it was many minutes before she made her way back to Charlie's house.

"I didn't get much," McKay told Carlyle as the three men sat at Charlie's kitchen table. "I was in every saloon in town tonight, but there was no sign of Hackett."

"Were you able to get into any back rooms?"

"Only the one at Rocky Point, but there was nothing more than a card game. I tell you I hate this, Carlyle." McKay was referring to the bars. "The sooner we wrap up this thing with Whitter and Hackett, the happier I'll be."

"You and Nick both," Carlyle told him. "That's the reason I'm here." The older treasury man now turned to his host. "When do you expect Callie back?"

"I haven't a clue."

"She's been staying here?" McKay asked.

"Yes." Charlie stopped himself from saying that he thought he'd seen her in the alley tonight with McKay, but hers was the type of disguise you didn't believe unless you saw it.

"Is she okay?" McKay wanted to know.

"She was when she left here."

"What was she going to do?" This came from Carlyle.

"Check the saloons, I'm sure." Charlie wanted to push McKay to find out if he'd seen her, but when he heard the front door open, he was glad he had remained quiet.

"That'll be her." Charlie rose, fully aware that Carlyle and McKay were on his heels. Once in the living room, he lit a lantern, and they all took in Pup's appearance. She was a mess. Holding her hat in her hand and covered with dust and mud where the bottle had broken down one side of her, she looked exhausted.

"You all right?" Charlie was the first to find his voice.

"Yeah." She sounded weary, which was enough to propel both Carlyle and McKay out of their surprise over her appearance and into action.

"Let me have the coat," Carlyle said as he began to remove it from her shoulders. It took a second for him to see why the pocket was wet. "Are you cut?"

"I don't think so."

"Here, let me get this." McKay's hands were there as well. He removed her hat from her hands and tossed it to Charlie. Next he took the wig from her head and then worked gently at the beard she'd adhered to her face. Her skin was red and chaffed underneath, and his heart clenched.

"Did you know it was me in the alley?" he asked softly.

"As soon as you spoke to me. I was about to say something when Charlie came up."

"I thought it might be you," their host commented, "but it's such a dark night."

"Sit down, Pup," Carlyle ordered. He'd taken the coat to the kitchen and checked to see if it was cut. The fabric showed no tears, but the smashed bottle indicated that her fall had to have hurt. Now as he came back to the living room, Nick's words rang in his mind.

If Pup has word, bring her to me. If she doesn't, tell her she can go home or continue her vacation. Either way, Carlyle, see to it that she's well. If she seems at all upset and won't come back to Denver with you, send for me.

Pup dropped onto one end of the sofa, and McKay pulled a chair up close to her. He sat down and looked at her dusty, weary face. He didn't think he had ever loved anyone more. She suddenly turned and looked at him. He was barely aware that Charlie had joined Pup on the sofa or that Carlyle had brought out another chair from the kitchen. He loved Callie Jennings, and he desperately wanted to tell her. Her gaze softened, and McKay knew she could see it in his eyes. Never married, but still wise to such things, Charlie Barnes watched them silently.

"Do you have news?" Carlyle sat in the chair and abruptly brought the group back to business.

"Yes." Pup made herself turn and answer.

"Then Nick would like to see you."

"All right. I can leave on the train in the morning."

"I'll go with you," Carlyle told her.

It took all of McKay's will not to tell Pup that she had to stay, but he managed to refrain. The timing was all wrong to tell her of his feelings. She was clearly upset by what happened tonight, and what he had to say would only add to her disturbance.

"McKay," she asked suddenly, "is there more than one Mr. Stuart in town?"

"I don't think so." He glanced at Charlie. Both men shook their heads. "No, I'm sure not."

"Who is he?" she wanted to know.

"A local banker. His bank is pretty small, but it's been established for years."

"Is he involved?" Carlyle wanted to know.

Pup only nodded her head yes, unaware of the way McKay's heart clenched for Brita and her mother.

"What about Paine Whitter?"

"He's here."

This was the first that McKay had heard of Nick's right-hand man in the head office. No wonder Pup had been pulled off her vacation.

"So is Jubal," she went on.

"You saw him?" McKay asked, since he'd been looking for her brother as well.

Pup's eyes dropped. "He was the one who threw me into the alley tonight."

If McKay could have done it, he would have taken her away right then and there. He'd have told Nick and Carlyle and anyone else who needed to hear that she was through. Any pain he'd experienced in this occupation was nothing compared to the way it felt seeing her hurt over her own job.

"Get some rest," Carlyle suggested. "We'll leave for Denver on the first morning train."

"All right." Pup stood.

"You're welcome to come to my house tonight," McKay told Carlyle.

"All right, McKay. Thank you."

McKay turned to Pup.

"Carlyle and I will be here to take you to the station in the morning. Wait until we come."

She nodded and looked into his eyes. *I want you to put your arms around me, McKay. I want you to hold me and tell me everything is going to be fine, but you can't do that.* She couldn't say any of this, so she had to content herself with the tenderness she saw in his eyes. A moment later she turned and went to a door off the living room.

Carlyle had a few more words with Charlie, and then he and McKay left for the night. There was some hilarity as they shared McKay's horse: The livery was long closed. In the morning they would use a wagon. For the most part the two were silent, Carlyle with thoughts that Hackett, Phipps, and the crooked treasury man were almost under wraps, and McKay with thoughts of the woman he loved and the pain he saw in her eyes. For completely different reasons, both men knew it would be a long night.

24

Pup scrutinized herself in the mirror and decided that the wig was on straight. It would have been easier to go as a man, but the suit of clothing she'd worn home from Denver last time was still in Boulder. Something told her that Carlyle would not want to travel with Morton Barnes.

Charlie had already given her a filling breakfast, so she now picked up her satchel and moved to the living room to await McKay's arrival. Her heart thundered at the thought of seeing him again, however briefly. From this point, it was anyone's guess when they would meet again. Charlie heard Pup come into the room and appeared in the doorway of the kitchen.

"Are you all set?" he inquired.

"I think so. I took the clothes and wig just in case Nick has plans."

Charlie nodded. "I don't think I would have any use for them anyway."

"Thank you for everything, Charlie," she said sincerely. He had turned into a real friend. "I couldn't have pulled any of this off without you."

"You're welcome," he said warmly, his look unlike any Pup had seen before.

She stood still, feeling slightly awkward. She knew she was something of a fascination to this man, but not until this moment had she thought his interest might go beyond work. His eyes, or rather the way they watched her, now told a different story.

Charlie knew well what he was doing. He'd seen the look that passed between McKay and his house guest the night before, but he wasn't going to assume, not where this woman was concerned.

"Do you think you'll ever be in Longmont again?"

"I don't know," Pup answered honestly. "I hope I'll be here to see McKay or his folks again."

Charlie nodded. It was what he had expected, but he had to try. Indeed, his estimation of her went up for her open honesty.

"I'll say it outright to you, Callie," Charlie went on. "If McKay doesn't see what he has in you, I hope you'll move on to someone who would really appreciate you for the woman you are."

There was no mistaking his meaning; he had all but proposed. "Thank you for that compliment, Charlie. Coming from you it means quite a lot."

He was embarrassed. "Tell Nick I said hello."

"I'll do that."

It was a relief to both of them when a knock sounded on the door. Charlie went to answer it and, not surprisingly, found it was McKay.

"Are you set?" he asked Pup after he'd come in and greeted Charlie.

"Yes. Thank you, Charlie," she said, turning to her host and holding out her hand.

Charlie shook it, and Pup moved away from him and out the door. McKay thanked him as well, and then Carlyle came in to have a few words with the Longmont contact. McKay walked Pup to the wagon and spoke only after he'd put her satchel in the back.

"Did you notice anything about Charlie's attitude toward you?"

"Yes," Pup said simply.

McKay stared at her for a moment; she stared back, not volunteering anything.

"Did he say anything?" McKay finally asked.

"Yes, he did. You'll have to ask me about it sometime."

"Why not now?"

But Pup ignored him and began to climb onto the wagon seat. McKay assisted her and then looked up at her. She was busy arranging her skirt and didn't look at him. He had so much he wanted to say. A glance over his shoulder told him it would all have to wait; Carlyle was coming toward them.

"Did you want to handle the team, Carlyle?" McKay asked out of respect.

"No, you go ahead. I'll sit here on the rear seat."

He settled himself with little ceremony and no talking. McKay had them at the train station in less than ten minutes. Carlyle took his bag and moved away from the younger couple in order to purchase tickets. McKay picked up Pup's bag and walked to the side of the stage office. Pup stopped in front of him. Hoping they would be left alone until the train came in, McKay looked down into her eyes.

"Take care of yourself, McKay," she surprised him by saying. "And tell your folks goodbye."

"I'll do that," he replied automatically. "I'm sorry I didn't know it was you last night in the alley."

"It's all right."

McKay's mind came to a painful halt. He couldn't say what he wanted to say in this short time. And what exactly did he want to share with her? He wasn't even certain, but opted for honesty.

"I have things I want to say to you."

"I know you do."

McKay couldn't go on. She never stopped surprising him; he now said as much.

Upon hearing this, Pup's mouth stretched into a slow, tender smile.

"I'll miss you, McKay," was her only comment.

"You make it sound like we'll never see each other again."

She gave a small shrug. "I don't know about never, but it could be awhile."

McKay didn't want that, but what did Pup want?

"How do you feel about that?"

"I just told you: I'll miss you."

This time it was McKay's turn to smile. She was always the same—not flowery in speech and not a waster of words.

"I'll miss you, too," he told her sincerely.

His last sentence was followed by a far-off whistle. The train would be in the station in just a few minutes. Pup's head moved as if she would turn away, but McKay caught her jaw. He didn't kiss her, but only held her head still for a moment longer so he could look into her eyes. It was then that he saw it again: the softening, the tenderness that he'd seen for a moment the night before. For now it was enough. Knowing her as he did, he knew that now was not the time to distract her with words of love. He reluctantly dropped his hand, his fingers sliding along the soft skin of her jaw. Picking up her bag in one hand, he took her arm in the other.

He walked her over to where Carlyle had been waiting, his eyes telling his boss that he was thankful for his sensitivity. Seconds later the train pulled in amid much noise and steam. Carlyle and McKay shook hands, and then McKay gave Pup a hug. She returned it warmly, all the while forcing her mind from personal things, namely how wonderful McKay Harrington was and how delightful it felt to be held in his arms. This was not the time to speculate on what her relationship with McKay might hold. She had to get to Denver; she had a job to finish.

Denver

"His uncle?" Nick questioned her again.

Pup nodded from her chair in the study, feeling the eyes of both men on her. She could only guess how difficult it must have been for Nick to learn of Paine's betrayal, and now this.

"That's what he said. I don't know who the one voice belonged to, but Mr. Stuart was questioning Paine, and Paine said Duncan Phipps was his uncle."

"Could he have been putting one over on this banker named Stuart?"

"I don't think so. It was as if he was hesitant even to admit it, and then his voice grew angry. He said for a time he'd been appreciated but no more; he said now he was going to go with someone who would take care of him."

Nick sat down heavily on the sofa, his hand going to the back of his neck. "It was never my intent to leave Paine out, but I've cracked down on security everywhere, not just with him. I never dreamed he was taking it personally."

"When I checked him out, Nick," Carlyle now spoke from the other chair, "I was surprised to learn that he lives a very solitary life. When I saw him coming and going from the Phipps mansion on several occasions, I naturally grew suspicious. Even at that, I never imagined the two to be related."

For a moment the room was silent. The three sat still with only the monotonous sound of the large clock on the wall breaking that quiet.

"I would love to get someone into that house," Nick said rather quietly.

"I can get in," Pup stated simply.

"How?"

"The maid's uniform and blonde wig."

"You're forgetting about Jubal," Nick reminded her gently. "He's bound to be coming and going out of that house."

"He didn't recognize me in Longmont."

"You won't be wearing a beard this time."

She patiently shook her head. "It's as I've always told you, Nick—people see what they want to see. He won't be looking for his sister. He may notice me, but he won't know who I am."

"And you're all right with this?"

"I've done a lot of thinking," she admitted quietly. "I wouldn't relish being in on his arrest, but neither will I continue to pretend that everything is fine."

Nick stared at her. A moment later she stood.

"If that's all, Nick, I'm going to go visit with Camille."

"Yes, that's all for now. I'll let you know if I need you to go out."

"All right. Otherwise I'm going to head for home on Monday."

She left the room, and the men, still comfortably seated in Nick's study, looked at each other.

"She and McKay seem to be getting closer all the time," Carlyle said quietly.

Nick's scowl was fierce. "He'd better not try to take her from me."

"I believe his intentions are honorable." Carlyle couldn't stop himself from standing up for his best agent.

"Honorable or not. I like things just the way they are." Nick's voice had become a bit threatening, his eyes on the cold hearth.

Carlyle wisely let the matter drop.

"And then I remembered, Camille." Pup's eyes shone with wonder. "As a child I'd come in faith and believed in Jesus Christ. As McKay talked, all the memories came flooding back. There's so much I still don't understand, but it's been so special to know that I'm truly a child of God."

Camille was silent, as she had been for the last several minutes. The women were sitting in Pup's room upstairs.

Miranda had brought them some coffee and sandwiches, and they'd been catching up for more than an hour. Just a few minutes earlier Pup had shocked Camille by suddenly telling her the story of her conversion. In truth, Camille didn't know what she believed, but never had she been this close to someone who'd had a religious experience. If Pup's eyes could be believed, something had really happened.

"I'm happy for you, dear, but I must admit that I was hoping you'd have more to say about McKay."

Pup laughed softly, her eyes turning dreamy. "He's in love with me."

Camille's eyes were just as soft. "I figured as much. Does he realize it yet?"

"I think so. He said he wants to talk to me."

"And you, Callie?" The older woman's tone grew excited. "Do you also want to talk with him?"

"Oh, yes, Camille," her voice was whisper soft. "I've never known anyone like him. Without even knowing it was me, he helped me up in an alleyway. I was dressed like a filthy drunk, and with gentle hands he bent over and helped me to my feet. And then when he hugged me goodbye at the station—" here she had to stop.

This was the first time in several hours that she had allowed herself to remember, and right now it was too much to take in.

"And this was all just this morning?" Camille asked.

"The hug? Yes. He took Carlyle and me to the station, and then we talked while Carlyle bought the tickets." She looked Camille in the eye. "Was it like this for you, Camille? Is this how you fell for Nick?"

Camille smiled. "He came to see my father on business. He was in a suit, so tall and handsome. I was young, only 17, but our eyes met when I brought them some coffee. I was so preoccupied that I burned my hand. Nick jumped to his feet and wrapped his handkerchief around it. I melted inside." Her eyes clouded then. "I thought I would die when he signed up to join the fighting. I thought he would never come home to me." Her voice caught, but she seemed to give herself a little shake. She looked into Pup's eyes. "But he did, and he brought you with him."

Pup smiled at her in genuine love, and the women embraced. They continued to talk until Nick sought her out and said that he and Carlyle were hungry. Only then did Camille remember that Miranda had already left for the night. The rest of the evening was spent preparing the meal, and around the table the discussion was all business.

Nick decided to let Pup go home on Monday. He liked the idea of getting her into the Phipps mansion, but he was in no hurry to move on it. Agents in the field were still gathering information. He would need Pup, but not for a while. As he looked across the table at her, he couldn't help but smile at the way she'd volunteered.

McKay's not going to take this woman from us, Carlyle, Nick thought to himself. *She's treasury through and through.*

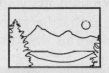

25

Longmont

Stan and Lisa had been married for more than 24 hours, but McKay felt he could still see them coming back up the aisle. Or was it someone else he was seeing?

What a time to attend a wedding, Lord, he prayed. *I put the woman I love onto the train and then have to watch my cousin marry and kiss his bride. There's something You want to teach me in this—I know there is—but right now I can't think what it might be.*

McKay lay on his bed, trying to get a nap in before the night's work began, but thoughts of Pup drove all fatigue away. A week ago she had sat in church with him, her whole body bent with intensity as she read his Bible. Now she was in Denver, or so he thought, doing the work to which she seemed so well-suited.

Actually, she could be headed home, McKay reasoned. *If Nick only wanted to debrief her, he might not have a reason for her to stay.*

McKay pushed the thought away. If he continued to dwell on it, he'd be headed back to Boulder and up the mountain like a lost sheep. If his time were his own, he could take that liberty, but he was still on the job. Carlyle had ordered him to spend the evening in town on Saturday night and again tonight. On Tuesday he was to start spot checks on two banks, one of which was Richard Stuart's.

He didn't think he was going to be welcomed with joy for the simple reason that spot checks were not standard in Longmont. It also didn't help that he was a local; Richard Stuart had watched him grow up in this town. However, he would do as he was told. The night Carlyle had come home with him, McKay had asked whether this spot check might spook Duncan Phipps. He was clearly behind the whole false mining operation they had unearthed, but Carlyle had said they wanted this.

"Duncan is too often at ease," he had said. "His setup is so large he feels he's above the law. If we close down some of the smaller banks it might make him sweat a little, and in the process make a mistake. At this point if he had just one slipup, we'd arrest him."

McKay now looked at the watch he had laid on the table by his bed. It was almost time to go. He freshened up at the washstand in his room and went down to the kitchen. His parents were at the table.

"I was just about to come up to find you," his mother said.

"I've got to go pretty soon."

"Again tonight?" His father's brows rose.

"Yeah."

"Oh, McKay." Liz's voice betrayed her disappointment. "We've asked the Stuarts over. I wish you could be here."

McKay shook his head, and his mother rushed to reassure him.

"I'm not pushing Brita at you, dear."

"I know that, Mom," he said kindly. In truth, Brita hadn't even come to his mind. He continued quietly, "I've been called back to work for the whole week, not just last night and tonight. I might as well tell you now because you're going to hear about it later: I start spot checks on two of the banks in town this Tuesday—one of them is Rocky Mountain Savings."

"Richard Stuart's bank?" Liz exclaimed incredulously.

"I'm afraid so," McKay told her quietly.

The three of them fell silent. McKay had remained standing during this whole interchange, so he now moved to the counter by the stove and prepared something to eat. There was leftover fried chicken from Sunday dinner and a hot potato dish. He grabbed an apple to add to his plate and joined his parents at the table.

"You understand that we're not upset with you, don't you, Mickey?" His father was the first to speak.

"I do understand, Dad. And I wish there had been an easier way to tell you."

"The shock is not so much that Richard's bank is under suspicion," the elder Harrington went on, "as it is the thought that the long fingers of crime have now stretched from Denver. There isn't a time that you leave us, Mickey, that we don't wonder if you'll come home alive, and we've had to surrender you to the Lord time and again. But the hint of crime right here in Longmont takes a little getting used to."

McKay nodded in understanding. He well remembered the way he had felt just a few nights earlier when Pup told him she was being called back to work but that she wasn't leaving Longmont. He felt a protectiveness so strong for the city in which he was raised that he could have burst with it. He was certain his parents were feeling the same way, but they also must be knowing some fear.

"I can't make any promises; you already know that," McKay began, "but I hope what I uncover will take some of the problems back to Denver."

Small bankers were easy prey for men like Duncan Phipps, and of course he was the man they were after. It would have further helped his parents' peace of mind to know that although Richard Stuart would have to pay for any crimes he'd been involved in, at least the main man was more than a hundred miles away.

"Be careful tonight, McKay," his mother cautioned, her voice a bit emotional.

He smiled at her. "I will, Mom. And when this is all over, I'll come and be here for a real vacation."

"With or without Callie?" she couldn't help but ask.

McKay stood and reached to where his hat hung on a peg by the door. When it was in place, he turned back to her.

"If I have anything to say about it, she most definitely will be *with*."

Before either of his parents could comment, he swung around and moved outside toward the barn.

Boulder

The train ride home this time seemed the longest ever. Pup climbed wearily from her seat, having already checked to see that her dark wig was in place, and moved with the others out into the aisle and onto the platform.

It had never before bothered her to come home on her own, but as she watched a woman embrace her children and reach on tiptoe to kiss her husband, she felt a strange longing. McKay's face came to mind, but Pup stubbornly pushed it away. This was no time to think of him. When she arrived at the cabin maybe, but not now. With a determined move she shifted her satchel to the other hand. Her destination: the livery.

"Hello, Pup."

Surprised to hear her name, Pup looked up to find she was walking right past Travis Buchanan.

"Hello, Travis."

"Just off the train?" the tall man wanted to know.

"Yes." She stopped before him. "Are you meeting someone?"

"No, but I'm expecting some supplies." He paused and looked at her for a moment. There was something different here, but he couldn't quite put a finger on it. He opted for a question.

"Have you seen or heard from McKay?"

"As a matter of fact I have seen him. He's doing well."

"Good. I'm glad to hear it."

"How's your wife?"

Travis smiled. "Still waiting. I don't think it will be long, but still we wait."

Pup smiled, too. She continued to look up at Travis. His height never failed to surprise her, but this time she studied his face, trying to gauge his response to her.

In turn, Travis could see that something was on her mind. His supplies were probably being unloaded right now, but he pushed work to the back of his head and told himself that if it took an hour, he'd wait to see what she had to say.

"You in a hurry to be off, Travis?"

"As a matter of fact, I'm not that pressed right now."

Pup nodded. It was so difficult when you couldn't get close, but she had some things she had to know.

"You go to the small church on Second Street, don't you?"

"Yes. My sons and I attend each week."

"What time does it get started?"

"The church service begins at eleven o'clock. We've just started a short service for the children that starts at half past ten. Pastor Henley's wife takes the kids for a short time and tells them a Bible story with pictures. During that time the adults have fellowship. The kids then come back to us, and like I said, the service gets started at eleven."

Her dark, intelligent eyes surveyed him.

"And your beliefs—" she began, "does Pastor Henley follow the Bible?"

"To the letter," he said softly but with firmness. "We're working our way through the book of Philippians right now. That's usually the way Pastor Henley works. He starts at the beginning of a book and preaches and teaches out of it until the last chapter and verse."

"Can you ask questions?"

"People usually don't ask questions during the service," he told her honestly, "but there are some small Bible studies that meet during the week. Those are good places to have your questions answered."

Pup nodded but didn't go on. The Lord was teaching Travis not to be surprised by anything, and never was he more thankful that he had remained calm.

"Do you think you'll join us, Pup?" he felt bold enough to ask.

"Yes," she surprised him by answering immediately. "I'll be there this Sunday."

"That's great," he told her sincerely. "I think you'll enjoy it."

She nodded. Travis could see that she'd gained the information she sought and was now ready to be on her way. Indeed, a moment later she thanked him and started off. However, Travis had one final thought.

"Pup," he called, starting toward her.

Pup's long legs had already taken her off the platform, so she turned and stopped, waiting for him to approach.

"I don't want to nose into your business," he said as he stopped before her, "but I just wondered where you're going to stay Saturday night."

"I was going to come partway down the mountain and camp in the woods."

He blinked at her. "There's no need for you to do that."

"It's no trouble, Travis. I've done it before."

He was again reminded that she was probably the most self-sufficient person he'd ever encountered. However, he was not going to let this drop.

"There are homes right here in town where you would be welcome on Saturday night—mine for one."

Pup surveyed him. Clearly the thought had never occurred to her. "Somehow I don't think your wife would appreciate that," she said.

"On the contrary," he told her sincerely, "she would be pleased to have you. The ranch house is huge, and we have folks in on a regular basis."

"Even now, in her condition?"

"Even now. Our housekeeper, Lavena, is doing a lot right now anyway, and she finds extra work a challenge. I assure you, Pup, you would be welcome."

Again Travis found himself under her scrutiny. He could see that she was considering his offer.

"I'll tell you what," he suggested. "We eat dinner about six o'clock; you're welcome to join us for that, too. On Saturday night we usually turn in around ten o'clock. You would be welcome anytime all afternoon, including for dinner, but if that won't work out, come before ten and one of us will show you to a bedroom."

He was serious. Pup had always known he was special, but never had she expected this.

"Do you need to know now?"

"No. Just consider it an open invitation." He couldn't help but add, "I want you to meet my wife and boys; I hope you'll come."

She was silent for just a moment and then said softly, "I just might do that. Thank you, Travis."

"You're welcome. Take care as you head up the mountain."

She acknowledged this with a nod and again turned away. This time Travis let her go, but he stood watching her until she disappeared into the crowd.

Who would have thought, Lord? I haven't seen her in weeks, and now she comes off the train and asks about the church. Bring her back to town, Lord. Bring her back so she can learn about You.

Travis would have been surprised to know that Pup was doing some praying of her own. The feeling of loneliness that had come with her on the train had lifted the minute Travis had asked if she would be coming back for church on Sunday. As Mickey saddled her horse, she stood quietly and savored the invitation.

It had to have been Your planning that I saw Travis, Lord. I was hoping to get down to church but hadn't given it much thought, and then he was standing there. He invited me to his home, and I know he meant it. Thank You. Thank You for caring about the small details.

Pup was so focused on this line of thought that she nearly forgot to pay the livery owner. It didn't get better when she finally left the livery. In fact, at the edge of town she had to backtrack to the mercantile, having almost forgotten to purchase supplies before heading up the mountain.

26

As McKay had suspected, Richard Stuart was not thrilled to see him on Tuesday morning. After asking Richard to speak to him in his private office, McKay quietly explained his presence. The bank owner had tried to keep his feelings masked, but the fleeting moment of panic and then anger was unmistakable. McKay waited patiently while Stuart got himself under control.

"Are you checking all the banks in town?" Richard finally asked.

"I'm not at liberty to discuss that with you, Mr. Stuart."

"Why my bank?" he tried again.

"Because I've been told to; it's part of my job."

It was not the answer the banker was looking for, but he fell silent. McKay felt himself being weighed. Mr. Stuart did not want to accept him at face value, and he now watched McKay's eyes to see if he could gauge an added motive.

From years of practice the treasury agent was able to arrange his features into a bland mask. The expression must have worked with Richard Stuart: Only a few seconds passed before McKay was directed to a table in the back and asked what years' books he wanted to examine. McKay had orders on this as well and requested January 1876 to June 1878.

The heavy account books were delivered by a silent bank employee. McKay thanked him and was left on his own. However, he knew he was not ignored. The table he worked at was in an out-of-the-way corner in the bank, but every time he glanced up he found Mr. Stuart's eyes either just leaving him or resting on him in thoughtful speculation.

❦

Boulder

A smile of peace and comfort lit Pup's face when she woke up Tuesday morning. She'd been away from the cabin for much longer periods of time, but never had she needed to get home more. So much had happened in her heart and life in the last few days.

Not surprisingly, McKay's face immediately sprang to mind. What was he doing? Had he been ordered back to Denver? Pup would have loved to see him, to look into his eyes again, and to hear his deep voice. But right now she needed to be home.

She rolled to her side and let her gaze roam out the window. The bed was too low to allow her to see anything but sky and trees, but somewhere beyond the glass she heard a mourning dove call to its mate. Pup never heard this sound in Denver, and this morning it made her want to lie in bed all the longer. So often when she came home she was filled with energy and determination to get things done, but today her heart was quiet, her body still. Last night she had been too tired to do anything save fall into bed, but this morning she wanted to pray.

I didn't know I could feel so secure. I didn't know I could be so sure. You're here. You're really here with me, and I know it. I believe this with all my heart, Lord God, and I see now more than ever before that You were here all along. I was wrong to go my way and live my own life. I hadn't thought about my childhood experience with You in so many years, but I know You tried other things to get my attention. I ignored them. That was wrong. I can see this now. Thank You for taking me back.

Pup felt her heart lift with her confession and realized that the last time the Lord had tried to arrest her attention had been while she was burying Govern. What an awful day that had been, and only two-and-a-half months past. Pup remembered her heart had felt as if it were going to burst, but she had pushed the pain away. She had desperately wanted someone here to share the loss and agony with her. She saw now that God had gently revealed to her that He was there for her, but Pup had not really understood or stopped to listen. Now her ears were open wide.

It's nice when we feel good, Callie. Mr. Harrington's words from one evening around the dinner table came back to her with startling clarity. *But our faith must be based on truth. No matter what we're feeling, good or bad, it's to be discarded if it's contrary to God's Word.*

It was then that Pup knew she needed a Bible. She could have kicked herself for not checking the reading room or even the general store when she'd come into Boulder yesterday. The thought of going back down to town did not thrill her, but she would do it if that's what it took to get a copy of the Scriptures.

Percy's face flashed into her mind so swiftly that for a moment she was completely still. A second later the covers were tossed back and she was jumping out of bed to climb into her clothes. Her boots were only half-tied when she went out the front door, gun in hand. Not caring if they were up or not, she moved swiftly toward Mud and Percy's. If Percy didn't have a Bible, she'd head to town. However, something told her he did have one, if not two, and she was just going to have to figure out how to talk it away from him for a time.

She slowed down as she neared the cabin and was relieved to hear voices. The brothers were up, and no one was shouting. Pup thought this might be a good sign, but in truth she never knew what she was going to find when it came to the Dougan brothers. They heard her coming even before she stepped into the clearing in front of their cabin, so both men were facing her direction when she appeared.

"Well, Pup," Mud said congenially upon seeing who it was, "you're home."

"Got in last night." Both men were sitting on a fallen log in front of their cabin. Pup didn't come in close, not sure if Percy would like it. She spoke from a distance.

"How've you boys been?"

"Can't complain," Mud said with a grin, "but then I'm not Percy. Percy can always find something to complain about."

Pup was further encouraged when Percy only laughed. It was then that she noticed a book in his hands. Mud must have gone out last night and come home this morning with a peace-offering volume. It wasn't hard to figure, considering that Mud's face was puffy, his shirt stained and torn, and Percy was intent upon the pages of the book.

"What can we do for you?" Mud asked. Percy kept reading.

"I wonder if you have a Bible I can borrow."

"Sure," Mud replied immediately, but Percy's head came up, his pleased face changing to a scowl directed at his brother.

"We only have Mother's," he informed Mud coolly.

"So?" Mud sounded indignant. "You never look at it, and what do you think Pup is going to do anyway—throw it into Lake Anne?"

Percy glared at him. "I say it stays."

"And I say she can take it. She never hurts any of your books."

"It's Mother's Bible," Percy repeated as though Mud hadn't understood. "I tell you, she can't have it."

"Well, for once you don't have all the say," Mud informed him. "Mother's Bible is just as much mine as yours, and I say Pup can take it."

Mud turned to tell Pup that he would go in and get the Bible, but when both men looked back to the clearing, they found their guest gone. Mud turned a fierce glare on his brother and slowly stood to his feet. He walked back to the cabin, but not before his eyes dared his brother to so much as say a word.

Pup had just finished saddling Ginny when she heard someone coming through the woods. She was not at all surprised to see Mud appear, but the Bible under one arm was another story. Pup had stepped out of the stable, and she now stood silently as he stopped and pushed the volume into her hands. She looked down. It was old, but the binding was intact and the pages did not appear to be torn or misused.

"I never meant to cause a fight, Mud."

"Doesn't matter," he told her. "Percy's always been stingy with his books. Usually I don't have a say, but this one was Mama's, and he can just get used to the idea."

Again Pup looked at the Bible.

"My mother never had a Bible," she said softly, "but if she did I would cherish it." She looked up. "You can tell Percy that no harm will come to this book. I won't take it out of the cabin until I'm bringing it back to you."

Mud shrugged irritably, still upset with his sibling. "It's not doing anyone any good just sitting on that shelf. You keep it for as long as you like."

Pup nodded and looked at him. Mud looked back.

"You're different," he said simply.

"Yes, I am," she agreed.

Mud's eyes dropped to the Bible. He knew that whatever she said, it would have to do with God and the Book she was holding. Mud looked again at the peace in her face. He didn't dread the coming conversation; on the contrary, he was frankly curious.

"You'll have to tell me about it sometime."

"I'll do that," Pup readily agreed.

Mud said goodbye and started away, but he was more curious than ever when Pup told him she wouldn't be around much come the weekend; she was going down to church.

Pup made herself work all day. She wanted to stop and read Mrs. Dougan's Bible but resisted. So much needed tending. When McKay had arrived on her doorstep, she had not been expecting to leave with him. Mud had watered the garden some, but now it was full of weeds and dried vegetables. The stable was in need of attention, and she had clothing to wash as well. She would not catch up in one day, but she forced herself to put some time in.

After a wearying day, evening was a welcome sight. The hot day began cooling, and the sunset sent a dazzling purple streak through the sky. She looked forward to bathing in the lake, but first she sat down to a meal of corn cakes, honey syrup, berries, and hot coffee. At her side was the Bible. She opened it to read, making herself pay attention lest she mark it with food.

At first she didn't know where to start. She paged through it slowly, not sure what she was looking for, when her eyes caught sight of the book of Jonah. She had heard of Jonah, but until she'd read the first chapter, she thought that the story of a man being swallowed by a huge fish was little more than legend. She now read all four chapters in Jonah with nothing short of surprise and awe.

There was so much more to the story than the great fish. Jonah was a prophet of God. She had not known this before. She had also not known of the plans God had for the city and people of Nineveh. God told Jonah to spread the news of judgment to the people of that city. Because of their wickedness, God was going to destroy them. He had not made any provisions to save them; they were doomed. But then the people had turned from their wicked ways, and God saw this.

Intent on the words, Pup read for a time and then sat back, her food forgotten. Did God change His mind? She looked at the text again. She read it over twice. God had not told Jonah that Nineveh was doomed *unless* they repented. He had said they were done for—no exceptions or promises otherwise.

Pup had never thought about God changing His mind. She would have to ask McKay about it, or maybe Travis when she saw him on the weekend. Right now it made her smile. What a tremendous display of compassion on God's part. The very second verse said that their wickedness had come before God, leading Pup to believe that it must have been horrific. But He had spared them.

"How often have You spared me, Lord?" she prayed alone at the table. "How many times did You see my sin and deal compassionately with me?"

No voice spoke from the air to answer her, but in Pup's mind there was no need. She simply wanted to voice the wonder inside of her. She went back to the book of Jonah and then prayed some more, her food still forgotten. It was several hours before she made her way to the lake and then was ready to turn in for the night. But until she fell asleep, her heart was amazed with the wonder of it all.

"How are you?" Travis spoke quietly to Rebecca as he came soft-footedly into their bedroom. Lying on her side, Rebecca smiled tiredly at him and didn't answer. Travis sat down next to her.

"You didn't sleep well, did you?"

"Not very," she admitted. "I ache, Travis. I don't remember feeling so achy with the boys, but this time I can't get comfortable."

"Are you still feeling that it will be soon?"

She made a face. "I certainly did yesterday, but right now I think I'm going to be expecting for weeks longer."

Travis leaned close and kissed her forehead. He then sat back up, praying all the while for his wife and unborn child. Although married, Travis and Rebecca had not been living together when she gave birth to their twin boys nearly seven years ago. Everything about this pregnancy was very new to him. Part of him loved being involved, but another part of him wanted to skip town until it was all over. Rebecca had not been overly moody or difficult, but seeing her so uncomfortable before her pains began caused Travis to dread the coming hours and days. It was a strong temptation to beg God to spare his wife and child, but he knew he needed to trust.

Rebecca watched his face, not able to keep a smile from her own.

"What's that grin for?" Travis asked.

"I know what you're thinking."

Travis smiled too. "What am I thinking?"

"You're wishing you could head out on the trail for a few days and return to find it all over."

Travis admitted to the truth of her words with an aggrieved nod.

"I'll tell you something else," Rebecca went on. "I wish I could get away for a few days and come back to find it over as well."

This made the chagrined husband chuckle and reach for her. Rebecca was definitely rounder these days, but she still fit in his arms and against his chest. He held her in silence for a time and then asked, "Do you wish I hadn't extended that invitation to Pup Jennings?"

"On the contrary," she surprised him by saying, "I'm hoping she'll come and take my mind off the way I feel."

Travis pulled his head back, his eyes taking in the morning blush of her cheeks, tousled honey-blonde hair, and the dark brown of her eyes. He was still studying her when their sons interrupted them. They didn't speak loudly or jump onto the bed, but crawled up softly and came close to their parents.

"Is the baby coming today?" Garrett wished to know, his voice hushed.

"I don't think so, honey."

"I'm glad," Wyatt informed them.

"Why is that?" Travis inquired.

"Because it's hot these days. I don't want the baby to get too hot. I want the baby to come before school starts again, but not if it's going to get hot."

"That's sweet of you, Wyatt," his mother told him, "but the baby will be fine. We'll work to keep the baby warm or cool, no matter what he needs."

"What if it's a girl?" one of the six-year-olds had to know.

"Whatever he *or* she needs," Travis filled in, a patient smile on his face. He watched as they both nodded with understanding.

Throughout the pregnancy the boys had been wonderful. Tender and caring with their mother and thrilled with the coming of the baby, they were nevertheless much more interested in having a younger sister than a baby brother. It wasn't hard to figure since the Buchanans' foreman had two little girls whom the boys adored.

"I think we should clear out now," Travis suggested, "and let your mother get up if she wants to."

"Are you coming down to eat breakfast with us?"

"I'm not very hungry," she told Garrett honestly, "but I'll come and talk to you while you eat."

The boys were more than satisfied with this, and after kissing their mother they scooted from the room. Travis followed them downstairs to the kitchen, his mind on Rebecca's condition. However, this wasn't his only thought. By the time his housekeeper, Lavena, poured him a mug of coffee, he was asking the Lord if Pup Jennings was going to visit before the day was through.

27

Pup hit the streets of downtown Boulder at 4:30 on Saturday afternoon. She had made better time coming down the mountain than she'd figured and now debated whether she should head straight to the Double Star Ranch. Somehow she felt unprepared. Social visits were not something she did often, and her baking was never good enough to share. But something told her she should take a gift of some type to this family. She didn't have a clue what it should be, but she stopped Ginny in front of the dry goods store and went inside.

The store was just the same as she always found it: fairly clean, well-stocked, and organized. Today, however, she didn't have a list; today she wanted something to catch her eye. She wanted something to leap from the shelf into her hand so she would know just what to take to the Buchanan home this evening.

It didn't happen that way. She first found herself spotting one item, knowing Travis would enjoy it, but doubting his wife would care for it. The next moment she would see something she thought the little boys might like but not knowing for certain. She was on the verge of giving up when she found the tin. There was just one, and on the side it said "Peppermint Sticks." It even showed a picture of the red-and-white striped confection. "Ready to Eat and Enjoy," the front of the tin proclaimed.

Pup lifted the can. It was heavier than she'd been expecting. It crossed her mind that it might have been sitting there for at least a year, but there was no sign of age or gathering dust. With a small feeling of contentment, Pup took it to the counter.

"Peppermint sticks," Jarvis said. "I usually sell these near Christmas."

"Is this old then?" Pup asked.

"No. In last month, I think, maybe two. They stay fresh in the can." His voice sounded confident.

Pup nodded. "I'll take them."

"You want the tin wrapped?"

"Yes, please."

Jarvis carried on a monologue as he wrapped the can and then accepted Pup's coin. It was his usual way, so Pup listened, not even attempting to answer the questions he asked and then answered himself before anyone else could. She thanked him for his help and was back out to Ginny a few minutes later. As she headed to the ranch, what she was about to do suddenly came to her. She didn't know Rebecca Buchanan from anyone, and although she was impressed with Travis, she didn't really know him, either. How would she stay with them and still maintain her privacy? Her heart sighed. Not for the first time she asked herself if the job was worth it.

Suddenly she was on the outskirts of town, her horse still headed toward the Double Star. With yet another soft sigh she let Ginny have her head, but Pup couldn't help but wonder what the next few hours or days would bring.

"Now you sit there, Rebecca Buchanan, and I mean it!" Lavena North, the Buchanan's housekeeper of many years, stood with her hands on her bony hips and scowled at her employer.

"I have more things I want to do," Rebecca stated calmly.

"No! You've got to rest. Why, this morning you looked so tired and worn-out that I thought you were going to have that baby today! And now look at you. Turning out closets and wanting to bake. I won't have it! If you don't sit still, I'm going to find Travis."

Lavena stomped from the room before she could see Rebecca smile, or the younger woman would have been in even more trouble. The baby chose that moment to change positions, and for a time Rebecca was content to sit and enjoy the boisterous movements.

She then realized Lavena was right. This morning and the past night she had felt terrible, but after the boys talked her into a little breakfast, she'd felt her strength returning, so much so that she had urged Travis to take the boys for a ride. Indeed, they were still gone.

The baby was quiet again, but Rebecca sat for a moment longer. The areas of the house that she wanted to check on came back to mind. With slow and now comfortable movements she stood. Walking softly from her seat in the large living room, she made her way to the front door and out onto the spacious wraparound porch. The broom was where she'd left it, and watching the windows carefully so as not to alert the zealous Lavena, she now went back to work on the webs and dust. She was still hard at work when Pup rode into the yard.

The relaxed and genuine hospitality she'd learned from Travis came swiftly to the fore, and the broom was set aside while she went to greet her visitor. Pup watched the lovely blonde woman as she began to navigate down the steps and swiftly called to her.

"Why don't you let me come to you?"

Rebecca stopped and smiled, waiting for Pup to approach on her horse.

"You must be Pup," Rebecca said from her place on the steps. She was still smiling, but in truth this woman was not at all as she'd been imagining.

"Yes. Thank you for having me." Thinking that the rumors of Travis' wife being a beauty were certainly true, Pup smiled kindly into Rebecca's deep brown eyes.

"It's our pleasure. My name is Rebecca by the way. Travis and the boys are out riding."

Pup dismounted and offered Rebecca her hand. The women shook, and Pup tied the horse's reins to the post and followed Rebecca as she moved back up onto the porch. Pup was much taller than the other woman; indeed, if Rebecca hadn't been expecting there would have been little to her. But at the moment that was the least of Pup's worries; she never figured on Travis not being present when she arrived.

For a moment Pup nearly panicked over what they might talk about, but she worked at staying calm. A moment later she let her head tip back. The porch was high and painted white. Most of it looked newly swept. The job was so thorough that it was immediately obvious where Mrs. Buchanan had left off with the broom.

"It looks as though I interrupted your work," Pup offered, opting for a safe subject.

Rebecca sighed and admitted, "I was so tired this morning that I could have slept all day. Now I'm so full of energy that I'm driving Lavena crazy."

Pup looked at her. "Your housekeeper?"

"Yes. If she knew I was out here, I'd be getting the sharp side of her tongue." She smiled. "Would you like to sit down?"

Pup shook her head. "I've been in the saddle for several hours, but don't let that stop you."

With that, the expectant mother watched in amazement as Pup picked up the broom and started on the porch where Rebecca had left off. The socially proper side of her wanted to tell her guest to drop the broom, but something in the other woman's face stopped her. A moment later she lowered herself onto one of the comfortable wooden benches that sat on the front porch.

"Is this what women call nesting?" Pup suddenly asked.

"What's that?" Taken off guard, Rebecca did not immediately catch on.

"Oh, you know, wanting to clean and get everything ready before the baby comes?"

"I think it must be. Now that I think about it, I did the same with the boys."

Pup brushed at a web and then looked over at her. "You had twins, didn't you?"

"Yes. Garrett and Wyatt."

Pup couldn't stop her eyes from dropping to Rebecca's distended waistline. "Is it twins this time, too?"

Rebecca chuckled, her hand going to her swollen middle. "No. Big as I am, I'm sure this is only one."

Glad she hadn't offended, Pup smiled and went back to work. "I've heard that women can tell if they're carrying a boy or girl. Is that true?"

"I've heard that, too, but I don't know. The boys want a baby sister. I guess I've been afraid to say too much and possibly disappoint them." She looked over to find Pup's eyes on her again.

But you know, Rebecca Buchanan, Pup thought to herself, *you believe you know what this baby is. I can see it in your eyes.* However, all she said aloud was "Do you hope for a boy or girl, or doesn't it matter to you?"

The younger woman smiled. "Only for the boys' sake. I'd like to see them get the baby sister they want."

Pup smiled as well and went back to the webs. A moment later she heard, "Well, of all things!"

She turned toward the front door to find a pint-sized woman whom she knew to be Lavena Larson. They had never met, but Pup had seen her around town over the years.

"I thought you were out here working; I tell you I did," she went on to the mistress of the ranch. "Travis and the boys are just back, and I was going to tell him if you were."

Rebecca smiled tolerantly at her. As a rule Lavena was very good about staying in the background, especially if they had company. But Rebecca's present condition had given her motive to throw off all caution. She was as protective of Rebecca as a mother hen might be, probably more so.

"Lavena," Rebecca spoke with some authority now, "please meet our guest, Pup Jennings. Pup, this is Lavena North, our housekeeper."

Surprised that she'd gotten the name wrong, Pup still came forward and offered her hand. "Hello," she said kindly.

Lavena shook it, but her eyes went to the broom.

"You're not going to continue with that broom, are you?"

"As a matter of fact I'm finished," Pup said smoothly, passing the aforementioned object to the bantam-sized woman.

Lavena thanked Pup with a low word and then turned back to the house. However, she didn't go before throwing a parting shot. "And you just stay seated, Rebecca, or you'll be hearing from me!" The door closed on this command, and the women exchanged a smile.

"At least she has your best interest in mind," Pup said to her hostess. "I'd hate to have her as an enemy."

Rebecca laughed in genuine amusement. "I'd never thought of that before. I have more to be thankful for than I realized."

Rebecca had just finished speaking when the sound of the boys' voices floated to them. They were coming around the side of the house and picked up the pace when they saw their mother seated on the porch. They ran to kiss her and then turned curious eyes on their guest.

"Garrett and Wyatt, I'd like you to meet Miss Jennings."

"Hello," they chorused together and even smiled at her.

Pup smiled in return. "Your mother tells me you've been riding." Pup studied their small faces, silently delighting in the differences between them: one dark, the other fair.

"We rode all over," Garrett told her seriously. "We went for a long one this time."

"Do you share a horse or each ride one?"

"Today we shared," Wyatt filled in. "Sometimes Gary gets Dixie and I get Feather, but today we shared Feather. She's Mama's horse."

"What's your horse's name?" Garrett wished to know.

"That's Ginny," Pup said as she looked over at the trim brown mare. "Do you want to ride her?"

"Can we?" Wyatt was already on his feet.

"May we?" his mother corrected.

"If it's all right with your mother."

Rebecca gave her consent with a nod, and Pup stood as the boys dashed off the porch. She followed them, removing her bag from the side of the saddle and untying the reins. Looking like little pros, the boys moved Ginny so they could climb into her saddle from the porch, and, faces serious, set off for a ride in the yard.

"Well, you certainly know how to make friends."

Pup turned with a smile and saw that Travis had come onto the porch from the front door.

"Hello, Travis."

"Hello yourself. Glad you could make it."

Pup came up the steps and shook his hand. He motioned to a bench, and Pup sat down before he joined Rebecca. Afraid that an uncomfortable silence would fall, Pup immediately opened her bag and drew out the tin of candy.

"I brought you a little something," she said, hoping she didn't sound as awkward as she felt. The can was passed to Rebecca.

"Thank you," she said kindly and then tore back the paper. "Peppermint!" she said with elation. "We haven't had peppermint since last Christmas. The boys are going to be thrilled."

"That was kind of you, Pup," Travis inserted. "Thank you."

"You're welcome."

243

The rancher smiled at her and then turned to the woman he was sitting next to. His arm was already along the back of the chair, and it now dropped gently onto her shoulders.

"Lavena tells me you've been naughty."

Rebecca turned her head to smile into his eyes. "She came out here to catch me in the act. You should have seen her face when she saw that it was Pup who was sweeping down the front porch."

Both women laughed at his expression.

"It was better Pup than me," his wife went on to tell him. "I was already in enough trouble."

"I can see I'm going to have to keep an eye on you two," Travis teased them, completely unaware of what his words did for Pup's heart.

Not until after she'd given the broom to Lavena did she think how strange her actions might have seemed. The last thing she wanted was to invite a bunch of questions or odd looks, but Rebecca had taken it in stride and so had Travis. She was still asking God to help her handle the rest of the evening as well when Travis called a halt to the boys' ride.

"Gary, Wyatt, come back to the porch. I think Miss Jennings' horse has had enough for now. After all, she came all the way down the mountain today."

"You live in the hills?" Wyatt asked when they neared, and Pup nodded her head.

"In a cabin?"

"Yes."

"Do you live with anybody?"

"I live by myself."

Clearly the boys thought this was great, and Travis could see that more questions were coming.

"You can talk to Miss Jennings at supper, boys," he informed them. "Let's take this little mare to the barn for the night."

"It's Ginny, Papa. Her name's Ginny."

"All right," Travis agreed, treating this with a sincerity that equaled his boys'. He tossed an amused smile at his wife and guest before heading to the barn with his sons.

"Why don't you come in?" Rebecca was saying as she stood. "I'll show you to your room, and then I think it must be close to dinnertime."

Pup picked up her bag and followed her hostess, once again pleased that no awkward silences or questions had assailed her. She was shown to a room off the kitchen and told that it had been Lavena's room before she moved to a small house on the property and married one of Travis' ranchhands. The mystery over the name was put to rest in Pup's mind.

Left alone, Pup found the bedroom spacious and comfortable. Although sounds could be heard from the kitchen, Pup knew they would not disturb her. She took a moment to check her wig in the mirror and wash her face and hands at the basin. The main reason for this visit came rushing back to her, and she forced herself not to worry about who she might be meeting Sunday morning. In many ways it was a temptation to saddle up Ginny and head right back up the mountain, but nervous as she was, her desire to be in church was stronger. In time she went out to enjoy the evening with the Buchanan family, thanking God again that He was watching over her.

28

No one was up the next morning, at least not early enough to be in the kitchen before Pup came from her room. She remembered the hospitality she felt from the Harringtons in Longmont and could honestly say that the Buchanans were no different. With that in mind, she moved quietly and started the coffee. It was just finishing, filling the kitchen with the familiar aroma, when Lavena came through the back door.

"Well now," she said simply, "first the front porch and now the coffee. Pretty soon I'll be out of a job."

Pup only smiled, knowing Lavena was not at all upset. She knew that Lavena would never be out of a job. The house was spotless and the food on the table the night before was some of the best Pup had ever tasted. Pup had to hide a smile as she pictured herself trying to do Lavena's job. Fiasco was the only word that came to mind.

"Are you ready for some breakfast?" the feisty housekeeper wanted to know.

"The coffee's enough for now. Thank you."

Lavena evidently didn't feel a need to comment again; she turned around and went to work. It wasn't long before she was filling muffin tins for the oven, and even before they went in, Pup could see that they would rise higher than her baked goods ever did. She wondered for the space of several heartbeats if it might be time to work on her own cooking skills, but a moment later she spotted a Bible. All thoughts of food and cooking disappeared.

There was a small shelf by the kitchen door and on the top of it rested a black Bible. Lavena, indeed the whole kitchen, was forgotten as Pup retrieved it and wandered back to the table. She opened it to the book of Ephesians. She'd been reading in that book in the Dougans' Bible before it was time to leave for Boulder. And forcing herself to keep her promise, she had left the Bible safely at home.

She immediately turned back to that book and took up where she had left off in chapter six. She'd read the first nine verses at the cabin and went over them again, but verses ten through twelve were new to her, and in the Buchanan's kitchen she read to herself with great concentration.

Finally, my brethren, be strong in the Lord, and in the power of his might. Put on the whole armor of God, that you may be able to stand against the wiles of the devil. For we wrestle not against flesh and blood, but against principalities, against powers, against the rulers of the darkness of this world, against spiritual wickedness in high places.

At that point she stopped and looked up, completely taken aback to see that Travis had joined her at the table. He stared across at her, his face open and kind, but he did not speak.

"It sounds like we're at war in here," she finally said in confusion.

"What book are you in?"

"Ephesians."

"'Put on the whole armor of God'?"

Pup could only nod.

"Those verses are referring to the battle with sin," he began. "When a person comes to a saving faith in Jesus Christ—"

"I did that," she cut in ever so softly.

"Okay," Travis nodded, pleased to hear it but wanting to answer her immediate question. "After salvation," he went on, "we see God's holiness in a new light. We see more than ever what sinners we are—even more so than at the point of salvation.

We recognize that a holy God was merciful to us, but we can't be content to live as we always did. However, old sin habits die hard. In Ephesians, Paul tells us—"

"Paul?"

"He's the writer of the book."

"How do you know that?"

"The first verse, or possibly the second, names him."

He watched as she looked back at the first chapter and then raised her head to stare at him again.

"Paul tells us how to fight against the sin we so naturally want to fall into."

"I'm not sure I do."

"Do what?"

"*Want* to fall into sin and need to fight against it."

This gave Travis pause. Had she really come to Christ? Or was she so young in the Lord that she just had a very limited knowledge of sin in general? He prayed about what to say.

"I must have completely missed that Paul wrote this book," Pup said, her voice filled with wonder. "I read those verses but didn't understand that's what he was saying. It makes me wonder how much else I've missed."

"Don't let it worry you," Travis assured her, still wondering how much he should share. He took a moment to think and then offered something that would cover her whether or not she'd actually made a decision for Christ.

"If you remain faithful with your study, Pup, you'll understand. God never hides from us."

She nodded, her face still intent. "Does Pastor Henley welcome questions?"

"Absolutely. He enjoys it. I've yet to see a Sunday when someone didn't approach him."

At that point Lavena brought a heavy stack of dishes down from the cupboard, and Pup and Travis' eyes were drawn to her. Although not aware of Lavena, Pup realized she'd been working in the kitchen the entire time. Was she comfortable with talk about God's Word? Did she know Christ? Somehow Pup didn't think so. Pup pondered on this for a few moments. The questions going through her mind must have been evident on her face. When she looked back at Travis, he slowly shook his head no.

If they'd been alone she might have tried to ask him, but not only was Lavena present, the boys joined them just five minutes later. They proclaimed to all in the kitchen that they were starving, and not until they mentioned food did Pup realize she was now ready to eat. It was the start of an enlightening day for her—one she would never forget.

Rebecca did not get up to eat breakfast or see Travis, Pup, and the boys off to church. As Pup gathered her things to leave, she wondered if this was because of her pregnancy or because she didn't enjoy church. Pup now remembered that the day she and Travis had talked at the train station, he had said he attended church with his sons. Pup had not taken him literally, but now thought she probably should have. After her things were ready and her room in order, she expressed to Lavena her thanks for the meal and a comfortable night. She went to the wagon to find Travis had already saddled Ginny and tied the mare's reins to the back; Pup had told him at breakfast that she would be headed home after services.

Pup and Garrett took the rear seat, and Wyatt joined his father as he handled the reins. The boys entertained the adults as the horses drew them closer to church, and for a time, Pup was not left alone with her thoughts. However, as they came to the edge of town the boys fell silent, and she was forced to think about what might lie ahead.

Many of the faces in town were not new to her, but she knew they considered her strange. After all, she was not given to small talk and she always came and went from the bank, livery, post office, and general store just as swiftly as she could. No one in town was ever openly rude, but Pup was good at reading people. She knew when someone didn't know what to make of her. Would it be any different with this church congregation? She reminded herself that at times she'd seen confusion and surprise in Travis' gaze, but he had also proved to be kindness itself.

"You've grown rather quiet back there." The object of her thoughts spoke from the front seat.

"Have I?" she evaded the comment.

Since Pup was not sitting directly behind him, Travis was able to turn his head and stare at her for a moment.

"You'll be welcome at the church," he said calmly, his eyes moving back to the horses. "I was sick to my stomach with anxiety the first time I came, but there was no need. I wasn't asked to sing a solo or even to stand and give my name. People were friendly and kind." He glanced behind him one more time. "They're still the same today, Pup."

The nervous woman nodded but did not reply. She sat still, thinking there was no reason not to believe Travis, but if that was the case, why did her stomach feel odd? She remembered the loving church family in Longmont and was reminded why she would be nervous. There was no fear that she would have to sing a solo; the apprehension came from the fact that someone might get close enough to expect her to talk about herself. And even if that didn't happen and she was able to get close for a few weeks, a telegram could arrive from Denver at any time. In the past, that mysterious aspect of her life was always very exciting, but not so today.

With subtle movements she touched the wig at her temple, praying that all was in place. Her hair was just now starting to fluff away from her scalp. It would be some time before she could leave the wig at home, but she was already feeling like a year at home wouldn't be enough. A moment later she mentally shook her head at her own musings. What foolishness. She knew she would be called back to work and that it would be far less than a year from now.

Garrett took that moment to announce the sighting of the church, so no one heard Pup sigh. But she knew then that the cramps in her stomach this morning were not just about church.

"I love this next verse," Pastor Henley spoke from the front, his sermon almost over. "In fact I know that my wife taught it to the children this morning. Verse four," he said, referring to the second chapter in Philippians where the sermon was centered that day. "Will you say it with me?" Pastor asked. Although he smiled encouragingly, little ones all over the church ducked their heads and lowered their eyes.

"I didn't give you much warning, did I?" he said with kind eyes, taking all the blame. "I'll do it for you, shall I? 'Look not every man on his own things, but every man also on the things of others.' Note that it doesn't say we're to ignore our own needs, but if we're *only* taking time for our own needs, we're disobeying. A church family can't function that way. We have to be mindful of each other.

"As you leave this morning, don't forget the first verse in the chapter that we've already gone over. Let's look at the list one last time. 'Comfort of love,' it says, 'fellowship of the Spirit,' and 'mercy and compassion.' This is how we're to act toward one another, and when we put the needs of others ahead of our own, this comes easily. It's when we're self-seeking that these commands get lost in the shuffle. Take this away with you today. Ask God to show you how you can exhibit these things in your own life, and others close to you will be blessed."

It was over before Pup could take a breath. It was hard to believe that more than an hour had passed since Pastor Henley welcomed everyone to the service. Pup had never taken her eyes from him, and now he was asking them to stand so he could lead them in the last song. *Had it been like this in Longmont?*

She honestly couldn't remember. The things Pastor Henley had said, the warm look in his eyes, and the gentle sound of his voice had thoroughly captivated her.

"I'm sorry the boys were a little wiggly," Travis was saying. They'd sat with the boys between them, but now the young Buchanans were gone. Pup turned to him. "They're usually better than that," Travis explained, "but one of them must have had ants in his pants."

Pup only looked at him. Had the boys been fidgety? Her look made Travis smile, and after a moment she smiled in return.

"I take it you didn't notice." His eyes were sparkling with humor.

"No," Pup said, feeling like laughing. It was a good thing she hadn't been eating—she'd have covered herself with food.

"How did you feel about the service?" Travis asked. He himself had been slightly preoccupied wondering what she was thinking.

"I enjoyed it," she said simply, but something told him there was a wealth of meaning behind the words.

"Would you like to meet Pastor and his wife?"

"Yes, I would."

Again the words were plainly said, but Travis was swiftly coming to realize that there was far more to Pup Jennings than probably he or anyone else would guess. Pup now stepped aside, and Travis understood that she wanted him to lead the way. He did so, feeling slightly uncomfortable walking in front of her, but she had clearly wanted this. As it was, Mrs. Henley was not at the front. Someone else had stopped the pastor, so Travis and Pup stood for a moment and waited. Pup's mind was just beginning to wander back to some of the things Pastor Henley said this morning when he turned.

"Travis," his voice told of his pleasure.

"Hello, Pastor Henley. I'd like you to meet Pup Jennings. She's a friend from here in Boulder who stayed with Rebecca and me last night at the ranch." Travis turned to Pup.

"Pup, this is Pastor Keith Henley.

The older man's hand came out. "Pup, is it?"

"Yes" Pup said, shaking his hand. "I go by Pup or Callie; it doesn't matter."

"It's good to meet you, Callie," the pastor replied, deciding in an instant not to use her nickname.

"I enjoyed your sermon," Pup felt compelled to tell him, unaware of the way her deep feelings showed in her eyes.

"Isn't that a great passage in Philippians?" he asked with a gentle smile. "It's one of my favorites."

Something melted in Pup's heart at that moment. She wasn't certain why she was so drawn to this man, but his faith was so genuine that Pup felt as though she could sit down with him and discuss the Bible for hours. For a moment she might have been that little girl so many years past who stood on the street corner and put her child's faith in the Son of God. Pastor Henley somehow had that effect on her.

"It was new to me," she offered hesitantly. "I mean, the verses—I hadn't read them before."

"Would you like to discuss those verses with me?" Pastor asked. "Was there anything that wasn't clear to you? I'd be happy to talk to you about them."

This was the last thing Pup had expected. She had asked Travis if she would be able to question the pastor, but she hadn't expected it to be this easy. For a moment she was so surprised she didn't speak. Pastor Henley suddenly turned to Travis.

"I suppose you'll want to be home with Rebecca since her time is so close, but may Beryl and I steal Callie from you for a time today?"

"Absolutely. Pup was going to head home from here anyway, so if she's available—" he let the sentence hang.

Pup suddenly found herself under the scrutiny of both men. She wasn't sure what she'd missed, but she waited silently for someone else to speak.

"My wife and I would be happy to have you join us for dinner today, Callie," Pastor told her.

It took a moment for the invitation to sink in, but then Pup simply said, "I'd like that."

A moment later, before anyone else could speak, they were joined by Mrs. Henley.

"Hello, Travis. How's Rebecca?"

"Still holding on."

Beryl grasped his arm. "You take good care of her, Travis." Travis smiled. "I will."

"Beryl," the pastor said, drawing his wife close with an arm, "meet Callie Jennings. She's going to join us for dinner today."

"I'm so glad," Beryl said sincerely as her hand came forward. Pup found herself liking this older woman from the first moment.

"I just asked Clayton and his family to join us, too," she added, telling Pup, not her spouse. "Have you met Boulder's schoolteacher, Callie?"

"No, I don't believe I have."

"You'll like Clayton and Jackie. They just had a baby girl."

It was all settled so swiftly that Pup wasn't given time to respond. Telling Pup she'd be welcome at the house next week, Travis was suddenly saying his goodbyes and leaving to round up his sons. Pastor Henley told his wife that he would be held up a few minutes and asked if she would walk with Pup and show her where they lived.

Pup met a few other people on her way to the door, her mind still trying to deal with how swiftly she'd been offered hospitality. Hospitality was nothing new in the West, but the warmth and caring behind it were so foreign to this mountain woman that she wished for some time alone to take it in. It wasn't to happen. Seconds later Ginny's reins were in her hand as she walked to the parsonage beside a woman she'd just met, her heart asking God to help her in the hours to come.

29

Seated comfortably in the Henley's living room, Pup looked down into the face of Katherine Alexa Taggart and couldn't stop her smile. At three months old, Katherine was the roundest, sweetest, most delicate child she had ever seen. Full cheeks that held an apple blush accentuated large, dark purple eyes. She didn't have much hair, but the soft fuzz atop her head was a deep red. Exquisite was the only word that would come to Pup's mind.

"Is she smiling at you?" Katherine's mother asked, and Pup looked up at the blinded eyes of Jackie Taggart.

"She's just looking me over," Pup told her. Wondering what it would be like never to see your child, she looked back down to the baby in Jackie's arms.

"She's smiling now," Pup said, thinking the baby might have needed to hear her voice to respond.

"I can feel it," Jackie said, an intense look of wonder and joy on her face. "Sometimes she smiles with her whole body."

"She's so pretty," Pup said softly.

"That's what Clayton and her aunt and uncle say, but I don't know whether I can trust anyone who's so biased by love."

"They're telling you the truth," Pup assured her softly, and for a moment they both fell silent.

"I don't always meet everyone who visits the church," Jackie said, "so I hope I won't sound nosy if I ask you whether you've come before."

"That's all right," Pup assured her. "As a matter of fact, this is my first time. Do you attend regularly?"

"Yes. Since the first Sunday I moved here. Did you meet Eddie or Robert Langley this morning?"

"I don't think so." Pup certainly knew who those people were, but she had never been introduced to any of them.

"Well, Eddie is my sister. I lived with them before Clayton and I were married."

The baby began to fuss, and Pup watched in fascination as Jackie "saw" her baby. She didn't just jostle her a bit and tell her to quiet down, but she shifted her bundle until she had one hand free. She ran that hand gently down the baby's head, face, and ears, checking stomach, arms, hands, legs, and feet—every part of her.

"I think you're fine," Katherine's mother told her baby. "You just ate, so you can't be hungry. I wonder if you might need to see Papa?"

"Do you want me to get your husband?" Pup hadn't met him but offered just the same.

"No," Jackie said with a grin, "I just say that to distract her."

Pup smiled in return, just as a voice spoke from the door.

"Sorry I'm late," Clayton Taggart said as he walked in with an easy stride. "Did Eddie drop you off?"

"Robert, actually," Jackie told him. "Clayton, meet Callie Jennings. Callie, this is my husband, Clayton."

"It's good to meet you." Clayton came forward and shook her hand.

"Thank you. Mrs. Henley tells me you teach at the school."

"Guilty as charged," he told her good-naturedly, taking a seat next to Jackie. He scooped his daughter from his wife's arms and held her to his shoulder. "Do you live here in town, Callie?"

"Up the mountain some."

"That's pretty country up there."

"I think so," Pup agreed with pleasure.

"Does living so far away make it hard to get to church?" Jackie wished to know.

"Not exactly hard, but it does take some planning. Last night I stayed with Travis and Rebecca."

"Don't you love that ranch and the house?" Clayton asked her.

Pup smiled. "It's beautiful."

"How is Rebecca feeling?" Jackie asked, well remembering the end of her own pregnancy.

"Tired, but in good spirits. When I got there she was cleaning everything in sight."

"Now, doesn't that sound familiar," Clayton chuckled.

"I was just awful," Jackie admitted, "and because of my vision I couldn't do everything I wanted. I probably drove Clayton mad."

But Clayton only smiled. "Let's just say I was glad to finally meet the little person who was causing all the disturbance." He had shifted Katherine to his arms and held her so he could smile into her eyes, but he still had a hand free to touch his wife.

Pup was surprised to feel something catch at her throat. What a special couple they were. She had certainly heard of them, and even seen them once or twice, but never would she have guessed how well they coped with Jackie's special needs. Indeed, until she'd met Jackie and seen her up close, she hadn't been aware of the blindness.

Beryl Henley came to the doorway at that moment.

"Keith is here now." Her smile encompassed them. "We're ready to eat."

Shifting Katherine to his shoulder again, Clayton stood and let Jackie take his arm.

"After you, Callie."

Pup went ahead of them, her nose catching the aromas of the meal. Beryl gently touched Pup's arm as she came from the living room to the spacious kitchen where the meal was laid out on the table. "Right here, Callie," she directed.

Pup had just taken her seat when Pastor Henley came in from a side door.

"It smells good in here, dear," he commented to his wife as he sat at one end of the table. "I hope I didn't ruin anything."

"Not at all. Your timing was perfect."

Pup watched them share a smile as the hostess claimed the other end of the table. Pup sat on Beryl's right, and the Taggarts were across the table. Even though there was an empty chair next to her, she felt warm and included. She also felt a rush of emotions, some so unfamiliar that she couldn't even name them. As they all bowed their heads to pray, Pup couldn't help but wonder if the emotions were *because* she felt included or *in spite* of it.

"So this verse is referring to verses above?"

"Yes. Words like "but," "therefore," and "finally," signal us to back up in the text because they refer to a prior thought."

Pup nodded, her face intent on the pastor and the open Bible in his hand. More than an hour had passed since Katherine had become very wet and Clayton and Jackie had taken her home. During that time Pup sat in the living room with the Henleys and discussed the day's sermon, or at least that's where the conversation began. Before long the subjects had ranged far.

The afternoon was growing long when Pastor Henley said, "Callie, I want you to rest in the Lord on all of this. The people of Paul's day clearly understood what was written to them. I want you to be just as confident in God and trust that He's brought His message to us in our common everyday language." With that, the wise pastor held his Bible up between them.

Pup sat back, her mind taking in all they had covered. It had been such a help to her. There was so much he'd been able to make clear with just a few words of counsel on how to study the Scriptures.

"Thank you for taking time with me today," Pup said softly.

"You're welcome. Are you settled on things for now?"

"Yes. Thank you, Mrs. Henley," she said, turning to her hostess.

"It's been our pleasure," Beryl told her. The older woman was tired, but getting to know Callie was worth the fatigue. It hadn't taken long to see that Callie Jennings could be a very intense individual, but her questions were sincere and well thought out. Beryl knew Keith would probably have to draw from years of study and pray for wisdom to keep up with her.

Pup had told them of her conversion, and Beryl had to admit to herself that she'd never heard the like. She'd also never known anyone who caught on so swiftly; Keith had not had to repeat anything. To top it off, she seemed as fresh as this morning. Beryl was tired just thinking about riding a horse up the mountain.

"Will we see you next week?"

"Yes. Travis told me I could stay with them again. I also heard Clayton say something about a Bible study at the Langleys'. Is that open to anyone?"

"Yes, it is. Robert teaches the study himself. They meet on Thursday nights, and I know you would be welcome."

Pup listened to directions to the Langley home even though the twins had pointed out their aunt and uncle's home that morning. She hadn't decided if going to a study would work for her schedule or not, and having grown intent on the thought, nearly forgot to say goodbye. At the last minute she recalled herself and graciously thanked the Henleys as they saw her to the door. However, her mind was swiftly back on all she'd heard as well as on the week ahead.

She'd been on Ginny's back for close to two hours when she looked down and saw some food marks on the lap of her dress. They immediately made her think of McKay. She wanted to laugh, as she knew he would have had he been present. Chagrined, she slowly shook her head. It had taken all she had not to forget herself during the meal, but clearly she hadn't been as successful as she had believed. Her next thought took the smile from her face and melted her heart to tenderness.

"I wouldn't be a mess if I'd gone to Longmont," she now told Ginny softly, the deep woods surrounding her. "McKay would have taken care of me. He would have wrapped a cloth around my neck and reminded me not to spill on my dress."

It was at that moment that Pup knew she must be tired. If she had not had hours still to go she would have stopped Ginny on the spot and sat down for a long, hard cry.

30

Silver Plume

McKay and Trent Adams, an agent he worked with on occasion, left the horses tied to a bush and walked behind the old-timer they'd tracked down at the boardinghouse in Silver Plume. He'd been a talker from the moment they approached him, and he didn't seem to have anything better to do. The incline up the mountain was proving to be steeper than expected, but they'd taken the horses as far as they could go and now set out on foot. Jed Cawley, 60 if he was a day, had told them he knew where the mine was located. He'd even offered to take them. McKay knew it was going to cost him, but it would be well worth every cent if this lead panned out.

Trent's hat came off for an instant, and he sighed as he wiped at the sweat on his brow. McKay was equally warm, but he'd been with this case so long that his interest and enthusiasm to solve it made the sun on their backs and the exertion of the climb seem insignificant.

"There she is." Cawley stopped and pointed. McKay noticed that the old miner didn't seem winded at all. "The William Tell."

"That's the William Tell mine?" McKay questioned; he had to be sure.

The smile Jed gave was gap-toothed. "I could have told you you fellas would be disappointed, but I knew you wouldn't have believed me. Hasn't been worked for ten years or better. The valuable mines are located in Brown Gulch. Why, you can practically hear the machinery from here!" The old man, who did in fact have time on his hands, stopped when he saw he'd lost the men. Their eyes were on the mine's opening and then on each other.

McKay was the first to lead off, moving farther up the incline to the mouth of the mine. He stepped gingerly to the opening. It was dark, and Jed was certainly right: No one had been here, let alone worked the mine, for a long time. McKay was on the verge of stepping into the gloomy interior when he saw the sign. It was on the ground and half-covered by dirt and rock. McKay picked up the board. In faded letters, it read simply, "William Tell."

"If you're thinking of buying, I'm sure someone will sell to you," Jed offered, his voice rather gleeful, "but you fellas look smarter than that. Now down in the gulch, that's the place to invest."

Trent had made the mistake of looking at the old man, so he rambled on for a time, but McKay wasn't listening. His mind was going over the things he had seen in Richard Stuart's bank—mining stocks in particular. Silver Plume was not what you'd call a stone's throw from Longmont or Denver, but this was the first mine listed in anyone's books to have been located within a reasonable traveling distance. The various mines and properties belonging to Duncan Phipps had been completely out of the area and sometimes out of the state. There were agents in those cities and states who could certainly check things out, but new assignments and the passing along of confidential information was not his job.

McKay looked back at Trent, who was listening to Jed with barely veiled tolerance. A few more checks in town, maybe with the old man himself, and they could head home and write up their report. McKay felt his heart swell with pleasure. Carlyle and even Nick were sure to be pleased.

Boulder

Wednesday did not begin well for Pup. She started, as she had the other mornings of the week, by beginning breakfast preparations and then reading in her borrowed Bible. This morning, however, she didn't reckon with the strips of bacon she left too close to the flames. Before she knew what was happening, she had a grease fire on her hands—not overly large, but a grease fire nevertheless. In trying to control things she lit a drying cloth on fire. The cabin was uninhabitable by the time she was through.

She knew she would have to clear things up and make some attempt to clean the black mess from the stove, but for now she picked up the Bible and went to the front porch. She didn't open the book but sat in the cool morning, the Bible on one side of her, her gun on the other.

She had read early that morning in the Psalms that God's creation alone declared His glory and the labor of His hands. Pup had long been fascinated with the workings of the forest and wildlife, but never had she thought about God's direct involvement and the way He ordained every leaf and twig. A tiny pinecone sat on the step near the toe of her boot. She picked it up and marveled anew at the miracle of it. The symmetry and smell of the cone intrigued her. She loved the smell of the pines, but never had she given God the credit and glory for their design and aroma.

I've been so blind, Lord, her heart now cried. *I don't want to be blind anymore. I want to see things as they are. I want You to be real to me. I know that my understanding has been childlike and I know You understand that things take time, but I want to know more. This limit inside of me feels stifling. Show me, Lord, please show more of Yourself and Your Word to me.*

For a moment her mind shifted to the Bible study that would take place the next night. She didn't know how she could work things to go down for that and be at church as well. Her head now tipped back and she looked at the woods around her.

Would You ask me to leave this cabin, Lord? Maybe take a place in town so I could be closer to others who believe in You?

She sighed, her mind running with questions. Was there any way to know if she should move? And if she did that, how would she come and go to work and still retain a low profile? Should she even continue her work for the treasury? McKay did it, but even he would be forced to admit that being sent on jobs broke up the continuity of one's life.

In the rush of emotions assailing her, Pup forced herself to stay calm. She told herself that God would not want her to pack her things immediately. It would be great to be at Bible study, but for right now she might have to make a choice. Her choice, at least for this week, was to be in church on Sundays.

She knew a peace then, but she was so deep in thought that someone had come nearly around in front of the house before she heard him. Her hand landed on the barrel of her gun just before Percy stepped into view. Pup had to stop her brows from rising at the sight of him. He stood uncomfortably for so long that Pup finally greeted him.

"Hello, Percy." Her voice was kind.

"Hello, Pup. I thought I smelled smoke."

"Yeah," she shrugged as she explained, "I burned some meat. It's all over now, but the cabin is a mess."

Percy just stared at her, and Pup thought she understood.

"The Bible is fine," she assured him softly. "It wasn't anywhere near the fire."

To her surprise he shrugged as if he didn't care. What Pup couldn't have known about was the big fight he'd had with his brother the day before. Percy knew it was his fault, but at the time the loaning of their mother's Bible was still eating at him. He told Mud he had expected to have it back by now and was headed down to demand it from their neighbor. Mud was so angry that Percy didn't recognize him. He thought Mud was going to strike him—something he'd never done, not even as a child. Instead his brother had yelled.

"Don't you see that she needs that Bible right now, Percy? What kind of inhuman fool are you? Her brother's been dead only a few months. Leave her and the Bible alone!"

"Her brother's dead?" Percy had questioned in surprise.

"I told you!" Mud had snapped at him, his patience gone.

"You did not. You said she had some shot-up man she was seeing to and might need your help. You never said anything about her brother dying."

The fight raged on for Mud, who continued to yell at his sibling, but Percy had lost all spunk. He felt awful for not having told Pup of his sympathy. Mud had taken off for town; indeed, he wasn't home yet.

"I'm not worried about the Bible," he now admitted to Pup. "I just thought I'd better check into the smoke."

"Thank you," Pup said quietly, but her mouth nearly dropped with surprise. She changed the subject. "Mud in town?" she asked.

"Yes. He went down last night. I expect he'll be back soon."

"Do you want me to tell him you're looking for him?"

"No," he shook his head. "If you see him, though, and there's any questions, you can tell him I said you should keep the Bible for as long as you need it."

"All right. Thank you, Percy. I appreciate that."

"I've got to get home."

"I'm glad you stopped by."

He raised a hand in a wave and turned from her, but he didn't move off. With his back to Pup and the cabin, he said, "I'm sorry about your brother, Pup. I didn't realize until yesterday."

"Thank you, Percy," she said again, and this time her visitor did walk away. He didn't speak or wave again but ambled quietly off through the trees. Pup pondered his visit for quite some time before she moved inside to clean up the kitchen. As she cleaned, the scene with Percy played over and over again in her mind.

I can keep the Bible for as long as I need. Imagine that, Lord. She was just finishing the work on the stove when she realized she desperately wanted to tell McKay about what had just happened. For a moment she missed him terribly. She shook off her mood, put some coffee on to boil, and found pencil and paper.

Denver

"It was abandoned," Carlyle stated, trying to assimilate the facts.

"Yes," McKay told him, "and not just last week. It's been vacant for years."

"And how many stocks have been sold?"

McKay stated a small amount, and he could tell that his superiors didn't understand why he was so excited.

"Have you contacted any of these stockholders?" Carlyle asked next, his tone telling McKay that this did not sound relevant.

"No, I didn't want to do that before I spoke with you."

"But you do think it ties in?" This came from Nick, his voice skeptical.

"As a matter of fact, sir, I don't. At least not directly."

Both men looked surprised, so McKay went on.

"I do think, however, that this is going to be Phipps' downfall."

"But this is Richard Stuart's mine," Carlyle reminded him.

"Yes, sir, but I've noticed that all of Phipps' mines are completely out of the area, yet he sells to investors in Denver. Enough of the mines are legitimate so he hasn't gained a bad reputation, but the ones that aren't let him collect money that goes straight into his pocket. Then a few months ago we turned up the heat, and that's when I think he involved Stuart and Brinkman in Longmont. Their banks are just far enough out of Denver to be out of reach, and they seem too small to be a threat."

"And how does this tie into the William Tell?"

"I think Stuart decided to try the scam on his own. I think he happily accepted the false stock certificates and money that went with them when Phipps offered them to him, but that was for the earlier mines. I think he recently decided to cut out the middle man."

"So how does this deliver Phipps to us?" Nick went straight to the point.

McKay looked resigned as he admitted, "Probably a bargain, sir. I've lived in Longmont my whole life, and I know that Richard Stuart enjoys his place in the town. I would hate to see him walk for these crimes, but he's the perfect man to sing like a bird about his business dealings with Duncan Phipps—especially if it means he can get off with a light sentence. I believe that Stuart's testimony alone could put Phipps away."

The older men exchanged a glance. McKay had no way of knowing exactly what they thought of his idea, but he'd certainly gotten their attention.

31

Boulder

On Saturday afternoon Pup arrived at the ranch certain she would hear the news of a new little Buchanan, but this was not the case. Rebecca smiled at her from the deep cushions of a living-room chair and invited her to sit down for a chat, but she was still obviously with child.

"How are you feeling?" Pup asked when she'd made herself comfortable.

"Like it's time. Earlier in the week I had energy, but along about Wednesday evening I went dry. For the past three days I've done nothing but sleep and wander from one chair to the next."

"Your color is good," Pup commented honestly, "but you do look a little drained."

Rebecca couldn't help but agree. "It's true, and the sad part is I just woke from a two-hour nap."

"Sounds like your time might be soon."

"The next hour would be fine with me."

"Did you have hard labor with the boys?"

"About normal I would say. I'll have to tell you after I've done this for the second time." It was no surprise that she didn't sound excited over the prospect.

Travis came into the room just then with a tall glass of water for his wife. She took it with a grateful if weary smile, and Travis turned to offer some to Pup.

"That sounds good, but I can get it myself."

"No, I'll get it for you," Travis told her and was gone in the next moment.

Before he arrived back, the boys joined them.

"Hi, Miss Jennings," they greeted her cheerfully and then went to hang on the arms of their mother's chair. Rebecca had a soft touch for each of them, and they smiled at her in a relieved sort of way.

Pup sat quietly while they told their mother what they had done that day and what they'd seen. A bird's nest was among their explorations, but a dead hawk was the most exciting topic.

"I think someone shot it," Garrett proclaimed.

Rebecca didn't argue with him, but her amused gaze met Pup's just long enough to cause Pup to bite her lower lip to keep from laughing.

"Do you have animals at home?" Wyatt suddenly asked their guest.

"Oh, yes," she assured them. "Mice and deer and everything in-between."

"Do you have raccoons?" Garrett asked, moving closer to her chair.

"Yes. They can be pests."

"Are they big?"

"Some of them are huge."

"Have you ever been bit?"

"No, never, but I've shot a few."

Both boys flanked her side now, their eyes huge as they listened. Pup glanced over to see that Rebecca's eyes had closed. With a finger to her lips she silenced the boys and then rose. They followed her quietly from the room and nearly ran into Travis, who was returning with Pup's water. The four of them settled into the kitchen, sitting comfortably around the table.

"I drew a picture of a raccoon," Garrett informed Pup.

"I wish I could see it."

She knew in a moment that she'd said just the right thing. Garrett jumped up and dashed over to the bookshelf, returning proudly with a drawing of the animal.

"This is very good," she told him honestly. "Do you get to draw in school, or did you do this here?"

"At school."

Pup whistled in appreciation. "It's been years since I've drawn anything."

"Do you want to draw with us?" Wyatt asked, enthusiasm lighting his little face.

"I'd like that."

They were busy until dinner. Even Travis, with occasional checks on his wife, took up paper and pencil. The boys begged Pup for a picture of her cabin, and she did her best. Travis turned out a horse that looked just like Feather, and the boys nearly woke their mother in their excitement.

When Rebecca did join them, she was delighted with the work they'd done, as well as with the gentle camaraderie she witnessed between Pup and her sons. The three of them volunteered to ready the table for the meal, and dinner was eaten with even more fun. As Pup was coming to expect, Lavena turned out a perfect meal, everything cooked to a turn.

The boys were ushered off to bed soon after the meal. The adults spent some time talking in the living room. Rebecca told Pup about growing up in Pennsylvania, and Travis entertained her with a story that happened right after he'd met Rebecca. It was a time years earlier when he'd been put in jail and kept there for weeks, all over a mistaken identity. Pup started to laugh in amazement, but cut off when she saw that Rebecca had fallen asleep at Travis' side.

"What did you do?" she asked softly.

"I waited it out." His face was rueful, his voice hushed as well. "What else could I do?"

"Amazing," Pup teased him. "You just don't look like the criminal type."

Travis grinned but then asked, "Can I ask you something serious, Pup?"

"Sure," she agreed, but prayed that it wouldn't be too personal.

"You said last week that you'd come to Christ. Can you tell me about it?"

Pup smiled with relief and did as he asked. His eyes were warm and slightly awed as she relayed the experience from her childhood, as well as the way McKay's words had brought it all back to her.

"That's wonderful," he told her. "I must admit that I've never heard the like."

Pup nodded, her face quiet, her manner humble. "I have a lot to learn, but then you know that. You must have wanted to laugh when I said I don't fall into sin and don't need to fight against it."

Travis' expression told her he understood.

"What I battle with the most is the future," she continued. "I worry about what's to come and how I'll handle it. Worry is a sin."

"That's a hard one for all of us," Travis admitted. "We're often tempted to try to do God's job. All He expects of us is to seek to know our own job and be very good at it."

Pup heard more of what Travis was saying, but her mind was still on the statement about God's job.

Rebecca chose that moment to sit up and apologize about falling asleep, and Pup suddenly realized she was tired as well. Knowing Travis would be taking Rebecca up to bed any moment, she bid the Buchanans goodnight and headed to her own room, her mind still on the rancher's words.

Pup had no idea what time it was, but the sky was still black. She lay in bed for a moment and tried to figure what had woken her. She heard the sound again and decided it was pans being moved in the kitchen. She let her head rock to one side of the pillow and saw a faint glow under the door. Someone was working in the kitchen, and with Rebecca nearly out on her feet by bedtime, it wasn't hard to figure why.

Pup slipped out of bed and into her robe, her bare feet moving soundlessly on the floor. She opened the door just a little and saw Travis in a pair of jeans and stocking feet. He stood over the stove, his face serious and intent. He looked up as Pup opened the door and joined him.

"Sorry to wake you."

"It's all right. Is Rebecca okay?"

"Her pains have begun."

Pup nodded. "Is there anything I can do?"

"I don't know," Travis answered honestly. "Have you ever assisted in a birth before?"

"No."

"I haven't either."

"Do you want me to go get Lavena?"

"She's already up there."

Pup now understood and said, "She told you to boil water."

Travis actually laughed. "No. I'm making coffee. I'm going to need it to get through the rest of this night."

Pup had to chuckle as well. "What time is it?"

"About 3:30."

They fell silent, both looking tired. Pup wasn't sure what to do next: go back to bed or pace downstairs waiting for word from the bedroom.

"I think you can help," Travis said suddenly.

"Sure, anything."

"Try to get some more rest. You're the only one who will have a chance, and whether or not the baby comes before morning, none of the rest of us are going to be up to handling the boys."

Pup felt her heart lift. It felt good to be needed.

"I'll plan on that and say goodnight again," she said softly. "I'll be praying for all of you, Travis."

"Thank you, Pup. We can use it. Don't hesitate to ask God to use this baby to touch Rebecca's life. I know I will be."

"I'll do that, too, Travis."

With that she turned to the door, slipped inside her room, and climbed back into bed. It hadn't taken long to see that Travis and Rebecca were not of the same mind. She knew he loved his wife and even felt that they had a good relationship, but clearly Rebecca did not agree with God's Word or some other aspect of Travis' faith. Nothing had been said, but Pup thought she knew the signs.

She began to pray. It took some time, but she did fall back to sleep. Pup woke as the sun was coming up. By the time the twins joined her, she was in the kitchen with breakfast ready.

"Good morning," Pup greeted Garrett and Wyatt as soon as they came through the door.

"Where's Lavena?" Wyatt asked.

This question stopped Pup because she assumed the boys had spoken to one of the adults before coming downstairs. She knew she had to be honest.

"She's helping your mother."

They both froze.

"Did the baby come?" Suddenly Wyatt's voice was hushed.

"Not yet. Your father was down about an hour ago and told me everything is going well, but it's going to take some more time."

"He's upstairs, too?"

"Yes, he, Lavena, and your mother are working together."

"Can we see her?" Garrett wanted to know, his eyes looking a bit moist.

"I don't think just yet, but I'll tell you what—you eat some of the eggs and ham I fixed, and then we'll have time to get outside for a walk."

"We can do that?"

"Sure. You boys are up early, so we won't have to leave for church for almost two hours."

"Is Papa taking us to church?"

"No, it's just the three of us this morning." They looked a little uncertain, so Pup thought fast. "I'm not sure I want to try and hitch the wagon on my own. I think maybe we should ride."

"The horses?" they asked at once.

"Sure. I'll ride Ginny and you boys can share Dixie."

"To church?" Garrett's eyes were huge. "We can ride to church?"

"I think so. I'll check with your father as soon as he comes down. Come and eat now."

It was just the right medicine. The boys sat at the table and started on their breakfast as if they'd been told the circus was coming to town. It went well for the first few minutes, but then things slowed down. There were no comments, but the meal was not as distracting as she'd hoped. Watching them, Pup didn't think they were remembering their mother's plight. She simply had to face facts: There was just no comparing her cooking to Lavena's.

"I see the head, honey," Travis coaxed his exhausted wife. "It's almost over now."

Rebecca clenched her teeth and strained with all her might, her face flushed like a flame, her hair wet from hours of effort. A huge gasp broke from her when she could push no more; she lay back spent, Travis' arms supporting her.

"I think one more—" Lavena encouraged, "two at the most."

Rebecca looked up at Travis, letting her eyes focus on his unshaven chin. When he looked down, she spoke.

"The boys. Did you tell me where they are?"

"Yes. They left with Pup less than ten minutes ago."

"Oh, that's right."

"She's going to take them to church for storytime. If they seem upset or too distracted, she won't stay for the service. If they do stay for the service, they'll come back as soon as it's over."

"It's so good to have her here, isn't it, Travis?" Rebecca whispered thankfully. "The boys like her so much."

"They rode horses," he told her, smiling a little. "You should have seen how excited they were."

And just that fast, the need to push rushed in on her yet again. Travis went to work as well, supporting her back and shoulders and whispering words of encouragement. Lavena was right. It was the second to the last push. The one that followed produced a wiggling, wet, baby girl.

"Do you have children?" Garrett asked.

"No, I don't."

"Are you married?"

"No, not married either. How about you boys," she looked over from Ginny's back. "Are you boys married?"

This produced the giggles and grins she'd been hoping for, and she smiled in return.

"Tell me about school," Pup said, still amazed at how easy it was to talk with these six-and-a-half-year-olds.

"We don't go in the summer."

"How do you get there?"

"Papa or Lucky."

"Who is Lucky?"

It was as if she'd released some pent-up steam. Words now tumbled one from the other, and Pup just listened.

"He works for Papa, and we like to play with Sarah, but Mary Ann is kind of little. She can't go to school. But we have desks—our own desks. We don't have to share. Sometimes we do if we forget the slate. Mr. Taggart doesn't get mad. He just gives us more work. Gary had to work one time."

They took a breath, and Pup tried to put it all together. It didn't take long before she said, "I met Mr. Taggart last Sunday."

"You did?"

"Yes. I had lunch at Pastor Henley's house, and he and his wife and baby were there."

"Katherine Alexa," Wyatt supplied. "She has red hair."

"I noticed that."

"I wonder if our baby will have red hair."

Pup looked over at them again, her heart feeling very tender. What an experience it was to have a baby come to your family. She vaguely remembered her brothers' births. That had been so long ago.

I trust You to guide and protect these little boys, Lord. It's too late for Govern and maybe too late for Jubal. Touch Garrett and Wyatt in such a way that they will never forget. Be with Rebecca now and that new little one. Keep her safe, Lord, but most of all touch her heart and help her to seek after You. Lavena, too, Lord. Thank You for all the care she gives. She's so capable, but without You, Lord, it will all be in vain.

"We're almost there," Garrett broke into Pup's prayer. She turned her attention to her two small charges. Their expressions were open and warm, causing her to think that they were quite willing to be there. As they tied their horses at the side of the church building, she prayed that she would be wise and aware of when the boys needed to head home.

"We have to stay for church," Wyatt told her just 30 minutes later.

"Okay," Pup said slowly, seeing the anxiety in his eyes.

"Yes," Garrett filled in. "We're doing a song today, one we learned in storytime. It's for the whole church, and Mrs. Henley really needs our voices; she said so."

"That's fine," she assured them. "I want to stay, but I didn't want you to worry about your mom."

"We're not." Wyatt's voice was matter-of-fact. "We prayed for her in storytime. We know the Lord Jesus is watching over her and the baby."

Pup's smile was very warm. *Oh, to have such faith at their age, Lord. It's wonderful to see.*

"Come on, Miss Jennings," Wyatt urged. "You've got to get close to the front so you won't miss us. It's two songs and my favorite—"

She allowed herself to be hauled to a second-row seat, and indeed, the children's singing, along with the verses they'd learned, was delightful. Both boys beamed at her when they came to sit on either side of her, and Pup felt her throat close. She told herself to keep an eye on them for signs of worry or upset, but her resolve didn't last very long. Pup was engrossed the moment Pastor Henley asked the congregation to open their Bibles. As it was, the boys were fine, but she never looked down at them until they stood for the closing hymn.

32

The boys' relaxed attitude after church lasted only to the edge of town. The three of them had not stayed around after the service but had gone right to their horses. Clearly the Buchanan boys were ready to go home and see their mother. Knowing how distracted they were, Pup kept the conversation to a minimum, and she sighed with heartfelt relief when they rode into the yard and found Travis waiting outside the barn.

"Papa!" The boys were out of Dixie's saddle in a flash.

"Is the baby here? Can we see Mama? Is it a boy or a girl?"

Pup heeled Ginny toward the huge barn, Dixie's reins in her hand. One of Travis' ranchhands awaited her and tended to the horses. Throwing Pup a grateful smile, Travis scooped the boys into his arms and moved toward the house. Questions still tumbled from their lips, but Travis only carried them inside. The kitchen was empty, and Travis spoke his first words.

"I want you to wash your hands."

"Right now?" Garrett looked thoroughly perplexed. "Are we going to eat?"

"No, just wash your hands, and we'll go upstairs and see your baby sister."

The import of his words took a moment to sink in, but then they rushed to the washstand. They would have soaked themselves at the basin had Travis not intervened. Without being told, they scrubbed their faces as well and turned to their father, eyes radiant.

"Come on," he said softly, fighting the fatigue that threatened to overtake him. "Let's go see her."

Somehow knowing it would be expected, the boys moved quietly. They nearly tiptoed up the stairs and to the doorway of their parents' bedroom. Rebecca was in the large bed, her eyes closed. Lying beside her, wrapped in a soft, white blanket, lay the baby. Removing their boots and approaching the bed in unison, the boys climbed carefully onto the mattress. They looked at their sister with awe and then at each other. They smiled in wonder, but anyone looking at them could see that they didn't know quite what to think of this little miracle.

She had been a lump under their mother's dress, and now she was on the bed beside her. Their expressions didn't go quite so far as to ask, Where did she come from? but the question wasn't far off. While their eyes were on the baby, Rebecca's opened.

"What do you think?" she asked softly.

"It's a girl, Mama," Garrett informed her, his smile huge.

"Yes." Her weary smile still showed her delight that the boys had gotten the sister they had wanted. "Are you pleased?"

He could only nod his head yes.

"What will we call her?" Wyatt wanted to know.

"We've been talking about that," Travis said, easing his way onto the bed next to his sons. "What do you think we should call her?"

The boys looked at each other again, and both were silent for a moment.

"I like Sarah," Wyatt admitted.

"Yeah." Garrett was clearly in agreement.

"We do, too," his father agreed gently, "but it could get a little confusing with Sarah Harwell right here on the ranch with us."

"We have two Tommys at school," Wyatt informed him.

Travis nodded. "So you boys know what I mean about two Sarahs."

They nodded in agreement, and then all four fell silent. Travis realized that young as they were, picking names was a rather overwhelming idea; at their age they didn't know many people.

"How about Kaitlin?" Travis suggested, voicing the one name both he and Rebecca liked the most.

The boys looked surprised and then pleased.

"Katie Buchanan," Rebecca added. "What do you think?"

"I like it," Garrett spoke up, but Wyatt was still thoughtful.

"What do you think, Wyatt?" his father asked.

He smiled sheepishly. "I forgot that she would be a Buchanan."

Travis smiled back at him and tenderly stroked his hair. Kaitlin chose that moment to move a little. The boys watched in amazement as she yawned hugely and worked to see, her eyes opening just a crack.

"She's yawning." Garrett's voice was breathless with delight.

Husband and wife exchanged a tender smile, but Travis could see how exhausted Rebecca was. He was well-spent himself. The boys had a few more questions, which Travis tried to field coherently before the boys asked to hold their sister.

Agreeing, Travis sat close to them, and as they nearly tipped her upside down, his hands hovered under the infant at all times. She slept through the whole ordeal. Rebecca, whose lids had been drooping low, was now fully awake and trying to keep the horror from her face as her sons "hugged" their infant sister for the first time. They worked with all their might to be gentle, but it was clearly an awkward task for their small arms. Wyatt, who was second to hold her, lasted an even shorter time than Garrett before asking his father to take her.

"Can she eat lunch with us?" Wyatt asked. He wanted to be near his sister; he just didn't want to hold her.

"I don't think she'd be too interested in the stew Lavena made, buddy," Travis replied kindly.

"Where is Lavena?" Garrett asked, having just missed her nearly constant presence of the last few months.

"She went home to get some rest, but dinner should be ready. Maybe you and Wyatt ought to head down to eat."

"What are you going to do?"

"I'll walk you down, but then your mother and I need to sleep. We were up most of the night waiting for the baby to come."

The boys made no argument to this, and after they'd kissed their mother and Kaitlin, they quietly left the room. Leaving the baby with Rebecca, Travis walked down with them. To his great pleasure, they found Pup in the kitchen putting Sunday dinner on the table.

"We had a baby sister," Garrett wasted no time in telling her.

Pup smiled at him and then stood aside while the boys went to the table.

"Will you be all right with them for a while?" Travis, coming forward, asked.

"Yes," she assured him. "Take all afternoon if you have need. I can sleep in the hills tonight if necessary."

"Why don't you just plan to stay over—not to be with the kids the whole time, but so you can have a fresh start in the morning?"

This hadn't occurred to her. "All right," she said at last.

Travis thanked her and gave each boy a tender kiss, hugging them to his chest. He left them with an admonishment to be "on their best" for Pup. They sat at the table, and both boys returned thanks for the food. However, they had little interest in their plates. As Pup was coming to expect, they began to chatter the moment they had a chance.

"We held her," Wyatt, who was the first to speak, said, "but I didn't know how."

"Her middle name is Gwen," Garrett filled in, forgetting that Pup didn't know the baby's first name. "It's for us. Mama thought it up. Gwen is spelled G-E-N."

"No, Gary, you forgot my letter," Wyatt corrected him. "It's G-W-E-N. The G is for Gary, and the W is for me."

"That's wonderful." Pup smiled with delight, knowing she would never have thought of such a thing.

"She's all pink and soft, and she didn't stink at all. Sarah said babies do, but ours doesn't. Sarah had a baby at her house awhile ago. Her name is Mary Ann. She had dark hair. What hair did our baby have, Wyatt?" Garrett suddenly couldn't remember.

"Dark, too, I think." Wyatt's brow furrowed with concentration.

"The baby Jesus had dark hair," Garrett said proudly. "Papa told us."

With the mention of Jesus, Pup's mind wandered. She had never considered what Christ might look like, but being of Jewish descent, dark coloring could only be expected.

"You put your knife in your coffee," one of the boys matter-of-factly informed her, and Pup gave a little start. It was true. She'd put her knife into her mug to stir the coffee, but she hadn't even added milk. She now mentally scolded herself. *You're in charge of those boys. You can't wander away like that.*

With that she pulled her mind back to the business at hand, the business of keeping two little boys occupied for the afternoon.

"A baby girl!" Margo Harwell exclaimed. "Did you hear that?" she turned to ask her husband, Lucky, who was Travis' foreman at the Double Star. "Wait until the girls hear."

"Come on in," Lucky was saying to Pup and the boys. As soon as they cleaned the kitchen, the boys had begged Pup to take them to see the Harwell girls, whose small home was right on the ranch next to Lavena's. Now that she was in their home and had met them, Pup realized she'd seen this couple at church both Sundays.

"I'll get Sarah and Mary," Lucky said.

"I told Lucky," Margo went on when he left, "when we didn't see Travis at church that I was sure Rebecca was having her baby. I could tell when I talked to her yesterday morning that it would be soon."

"Hi, Sarah; hi, Mary," Garrett was the first to say as two small, dark-haired girls, one struggling to remain on her feet, came from the other room. "We had a baby girl."

"You did?" Sarah looked pleased.

"Yeah. You wanna see her?"

With that the boys were off. They explained about the name Gwen and that her real name was Kaitlin. Their words tumbling over each other, the boys further announced that they could call her Katie and that her last name was Buchanan just like theirs. Pup felt her heart melt all over again as she listened to them.

At one point she thought the children might disappear and leave her to find her own conversation with the Harwells, but the boys were not yet willing to be far from home. Sarah asked them to stay and play, but they said they wanted to get back.

Pup knew her own sense of relief and thanked Lucky and Margo for their brief hospitality. The three of them trekked back toward the ranch house, and Pup found that they didn't even need to go inside, only to be closer to home. They checked out the barn and fed some sugar to the horses. Next they sat on the porch, fanning themselves with papers they had folded. Then the boys caught and played with as many crickets as they could find.

Pup had just offered to get them something cold to drink when Travis came out the front door. The boys were thrilled, and Pup could see that he felt he could act like their father again.

"How's it going?" he asked as he took a seat.

"Just fine. We've been to see the barn, we walked the trail for a time, and we even visited the Harwells."

"Sounds like quite an adventure."

"Indeed. How is Rebecca?"

"She just woke up and says she feels great. She's feeding the baby right now but would still like you to come up."

"I'll go then," she said with a smile. After Travis explained which bedroom to look for, she went inside, washed up a little, and took the stairs on quiet feet.

To her surprise, Rebecca was in a large chair, her feet on a footstool, a cradle right next to her. She was just putting the baby to her shoulder when Pup appeared at the door.

"Come in," she said softly, smiling at the other woman.

"How are you?" Pup's voice was hushed, too.

"Fine now, but for a little while there I didn't think I was going to make it."

Pup smiled compassionately and came close. Rebecca shifted her bundle so the other woman could see.

"Oh, my," Pup whispered softly. Kaitlin was precious. For a moment Pup couldn't take her eyes off the sleeping infant. She had thought that Katherine Taggart was small, but newly born Kaitlin Buchanan was especially petite. Pup took in the fair eyebrows that weren't even half the length of her own small finger. The back of Kaitlin's hand didn't look more than half an inch across.

"Pretty amazing, isn't it?" Rebecca commented.

"Yes, it is. She's so tiny and sweet."

"The boys were thrilled."

"Oh, yes. We've already been to see Harwells so they could hear the news, and of course the boys told them all about Gwen. That was pretty ingenious on your part."

Rebecca smiled with pleasure. She had been proud of that idea. Kaitlin was put into her cradle, and after Pup had taken a seat, the women fell into easy conversation. Pup questioned Rebecca about being out of bed, but Rebecca simply told her that she didn't try it unless someone was in the room with her. After all the hours of delivery, she said, staying in the bed was intolerable.

They had been talking for more than half an hour when Travis and the boys joined them. Again the twins were pleased to see their mother and baby sister, but it wasn't long before they grew restless. Kaitlin was still asleep, and Rebecca was ready to go back to bed, too. Travis assisted her and then took his sons on a walk.

When Pup gained the kitchen, she found Lavena already working on supper preparations. Seeing this, Pup went on a walk of her own. She prayed for this special family, thanking God for the hospitality they had shown. She included Lavena as well, and sincerely told the Lord that it was going to be hard to leave in the morning.

33

Pup left the ranch before eight o'clock Monday morning. She could already tell that the day was going to be hot and was eager to be well into the hills before the sun rose too high. Her talk with Travis on Saturday night, specifically the part about God's job, was still on her mind.

There's so much, Lord, I think I could become overwhelmed. Travis reminded me not to try to do Your job but just to be very good at my own. I'm encouraged by that, Lord, but I don't know if I understand what my job is. He couldn't have been talking about the treasury department because he doesn't know about that. Show me what he meant, Lord. Show me exactly what You want me to know.

And such was her prayer all the way through town. She was so centered on what she was thinking that once again she nearly passed up the general store. She was certain to be back next week—both Travis and Rebecca had made it clear she was welcome—but it never hurt to lay in a store for the week. She came jolting back to earth when she got her mail. Alone with her thoughts and just one small piece of paper, Pup read: "Need you in Denver ASAP NW."

It was over. Her time off as well as the opportunities to go to church had come to an end. How would she get word to Travis? How would she explain? For a moment she asked herself if getting close to these people had been worth it, but her mind had no more asked when she had her answer: It had been completely worth it. Indeed, at this point she would almost be willing to give up her job in order to stay here to learn and fellowship some more.

In the next instant Pastor Henley came to mind. It wasn't at all hard to visualize the kindness in his eyes. Knowing she had to see him, she walked from the post office wondering just exactly what she would say. However, not knowing did not stop her from stowing her things on Ginny's back and heading to the parsonage.

Just minutes later she was tying the horse's reins to a post on the street and approaching the door. From outside it sounded as though someone was singing. Pup hesitated. A moment later, however, the music stopped, and she knocked before she could change her mind. Her summons brought a warm-smiling Mrs. Henley to the door, and Pup knew in an instant she'd done the right thing.

"Hello, Mrs. Henley."

"Well, Callie, it's good to see you. Come in."

Pup entered the neat surroundings of the Henleys' living room and remembered the warm hospitality from a week before.

"Do you know if Rebecca had her baby?"

"Yes. A girl," Pup was able to report with a smile. "Kaitlin Gwen."

"The boys must be thrilled," the older woman said sincerely. "They both told me they wanted a baby sister."

"They're pretty excited."

"I'll bet they are. Can you sit for a while?"

"Well, actually I came to see Pastor Henley. Is he available?"

"He sure is. Sit right down, and I'll go get him."

Pup knew she was welcome, but she didn't sit. Questions assailed her: *What will I say? How will I explain? I can't tell him anything. Right now I don't even know what I'm doing here.*

"Callie," the pastor called kindly as he entered, Beryl right behind him. "This is a pleasant surprise. Can you stay awhile?"

Pup sat in one of the two rocking chairs and then glanced between them. She felt awkward and almost anxious. Desperate to make Pastor Henley understand that she had to leave but didn't want to, Pup felt the familiar frustration of not being able to even tell him why. Seeing the look, Mrs. Henley thought she understood.

"I'll go into the kitchen," Beryl offered.

"No," Pup assured her, "it's all right. I just needed to let you know something." She paused here, wondering how this could be so difficult. "I have to go away for a time," she began simply.

"All right." Pastor Henley's voice was gentle. Whenever he looked at her kindly, Pup felt emotions that were new to her. They somehow made her want McKay to be with her, to hold her hand or put his arm around her.

"I would like to keep coming to the church," she was able to add, "but I'm needed in Denver. I don't know how long I'll be gone." She swallowed and made herself continue. "I've really enjoyed the last two Sundays. I wanted you to know that."

"I'm so glad, Callie," the pastor put in. "We've enjoyed having you. Whenever you come back, you'll be welcome."

Pup nodded with relief that was visibly evident to the couple watching her.

"Travis and Rebecca let me know that I'd be welcome back at the ranch, but I'm sure I won't see them to tell them I must go."

"We'll tell them you've been called away, Callie. They'll understand."

Again she nodded with relief and this time spoke very hesitantly.

"I don't want to presume, Pastor Henley—I mean, you've already done so much, but could you pray for me?"

"I pray for you every day," he told her quietly, and Pup knew her mouth had dropped open. "And so to answer your question," he finished, "I will pray for you, *continue* to pray for you that is, every day."

They were silent for a time, letting their guest take this in. Her faith was so new and tender and her knowledge still limited, but her enthusiasm was such a reminder of all God had done for a dying, sinful world. They would genuinely miss Callie Jennings' presence in the weeks to come.

A few moments passed, and then Beryl asked gently, "Will you stay and have coffee with us, Callie?"

They weren't going to question her. They weren't going to put her on the spot. Pup sagged with relief. Instead, she said, "I'd like to, Mrs. Henley, but I've got to get home if I'm going to get back down for the train tomorrow."

"Another time then."

"Yes." Pup's smile was serene. "Another time."

"Do you have a Bible?" Pastor Henley suddenly asked.

"Just one that I read at home."

"So you won't be taking it with you?"

"No, it's borrowed, and I need to be careful with it."

"I have one I'd be happy to give you. Are you interested?"

"Yes." The word was said quietly, but there was a wealth of emotions behind the dark eyes that watched him. Pastor Henley went to the other room and returned with a black, leather-bound Bible. Not aware of the loving way in which Beryl looked at her, Pup sat in utter silence.

"Someone left this at the church some years ago now," Pastor Henley explained as he handed it to her. "Beryl and I both have one, and we'd like you to take this."

For a moment Pup couldn't speak. Looking down at it, she wanted to open it on the spot and read, but turning it in her hands, kept herself in check.

"Thank you," she managed at last, her mind still reeling.

"We won't hold you up, Callie," the pastor suggested, seeing that she needed to be alone. "But if you can spare a minute, let's pray now before you go."

As she bowed her head, Pup's heart was so full that all she could do was marvel at this man. *He's been praying for me,*

Lord. I didn't know. I didn't have any idea. And a Bible, Lord, I have my own Bible! The prayer was brief, over before she could begin listening, but it meant so much. She was shown to the door by both of them, and Pup knew that everything they had said was true. It was as if the Bible itself gave testimony to that fact: She would be welcome here again anytime—not just at the church but their home as well.

I don't really want to go back to work right now, Lord, but I can't let Nick down, she prayed as she left. *I'll take the job if it's tied into Duncan Phipps; I need to do that much for Nick. Knowing that Pastor and Mrs. Henley are here praying for me makes it easier to go. Help me to come home soon, Lord, and if at all possible, let me see McKay again.*

Denver

McKay barely tasted his food. Mrs. Meyer's evening meal was as palatable as ever, but McKay was preoccupied to the point of distraction. For as long as he had lived there, Mrs. Meyer handled the mail in the same way. She always placed that day's arrivals next to their napkins. Tonight there was a letter by his plate. The postmark was Boulder, and without having ever seen her handwriting, McKay somehow knew it was from Pup. He managed to answer a question that was directed at him and even remembered to thank Mrs. Meyer for the good meal, but he left the table as soon as propriety would allow and escaped to the privacy of his room.

His hand shook like that of a schoolboy with his first love note, tearing the envelope just a little. Finally the pages were in his hand. It was dated at the top and began simply,

> McKay:
> *You'll never believe what happened today. Percy came to see me. I'm still amazed over it. Mud wasn't with him;*

Percy said he'd gone to town. A few weeks back, I borrowed a Bible from them, one that had belonged to their mother. At first Percy didn't want me to take it, but he came today to tell me I could use it for as long as I'd like. He also told me he was sorry over the death of my brother. Even as I write this, I still feel amazed.

I've been reading the Bible every day. It's a remarkable book. I'll read a verse and think it's the most wonderful and then read another and change my mind. I've been reading in Romans. There's so much I didn't realize. I thought Jonah was a legend, and then I found him right in the Bible. I have some questions I want to ask you about that book. Actually, I have some questions on just about all the books. It's helped to talk with Pastor Henley. Have you ever met him? I've gone to the church twice now, and one time I was able to speak with him at length.

"I'm back now," the letter went on, "I boiled the coffee over on the stove and had to clean it up. I managed to salvage one cup for myself."

For a moment McKay had to stop. He'd sat on his bed when he had come in and now lay back, a smile on his face, his shoulders moving with silent laughter. It was so like her to burn something in the middle of writing a letter and then to tell about it as a matter of course. McKay's eyes closed.

He couldn't believe how much he missed her. She was a ray of sunshine in his day. He had known women who were more bubbly, but they all paled in comparison to Pup. She was like the moon, he decided. Not so bright as the blazing sunlight but constant in his mind, especially when things seemed dark. How he wanted to see her. He lifted the letter again.

Are you working hard? Do I know about your latest case? I wish I had time to go back to see your parents. I'm not sure they really understood how much I appreciated their welcome of me. I realize that's my fault for leaving so abruptly.

When I arrived home I saw Travis Buchanan. He's the reason I'm going to the church. He offered to let me stay at the Double Star on Saturday nights and even join his family for supper. His wife, Rebecca, is expecting soon. I've met his boys, too. They're sweet. Not identical twins, but similar in many ways. One is dark and the other is light, but you could pick their faces out of a crowd. Travis is doing a good job of teaching them about the Bible. They enjoy church and the special storytime for children that Mrs. Henley teaches before the service. The adults fellowship at that time, and I must admit to you that I wished I could have gone with the children. A Bible story with pictures sounded like a good time.

I've yet to hear from Nick, and I must admit that this suits me fine. I think I need some time to sort things out. My head feels clearer in the mountains. I do know one thing—I think about you and wonder if you are well.

Pup continued to write about the Bible, the weather, and even her garden. She didn't get personal again, but McKay was coming to know her well enough to understand what wasn't put down in writing. He finished the letter—she signed off with just her name—and immediately went to his desk to start one to her.

He began to write, knowing some very good things had come from their being separated, things he had not been able to see while standing at the Longmont train station. For days now, he'd been wrapped up in the Phipps' case and the mine scandal, but there had been plenty of time to think about his relationship with Pup. His mind had actually moved to marriage before he'd started to think clearly. Not that he thought marriage to Pup was wrong, but it was definitely too soon.

He thought about the way she'd remembered that moment when, as a child, she'd come to Christ on the streets of Boulder. He believed with all of his heart that her conversion was genuine, but the fact that she was a believer didn't mean they needed to rush into marriage. If, in fact, marriage was also on her mind, they both needed to be reminded that this was not something that could be entered into quickly. His emotions told him to run and find her and never let her go, but his heart, led by the Holy Spirit of God, was counseling him to go slowly.

McKay traveled so much that at times regular church attendance was difficult. Yesterday had been different. He'd been in town and able to attend the Denver church that he had been a part of for several years.

The pastor had been there for only a year, but McKay liked him immensely. He was a man who often made jokes from the pulpit, loving it when the congregation howled with laughter. There was no mistaking his sincerity, though, when as a group they turned to study the Scriptures. Newly married, Pastor Adair MacKinnon was three years younger than McKay. For a young man he had deep wisdom and a heart to know God more. He also had a heart for the unsaved in the city. The church had grown tremendously in the last several months.

After the service, several people were crowded close to question the pastor, but McKay waited his turn and had a chance to talk with him as well. The treasury agent was amazed to learn that he'd been on Pastor MacKinnon's mind.

"I've been praying for you, McKay," he told him in his soft Scottish burr.

"You have?" McKay's raised brow was genuine.

"Indeed. I know your job takes you hither and yon, and I've often wondered if that doesn't lead to temptation for a young man."

McKay nodded. One time he had confided in Adair that his job sometimes took him into saloons and dance halls.

"Every man is tempted, McKay," the large Scot went on, "but it's easier at times to come home to a wife, hopefully one you can confide in and know she's praying for you while you're out."

"I've met someone." McKay said these words before he actually realized how much he wanted to talk to this man. "She's very special, but our circumstances are not normal."

Adair smiled. "That can mean a merry chase or a grand headache. Which is it with you?"

"Neither one right now, but her conversion was different. I believe it's genuine, but I've just realized that our relationship should go slowly—or rather *I* should—since I'm not sure if she's moved as fast as I have."

"I think proceeding with caution is wise. What do you think she'll say?"

"That's part of the problem. She doesn't live here, so I don't get to see much of her."

Adair studied him with shrewd eyes. "You're in love with the lass."

McKay nodded. "Yes, I am."

"But you're not sure if she truly believes."

"I do feel sure, but without time with her—time when we can talk and I can watch what she does with her new faith—I don't think I can really know what God has for us."

"Have you asked God to give you time together?"

"No," McKay admitted, "I'm busy at work right now, and she has responsibilities of her own. That never occurred to me."

"Ask, McKay. God may say no, but you'll not know unless you bend your knee."

The pastor's words came back to McKay as he sat alone in his room, and before he wrote one more word to Callie, he asked God for wisdom and patience. However, he stopped short.

"I really didn't hear anything Adair said," McKay admitted quietly to the Lord. *"I've already been asking for wisdom and patience, and I think You've given me that. Now I need to do as he advised and ask You to bring Pup and me together. I know You brought her into my world for a reason. I think that reason is a life together, but I can't know for sure unless I can be with her. Please put us together again, Lord, and when You do, remind me of how much I need to wait on You. Remind me that I can't rush, and that Your timing has to be my goal.*

"Thank you for Pup, Lord. Thank You for the special, beautiful person she is. Thank You for saving her. Help her to keep reading and learning about You. A marriage built in You would be the sweetest of all, Father. Show us the way. Make the path clear so that I'll know where to walk. And wherever Pup is this night, bless her, keep her, and remind her of Your love.

McKay could not have known that Pup was just coming from a bath in Lake Anne. Night sounds and the smell of pine were all around her. She felt clean and refreshed and ready for one more sleep in her own bed, her heart wondering when she would be back to bathe in the lake again.

34

The train ride to Denver was the fastest Pup remembered. Dressed in a plain, dark dress, wig in place, she drew no attention whatsoever. With her nose buried in her new Bible the whole way, she wouldn't have noticed if she had. At times she looked up, but only to stare sightlessly out the window, her mind thinking and working to understand and remember all she'd read.

The Denver train station was the same, but Pup realized the difference in herself. How many others around her believed as she did? This question hung in her mind until she hired a hack to take her to Nick and Camille's. It was at that moment she realized how little praying she'd done for her friends. Nick and Camille probably didn't believe as she did. She didn't know everything the Scriptures had to say about this subject, but it seemed to her that the verses she had read made it clear that the only way to God was through His Son, Christ Jesus. Pup felt concern for the Wallaces. She knew better than to barge in and start lecturing, but she loved them dearly and now prayed that something she would do or say would make a difference in their hearts, much the way Travis had wanted her to pray for Rebecca.

Before she knew it, she was paying the driver, her keen mind having taken a moment to figure out the fare before he charged her. Since he'd been honest with her, she tipped him generously and went up the front walk to the Wallaces' double front door. Miranda answered the door and then hugged her when it was closed against the street.

"The Missus said you were coming."

"Here I am," Pup said with a smile.

"How have you been?"

"I'm doing well. Yourself?"

"Can't complain."

"You never do, Miranda," Pup told her with kind eyes. The two exchanged a smile before Pup put her bag down and ran Camille to earth in the pantry.

"Callie! I didn't even hear you." The younger woman felt herself being hugged again. "Nick has plans," she told her dramatically as she led the way through the kitchen, her hand on Pup's arm. "You should hear the man."

"The blonde wig and maid's uniform?"

"Yes, how did you know?"

"We talked about it before I left last time."

"Oh, that's right. Well, come on. He wants to see you outfitted when he comes home." Camille stopped suddenly. "How long is your hair these days?" She stared at the wig as though she could see beneath it.

"It wouldn't matter," Pup dashed her hopes. "I'm too recognizable without the blonde wig."

"I suppose," Camille gave in. "Well, come on. Let's get this over with." She sounded completely chagrined at the idea, but the two were having fits of giggles just 20 minutes later.

"It completely changes you," Camille said with a gasp. "I wouldn't have believed it if I hadn't seen it with my own eyes."

Pup did a silly pirouette, her eyes crossed, her movements awkward. Camille was off again into gales of laughter.

"How does the wig fit?" she finally managed.

"It's all right—a little loose maybe. My hair must have been longer when I used it before, but I think it will stay in place."

"Are you going to pad yourself?" Camille wanted to know. Her eyes took in the front of the dress. It needed something.

"I don't think I'd better. The last thing I want to do is draw attention. A straight figure is handy when you don't want someone pawing at you."

"Has that happened?" Camille was all concern, the bodice of the dress forgotten.

"Only a few times. I was never in a position of complete vulnerability, but I would just as soon not have it happen again."

The older woman nodded. *How long can you keep this up, Callie? How long can you go on in this type of work?* Camille couldn't keep the thought from her mind. She knew that Nick wanted Pup to go on spying for him forever, but suddenly the wise Mrs. Wallace knew that would never be the case.

And why should you go on? she asked Callie mentally as if she could hear. *If you have a chance to settle into a life of fulfillment and happiness, why shouldn't you take it? The rest of us are doing what we want. Oh, Nick,* her heart cried, *why can't you understand that? Why can't you let this girl go?*

"Camille, are you all right?" Pup's voice broke into her turbulent, one-sided conversation.

"I think so." Her voice was soft when she admitted, "I was just worrying about you."

Pup sat down next to her on the bed. "What about?"

Camille looked into her eyes. "How long can you do this? I know you enjoy it, and I can't imagine Nick being as successful without you, but it has to be disruptive, Callie."

"Yes, it is," the younger woman quietly acknowledged. "In fact, I determined when I got Nick's cable that I would only take this job if it involved Duncan Phipps. I want to see this case through for Nick; but you're right, the summons didn't come at a very good time."

"You and McKay?" Camille's thoughts were instantly romantic.

"No. I wish he had been in Boulder, but that's not it. I've gotten involved with the church there, and it's really helping me."

"Callie." The older woman's face was concerned all over again. "Who are these people? You can't be too careful. I've heard of churches that took people's money and time—all in the name of God—and they got nothing in return. It scares me a little."

"It's not like that," Pup reassured her. "Money hasn't even been mentioned. They love me and invite me into their homes like they've known me for years."

Camille nodded with relief. It wasn't hard to see the truth in the younger woman's eyes.

"I'm happy for you, Callie—I can't tell you how much."

"Thank you, Camille. The pastor gave me a Bible. I read it all the way over on the train. I can't believe how much I didn't know."

Camille studied her eyes again. Pup was a master at covering all emotions, but right now her eyes were alight with joy. She saw something else there as well. *Was it yearning?*

"I wish I understood why it mattered, Callie. I mean, what was wrong with your life before?"

Pup sighed. This was a hard one. "I don't know quite how to say it, Camille, except that I knew something was missing. I know I'm good at my job and that it's a very exciting one, but I couldn't shake the feeling that there must be something more. McKay Harrington understood, and he has that something more. He works hard at his job with the treasury, just like I do, but because of his faith in Christ, his job means more. I want the same meaning for my life."

Pup was afraid she had sounded ridiculous. "Does that answer your question?" she asked.

"Yes, it does," Camille told her truthfully. "I'm not sure it's for everyone, but I think I understand what you mean."

"I've never told you this, Camille," Pup now said sincerely, "but the way you've always been here for me, the way you've never really wanted anything for me except to be myself, well, it's meant a lot to me."

Camille embraced her and thought not for the first time that she'd never met anyone like her. They held each other tenderly for a long moment, breaking apart only when Nick's voice called from downstairs.

"Are you ready to show him the latest disguise?"

A sparkle lit Pup's eyes. "When he asks if I'm ready, just stall. I'll sneak around to the kitchen and come in with the coffee tray. He's seen this wig before, but it's been years. Don't say anything, and we'll see how long it takes him to notice."

Camille couldn't help but give her one more hug. She then chuckled all the way to the door.

"We don't need any other house help," Gerard told the tall, blonde woman standing in a maid's uniform before him, but she just didn't seem to understand. He didn't know if she was Swedish, Dutch, or something else, but she wasn't catching a word he said.

"I sveeep," she told him with pride. "I do cook, too."

Gerard tried again, his voice rising as if this would help her understand. "We have all the help we need."

"I bake cake for you," she said with great pleasure.

Gerard began to shut the door, but with a hand pushing an old bruise on her hip and her mother's face in mind, Pup actually managed to bring tears to her eyes, trembling lips and all. Gerard stopped. He should have known better, but he couldn't take the eyes. They were the most hopeful he'd ever seen—dark like shoe buttons and yearning to please. He sighed and opened the door again.

Pup came in, a genuine smile lighting her face. Once inside she immediately turned to the man as though ready to hang on his every word.

"What's your name?" he asked a little tiredly.

Pup looked confused.

"Name," his voice came up again. "Do you have a name?" Pup nodded like an obedient child.

"Is Inga."

"Inga?"

"Yah, das me, Inga."

"Okay, Inga, come this way."

Checking to make sure she followed, Gerard led her through the back hallway to the kitchen at the rear of the house. Pup was careful to be looking at him every time he glanced her way, wanting him to think she was eager for his every command. There would be time to look around later.

A few minutes later she was introduced to a cook who looked at her with long-suffering. Again she smiled hugely, and after much nodding she gave the appearance of understanding that she was to peel potatoes. She set right to work—ready, willing, and able, at least to start. By the tenth pound of spuds her head was thumping and she was asking herself how she could have possibly agreed to do this job. Nick would surely laugh if he could see her, and she most assuredly would have thrown the whole ten pounds at him.

McKay was not a snoop, but for some reason the paper on Nick's desk caught his eye. It was a Denver address and the initials at the bottom read PJ. Since the start of the problems with Paine Whitter, who was still completely ignorant of the fact that he was under constant surveillance, Nick had been more careful than ever, but Paine was out of town right now. Finished for the day, McKay had some papers to leave on Nick's desk. He touched nothing, but his eyes lingered on the small sheet of paper and Nick's bold writing. He then caught himself. It didn't matter what he saw. He moved swiftly from the empty office, closing the door securely and telling himself to ignore what he'd just seen.

He worked at doing just that as he left the office building and walked home. However, the initials and Camden Street number lingered in his mind all the way through dinner. He knew he was being fanciful but couldn't shake the feeling that those initials were Pup's. The meal ended, but McKay didn't hurry away as he would have liked.

Again he tried to forget what he'd seen, but it was no use. He told himself that he just needed to stretch his legs, but it wasn't long before he was on Camden Street, just two doors down from number 32. He stood still for a moment and then got a hold of himself. *Don't be a fool, McKay, you could be blowing someone's cover by standing here.* With this scolding he made up his mind to head back to Mrs. Meyer's.

With just this purpose in mind, he turned and nearly ran straight into Pup. It took a moment for him to see who it was, but by then she had lifted her chin with a haughty air and started to move around him. He spun, desperate for more of her, his voice coming softly to her ears.

"Can I see you?"

She turned back to him so suddenly that he started, and then amazingly, stood stock still while she slapped him full across the face.

"The park in a half hour," was uttered so quietly that he barely heard her. However, he was given no time to reply. She turned as if he'd suggested the most offensive insult and marched her way up the street. She disappeared into number 32, the door closing with a resounding thump, and McKay was left alone in the street. He didn't look around to see if anyone had witnessed the act but stroked his cheek as though irritated. He then moved off in the direction of the park, marching almost as fast as Pup had. He was on top of the grass and amid the flowers in full bloom before he slowed his pace. He walked to the edge of the small lake, his eyes moving over the water, his mind still on Camden Street and a woman who never failed to take him by surprise.

It was fully dark by the time Pup gained the park. She knew it wasn't the safest thing to do, but nothing was going to stop her from seeing McKay. The lamps lining the cobbled street that circled the park were already lit, but Pup stayed clear of them. When she finally stopped beneath a tree, McKay was in front of her, his face to the water. Pup was debating what to do next when he turned.

There must have been just enough light coming from behind her to give him an idea who she was because he approached immediately. Stopping just two feet in front of her, he stared.

"That's better," he said cryptically.

"What is?"

"Your hair. I don't like you as a blonde."

Pup wanted to smile, but she was too concerned. "How's your cheek?"

She heard him laugh. "You certainly know how to surprise a man."

"I'm sorry." She surprised him again by reaching up and laying her hand along the cheek she'd struck. McKay covered it with his own, and Pup's heart melted at the gesture. A moment later he captured her hand within his own and pulled her along to walk beside him. He started around the perimeter of the lake, only their hands touching.

"I got your letter." McKay was the first to speak. "It sounds as though you're doing well."

"I think I am doing well, but it feels like I wrote that a long time ago."

"Evidently a lot has been going on."

"It has. I stayed with Travis and Rebecca again last weekend so I could go to church."

"When did you get here?"

"Just yesterday."

He nodded in the dark, but Pup couldn't see him. "How are the Buchanans?"

"They're doing well. Rebecca had her baby—a girl. The boys were ecstatic. I didn't leave there until yesterday morning, and that's when I got word from Nick."

"And your job this time actually calls for a blonde wig and a maid's uniform?"

"Yes." He could hear the laughter in her voice.

"Let me see," he tried to guess. "One of the hotels in town?"

"No." She still sounded as if she was laughing.

"Then it must be someone's mansion."

"Well, now," she said with admiration, "you're good."

"I'm surprised," McKay admitted.

"Why?"

"Because I thought you'd still be on the Phipps case."

"I am."

McKay came to a halt so swiftly that Pup nearly stumbled.

"Don't tell me he has you inside Phipps' mansion."

"Someone has to penetrate there, McKay." Her voice was calm; as always she had a job to do.

McKay felt as if he'd been hit. It was so dangerous. She'd already come face-to-face with the man as Bryan Daniels, and now this. McKay's next move came spontaneously. They were in a public park after dark, but he couldn't help himself—and in truth he didn't want to try. He let go of Pup's hand and gently drew her into his embrace, his arms going full around her. Only a few inches taller than she was, he let his jaw come to rest against her cheek. Pup let herself be held, her heart burgeoning with pent-up emotions.

"What has you so worried, McKay?" she asked quietly when she could speak.

"Duncan Phipps. He's not a man to be trifled with, and he's already seen you as Bryan Daniels."

"You're forgetting what I told you."

"I know." He sounded tired. "People don't really look at you. I'm still not thrilled with the idea."

They were silent for a time, and then Pup pulled from his embrace.

"If you didn't know I was working on this case, McKay, how did you find out where I lived?"

"I'm rather ashamed to admit it, but there was a piece of paper on Nick's desk that listed an address and your initials. I've never done that before—look on his desk, that is—but when I spotted the note, I couldn't get it off my mind. I had just decided that I had no right trying to learn who was at the address when I turned and nearly ran into you. Are you angry?"

"No." Her hushed voice told him she understood and was pleased. "I saw you the moment I started down the street. I didn't have to be seen, McKay, but you do know how careful I have to be. I wouldn't give up this time with you for anything, but I think I'd better head back now and not meet you again. I would feel just sick if I blew this for Nick."

"I understand. Just tell me you'll be careful."

"I will."

"I still have things I want to talk to you about."

"We'll do that, McKay, as soon as this is all over."

He took her hand and walked her back to the tree. Neither one wanted to say goodbye, so after a moment of just looking through the darkness at each other, Pup abruptly turned and walked away. McKay followed at a distance, staying well back, but making sure she was safely inside.

It was a relief not to find anyone up at Mrs. Meyer's. McKay took the stairs on quiet feet and was relieved to gain his room. He had so much on his mind, namely that just 24 hours ago he'd asked God to bring Pup back into his world. That thought alone led him to believe he would never sleep. Added to that was the concern he felt over Pup's current job. But he hadn't reckoned with how it would feel to see her again: It had done his heart a world of good. He slept almost as soon as he blew out the lantern.

35

She had been told to dust the front hall, but she wanted more. It was already Thursday morning. She'd been on the job for 24 hours and hadn't gotten anywhere. The kitchen was all she'd seen. Gerard had been to check on her a few times, but after the first few hours he'd left her at the mercy of the cook. It hadn't been too bad on Wednesday morning, but by Wednesday afternoon the woman had tried to work her into exhaustion.

Pup didn't live at the Phipps mansion; the apartment Nick rented for her on Camden Street was a few blocks away. Walking to it made her all the more tired when she arrived home Wednesday night.

It had been her plan all day to check in with Nick that night, but by the time the day ended, she was too tired to do anything more than walk back to the apartment, remove her wig and dress, and fall into bed. She knew that if she didn't go see Nick, he would come to her. With that thought, she drifted immediately off to sleep.

Back at work Thursday morning, a noise stopped her reverie and caused her to remember who she was: Inga the maid. She ran her cloth over the top and down the sides of a gilt-framed mirror, careful to concentrate lest she tip the whole thing off the wall. From there she moved to an entry table and a plant stand. She was just finishing when one of the numerous wooden doors that opened into the hallway squeaked. The door opened completely and a young man emerged. He walked past Pup without even looking in her direction and left the door wide open.

Pup took a swift glance around. She sidestepped carefully, dusting as she went, until she was almost opposite the portal. It was an office, and from what she could see, no one was inside. This was the first time Pup had even had a glimpse at the interior of any of these downstairs rooms. It didn't take her more than an instant to see that this was the room she wanted, and she had to stop herself from doing a triumphant cheer. Her cloth going rapidly and her face intent, she dusted her way across the threshold. The room *was* empty. It was tempting to turn and close the door, but she refrained.

Cloth moving again, her hand dusted while her eyes moved. She didn't want to be caught looking directly at the desk, so she polished a chair nearby, her arm moving so vigorously that it seemed she would put a hole in the leather. She didn't stay at it long, however, since the top of the desk offered nothing.

Her eyes roamed again and found a series of filing cabinets in one corner. Again she was off, buffing and polishing as she went. She had just gotten close, her back to the door, when she heard voices and footsteps approaching. As two men entered the room, she recognized Duncan Phipps' voice immediately. Remembering Bryan Daniels and her work at the First National, she had to force herself to act naturally.

"I want you to be in touch with Stuart."

"What about Brinkman?" the other man asked.

"No. It's Stuart who decided to do a little business on his own, and now the heat's been turned up. Get word to Stuart. Tell him we need to have a little meeting next week," Duncan's voice was frosty. "Thanks to him everything has to be stopped until we can be certain they're not suspicious of those—" he stopped abruptly. "Who is that?" he barked.

"Just a maid," the other man said dismissively, "I'll get rid of her."

"You do that, Nelson." His voice was cold.

Pup heard Duncan's man approach, but by now she was on her hands and knees, her rag moving along the baseboards.

"You can do this room later," Nelson spoke to her back.

Pup didn't turn or acknowledge him in any way.

"Excuse me," he tried again, his voice gaining an edge.

Pup kept on with her work a moment longer, until she pretended to glance to the side and notice the man.

"What are you *doing?*" He was downright testy now.

Pup scrambled to her feet. "Inga," she told him proudly. "Yah, Inga cleans."

"What?" He was so surprised by her voice that he faltered.

"You need coffee. I bring for you," she offered, a huge smile lighting her face, nodding all the while.

"No!" He snapped out of his momentary trance. "We don't need things dusted right now. You can leave."

Pup's face showed nothing but confusion as she tried to continue her stall, but Nelson had had enough. With a hand on her upper arm, he saw her firmly to the door.

"Get out," his voice was now low and furious. He was dressed in a well-cut suit, but Pup felt he could be a dangerous man if provoked. He put her in the hallway none-too-gently and closed the portal with a slam.

Once outside, she thought of the way Duncan Phipps' head had been bent over some papers. He'd never even looked up. She was thankful for that, but under her feeling of gratitude was a niggling of discomfort. The man named Nelson had been positively flabbergasted when she spoke to him. She had slipped past Gerard on Wednesday when he'd hired her for the job, but in truth Pup thought her accent a bit weak. However, Nelson was the most recent of at least 15 people who worked in this mansion, and he found her believable as Inga the maid.

Wasn't that what she wanted? After all she was an undercover agent. Pup's heart was thoughtful as she finished in the hallway. What would Christ have to say about her duplicity? Would He excuse the subterfuge because it was all done in the line of duty? For the first time Pup honestly had to tell herself no.

She had told McKay she couldn't see him again, but right now she was desperate to talk to him. Should she continue in this job? That was the question she would ask him. For the moment she kept dusting and worked hard the whole day, but only because she didn't know what else to do.

It was almost dark by the time Pup arrived home that night, and fuzzy as her mind felt, she was not at all surprised to find Nick sitting in her apartment.

"Were you seen?" she asked the man.

He smiled. "I may not be as good as you are, Pup, but I do know what I'm doing."

Pup's smile was self-disparaging. "Don't mind me. I'm tired."

"Hard work?"

"Awful," she admitted. "I've never cleaned like that in my life." She studied her hands. "My fingers are ruined."

"What are the stains from?"

"Peeling potatoes."

As she'd known he would, Nick chuckled.

"You'd better stop that or I'm not going to tell you anything," she threatened good-naturedly. She had dropped into the room's only chair and pulled off her wig.

Seeing her fatigue, Nick was suddenly serious. "What have you found?"

"A room. The only problem is getting into it. I was inside, but Duncan and another man named Nelson came in and interrupted."

"Nelson Case," Nick said almost absently. "Were you recognized?"

"No, Duncan didn't even look at me."

"Good. What did the room have?"

Tired as she was, Pup smiled. "Files. Drawers and drawers of files, and there's more. I heard Phipps tell Nelson that Stuart decided to do some business on his own. He wants Nelson to meet with him next week."

"We've got to move fast. If Duncan gets to Stuart before we do, it could blow our case apart. Can you get into that room?"

"I'm going to try."

"Is it dangerous?"

"The job? Not at this point. Right now I'm just a maid. I don't think anyone gives me a second glance."

"Good. You know I want you to penetrate that room, but not if it puts you at risk."

"All right."

"I'll let you get some rest now. I want to talk to you again tomorrow night," he said.

Pup nodded and stood when he did.

"When are you off?"

"I don't know. I'm afraid to ask. Hopefully this weekend sometime."

"Well, come to the house if you can. Camie's been asking about you."

"Tell her I'm exhausted. On second thought, tell Miranda and then thank her. I had no idea what it took to clean these huge homes."

Nick smiled and moved to the door. Pup locked it behind him. She knew she should eat something but was too tired to care. She went to bed hungry but woke early. Once up, she made a large breakfast for herself and spent some time reading her Bible. The question about her job still lingered in her mind, but she knew Nick would never understand if she walked out on the case right now. She simply couldn't do it to him when they were this close to cracking it.

It was time to go. She climbed into her maid's uniform and adjusted her wig, making sure all was in place. Usually, just donning the costume was enough to get her going, but this time she didn't drop into the role of Inga until she was at the kitchen door of the mansion. She had too many other things on her mind.

"Hello," McKay spoke kindly and removed his hat. "I'm McKay Harrington with the U.S. Treasury Department. Are you Mr. Robinson?"

"Yes. Come in," the older gentleman bid him.

"Thank you." McKay turned to him the moment he was inside. "I'm sorry to bother you on a Saturday morning. Did you receive my letter, Mr. Robinson?"

"Yes. Earlier this week. I can't think what the treasury could want with me, but I got your letter."

"The business dealings of a certain banker have come under suspicion, Mr. Robinson. The investigation isn't directed toward customers like yourself but toward the banker. I'm afraid that some mining stocks have been sold illegally. Have you purchased some mine stocks recently, Mr. Robinson?"

"Yes, I have." His voice had dropped a notch.

McKay's look of compassion was very real. "I'm afraid you might be one of the customers who have been duped. I'd like to ask you some questions."

McKay had been doing this for years and knew exactly how to gain information. He had the bedside manner of a doctor, and by truthfully telling the man that he might have been cheated and that someone else was under investigation, he not only gained the man's interest but put him at ease concerning his own involvement. As he expected, Mr. Robinson asked him to sit down and then to wait while he asked his wife to join them.

Pup was not able to gain entry to the room again until Saturday morning. She had met briefly with Nick the night before but had nothing new to report. This morning the whole mansion was on the quiet side. She'd been told to dust the library, which happened to be right next to the room where she sought entrance. It was easy enough to flip the door lock on the room with the files, hoping that if she were caught, Gerard would fall for her act of not understanding which room she was to dust.

As it was, she saw no one. But that didn't make the search as successful as she'd hoped. The files held nothing. She had to rifle through them swiftly but knew enough to realize there was nothing to interest Nick. She closed the drawers softly, when in fact she was tempted to slam them.

In order to maintain her cover, Pup had to put some time into actually dusting the library, and she had already taken more time with the files than planned. She was moving from the room, reminding herself to lock the door behind her, when she spotted a panel. Experience told her it was a hidden doorway. She had no choice but to let it go. Frustrated and none too happy to have run out of time, she went back to the library and dusted swiftly throughout the room. She was just finishing when Gerard checked on her.

"What day were you given off this week, Inga?" he asked with genuine concern.

She momentarily wondered whether she looked as flushed and harried as she felt, but for Gerard she tried to look as vague as usual. He tried again.

"What day did you have free time?"

"Free? You wish Inga to work for no payment?"

"No, no." As usual his voice went up. "You came to work Tuesday." He had his hand up, counting on his fingers.

"Yah."

"And then you worked Wednesday and Thursday. Is that right?"

"Yah, das right."

"How about yesterday? Did you work Friday?"

"Yah. Inga work Friday."

"Take tomorrow off."

She frowned at him.

"Don't come to work tomorrow. Come Monday."

She managed to maintain her act long enough to show comprehension and then feigned delight over a day off. She kept the smile on her face until he turned away. He told her to go to the kitchen and help the cook. Pup had no choice but to obey.

It wasn't potatoes this time, for which she was thankful, but neither was it work in the hallway where she needed to be. She should have been thrilled with a day off, but all she could see was the camouflaged panel in the wall of the room.

"I have everything I need," McKay told Carlyle. "The Robinsons have dealt with Duncan, as well as Richard Stuart whom Duncan recommended to them. The mine stocks are for the William Tell in Silver Plume."

"Excellent." Carlyle's praise was sincere. "Head to Longmont in the morning, or tonight if you can get a train. Just be there by tomorrow night. Lie low for the first few days, but keep an eye on things. Adams is already there and has reported that Stuart got word from Denver. However, Stuart hasn't made a move to leave the city. See to it that he doesn't. If he does, cuff him and bring him to Denver—Stuart and anyone else you think may be involved."

"Yes, sir." McKay stood up to leave, but Carlyle's voice stopped him.

"We'll wrap this up this time, McKay; I can feel it in my bones. And when we do, you'll have those two weeks you wanted."

"Thanks, Carlyle. I'll count on that and keep you posted."

The men parted then, both eager to close this case, but for entirely different reasons. Carlyle had never seen Nick so anxious, and working with the man, along with keeping his guard up with Paine, was coming to be something of a strain. McKay's impetus was the two weeks Carlyle promised him, not just because he needed the rest, but because he planned to spend every moment with Pup Jennings.

36

The downstairs was completely lit up, telling Pup that the Wallaces probably had company. She let herself quietly in the back door and stood still in the empty kitchen. She had taken the time to put her dark wig back on but had only thrown a sweater over her uniform. She had also put her Bible and a few personal effects in her bag before leaving the apartment. Fatigue threatened to overwhelm her. The letdown over not getting back into Duncan's office had abated; she needed the day off tomorrow.

"I didn't hear you," Miranda said, suddenly coming through the door.

"I just got here."

"You look all in."

"I am. I have the day off tomorrow. Nick told me to come if I had the chance."

"And a good thing you did. Have you eaten?"

"No, I'm too hot and tired."

"Well, you get on up those back stairs and I'll come and fix you a bath."

"Aren't you needed down here?"

"Dinner is over, and I just took the coffee in. I'll check with the Missus, but she'll tell me to take care of you just like she always does."

Pup would have thanked her, but she was too tired to speak. She made for the back staircase, and just 20 minutes later sank down into a warm tub of water. It would have been lovely to soak for a time, but she knew she would fall asleep in the bath if she did.

"I'm going down to get you something to eat," Miranda told her as Pup climbed from the tub. "You get ready for bed, and I'll be right back."

Miranda was as good as her word, returning a short time later, and even bringing Camille with her. But Pup could not eat. She had already climbed into bed and fallen sound asleep.

Sunday morning McKay was on the earliest train that left for Boulder en route to Longmont. It was hard to leave the city. The only reason he hadn't sought out Pup was because he had to leave. He knew that she wanted to be careful, but he was quite certain he could have come and gone without notice. Recognizing that he was starting to think and sound like a man possessed, he finally closed his eyes and asked God to help him maintain a balance.

I need to trust You with Pup. She's in Your care, and I've got to let her go. I keep seeing her in that uniform and blonde hair, and then I worry. I'm not going to keep doing this, Lord. I'm going to believe the truth of Your Word that You will be with her. Thank You for seeing to her every need. Thank You for bringing her into my life. Help her to know Your presence and to remain in the Word.

That was not the end of his prayer, but he had become more restful. He knew that obedience was a constant, daily choice, and joy always came when he claimed God's truth and obeyed. He knew that Pup would still be on his mind, but he didn't have to worry. Indeed, he didn't have time for worry. He had a job waiting for him in Longmont, a job that in one way or another would affect the whole town. With this in mind, McKay turned his attention to the people of

Longmont and the case. These thoughts occupied him for the rest of the trip.

"You need to take it easy with her, Nick," Camille warned him in no uncertain terms, her look stern.

"What do you mean?"

"I mean that girl looks exhausted, and she slept all night. She'll be down for breakfast in a few minutes, but you let her eat before you begin the interrogation." It was an order she expected to be followed.

Nick frowned at his wife but didn't argue. He knew he was slightly berserk when it came to this case, but he was sick to death of Duncan Phipps and wanted nothing more than to put the matter to rest. If they all had to work a little harder to accomplish that, well, so be it! Then they could all breathe easier.

That was the way he felt *before* Pup joined him in the dining room. One look at her too-thin face and he changed his mind. Never one to carry extra flesh, his top undercover agent was losing weight. Even Nick could see the difference.

"Ready for breakfast?" he asked solicitously, working to hide his emotions.

"Yes." Her voice was fervent. "I think I must have fallen asleep last night before Miranda could come back with a tray."

"You're certainly right about that," the aforementioned woman said when she came in with fresh coffee. "You were out cold when I returned. I want you to eat up this morning."

"You can count on that." Pup's smile thanked her before she began to eat the sumptuous meal. Eggs, muffins with butter, ham and potatoes, hot coffee, and juice were the fare, and Pup felt as though she hadn't eaten in weeks. Watching her tuck into the food, Nick kept the newspaper in his hand and forced his questions to remain inside of him. He didn't think she had any new information or she would have said so immediately. He was wrong.

"I'm sorry to keep you waiting," she suddenly said, her food half gone and only a little on her front. "I was just so hungry I had to get a little in me."

"It's all right." Nick kept his voice light. "I take it you have news."

"Good news," she replied, clearly pleased.

"The files?"

Pup shook her head. "Nothing you're looking for, but there is a panel in this room—I guess you could call it an office—that's not a part of the wall. It's a door if I've ever seen one. It's subtle. I'm very impressed, and although I didn't have time to do anything with it, I know a secret door when I see one, and our Mr. Phipps has one in his office."

Pup stopped talking and went back to her food, which was fine with Nick. He didn't need her to find a way into this door, just knowing it was there was invaluable. It wouldn't be long before they would raid the Phipps mansion. Nick would see for himself what sat behind the door. By then Pup would be pulled from the case; he couldn't have her at risk. When it came time to shake the house down, she would be long gone. He opened his mouth to ask her to describe the panel to him, but Camille chose that moment to join them.

When she saw that Nick was letting Pup eat, she looked at him with loving eyes. His heart swelled with the fact that he'd done well; indeed, she was still tenderly gazing at him. The wink he gave her was playful and turned into a huge smile when she blushed.

"Do you want more coffee, Callie?" Camille asked from behind Pup, hoping to divert attention from her flushed face.

"Yes, please. The cook at the Phipps' can't make Miranda's coffee."

"Do they feed you meals at all?" Camille asked and sat down.

"Only lunch, and that's because I'm in the kitchen. By dinnertime I've been sent upstairs to dust or mop, and no one ever thinks to offer me food. By the time I leave in the evening, the kitchen has been totally cleaned."

"You don't do anything but clean?"

"That's about it. I work in the kitchen some, chopping or peeling potatoes. One evening they wanted me to serve dinner to Duncan and his men, but I dumped a tray and broke several cut-glass dishes. I wasn't asked to serve again."

"Well, you don't have to worry about any of that today," Camille told her. "You can lie around all day, go for a walk, or attack the bookshelves in Nick's office."

"Lying around sounds wonderful," she said, her hand covering a yawn. "I feel I could take a nap right now." Pup was done with her food and pushed the plate away.

"Maybe this afternoon," Nick inserted, keeping his voice neutral, "you could give me the layout of the house and office."

"Sure. I'll draw it and go over it with you. You don't mind waiting a bit?"

"Not at all."

Pup stood. "I'm going through the kitchen so I can thank Miranda, and then I'll be in my room."

Both husband and wife told her to sleep well. Camille's eyes were still on the doorway to the kitchen, so she was unaware of the way Nick had approached. She turned and found him standing close, one hand on the table and the other on the back of her chair. He was bending slightly over her. Their eyes met and he bent the rest of the way to kiss her, a sweet lingering kiss. Camille spoke when Nick moved slightly away, but his lips were still close.

"Thank you for letting her rest."

"You're right; she's tired."

Camille could only nod and try not to worry.

"Are we having company again tonight?" Nick asked.

"No," Camille answered, a little surprised at the question.

As Nick studied his wife's face, his eyes lit with a slow, intimate smile that went straight to his mouth. Camille found herself blushing all over again.

Longmont

McKay was both surprised and pleased to find Trent Adams waiting for him at the train station. The men talked as McKay walked with Trent back to the hotel, the other agent filling him in. Trent had still more to report, so McKay accompanied him to his room on the second floor, and the men exchanged notes there. McKay was relieved to learn that Stuart hadn't made a move. The senior agent asked Trent to stay on the alert the rest of that day, at least until the trains stopped running that night. McKay would go on duty the next day, but Trent would stay in town. McKay said his goodbyes after making sure Trent knew where he would be that night.

From the hotel McKay went to the livery. He rented a horse and headed home, that sight alone doing his heart a world of good. His father was at a neighbor's, but his mother was there to greet him. After she'd hugged him, McKay put an arm around her and led her to a chair. They made themselves comfortable in the living room.

"Welcome home," she offered with a smile.

"Thank you. It sure feels good."

"Is this business or pleasure?"

"Business, I'm afraid."

"For how long?"

"Maybe a few days, or possibly back out on the train tomorrow. In fact, I might need to leave town in a hurry. If that happens, I'll do my best to get word to you."

Liz's brows rose. "Sounds important."

"It is, but I hope it's also coming to an end. I wish this business didn't involve people in town, but it does."

"I've prayed for the Stuart family every day since you told us."

"I appreciate that, Mom. They're going to need it."

"And what about you? Beside the obvious needs of safety and wisdom, what should I be praying about for you?"

"Mostly that I don't lose my mind over a certain woman."

"Callie." His mother didn't even try to keep the satisfaction from her voice.

"Yes."

"Have you two had trouble?"

"No, but it's just so hard to get time together, and sometimes I worry about her."

"I think I can relate."

"I don't know, Mom," he sounded doubtful, knowing he could be honest. "You and Dad saw each other one day, talked nonstop for the next three months and then were married. Callie and I can't seem to get any time together for more than a few days, if that."

The room was silent for a few minutes before Liz spoke quietly.

"You were little more than a baby when your father went to work at the cannery."

"The cannery?"

"Yes, before he gained an interest in pharmaceuticals. Did we never tell you?"

McKay shook his head no.

"It was a night job," Liz went on. "All night, every night, and I hated it. For the first six weeks all I did was sit up at night and worry. Would he be hurt? Would he do a poor job and be fired? On and on I went until I was nearly ill with exhaustion.

"If you hadn't been born, it wouldn't have been so bad, but I was up all night worrying about your father and then had to work all day in this house and take care of you. Things became unbearable. In the little time your father and I had with each other, I was short and angry with him. I would start an argument just as he was walking out the door and say horrible things to him. Because he was leaving, there was no time to resolve issues."

McKay stared at his mother. He had never heard any of this before.

"One night the situation became very bad. I said such awful things that I was sure your father would never want to come home. He rarely grew angry with me, and I'm ashamed to this day over the way I acted, but this night as he was leaving, he snapped. He shouted at me, scaring you to tears in the next room."

"What did he say?"

"He said, 'I have a job to do, Liz. Will you please just let me go and do it!' It doesn't sound like much right now, but he got my attention. Your father had a job to do, and so did I. I didn't have to figure out how to do his job or even answer for him if he didn't do well. I just had to do *my* job. That was all God would ask of me.

"I'll never forget that night of understanding. I put you to bed early and then fell on my knees. I didn't pray long—I was too tired to last—but when I climbed into bed, I'd given it all to God. That night I slept through the night for the first time in six weeks. When I woke in the morning, your father was in bed with me. I hadn't even heard him come in. I left the room as quietly as I was able and came down here to pray. I decided then and there that I would start and end every day by praying and asking God to help me do my job, and my job alone."

McKay could only stare at her. How wrong he'd been to think she wouldn't understand his worry. How foolish and naïve to think that all problems disappear once a person is married.

"Thanks, Mom," McKay said sincerely. "I told God on the train today that I would let Him do His job, but I still don't have it right. I just have to do my job." McKay said the last words with the feeling that he had finally gotten the point.

"Will you try to see Callie on your way back through Boulder?" Liz couldn't resist asking.

"She's not in Boulder. She's working in Denver, and I don't know when I'll see her."

Liz was more curious than ever but didn't press the point. McKay was silent for a time, his mind on other things. Thinking they could both use some quiet and something cool to drink, Liz gave him his peace. She had just brought tall glasses of cider to the living room when Harry came in the back door.

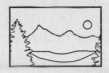

37

Denver

"The desk sits here." Pup gestured to the simple map she'd drawn of the office. "There are bookshelves back here," she put a finger behind the mark which stood for Duncan's desk, "and over by these windows are the filing cabinets. The door is here, on this paneled wall." Again she pointed.

It was Sunday evening. Pup had rested all day and was now ready to talk about the layout of the house.

"It's a well-done job, Nick. You'll really have to look. The door sits on the same wall as the hallway, so the room can't be very wide. It might be full of the filing cabinets you really want, or possibly it leads to a stairway that could go either upstairs or into the basement."

"What about Duncan's bedroom? Have you ever seen it?"

"I don't think so. When he's in the house, there are men everywhere. I do know that all the bedrooms are upstairs."

He tapped the paper. "This is excellent. You've done a great job, Pup."

She nodded. It had been fairly routine for her, but she was still pleased.

"Just take it easy in the days to come," Nick told her, but without warning Pup's mind wandered. She had been so uncertain if she was even to continue the job, and now she sat as pleased as a child with candy over the praise Nick was giving her. She suddenly realized Nick was still speaking to her.

"It hasn't gotten dangerous, has it?"

"No," Pup answered truthfully, albeit absently.

Nick nodded, telling her she'd probably be out of Phipps' house by the middle of the week, if not sooner. But again Pup's mind was on other aspects of the case. This time Nick didn't notice. He never did become aware that Pup had missed his comments about the job finishing soon. And since she'd missed them completely, she asked no questions. Pup left for her apartment just before dark with no plans to see Nick until Monday or Tuesday night.

By the time Pup returned to work Monday morning she was ready to be back on the job. Her goal: the paneled door in the office. She hadn't lifted a finger on Sunday, and she now felt refreshed and more than ready to complete the job. Part of her enthusiasm stemmed from the fact that after arriving home from Nick and Camille's, she had spent two hours praying and reading her Bible.

She was coming to the very solid conclusion that spying was not a job she could continue with a clear conscience. At the same time, she could not justify walking out on Nick. As soon as this case was wrapped up, she would talk to him and try to explain. This above all else gave her a strong reason to penetrate the office and the hidden door. But no one at the mansion would accommodate her this day.

She cleaned in the upstairs, the library, and the formal dining room, and then worked in the kitchen. Since there were men everywhere, she surmised that Duncan was in the house, but she saw nothing of him. The few times she needed to pass by the office, the door was closed and a man, someone she hadn't seen before, sat on a chair outside. The closest she came was the library, where she cleaned at a snail's pace in an effort to be near the office. It was no use. The door remained shut and guarded all day.

"You need to go to Longmont," Duncan told the man sitting across the desk from him. "You need to see a banker for me."

The man's dark eyes regarded him with little interest, and Duncan asked himself, not for the first time, why he knew he could depend on Jubal Hackett. There was nothing overly flashy about him that would draw attention, but in his quiet way he was rather amazing. There was little Duncan didn't know about the people who worked for him, and the reports back from his closest men told him that Jubal was his type of employee.

With his light brown hair, dark eyes, baby-smooth complexion, and shy smile, he could cajole an old lady out of her life savings or work a man over with his fists until he was ready to agree to anything Jubal demanded.

He and his brother had been doing jobs for Duncan for years. Govern had been the more brutal of the two, more easily riled and violent, but Jubal was cool, keeping his head in the tensest situations. Men like Govern were a dime a dozen, and Duncan had not even missed him, but Jubal's talents were a treasure. Duncan knew well that Jubal would get Richard Stuart to Denver if he died trying.

"Tell Richard Stuart I'd like to see him as soon as possible," Duncan went on smoothly. "You can give him this. If that doesn't convince him, do what you need to do." Duncan handed Jubal an envelope. Pup's brother put the message in his coat pocket without even looking at it.

"I'll expect you both back no later than tomorrow night."

Jubal saw no reason to answer. He rose and moved toward the door. He had a job to do and he would get it done. It was just after two o'clock now. He knew that a train left at three. He'd be in Longmont that evening and at the door of the Rocky Mountain Savings first thing Tuesday morning.

Nick could not believe he'd forgotten his anniversary. It was the first time in 34 years. Camille had met him at the door, dressed for an evening on the town, and she could tell by the look on his face that he had not remembered. She fought back the tears, but they would not be stemmed. He had always bought her flowers, she reminded him. The only years he'd missed had been during the war. And now his head was so full of this case that she almost didn't know him anymore. Nick had to admit that it was all true.

There had been no choice for him—he had to repair her heart. He'd held her, told her they would go to dinner anyway, and made himself push the case from his mind. He'd been headed to see Pup to tell her she didn't have to go back the next day, but one more day probably didn't matter. Word had come from McKay that Stuart hadn't made a move. Nick forced himself to relax. He was tense enough about this case, and Camille was right—it wasn't fair to her or their marriage when he brought his work home with him.

In spite of such a dreadful start, the evening ended like a lovely dream. The meal at the Brown Palace was perfect, and with the stars bright overhead, the ride through the park in the open carriage set the mood for the rest of a lovely night.

As for Pup, she came home at the regular time, not quite as tired, and fixed herself a good meal. She gave Nick little thought. He had said he'd be by to see her on Monday or Tuesday, so his absence meant nothing. After dinner she read for a time and then began another letter to McKay, missing him more than ever. A walk in the park was tempting, but it was already dark. She turned in a little early and went back to the mansion first thing Tuesday morning.

Longmont

Jubal crossed the threshold of the Rocky Mountain Savings as if he'd lived in Longmont all his life. He had on a clean shirt and string tie and had taken time to have his jacket and pants pressed. Not one teller looked at him with suspicion. However, Richard Stuart's face blanched white upon seeing him.

"Good morning, Mr. Stuart." Jubal's voice couldn't have been more polite. "Mr. Phipps asked me to visit you. He sent you something."

"Come into the office." Richard's voice was low, his eyes shifting to see if they'd been observed by any of the bank patrons or employees. All looked in order, and the banker led the way inside.

Once in the office, Jubal took a chair as if he had all the time in the world. He brought forth the envelope and placed it gently on the desk. For a moment Richard only stared at it.

"You do understand, Mr. Stuart," Jubal continued, his voice polite if not mildly bored, "that it's nothing personal. I have a job to do. Mr. Phipps would like to see you, and I simply can't return and tell him that you didn't want to come. You do understand, I'm sure."

Richard Stuart licked his lips. He looked at Jubal and then at the letter before slowly picking it up. He swallowed hard, opened it, and read.

> *Greetings Richard:*
>
> *I was surprised that you didn't accept my offer to join me in Denver. I know it would be hotter here in the city, but you never know when the temperature might change in Longmont.*

I've asked an associate of mine to come back with you as I understand your failure to join me might stem from a reluctance to travel alone. I'll expect you here no later than Tuesday night. I look forward to seeing you, Richard. We have much to discuss.

It wasn't signed, and without looking at Jubal, Richard felt a chill go down his back. He had been to see Duncan in Denver some time ago, but that was before he decided to branch out on his own. Things couldn't have been friendlier. The Denver banker must now be on to him. Richard studied Jubal. There was nothing in his face or posture to indicate any threat of violence. He might have been a customer looking for a loan, but Richard believed any man Duncan sent to be capable of anything.

"I'll have to talk with my wife," he nearly whispered.

"Certainly." Jubal managed to look compassionate. "I must gather my own things from the hotel. Shall we meet back here in, say, 30 minutes?"

Come to the bank with his traveling bag! Richard nearly panicked, and on the heels of this came anger. He knew he had to take back control, albeit slightly.

"No." Richard felt relieved just saying the word. "I'll meet you at the train station, and I need an hour."

Jubal's face was expressionless, but Richard didn't care. He was angry enough right now to physically fight this man, but he wouldn't. However, he wasn't going to let him completely control his life. His wife was going to be upset enough to have him leaving so suddenly, let alone with a half hour's notice. Not caring what Jubal thought, Richard took his jacket from the coat rack near his chair and slipped into it. He then slipped the letter into his shirt pocket. His briefcase was next. He picked it up and then looked expectantly at his visitor.

Only then did Jubal rise, and he did so slowly, still feeling he was in control. He motioned with a hand for Richard to precede him out the door, but the banker looked at him coldly.

"You may have a job to do, Mr. Hackett," Richard said, keeping his voice low, "but this is my bank, and I am a respected citizen in this town. One call to my tellers explaining that you have threatened me, and you will be a hunted man in Longmont. Now you may still get your job done, but not without great delays and time spent behind bars. Indeed, I could probably keep you locked up for a very long time."

Jubal's respect for the man rose. He saw no harm in letting the banker think he was having his way. Seemingly in complete compliance, Jubal preceded the banker out the door. In truth he had nothing to pick up at the hotel; he always traveled light. He would let Mr. Stuart think he was going home and to the train station on his own, but Richard would never be out of Jubal's sight.

"I've had him in my sight since six o'clock," McKay told Trent.

"Did he go to the bank?"

"Yes."

The men were walking the streets as if they had all the time in the world. It was a little trickier for McKay since he was known in this town, but so far few people had done more than nod and say good morning.

"My guess is that Stuart has gone home to pack his things."

"So the train station will be next."

"Exactly," McKay affirmed.

"I'll meet you there."

Trent wandered from McKay's side with the smoothest of moves, slipping into a shop, browsing for several minutes, and then exiting to head in the opposite direction—toward the train station. McKay continued his pursuit up the street, seeing that Jubal was trailing Richard. McKay wasn't so foolish as to think that he wasn't being watched as well, so he not only kept an eye on Jubal, but also on the happenings behind him. So far, so good. His palms began to sweat, which was always a good sign. The adrenaline rush of a near victory pumped through his veins. Jubal seemed completely under control. McKay knew he had him.

Denver

Gerard's words had been, "Dust the hallway."

Pup could have sang. No one was positioned outside the office door today, and things seemed a little quieter. She started out dusting, but not even ten minutes passed before she knocked softly on the door, her ear pressed against it. Nothing. No sound at all. A moment later she was inside, locking the door just as she'd found it.

The first thing she noticed were the drapes. They had been pulled over the windows, and the room was much darker than her last visit. She debated what to do. It was going to be hard enough to figure out the secret door, let alone do it in the dark. She could light a lantern, but it would be harder to get to and blow out if she was disturbed—the window covers wouldn't be easy either.

She opted against both. Maybe her hands would tell her more than her eyes anyway. Feeling along the wall, she located the door right away. She fingered the entire seam, the inspection telling her it was a little narrower than normal. So far there was no hint of a hinge or handle. Trying to gauge which side would open, Pup moved her hand down to where a handle could be. Nothing. Not knowing how much time she had made it so hard. She would have to have some light and decided on the drapes.

Duncan Phipps, just coming from an early breakfast meeting, watched from outside as the curtains in his private office opened. Standing at his side, Nelson had seen the action as well. They couldn't make out who was standing to the side of the window, but it looked like the blonde maid.

"She must be in there by mistake," Nelson commented.

Duncan only grunted his agreement. One of the clients with whom he was supposed to meet, a Mr. Robinson, had not shown up. His mind was also still occupied with Richard Stuart and that banker's mine stocks. Was Robinson involved? Duncan hated to be played for a fool.

"We'll just tell her to get out when we get there," Nelson said to comfort him.

"You do that" was the banker's automatic reply. Duncan gave it no other thought. Nelson looked forward to throwing her out again. The men continued their almost leisurely walk toward the house.

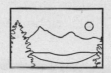

38

Longmont

"Mr. Stuart," McKay approached the man and his companion, his voice almost gentle. "May I speak with you?"

Richard Stuart turned, his anxious face relaxing when he recognized McKay. After the inspection, he'd never heard back from the treasury man and assumed that he'd done a good job on the books.

"Hello, McKay."

"I'm sorry to bother you, sir, but I need to speak to you. Could you come into the railway office?"

"As a matter of fact—" Richard began. He was going to tell them he was headed out of town, but Jubal cut in smoothly.

"He'd like to, but something important has come up. We're headed to Denver." As always his voice was calm. Not above lying, he still believed in telling the truth for as long as possible. "Maybe when he returns you can see him about your loan or whatever you need."

"I quite agree with you, Mr. Hackett; the two of you will be going to Denver, but not exactly the way you'd planned."

The quiet sound of Jubal's name coming from this man's lips registered just a second too late. His hand was reaching for his inside coat pocket, but another voice spoke into his ear.

"Don't even think about it," Trent told him, a gun surreptitiously pressed into his side. "Just head to the railway office as you've been asked. That's right; keep those hands where I can see them."

McKay led the way and was not at all surprised to see Stuart's expression showing his quandary: Had he been caught, or was this a rescue? Jubal's face showed nothing at all. For a moment he had lost his calm, but he was now back under control, walking to the stage office as though he visited there often.

~

Denver

She had found the latch. She wouldn't have found it without the light, but now her hand was on it. It was a narrow strip of wood so subtly put into the wall that it was nearly impossible to see. At the top was an opening. Pup put her finger inside the half-moon hole and pulled down. The door opened with a low groan, one that disguised the unlocking and opening of the outside door. She was in the process of pulling the paneled doorway open when Duncan spoke.

"Well, now—we thought you'd come to dust."

Pup spun, her heart thudding in fear. She recovered swiftly, picking up the dust cloth at her feet, and began to babble in her Swedish accent.

"Inga broke, Inga sorry, so sorry," and on she went, practically crying as she rubbed the cloth up and down the wall to show what she'd been doing. Amazingly her story worked. Eyeing her coldly, Duncan told Nelson to get her out.

Nelson came forward, more than happy to oblige, but in his enthusiasm he grabbed her arm and violently jerked her whole body forward. She felt her wig slip down onto her forehead and was afraid to touch it lest she draw attention. Pup didn't think she would be spotted, but Duncan must have been looking directly at her. He raised his voice for the first time.

"Stop!"

Nelson turned, his hand still holding Pup. Pup kept her eyes toward the door so she knew exactly when they were joined by two other men. She didn't have to feign fear as Duncan stepped in front of her. His eyes cold on her face, he reached up and removed the wig.

"Well, well," he spoke, his voice little more than a whisper, "if it isn't Bryan Daniels."

Pup's gaze was transformed in a moment. Composed, sure of herself, and even slightly amused, she looked boldly back at Duncan Phipps. Even if she were about to die, there was one comfort: She was not the criminal.

Duncan watched her for a moment and then jerked his head. The door was shut, and the two other men remained inside.

"I want your name, and I want it now."

Pup hesitated without looking unsure. She wasn't certain if he thought her a man or woman and wanted to figure which gender would be to her best advantage.

"I'm waiting."

Pup's brows rose. "Considering the fact that the last two names I've given haven't been mine, how could you possibly know I'd be telling the truth?"

She was surprised when an admiring smile covered his mouth.

"Go ahead." Genuinely amused, he liked anyone who could match wits with him—at least for a time—as long as he eventually gained the upper hand. "Tell me a name anyway."

"And if I refuse?"

Duncan shrugged. "I guess it doesn't really matter. It's not as if your grave will be marked."

Pup now shrugged as well, impressing Duncan again because she showed no fear. He studied her some more.

"You're good, but then you probably know that. When I think back on Bryan Daniels, I realize now that if I had really studied you, I'd have known your gender." He paused and weighed her a little more. "You're very good."

Pup said nothing. She showed not one flicker of emotion.

"Show our mystery lady to an upstairs room," Duncan ordered Nelson. "I'm sure she can tell us quite a lot." He turned back to Pup. "You might not be so reluctant to talk in the future."

"You've already stated your plans to kill me; why should I talk?"

"I may have spoken rashly." He was the smoothest she had ever seen him. "Indeed, I think the two of us could get along very well together. I'm sure whomever you work for couldn't possibly match the salary I'd be willing to pay you."

Pup managed to look bored.

"Take her upstairs." She hadn't been impressed with his offer, and the frigid tone came back into his voice. "See to it that she doesn't leave us anytime soon."

Feeling she had nothing to lose, Pup boldly took the wig that still hung from Duncan's fingers and put it back on her head. Again the banker was impressed but tried not to show it. A moment later she was taken away, each of the men at the door holding one of her arms. Escape was impossible. Nelson led them upstairs. He did nothing to disguise his loathing as he opened a bedroom door and watched her walk in. He slammed it a little too loudly, and Pup listened to the turn of the key. This was no time to lose her head, but her knees suddenly turned to water. She sank down on the nearest chair, her mind racing with what she should do next.

Longmont

"Hello, Mr. Stuart," Happy Conway, the train station manager, greeted the men as they came in. "What's up, McKay?"

"Hello, Happy. Could we use your back room for a few minutes?"

"Sure, help yourself," he offered, his eyes frankly curious as they went in and shut the door. McKay wasted no time in taking Richard Stuart aside. Trent, his gun already out, dealt with Jubal.

Phipps' man was completely searched and divested of a gun and two knives. Determined not to let Jubal get away or harm anyone, Trent went over him twice, even holding the gun on him while he asked Jubal to remove his shoes. While this was going on, Richard and McKay spoke.

"Does this have to do with your inspection?"

"Yes."

Richard looked regretful. "When I didn't hear back from you, I thought that things were all clear."

"I'm afraid not."

"How did you know that was Jubal Hackett?"

"We know a lot of things."

The men stared at each other. "I need to search you and the case, sir."

Richard nodded. It was humiliating, but it could have been on the platform; he had to thank McKay for that small courtesy at least. It didn't take long to find him clean, and after giving the banker a measured look, McKay went to Trent and Jubal. Jubal was now cuffed from behind and sitting on a crate. The two treasury men spoke briefly, and then McKay exited. No one had to tell the apprehended men that he was going for two more train tickets. It was as McKay had said: They were headed to Denver all right, but not the way they'd planned.

343

Denver

The day was getting long. In fact, Carlyle was headed home very soon. He had a few more papers to clear from his desk and then he would leave. In the midst of deep concentration, a messenger knocked. Carlyle tipped the lad, asked him to stay around outside, and opened the letter. He smiled at the words he read and made a call on the interoffice telephone. Nick answered almost immediately.

"Is Paine with you?"

"No."

"Now might be a good time to send for him."

"Give us five minutes."

Both men hung up and, just as planned, Carlyle knocked on Nick's door five minutes later.

"Come in," the older man called. "What is it?"

Paine was in the chair in front of the desk, and Nick was in his seat. Carlyle shut the door and approached, reading as he went.

"News from McKay. He's brought Stuart and Hackett back from Longmont. He's waiting at the jail for word from us."

"Excellent." Nick held his hand out as if he wanted Carlyle to give him the note, but then he glanced at Paine.

"What is it, Paine? You look ill."

Nick's chief aide licked his lips.

"McKay has brought in Richard Stuart and Jubal Hackett?"

"Yes. Didn't I tell you that he and Trent Adams were on the job?"

A sick smile crossed Paine's face. "Of course," he tried to bluff. "I must have forgotten."

"All right. Well, let's finish this letter," Nick went on, business as usual. "Here, Paine, read Carlyle what we have."

But he couldn't do it. He stammered and began to sweat.

"I don't think I feel well, Mr. Wallace," he finally whispered and stood. "I think I'd better go home."

"Are you sure there isn't something you want to tell us, Paine?" Carlyle now inserted, and the man really looked at both Nick's and Carlyle's faces.

"You know. You've known all along." He was growing angry. "You've known all along, and you've played me for a fool!"

"You are a fool," Nick said without compassion, "to think you could get away with this."

"You can't pin anything on me!" Paine now said rashly, his face going from white to red. "I don't know anything!"

"You know plenty, Paine, and before this is over you're going to tell all," Carlyle spoke up, careful to keep his body between Paine and the door.

Paine was shaking his head wildly, and Nick came to his feet. His voice was hard.

"We're going to send Duncan Phipps to jail, Paine; you can help us do it, or you can go with him."

The younger man looked as if he would panic and run, but the uncompromising look on Nick's face seemed to take all fight out of him. He sank back down into the chair, slumped over, his hand to his head.

Carlyle went back out and gave three messages to the boy who waited. One was to his wife telling her he would be late, another was for Camille Wallace so that she would know not to expect Nick, and the third missive was to McKay Harrington at the jail, telling him the three of them would be with him shortly.

Pup was surprised when dinner was delivered to her. She had expected to be killed, tortured, or starved at the least, but not fed. The meal looked good, but part of her was afraid to touch it. However, it had been hours since she'd had food, and she knew she had to take the chance. There was nothing to fear. It didn't taste odd, and she didn't feel sick or faint, but neither could she eat very much. She was much too tense.

Darkness fell, and since she couldn't get the windows open, the room was warm. Praying all the while for strength and wisdom, she was able to light a lantern and, at one point, she even tested the bed. When a clock down the hall chimed 11 times, she gave up, removed her shoes, and lay down. Less than an hour later she fell into a fitful sleep.

Back at her apartment, Nick's stomach churned and his heart hammered in his chest as it had been doing for hours. Stuart, Hackett, and Paine were all behind bars. So where was Pup? Pup was working at the enemy's mansion, a place she no longer needed to be—but it was too late to tell her. Something had gone wrong, terribly wrong; he could feel it in his bones.

He waited until midnight and then went to Carlyle's, rousing the man from bed. He gave him orders to have undercover men guard the Phipps mansion effective immediately. Carlyle called on some of his best, assuring Nick that they would handle it.

Nick finally headed toward home, his heart still sick with worry. It wasn't just Pup who was on his mind. He knew now that he should have pulled her Sunday night, or even pushed the point with his wife the night before, but he didn't and now it was too late. His heart clenched in agony as he tried to figure out how he could have been so lax. It clenched further when he asked himself how he would ever break the news to Camille.

39

"Well, now," Duncan's voice was almost congenial as he addressed Pup, "I was hoping you were an early riser. It looks like you had a comfortable night." His eyes surveyed the room and then focused on Pup.

The captive maid didn't see any point in answering. They had brought her breakfast, and she'd eaten a few bites. The rest sat on the tray near the door. If he was hoping to be thanked, she knew she would disappoint him.

"Have you been keeping busy?" Duncan asked, as if they were enjoying a day in the park. Again, Pup didn't respond. She didn't wish to antagonize the man, but neither was she going to make things easier for him.

Before breakfast had arrived, she'd gone to work in earnest. The windows were her first focus, but they held fast. She had checked the entire room for panels, a hidden door, anything—she'd come up blank. She'd even lifted the rug and checked the floor and then stood on a chair to get a closer look at the high ceiling. Again, nothing.

"Still don't feel like talking?" Duncan's voice was losing its charm, and Pup realized she'd remained quiet long enough.

"I told you yesterday, I don't see any point."

"Meaning?"

"Meaning that you'll just kill me, so why should I tell you anything?"

Duncan looked as though he were considering something. "You're obviously an intelligent woman; you must know that death can come very slowly."

"True, but you don't strike me as the type who likes getting blood on his rugs."

"You're right, I don't, but sometimes I can make an exception." Duncan studied her again. When she still displayed no fear of him or his power, he went on. "It looks as if someone needs to give you a point, a reason as it were, to tell me what you know."

Pup remained quiet this time.

"I think you'll find that I'm a fair man." His voice was mild; after all, he held all the cards. "So I'll tell you what. I'll give you one hour to think about talking to me, and to be extra fair, I'll tell you what I want to know. I want to know if your presence here has anything to do with the fact that one of my men and one of my business associates never returned to me last night as they'd planned. I also want to know for whom you're working and how much they pay you. I want to know if the name Richard Stuart means anything to you. Am I making myself clear?"

"Very."

"Good. You see I have a few men who don't specialize in banking and finance as I do. Their talents abound in a more physical realm, such as pain levels and the art of convincing someone that her loyalty is no longer worth the price. I assume this is also clear to you?"

Pup nodded.

"I hope it won't come to that. In fact, at anytime within the next hour you only have to knock on the door, and the man waiting outside will come for me." He turned and started back toward the door but stopped. "I do hope you'll make the wise choice. Nothing is worth that much protection."

Duncan went out the door on those words, and Pup was left alone. She had never been in this situation before—not just having her identity revealed, but being held captive as well.

I have no idea what to do here, Lord. Does Nick even know that I'm in trouble? If he didn't try to see me last night, then he probably doesn't know anything. Would Nick want me to keep my mouth shut during torture?

Somehow Pup didn't think he would, but what if she revealed something that compromised the whole case? The thought was intolerable to her; they had all worked so hard. She also realized there was nothing honorable about Duncan Phipps. He tried to be smooth, but he was a criminal. He said they could work together, but he was a liar. He was better at deceit than banking. Her mind was made up. She would tell Duncan nothing. She might die in the process, but she knew that even if she did tell him he would kill her. She might not be here to see Phipps go to jail, but Nick would still have his case.

A clock chimed down the hall. Pup lost track of the bells, but she knew it must be around seven o'clock. How long had Duncan been gone? Suddenly Pup didn't know, but however long it had been, she had less than an hour before the torture began.

Not in all the years McKay had worked for him did Carlyle ever need to seek him out at the boardinghouse. It was a surprise to have anyone knock on his door in the morning, but to have Carlyle waiting in the hall outside his room was stunning. What did it mean? McKay could only stare.

"May I come in?"

"Of course." McKay recalled himself and stepped back. He shut the door automatically behind his superior.

Carlyle came right to the point. "Pup never came back to her apartment last night. I've got agents surrounding the mansion. As you know, the plan was to invade and search the premises tomorrow, but with Pup possibly being held inside we're going now—in about an hour. I want you with me."

McKay would have told him that nothing could keep him away, but he couldn't speak. She was in danger. She was trapped in that mansion, and for a moment he couldn't breathe.

"Are you going to be all right for this, McKay?" Carlyle's voice became firm. "You can't run this one on emotions; you've got to have a clear head."

McKay took a deep breath. He felt resolved but also calm. "Yes. I'll do all I can, and I'll be fine. Just tell me what you need me to do."

Carlyle mapped out the plan, giving several alternatives if things didn't proceed as they figured. The men left McKay's room just 15 minutes later. Both were armed and headed to meet with Nick and Paine. Pup could already be dead; there was not a minute to lose. The time had come to shut Duncan Phipps down for good.

"You didn't knock on the door," Duncan said as soon as he entered Pup's room. This time he wasn't alone. A rather small, wiry man was with him. His eyes were flat and remote, and in his hand was a rope.

"No." She had to drag her eyes from the other man. "I didn't see any point."

"I had hoped you would feel otherwise."

Pup cocked her head to one side, trying not to fear what lay ahead. "You know, you've really made quite a few presumptions. What makes you think I have anything to tell you?"

"I've thought of that," Duncan admitted, "and had you only been here at the mansion I wouldn't assume anything, but you were also at my bank—and not just at my bank, but at my special office."

"Ah, yes," Pup returned, looking satisfied. "I'd forgotten about the special office. You know, Mr. Phipps, you're not really so much a banker as a thief."

Duncan looked at her indulgently.

"You've been misinformed."

"I don't think so."

Duncan smiled. "You delude yourself. You don't know as much about me as you think you do."

"On the contrary, I know quite a lot. I'm going to tell you something, Mr. Phipps." She spoke slowly now, drawing the words out to make sure she had his attention. "I'm going to tell you something that not many people know. My brother works for you." It was out. Pup had debated what to do or say, and she now felt a weight lift off her shoulders.

The men were in place. Paine had gone to the front door, and treasury agents were across the street, in the bushes around the house, everywhere. There were no plans for a shoot-out. If Duncan would let them in, they would handle this civilly. They would search every room and probably arrest every member of the household, but unless Duncan put up a fight, no shots would be fired.

McKay positioned himself at the rear of the mansion. There were tall bushes all along the edge of the house. He had a clear view of two doors, one of which was very near. Trent Adams was not far away on his other side and closer to the other door. Every so often McKay's gaze would move upward, giving him a view of all the windows on the second floor.

She's up there somewhere, Lord. She might be hurt or frightened. Please watch over her. Help her not be afraid. And even if I never see her again, Lord, help her to know that she's the only woman I've ever loved.

With Pup's announcement, all amusement fled. The banker looked intently at his prisoner, his eyes showing disbelief.

"Govern," he finally whispered. "Govern and Jubal Hackett."

"I'm impressed," Pup commended him. "I thought I would have to spell it out for you."

All thought of torturing this woman flew from his head. If she was anything like her brother, nothing could force her to talk before she was ready. Not aware of the way Pup watched him, he moved around the room, his mind working things out.

He would just keep her. Whoever had sent her would eventually come looking for her. In the meantime she would enjoy his hospitality. He wouldn't starve her or harm her in any way, but a few weeks in this room might loosen her tongue or bring her boss out of the woodwork. And then there was Jubal. A visit from her brother might do a world of good.

"I suddenly find you much too valuable to harm, Miss Hackett," Duncan said firmly as he now faced her. "I believe I will enjoy your company for a bit longer. If you need anything—food, reading material, anything—just knock on the door and ask."

This was the last thing Pup had expected. She was working desperately to frame a reply when someone knocked on the door. Duncan scowled but went to answer it.

"I was not to be disturbed," he said. His voice could be so cold.

"I'm sorry, sir." Pup couldn't see him in the hallway, but she recognized Nelson's voice. "It's your nephew. He says he has word on the men you were expecting last night."

"What is he doing here during the day?" Duncan growled. "He'll have the whole treasury department down on my head."

Pup heard the last of this as Duncan and the rope man went out the door. Her relief was so great that she began to tremble all over. For an instant she had thought he might make a connection between her and the treasury department, but he'd been too angry with his nephew—Pup assumed it was Paine—to give her any more thought.

She stood for a moment, her mind racing in frantic thought. Then it occurred to her: She hadn't heard the door lock. Terrified to hope but determined to try, she moved silently toward the closed portal. The knob turned under her hand and her breath caught in her throat. She froze, knowing if someone was outside she'd be caught in an instant. She heard nothing, no voices, nothing. Still moving as soundlessly as she was able, Pup pulled the door open and paused yet again. There was still no sound or movement.

She put her head out. The heart that had nearly stopped a few moments ago now raced in her chest when she saw that the hall was completely empty. Keeping her head long enough to remember to shut the door behind her, Pup moved into the passageway. No longer was she thinking of secret panels, file cabinets, or information. She had worked in this house for days. She knew every door, hallway, corridor, and stairway. And right now she was getting out.

"Why did you have to come now?" Duncan asked Paine for the fifth time.

Paine's fear and nerves were not feigned; he was not a good liar. "I just got the word, and when Mr. Wallace asked me to run an errand this morning, I thought I should tell you right away."

Duncan scowled at him but then asked, "Did you actually see them in jail?"

"No." This was true, although he'd been at the jailhouse himself. "But Mr. Wallace wasn't even talking to me; it was Mr. Crawford who brought the news." Paine slowed down now. What if they had been playing him for a fool yet again? Then he remembered the night he'd just spent in prison. A shudder ran all through him. He couldn't take the chance.

"I'm sure it's true," Paine went on. "After all, you just said they didn't come last night as planned."

"I know what I said!" Duncan snapped. He would have gone on, but a knock sounded at the office door. Nelson answered it.

"A Mr. Carlyle Crawford is here to see the boss."

Duncan had been moving to the door, but now rounded on his nephew. "You fool! You were followed."

"No, I'm sure not." Paine was certain that this was not part of the plan.

Duncan cut him off with a downward slash of his hand. "Get out of sight!" he whispered furiously. "I'll handle this."

Paine stood frozen while Nelson and his uncle left the room. He'd never been so frightened in his whole life. Completely forgetting that there was another door he could use, he hid underneath the desk in terror.

It was impossible to know if the mansion staff knew she was being held captive. So for this reason alone Pup was determined to keep out of sight. She had arrived on the main level, but the door she usually used exited through the kitchen. Someone was always in the kitchen. At one point she heard footsteps moving rather fast in the hallway and had to hide behind a corner. No one had approached, but she thought her heart might stop before the person turned and entered a room without discovering her.

At last she had made it. She was at the door to the wine cellar. She wasn't certain if anyone would be in the cellar, but right inside this door was a door that led to the back of the house. It was on the same side of the house as the kitchen door but was separated by many high bushes. If she could just gain that door, she knew she was home free. Even if it meant hiding at the back of the house for the rest of the day, she would be safe.

Pup breathed a prayer of thanks when she found the cellar door unlocked. She wasted no time, swiftly slipping inside and trying the outside door. The key was in the door, so she turned it, moving slowly in case this entry was being guarded from outside. She opened it just a crack and saw nothing. Determined to put up a huge fuss if she was grabbed, Pup went ahead, every movement subtle. Opening it just enough to slip out, she remembered again to close it behind her.

She saw no one. Her heart soared as she took the steps on swift, silent feet. She was almost free. Walking carefully along the bushes, she knew just where she was going to hide. Pup never made it. Arms roughly grabbed her from behind, one hand going hard over her mouth. Before she could think about struggling or screaming, she was dragged off her feet and into the thick foliage at the back of the house.

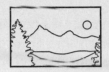

40

"My files?" Duncan managed to look pleasant, but Carlyle wasn't fooled.

"Yes, sir, we have some questions on several accounts and would like to verify the facts with you."

"That sounds like bank business."

"We think so, too, sir, but there are no such records of these accounts with your banks, and we have people who say they've worked with you."

"Of course." Duncan looked as if he'd just remembered. "I do have some private dealings, and the files for those transactions are right here in my office. I'd be happy to show you."

"Very well. I'll get my assistants, and we'll begin."

"Assistants, Mr. Crawford? I really don't think you'll find that much."

"But this will speed things along, Mr. Phipps."

"How many men are we talking about here?" he still sounded only mildly interested.

"Just two."

He hesitated for only a moment. "All right. I'll wait for you here and then show you the files."

Carlyle nodded pleasantly and walked to the front door. Gerard was there to let him out, his manners impeccable. The door closed behind him, and all Carlyle could do was hope that they would be allowed back in.

Nick couldn't remember if Duncan Phipps had ever seen him. It had been nothing short of torment to send Carlyle in where he wanted to be, but he couldn't take the chance. He comforted himself with the fact that, either way, they were going to get him, and Nick would get inside. He would be called in as one of Carlyle's assistants. If that didn't work and Duncan put up a fight, they would raid the mansion. It was just a matter of time before he had the information he so desperately sought.

He felt his palms sweat. It was almost impossible to keep Pup from his mind, but he forced himself to stay calm. His wife was another worry. She had been inconsolable the night before, almost ill with the tears she'd shed, first with worry over how late he had been, and then over the news concerning Pup. It was a temptation to hide it from her, but he knew that wasn't fair.

I've got to take Pup home to Camille, Nick said to himself. *She has to be all right. I want Phipps. I want him badly. But no matter what else happens, that girl has to be all right.*

Pup's huge eyes looked through the gloom at the man holding her, and she nearly collapsed with relief. Only then did McKay remove his hand from her mouth. Both arms crushed Pup against him for a moment, and then he held her away so he could look into her face.

"You're going to be the death of me," he whispered almost faintly.

"I was so scared." Her voice was just as low.

"It's over now. Stay here."

She wanted to hold on to him, to tell him not to leave her, but she realized all too well that he had a job to do. McKay shifted her so she could lean against the wall. Weak with exhaustion, Pup slumped against it. He then moved through the bushes along the house toward Trent.

"Is everything all right?" The other agent had heard the scuffle.

"Yes. Get out front. Tell Nick that I have Pup."

"Pup?"

"That's right. Get to him immediately, even if he's already gone inside. Tell him or Carlyle privately."

Trent moved to do as he was told, and McKay returned to Pup.

Carlyle came down the steps, and both Nick and Kelsey Frost, the other man they'd chosen, stepped down from the buggy where they'd been waiting. Nick was just about to stride up the walk when he heard his name. He stopped in the guise of tying his shoes.

"Is that you, Trent?" he asked without ever looking in that direction.

"Yes. McKay sent me from the back. He has Pup."

The young agent had no idea what his words did to Nick's heart. For a moment he couldn't breathe. He could still see Camille's stricken face and wanted to weep with relief for all of them.

"Thank you, Trent."

A moment later, Carlyle was beside them. He reached into the buggy and, as planned, brought out a slim briefcase. Nick finished with his shoe and spoke, his lips barely moving as they walked toward the house.

"McKay has Pup," he told his closest agent. "Nothing will stop us now, Carlyle. We've got this man dead to rights."

The moment he was close enough, McKay took this special woman back in his arms. They were both going to be covered with scratches, but neither cared. Wanting to see the real Pup, McKay pulled the wig from her head and stared at her for a full minute. He had almost lost her. She was so much a part of him now, and he had almost lost her. Emotions threatened to overwhelm him.

It was not the moment McKay would have chosen for such a thing, but before anything else could happen, he kissed her. Still holding her close with one arm, his free hand cupping the back of her head, he kissed her full on the mouth.

"Please do that again," she whispered the moment they broke apart. McKay was happy to oblige.

"I was so scared," she repeated. "I didn't think I was going to make it."

"It's over now. You never have to go in there again."

"Duncan will be furious when he realizes what he's done."

"What's that?"

"Paine must have come to see him."

"That was the plan," McKay told her.

"Duncan was questioning me, but he was so irritated that he left the door to my room unlocked and unguarded. I simply let myself out."

After that she couldn't talk any more. She laid her head on McKay's shoulder, wishing more than anything that she could just go to sleep.

Carlyle introduced his workers to Mr. Phipps, his eyes watchful. They had been outside only a short time, but anything could have happened. His concerns were groundless. Still certain he knew more, Duncan smiled hugely as he showed them to the filing cabinets in the corner.

Carlyle started on one, but Kelsey took a little longer. He had two guns on him, and he wanted to be in a position to stop Phipps if he tried to leave. Nick made no attempt at pretense. He immediately began an inspection of the wall Pup had described. It could be a lost lead. After all, if they'd caught Pup because of this secret door, the files might have been moved; Nick could only hope that they felt too secure for this.

Duncan took a seat at his desk. He realized almost instantly that Paine was in front of his feet, and in his present mood, took perverse pleasure in giving him a hard kick. He tried to ignore the treasury men and work on his papers, but Nick caught his eye.

"The files are over there," Duncan directed him.

Nick ignored him.

"You there, by the wall. The files are over there."

Nick looked at him for a moment but went back to his inspection. He'd found the outline of the door but had no clue as to how to get in.

"Did you not hear me?" Duncan began, but then cut off. Nelson had come through the door, gone right to the desk, and whispered something into his ear. The banker's face flushed a furious red. He stood and cleared his throat, trying to maintain his calm.

"I know you gentlemen will want to get on with your work, so I'll just leave my assistant, Mr. Case, to answer any questions you might have."

"We'd rather you stay here." Kelsey had stepped forward now, his gun pulled. "You too, Mr. Case. Both of you gentlemen can take a seat over here."

"This is an outrage!" Duncan began, but closed his mouth when Kelsey leveled the gun in his direction. He sat on the leather davenport, Nelson beside him, and tried to contain his fury. It didn't work. Seconds later he had to lash out.

"Get out here, Paine—you sniveling little coward!"

Carlyle gave up his act at the filing cabinets, pulled his own gun, and turned to see Paine climb from beneath the desk. The clerk's hands went into the air as soon as he saw the weapons. Kelsey motioned him to join his uncle on the sofa, and he did so without speaking. For a long moment the occupants of the couch watched Nick's fingers on the wall. Carlyle knew what he was after but opted to stay out of the way.

A few minutes later, Nick slammed his hand against the paneled wall. His fierce gaze swept the room before he took a gun from under his own coat. Certain that by now his men had secured the entire mansion, he nevertheless moved carefully to the entry hall and out the front door. It was busy out there, agents and mansion employees everywhere, but he spotted Trent almost immediately and motioned him over.

"Find McKay. Tell him I need Pup. He's to stay with her at all times."

"Yes, sir."

Nick paced until Pup came into view, McKay beside her. He took in her appearance—white face, scratches on her arms, and her dress looking like she'd slept in it. Her wig was in place, but the blonde hair made her look even more pale.

"You need me?" she asked before he could speak, telling him that she was all right.

He nodded. "For just one thing. Did you get into that wall?"

"Yes. I'll show you."

Pup led the way indoors, Nick and McKay on her heels. She didn't even look at the men in the room but went straight to the panel. Not five seconds later she had pulled the strip down, and the door creaked open. Carlyle lit a lantern that Nick held high. The head treasury man allowed Pup to step in ahead of him; this was her moment as much as his. Carlyle followed. Not only were there file cabinets, but just past them a stairway led up to what must have been the attic. Pup had been right on both accounts. Nick didn't need to see any more. He was happy to leave Carlyle to the inspection. He returned to the room, Pup with him.

"Well, gentlemen, it is our belief that you have a lot to answer for."

Duncan's mutinous expression told Nick they'd hit gold, but he also knew the crooked banker would deny all involvement to his dying day. No matter. Nick knew they had enough to convict.

A bustle of activity followed in the next few minutes, and then Pup stood before Nick just outside the wide front door. He stared down at her, unable to speak. A moment later he hugged her. Pup's eyes closed with comfort. She hadn't known if she would ever see him again.

"I'm headed to your house now," she told him when she could speak. "I've asked McKay to take me."

"Good. Camie's pretty upset, so steel yourself."

Pup could only nod. McKay stood waiting nearby. She began to turn away, but Nick's voice stopped her.

"Thank you."

Pup smiled. "You're welcome. Duncan knows who I am. It's the only reason I wasn't tortured for information. Finding out that I was Jubal's sister stopped him in his tracks."

"I can see how it would. Jubal has worked for him for so many years. Duncan must have been asking himself if Jubal had been playing him all along."

"He mentioned that one of his associates and a worker didn't show up last night. Was it Jubal?"

"Yes. He's behind bars." Nick watched her. "You can see him, Pup. I will arrange it."

"I'm not up to it today, but I'll bank on that. I'll see you at the house tonight. I'm too tired to clean out the apartment right now, Nick. Can it wait?"

"I'll see that it's done and get your things back to you."

"Don't miss my Bible—I need that."

"Of course. I'll see you tonight at the house, and I'll have your things."

Having heard every word, McKay stepped forward then and gently took her arm. They were silent as they made their way to the street. A buggy was on hand, and McKay asked the driver to take them to the Wallaces' house. Pup began to feel numb and passed the next minutes in something of a blur. First she was in the buggy, McKay beside her, and then she was leading the way into the Wallaces' kitchen, whereupon McKay ceremoniously removed her wig for the last time.

At first she didn't move; she was too tired. Miranda, thinking she had heard the door, came through from the dining room and stopped short. She didn't speak but put a hand to her heart and went right back out. A moment later Camille walked hesitantly into the room. Clearly she had been crying for hours, and even now tears welled in her eyes. The two women came together, and McKay stood aside while Camille held Pup and sobbed.

"I just can't . . ." Camille tried to speak, but was too overcome. "I'm sorry. I was just so afraid."

"It's all right now," Pup told her. "It's over. Nick is safe. Duncan Phipps has been taken to jail. I'll be here the rest of the day."

Camille let go of her to reach for a hankie, and Pup turned to McKay.

He was the first to speak. "Are you going to be all right?"

"I think so. I'm tired."

"I've got to get back to the house, but I'll be back. You'll be here?"

"If you're coming back, I'll be here."

McKay smiled. He stroked her cheek with the back of his fingers before capturing her jaw to kiss her ever so softly. He then handed her the wig.

"Don't be wearing this when I come back." He reached toward her again.

"All right." She would have agreed to anything while he was touching the black curls at her temple, his eyes alight with love. Pup turned as he slipped back out the door, knowing that he had to go but needing to see as much of him as possible. She then turned back to the room. Both women had been watching them unashamedly. A moment later the three of them were in tears again.

41

Camille sat very still at the side of Pup's bed. Pup was already asleep, and she herself was tired to the bone. Yet something compelled her to remain close to the girl. It was just too much of a miracle that she was alive. You couldn't live with Nick Wallace and not understand what type of man Duncan Phipps was. Camille had been certain Pup had been discovered and killed, and then she'd walked in to find her standing in the kitchen.

Miranda had come to the living room where Camille had been trying to stay busy arranging flowers and writing letters, and with just two words had brought her back to life. "She's here." Camille knew she would never forget it.

Nothing has ever made me want to believe in You, God, Camille now prayed, *but this does. You brought her back to me. I know You did. Even if she marries McKay Harrington and I won't see as much of her anymore, I don't care. She's the daughter I never had, and You brought her back to me. She trusts in You so much. She reads Your Bible, and has found peace—a peace I've never really known.*

Camille bit her lip. She had never admitted this to anyone. What would Nick say? He'd be totally crushed if he thought she wasn't happily married to him. Could she even explain? Could she ever make him see that it wasn't about him or their marriage but about what went on inside of her?

As she had been through the night and during the day, Camille was once again overcome by emotion. She sat by Pup's bed and cried, silent tears pouring down her face. She tried to stop; all the tears had already given her a headache, but it was no use. Afraid she would wake Pup, she walked to her own bedroom. It felt good to slip out of her dress and lie on the bed: She'd spent so little time in it the night before.

Tired as she was, sleep never came. Her eyes felt weighted, but it was no use trying to sleep when Nick wasn't in the bed with her. She'd always had a hard time sleeping without him. But today *he* wasn't on her mind. Pup was—Pup and her relationship to God. The older woman knew she could ask her about it, but the answer might be a fearful thing. What if Pup told her that it wasn't for everyone? Camille didn't want to think that way, but the idea persisted. *Why does Pup have such assurance while still a young woman, while I, who am old enough to be a grandmother, am still searching?*

She rose and dressed just an hour later, not feeling refreshed, but knowing she needed to be available for Pup when she came downstairs. Her mind shifted to Nick as she took the stairs, and she remembered again with relief that he was all right. She sighed a tired little sigh. She would sleep tonight. Nick would be in the bed with her, and Pup would be down the hall. She just needed to get through the day.

McKay felt as if the paperwork would never come to an end, but still he kept on. Reports had to be filed. His every action on the job this morning, as well as in Longmont, had to be recorded. It was tiring. Finally he finished and he felt his spirits lift as the Wallace home came into view. *She* was inside, and he was going to see her. He knocked on the front door, his heart beating a little faster as he waited. Miranda answered.

"Well, Mr. Harrington." She never seemed to forget names. "Come right in."

"Thank you. Is Callie up to a visitor?"

"I'll ask her."

McKay's heart did erratic things when Miranda came back to take him to the study. He stepped to the doorway and found Pup sitting inside on the sofa, a book in her lap. She didn't have her dark wig in place, but she was still in a dress, and even with the short hair, she looked very feminine. She had never looked like a man to him, but now her dress of dark blue with white cuffs and collar only added to the attraction. McKay was so taken with her that he almost forgot to thank the Wallaces' housekeeper before making his way across the room. Pup watched him approach.

"Hi," he spoke quietly when he'd seated himself beside her.

"Hi, yourself."

"You look as though you feel better."

"I slept and ate."

For a time they just looked at each other.

"Did they need you back at the mansion?"

"No. I ended up at the office working on piles of paperwork."

"Did you get done?"

"Yes."

Words died out. They were content just to be near each other. McKay had picked up her hand, and Pup loved it when he wove their fingers together. It helped her forget a little bit of the fear she had known just that morning. Had it really been only a few hours ago? So much had happened. It was hard to believe it was over, and for Pup it was over in more ways than one.

"I can't do this anymore, McKay," she said quietly, her eyes looking across the room. He watched her profile. "I can't keep this up."

Those words were music to McKay's ears, but the discussion couldn't end there.

"Can you tell me why?" he asked.

She turned her head. "I can't handle the deceit. It has really bothered me these last few days. People are fooled so easily by what I do. Shouldn't I be more concerned for their souls than I am with making sure I get past them or pull the wool over their eyes?" He had never heard her so passionate.

"So you think all undercover work is wrong?"

"No." She was sure about that. "But it is wrong for me. It's impossible to be playing a role and still tell someone about Christ, because I can't get that personal. And I don't like that. It doesn't feel right. I was glad to help Nick with this case, but I can't even stay and fellowship with my church family without getting called out on a job. And when I think of the people I've deceived—not crooks like Duncan Phipps—but innocent people like Mrs. Meyer and others at the mansion, I feel sick. I just can't do it anymore, McKay. I just can't."

"All right." He dropped her hand and put an arm around her.

She was still upset. "I care what you think, McKay. Tell me if I'm wrong."

"You're not wrong, because obviously the Lord is leading you. I can see how it would bother you, especially not being able to get close to people, but your type of job is also very special. Your talent allows the law to pull criminals from the street. That's one of the reasons I stay involved. I believe in our system. It's not without its problems, but Phipps is now behind bars. Think of the people who will be spared his manipulations because of that."

Pup laid her head on his shoulder. McKay kissed the top of her head.

"Somehow I thought you would be more enthusiastic."

McKay immediately shifted so he could look down into her face.

"You misunderstand me." His eyes were warm, almost smiling, and his voice low. "I'm all for your leaving this job.

My plans for us do not include your moving about the countryside in various disguises."

Pup smiled. "What do they include?"

"First of all, getting to know each other very, very well. Time with you and your church family. More time with you in Longmont with my parents and church family. Time to talk, plan, and dream a little."

Pup stared at him. "To what end, McKay?"

It was McKay's turn to smile; he loved it when she was direct. "If you haven't figured out that I'm in love with you, you're not half as bright as I've given you credit for being."

"I know when it happened for me," she told him, her voice full of wonder. "It was the night you picked up an old man in the alley and dusted him off. I knew that if I looked forever, I'd never find another man in all the world who was like you."

McKay kissed her. He didn't even try to fight the emotions surging through him. He loved this woman and wanted to kiss her. For right now that was all he needed.

"You look tired," Pup said after a while.

"I am tired, and I know Nick is going to come home just as tired, so I'm going to take off. What are your plans for the next few days?"

"Tomorrow I want to see Jubal. I wish you could be there with me, but I know you're working."

"I can ask."

"Okay. Did you bring him in?"

"Yes. I'm sorry. I wish it could be different for you."

"Do you remember that day we stood over Govern's new grave, the day you left my cabin? I told you then, McKay, and I'm telling you now—he made his choices. I didn't have a chance to tell Govern about Christ, and you can believe that I'll tell Jubal, but it's still the same. He's got to make his own choices."

McKay put his forehead against hers and kept his eyes closed. She was so special. He had shot one brother and arrested another, but there was no anger in her. *Choices.* She had used that word with him several times. McKay realized that she had made her choice as well—a good choice.

"Are you really going to ask if you can go with me tomorrow?" Her voice broke into his thoughts.

He opened his eyes. "Yes. I'll let you know if it's going to work. And now I'd better get going."

"All right."

He tried to rise, but Pup held onto his shirt.

"If you can't go with me tomorrow, when will I see you?"

McKay's heart melted. He had never seen her like this.

"Either way I'll come here tomorrow night at seven o'clock and we'll go out for dinner and spend the whole evening together. I've got something special in mind."

Pup bit her lip and wanted to cry.

"I'd better go." He could see she was feeling teary and thought she might need some time alone. Either that, or he might end up staying longer than was wise.

He kissed her gently and made himself walk from the room. It wasn't his choice to leave her, but something told him that Nick would not want to come home and find the two of them talking in his study. At some point his relationship with Pup was going to have to come to the surface, but not today. Today had been full enough.

"This meat is delicious," Camille told Miranda that evening.

"It was a good cut," she said modestly, as she put a bowl of fresh potatoes at Nick's elbow.

"Thank you," Nick spoke to the housekeeper, and then looked back to Pup. "Did you decide if you wanted to see Jubal?"

"Yes, I would like to. I asked McKay if he could take me tomorrow, and he said he'd have to ask."

It was slight, but Pup caught it. Nick's movements paused for little more than a second before he went back to eating. Pup was no fool. She had not pressed McKay, but she knew very well that it had been more than fatigue that had sent him from her side before Nick came home.

"Is there some problem, Nick?" As usual she came straight to the point.

The man stared back at her.

"I mentioned McKay, and you looked uncomfortable. Is there something you want to say or something I should know?"

"I'm just not sure you know what you're doing."

"With McKay?"

"Yes."

"You'll have to be more specific, Nick."

"I just don't want you to get hurt," he said, a frown between his eyes. "Romance and the treasury department don't mix."

"What if I wasn't with the treasury department anymore?"

"Don't be ridiculous! Of course you'll be with the treasury department." And that was the end of that. Nick was not in the mood to be reasonable about the matter, and Pup felt it useless to argue with the man. The last thing she wanted to do was part on a bad note. She went back to her food, but not before glancing at Camille. Mrs. Wallace was looking right back, her eyes telling Pup she was on her side.

"What is it that makes you so unreasonable about the matter?"

Nick looked over at his wife. She usually didn't wake as early as he did, but something told him she'd been lying there awake for some time.

"I just don't want her hurt."

"Then you haven't seen McKay's face when he looks at her. How could you possibly deny her that kind of happiness?"

"She's happy now. I'm not denying her a thing." He turned away to tie his tie, and for a moment Camille was silent.

"I can still see you," she began softly, Nick's back still to her. "You came in the front door of my parents' home, and I thought I would die. You were the most handsome man I'd ever seen. And the way you looked at me . . ." She sighed. "I blushed for a week."

Nick had turned to look at her now, but her eyes were still on a distant spot.

"I can still see it as though it were yesterday." She now looked at Nick. "I know that nothing would have been the same without you, and up to now I thought it was the same for you."

"It is the same for me; you know that, Camie."

"Then you can't tell me she's happy and should just settle for her job. She's met McKay, and now her heart wants more."

Nick's eyes closed in agony. "She's like a daughter to me, Camille. Can't you see that?"

"Of course I can. Don't you think it's the same for me, Nick? I think we've been with Callie more than if she had been our daughter. A daughter might have moved hundreds of miles away; we have Callie off and on all through the year."

She thought she'd gotten through to him, but a moment passed and the shutters dropped over Nick's pain-filled eyes again. He came to the side of the bed.

"Tell Pup that someone will be here to take her to the jail this afternoon, probably between one and two." He bent and kissed his wife, his touch as gentle as always. He stood to full height then. Although his eyes were on Camille, they weren't really seeing her.

"He can't have her."

Nick probably wasn't aware of having said the words aloud, but they were out and Camille's heart clenched in pain. A moment later he left without remembering to tell her goodbye.

42

Pup lay on her side in bed, her Bible open to Ephesians 2:10. The verses leading up to this passage had spoken of salvation and God's grace, and Pup had read them while still at home. But she didn't remember seeing verse ten before.

For we are his workmanship, created in Christ Jesus unto good works, which God hath before ordained that we should walk in them.

"Your workmanship, Lord. That makes me feel so special and loved," she prayed softly. "And Your plan. All along You had something You wanted me to do. *Before ordained that I should walk in them.* I love that. I want to walk in the plan You have for me. Please help me to be certain about this job. Nick thinks my thoughts about leaving are because of McKay, but they're not. Help me to make him see."

The door opened, and Camille put her head in.

"Have breakfast with me?"

"Can you give me about ten minutes?"

"Certainly. Miranda is going to want to know what you're hungry for."

Pup thought for a moment. "I haven't had that hot cereal she makes for ages—you know, the one with the raisins."

Camille smiled. "I'll see what I can do."

Upon Camille's departure, Pup got out of bed and started to dress. She didn't move very fast, and it struck her, not for the first time, that when she wore a wig, there wasn't much she had to do with herself. Nick had brought her things, the dark wig among them, from the apartment the night before, and she was now able to be more comfortable in a dress. It wasn't a problem with McKay or the members of this household, but should so much as a messenger boy come to the door, a woman with hair almost as short as a man's would certainly draw attention.

It was a given that she would wear the wig tonight, but what dress? Pup stood at the wardrobe and pondered the matter. She'd had the navy on when McKay came yesterday. Maybe she should wear that one again.

"Are you coming?" Camille was at the door again, and Pup knew she'd been dawdling.

"Yes. I was just thinking about tonight."

"You're not headed home, are you?"

"No, McKay is taking me to dinner, and I'm wondering what to wear."

The women took the stairs, walking side by side.

"You've fallen rather quiet," Pup commented when they reached the landing.

"I was just wondering if the reason you didn't mention your plans to go out tonight had to do with Nick."

"Yes. He's upset enough already."

"I know he is, Callie, and I feel for him, but you can't live your life around Nick's wishes. You'll just have to tell him that you love McKay more than you love the job."

They both took seats at the dining room table. Miranda had already put the food on and the women began to eat.

"I guess that's the problem, Camille. This is not really about McKay, and I just don't think Nick will understand."

Camille could have told her that *she* didn't understand but made herself stay quiet. If this wasn't about McKay, then what or whom?

"It seems to me that Nick sees McKay as the problem," Pup's hostess said slowly. "Why don't you think he'll be pleased to hear the real reason?"

"First of all, I don't think he'll be pleased because even though it's not about McKay, I'm still leaving the treasury. My biggest fear is that he'll think *I* think I'm better than everyone else."

"Why would he think that?"

"Because of my beliefs. I need to leave this life of undercover work because I think it's wrong for me to keep up this constant false front. Before the Lord I can't do it anymore. You've always listened to me, Camille, so I feel free to share with you, but when I asked Nick for my Bible, he got a strange look on his face."

Camille sighed. "That's certainly the truth. Just yesterday I was thinking about how crushed Nick would be if he knew I yearned for spiritual things. He prides himself in being a fine provider, and he is, so I think he'll take it personally if I ever tell him I want more."

"I didn't know that, Camille," Pup said quietly.

The older woman looked down at her food. "The first time you talked to me, I didn't know if I agreed with you or not, but when you went away there was a hole inside, a hole that has been there all along—one I've never known how to fill." She shrugged uncomfortably. "I don't know. Maybe what you have isn't for everyone."

Pup had to think on that. She had never considered that some might not be included in God's plan to save souls. It didn't make sense to her.

"I think you should keep searching, Camille," she told her friend sincerely. "I mean, there are so many verses that say Christ died for the whole world. That sounds to me as if He means everyone."

"I have so many fears," the older woman admitted, and Pup's heart broke when she saw the tears in her eyes. "What if I can't do it, Callie, what if God asks more from me than I can give?"

Pup bit her lip. "I wish I knew more," she said fervently. "I wish I had all the answers for you." She paused, her mind racing. "I think you might need to ask yourself one question, Camille."

"What's that?"

"Could my coming to God make me more empty or miserable than I am now?"

It was Camille's undoing. She covered her face with her hands and sobbed. Pup rose and immediately went to her side. She put her arms around her and simply held her while she cried. Miranda came in with coffee, her concerned eyes intent on her friend and employer, but she left without speaking. When Camille seemed to be in control again, Pup pulled a chair close.

"Do you have a Bible?"

"Yes," Camille whispered.

"Read it, Camille. It's all in there. Everything you need to know is there. I refuse to believe that God would hide from anyone; He's too loving for that. If you seek after Him, you'll find Him. In fact, I think these feelings of wanting to know Him are *from* Him. Does that make sense?"

Camille nodded. She felt a headache starting, but her heart was lighter. She didn't have to be left out. She could search like anyone else.

"Thank you, Callie."

"I don't feel I did much."

"You did quite a bit."

They went back to their food and continued to talk through several cups of coffee, Camille wanting to know what Pup was going to say to Nick. Pup had to admit that she wasn't too sure. The older woman also had to know if Pup was ready to go to the jail. Pup responded that she'd have to be since she'd made up her mind to see her brother. She just hoped that McKay could be with her.

"I'm still confused about one thing," Camille remarked. "If McKay's not a main part of the picture right now, why do you want him at the jail, and why are the two of you going out tonight?"

Pup blinked. "I didn't explain myself very well. McKay is very much a part of the picture. I'm in love with him, but whether or not we'd ever met, I'd still be leaving the treasury."

"So McKay hasn't pressed you to do this?"

"No."

Camille's brows rose. "I don't think Nick knows that."

"No, he probably doesn't. He was in no mood to be reasonable last night, so I couldn't tell him."

They ran out of words then, both busy with their emotions and thoughts. They thanked Miranda for the meal when she came to check on them, and then the women went off in various pursuits: Pup to pray about seeing Jubal and confronting Nick, and Camille to find the family Bible. She had some reading to do.

The Denver courthouse and jail was not a cold structure, but Pup felt a chill go over her. It wasn't the dark brick of the building or the bars on the windows; it was the fact that men chose to come to this place. They would never see it that way, but it was still true. Choices were made and consequences were often paid within these walls.

This was strongly on Pup's mind as she and Nick made their way inside. That he was a familiar figure was obvious from the greeting he received from several men. Both Nick and Pup had to sign in, but it wasn't long before they were shown to a doorway and led inside. Nick had a few words with the guard escorting them, and a moment later the guard left them alone, closing the portal in his wake.

The hallway was dim. Pup had feared that she would have to walk down between rows of cells, but instead she was taken to a section with roomlike enclosures. The walls between the cells were solid, sporting bars only on the front. After they had entered, Nick told her which cell it was and that there was no one else there, but she still felt frightened. However, she was pleased that Nick hung back, allowing her to step before Jubal's cell alone. She did so now, the light from a high window coming full on her face.

"Pup?" her brother's voice came to her, and he rose from a solitary bunk. "Is that you?"

"Hi, Jubal," she said softly, watching as he came to the bars. For a moment they just stared at each other, the years falling away. To Pup's mind he didn't look tough at all, not like she was expecting. Jubal thought Pup looked just like Govern and Papa.

"How did you know I was here?"

"A friend told me. Are you all right?"

Jubal looked away. He'd never been caught before. He'd never spent even one night in jail, and now it looked like he'd be spending the rest of his nights in jail. He finally looked back at her.

"Is it true about Govern, Pup? Did he die at the cabin?"

"Yeah," tears filled her eyes. "I buried him next to Mama and Papa."

Jubal had to look away again.

"Do you ever ask yourself how you and Govern got to this place, Jubal? Do you ever think about that?"

He shrugged. "Only if I think of Mama. I'm just glad she can't see me now." He looked at his sister. "Were you with her when she died, Pup?"

"Yes. She got sick and wouldn't go down to see the doctor. I was afraid to leave her. She died one night in her sleep."

They looked at each other again.

"I went back to the cabin once, but you weren't around."

"When was that?"

"'Bout five years back I guess."

Pup nodded; she could have been anywhere.

"I need you to know something, Jubal. I'm on the other side of the law from you. The man who brought you in is the friend who told me you were here. He's very special to me."

To her infinite relief, he only nodded. "Harrington's all right. He was just doing his job. He doesn't rough a man up when his hands are cuffed behind his back."

"You're right; he would never do that."

"So you're living here in Denver now—with him?"

"No, it's not like that. I don't live with any man. I'm still at the cabin."

Jubal looked her up and down, not able to miss the fine cut of her dress. "You look good."

"Thank you."

"Did you and Govern talk before he died?"

"Not really. He was angry and wanted money." Even if Jubal never wanted to hear from her again, she had to lay the truth between them. "Do you know who shot him?"

"I heard it was Harrington."

"It was."

"And that doesn't bother you?" His voice was surprisingly mild.

"Of course it bothers me. It would bother me no matter who it was. McKay nearly died from the wounds Govern inflicted. That bothers me, too." She knew she had to be blunt. "There was no talking to Govern, Jubal, and you know that. He shot first. It was a mess."

They fell silent for a time. Pup couldn't tell if he wanted her to leave or not. She remembered the basket in her hands.

"I brought you some cookies and a small loaf of bread." She pushed the basket toward the bars which separated them. Jubal took it.

"You make these?"

"No, I'm an awful cook. Camille Wallace made them." She again forced herself to be brutally honest.

"Camille Wallace," Jubal said the name slowly, "as in the wife of Nick Wallace, head of the treasury?"

"Yes. I stay at their house when I'm in Denver."

Jubal's whistle was whisper soft. "You *are* on the other side of the law."

Pup nodded, regret filling her. Not regret that she'd chosen the right path, but that, standing here now, she believed with all her heart that Jubal could have done anything, been anything, but he'd chosen crime.

"I've been learning some new things lately, Jubal. I'd like to share them with you, but I'm not going to be in town much longer."

He nodded, his eyes still on hers.

"Will they allow you mail in here?"

"I think so."

"If I write to you, will you read my letters and write back?"

"Yeah." He seemed surprised that she would want to keep in touch. "I'll write back to you."

It was more than she could have hoped for.

"When's your trial?"

"I don't know. Do you know what I'm up for?"

"Yes, do you?"

"They told me yesterday." His voice couldn't hide his fear. They had everything on him. They knew about every dirty deed he'd done for Duncan Phipps.

Pup had to get away. The list of his crimes was a mile long. She was going to come undone if she stayed.

"I'm not sure when I'll be back, but when I am, I'll come to see you."

"All right."

"And I'll be here for your trial."

All he could do was nod.

Her heart felt as if it would break. She put a hand on the bars to steady herself. She spoke with tears in her eyes. "If you ever get out of this place, Jubal Hackett, you come to me," she whispered furiously. "You come to me, do you hear? We should never have gotten this far apart."

Jubal covered her fingers with his hand, tears filling his own eyes.

"I love you, Jubal." She barely got the words out, her hand turning to clasp his tightly. Just an instant later she turned and fled down the hall, harsh sobs breaking in her throat. Nick met her halfway, his arm going around her as he led her outside.

As soon as the door shut she turned into his arms and cried. Nick held her for a few minutes before they began to maneuver their way out of the building. Once out front, he gently helped her into his buggy. It wasn't long before they were back at the house, but part of Pup wondered why she'd bothered to leave: She saw nothing but Jubal's face for the rest of the afternoon.

43

Nick came home in a great mood. The hidden files at the Phipps mansion had turned up a wealth of incriminating evidence; a good case was being put together. Duncan had hired Miles Jefferson, the best lawyer in the territory, but Nick wasn't worried. No jury could fail to see this man for what he was and send him to jail—hopefully, for a very long time.

Richard Stuart's arrest had paid off, just as McKay had speculated. He was already offering valuable information in exchange for a lighter sentence, and because of his no-record status and his standing in his hometown, he was soon to be released. As it was, Nick nearly skipped through the door that night, his heart lighter than it had been in months.

The kitchen was empty but smelled of a promising meal to come. Mr. Wallace made his way through the dining room and headed toward the stairs. He stopped short when he saw Pup coming down.

"Well, now," his voice was as joyful as he felt, "what's the occasion?"

Pup smiled. She had let Camille style her wig and was wearing a dress that she had picked out for her. The older woman had not liked the fact that she'd worn the navy just the day before, so she put the dark rose on. It was more feminine than her other gowns, and Camille had insisted it was just what she needed for the now-softer curls in her wig.

"I happen to be going out tonight."

Nick smiled hugely. "I suppose I'll be expected to pay."

"Not in the least," Camille spoke as she came down behind Pup. "McKay should be here in less than an hour, and I can tell you right now that you and I are not invited to join them."

All joy left Nick's face. Pup looked at him in compassion, but she was not going to spare him.

"A message was delivered after you dropped me off. It was from McKay. He said he'd been kept busy all day and would see me tonight. I find it hard to believe you would stoop to such tactics, Nick, but I know that's what you did. You knew I wanted McKay there with me when I saw Jubal."

His eyes drilled into hers, but she did not back down. She kept her voice kind but resolute.

"We have to talk, Nick. Obviously not tonight, but soon." She turned to Camille. "Do the two of you have plans for tomorrow night?"

"No, I'm sure not."

Pup looked back at the man who had been the closest thing to a father to her for more years than she could count.

"If McKay wants to see me tomorrow night, I'll tell him I'm busy. Please, Nick. You and I have to talk. I'm probably going home first thing Saturday morning. Please don't send me away with this unresolved."

There was nothing else she could say. This home had been a haven for her. She felt loved and comforted within these walls, but if things remained so tense with Nick, she would feel unwelcome for the first time.

"Nick?" his wife now urged him gently.

"All right, Pup." His voice was hard. "I'll plan to be here tomorrow night, but I have some things to say to you—things you might not want to hear. I think this man's attentions have turned your head. You're thinking with your heart. Are you willing to hear how I feel about the matter?"

"Yes. Just so long as we're able to talk."

Turning away, he retreated into his study and shut the door.

"Will this ruin your evening?" Camille wished to know.

"No, but I'm a little worried about you, Camille. You have to live with Nick after I'm gone. If he feels we've ganged up on him over this, he's going to resent you."

Camille smiled. "You wouldn't believe the things we've fought about over the years, my dear. Nick never holds a grudge against me. Even if he thinks I'm wrong, he never mentions that subject again."

"You're sure?"

"Absolutely. Now, you go into the living room and wait. I'll let McKay in and bring him to you."

Pup's look was indulgent.

"Don't you give me that look. It's all part of the fun. You just go."

Pup did as she was told, but not before shaking her head. Camille watched her go and even caught the little trip she made on the carpet. It was her turn to shake her head. It was a good thing McKay was already in love with her; otherwise, he might be scared to death.

For the next few minutes she worried about the food Pup might get on that rose gown, but then came a knock on the door. It wasn't quite time, but Camille only smiled. The gentleman was anxious.

"Good evening," McKay said as soon as he saw Mrs. Wallace.

"Hello, McKay."

"I'm early; is that going to be all right?"

"Of course. Callie's all ready and waiting for you in the living room."

Camille had been brought up to think that it was more romantic to keep a man waiting, but she saw now that those were childish games. This couple didn't need those ploys to add interest to their relationship. No indeed. The interest was so apparent you could almost feel it.

"Come this way," she offered, showing him to the living room. She made herself stay back away from the entrance. Hearing the couple greet each other, she went to the kitchen to report to Miranda.

"You look nice," McKay said as soon as he could think straight again. He'd never seen her in this color, and her hairstyle softened her face.

"You're early—you must be hungry."

McKay smiled. "Hungry," he repeated. "If that reason works for you, we'll go with it."

Pup laughed. "I'm ready when you are."

"Good. Our reservation is for 7:15, so we'll just ask the driver to go slowly."

Pup smiled at him, her heart burgeoning with love. She slipped past him to tell Miranda she was leaving and found Camille too.

"Have a good time," they both bid her and beamed at her as she passed through the door.

McKay was waiting just inside the front door, and he watched her carefully as they moved outside. As soon as his hat was in place, he pulled her hand through his arm and walked her to the waiting hack. Pup kept looking at him, and in so doing tripped just a little on the front walk. McKay welcomed an excuse to slip an arm around her waist.

A moment later he had her in the buggy, his hand holding hers as the driver took them down the street. They had eyes only for each other. Neither one was aware of the man who stood at the window of his study, his brow lowered disapprovingly as he watched them leave.

"I thought about you so much today." They were at the River House, one of Denver's finest restaurants, their meal ordered. "Did you get to see Jubal?"

"Yes."

"How was it?"

"Hard. But I'm so thankful, McKay. He talked to me. I wasn't sure if he would want anything to do with me, but he talked. I was very honest—he even knows about you—but he was still willing to correspond with me. I told him I would be at his trial."

"I can probably get those dates for you."

As was becoming the custom between them, they fell silent. There was so much to say, but there was also no hurry. For the first time since they'd known each other, nothing hung over their heads. There was no fear that Pup would suddenly have to garb herself in a new identity and be off. During their silence the food arrived, and after McKay held her hand and thanked God for the food, they resumed their conversation.

"How is your meal?" McKay asked.

"Wonderful. Taste these potatoes. Is that a cheese sauce?"

"I think so. It's excellent. I didn't see Nick when I came. Was he there tonight?"

"Yes. He had taken himself off to the study. He's agreed to talk with me tomorrow night, but he is not happy about tonight."

"What did he say?"

"Only that he had some things to say that I wasn't going to like."

"You've upset his world," McKay told her. "I can't see him lashing out in anger, but this really has him bothered."

"At least Camille sees things the way they are. We had the most wonderful conversation this morning. She has such a heart for spiritual things. I wish I knew more."

"I'm sure you did fine."

Pup made a face. "I don't know. Christ died for all of us, didn't He, McKay?"

"Yes, He did. First John 2:2 says 'He is the propitiation for our sins, and not for ours only, but also for the sins of the whole world.' And I could show you many more verses on the subject."

Pup nodded with satisfaction and went back to her food.

"Watch your knife," he said softly as he moved her water out of harm's way.

Pup smiled at him and gave a huge sigh when McKay winked at her. He was the most wonderful man she'd ever known.

They ended the evening with a walk in the park near Camden Street. McKay held her hand as before, but this time she would not be headed back to the Phipps mansion. This time there was no worry of being seen together. Both of them were aware of this, and the excitement of being together escalated. They didn't have much silence as they walked; their conversation roamed from one topic to the next. Pup had many questions about Scripture passages she had read, and, in truth, McKay didn't know every answer.

"Why don't you come to church with me Sunday morning? I know my pastor here in Denver, Adair MacKinnon, would be happy to talk with you."

"I would if I were going to be here, McKay, but I was planning on leaving for Boulder Saturday morning."

McKay brought her to a halt. He hadn't been expecting this news. "I understand your need to go home, but I can't help but wonder how we're going to get to know each other if we're not together."

"I've wondered that myself. Did you think I was going to move here, McKay?"

"It's crossed my mind. What do you think?"

"I'm not sure right now. The chance to see you every day would be wonderful, but I'm just not sure if I'm supposed to do that." She gave a small laugh that ended in something that sounded much like a sob. "I can't believe I just said that. You've given me an open invitation to join you here, see you, and be with you all week long, and I tell you I have to think about it."

"It's all right," he said gently. "I know you want to be with me as much as I want to be with you, but the details just haven't been worked out yet."

"It's my fault."

"Why is that?"

"I haven't been praying about it. With everything else, it hasn't even been on my mind. How can God bring us together if we don't ask?"

McKay laughed. "So you think God can't work unless we tell Him what to do?"

Pup opened her mouth to argue but realized that was exactly what she'd said. She laughed as well.

"I think I'm a little too used to having my way," she admitted.

"Be that as it may, as long as you pray wanting God's will over your own you can ask for anything, even thanking Him ahead of time whether His answer is yes or no."

Her chest lifted on a huge sigh. "I think you're wonderful."

McKay pressed his lips to her brow. "I love you, Callie Jennings."

"I love you, McKay." She smiled suddenly. "Jubal called me Pup today. After all these years, he still thinks of me as Pup."

"That name must hold warm memories for him, and right now you're the best thing that's ever happened to him. If he's half as smart as his sister, he'll have figured that out already."

"Thank you, McKay. I wish I could see you tomorrow."

"Maybe I can check with you in the afternoon about your plans to go home."

She was silent for a moment and then admitted, "I hope things go well with Nick, but even if they don't I'm catching an early train home Saturday morning."

"All right." He accepted her decision with equanimity. "What time should I come by to get you to the station?"

Pup could have hugged him. Instead she gave him the time and thanked him with a kiss to the cheek. After that it was time to head back. They walked the blocks to the Wallaces' home, and McKay saw her to the door. He kissed her gently goodbye and told her he'd see her no later than Saturday morning.

Pup made her way inside. It wasn't too late, but she still tried to be as quiet as possible—completely unaware that Nick was still in his study waiting for her return and that Camille wouldn't be sleeping because Nick wasn't in bed. The head of the regional treasury department waited just a few minutes for her to go upstairs. Finally able to seek his rest, he followed her.

McKay knew he had to work in the morning, but he did not let himself sleep. It helped him to remember what an awesome, loving, creator-God he had when he knelt to pray. This was the reason he was on his knees this night.

You know my heart better than I do, Lord. You know how I feel about that woman. I can't think right now how we're going to get together, but I'm going to trust You. It will be so hard to see her go, but You will bring us together again in Your time. Of this I'm sure.

McKay stopped before he could give in to the temptation of telling God how he wanted things handled. Reminding himself just how good God was to bring Pup into his life in the first place, he climbed into bed and fell asleep almost instantly.

44

Carlyle called McKay into his office first thing Friday morning. The younger man took a seat across the desk from his first in command, having shut the door as he was asked.

"I've just finished with your reports. Thank you for the detail."

"You're welcome. It was clear?"

"Yes." Carlyle smiled. "You didn't elaborate, but I assume you scared Pup Jennings nearly out of her wits when you grabbed her."

McKay smiled in return. "I'm afraid so. I saw no other way to handle it."

Carlyle studied him for a moment. It was going to be hard for him to say what he was about to, but Nick Wallace had taken a true aversion to this young agent, and with that in mind Carlyle knew it was best for all concerned. However, he knew how much he would miss him.

"Are you still interested in a posting closer to Longmont?"

"Yes, sir, I am. I guess I'll always be a small-town boy."

"Well, something has come up—two posts actually. One in Evans, which wouldn't put you closer to Longmont but would get you out of the big city."

McKay nodded. "And the other?"

"Boulder."

McKay let his head fall back for just a moment, his eyes on the ceiling. *Boulder. Did You hear that, Lord? He said Boulder.*

Thank You, heavenly Father. Thank You, Lord of all. McKay looked back to see Carlyle watching him.

"I take it you're interested."

"Yes, Carlyle, I am. In Boulder, specifically." Carlyle was about to go on, but McKay had more to say. "It sounds like just what I've dreamed of, but may I give you my decision Tuesday?"

"Yes. I'm in charge of this posting, and you have first choice. I won't make a move until I hear from you."

"Thank you. I appreciate it. I did tell you that I'm taking Monday off?"

"Yes, and then two weeks at the end of the month or possibly the first two weeks of September."

"Yes."

"Well, that's all for now," Carlyle told him by way of dismissal. "Plan to see me when you get in Tuesday. I'll expect your answer then."

"Yes, sir."

McKay exited, knowing that if there had been any way to see Pup right then, he'd have done it. He wanted to skip from the room. He wanted to stand on the roof and shout to everyone that God's provision went beyond anything he could ask or think. He had completely forgotten that he'd told Carlyle he would eventually like to get out of the big city. He loved Denver—it was a great place to live—but the small-town warmth of Longmont and many other small towns he'd visited in the state was never far from his mind.

Back in his office, he forced himself to focus on the letters he was writing, which confirmed a few more facts for the case. His inter-office speaker sounded. It was Sam Binks, Nick's new assistant, calling to say Nick wanted to see him. Without even hearing Nick's voice, McKay knew something was up.

Not having seen Nick the night before, McKay nevertheless had a premonition that this man, whose relationship with Pup was so intense, was ready to have it out with him. He walked to the head-man's office, his heart asking only one thing of God: that he would maintain his testimony before Nick Wallace.

"Sit down," Nick instructed as soon as he let McKay into the office. He had indicated the comfortable area of the office, the section with the small carpet, sofa and chairs, but McKay was not fooled. This was not going to be a warm, good-to-see-you conversation. Nick's face told him he had things on his mind.

"First of all," Nick started as soon as they'd both sat down. "I want to thank you for all your work on this case; it's been invaluable. Much as I appreciate your efforts, I still want you to stay away from Pup."

McKay was relieved that he'd been expecting the worst. His face was more impassive than he felt when he respectfully asked, "Why is that, sir?"

"Because she's young," Nick said firmly. "Not in age but in experience. She's never had a man interested in her before, and quite frankly it's turned her head."

McKay didn't believe that no one had ever shown interest in Pup, but for a moment he didn't reply. There was so much he could say, but not all of it was wise. He tried again, keeping his voice even.

"Have I done something that makes you think my intentions toward Pup are not honorable?"

"Of course you have!" Nick was becoming agitated. "She's leaving the treasury, and for what? To go off with a man who may or may not be interested in marrying her."

These were serious accusations in McKay's mind, but again he forced himself to remain calm. The type of man Nick had just described was a reprehensible creature. If McKay had chosen to, he could have been quite offended. He knew he wasn't that kind of man; if only he could convince Nick Wallace of that fact.

"Have I made myself clear, McKay?"

"I believe so, sir. Do you care to hear anything I have to say?"

Nick nodded immediately. Nothing would change his mind, of this he was certain, but it was only fair to let the man talk.

"With all due respect, sir, I think you're selling me short. I know that you've called me in here today out of concern for a woman who is very dear to you, but have you considered Pup's happiness? She has the same right to have a husband as any other woman."

"Husband?"

"That's right, sir. I'm sorry you've had the impression that I'm just playing games with her. The truth of the matter is, I'm in love with her."

"Have you asked her to marry you?"

"No, sir, I haven't, but—" McKay tried to explain, but Nick wouldn't let him.

"You can't have her," he said bluntly, and McKay knew it was time to put things on the line. Nick glowered at him, but McKay looked steadily back, determined to have his say.

"I have no wish to antagonize you, sir. I realize you can fire me in an instant, but I'm still going to tell you that you don't own Callie Jennings." Nick's expression grew black, but McKay kept his cool. "Her days with the treasury department are numbered, if not already over."

"The only thing that's over is this discussion," Nick said, coming suddenly to his feet. "I don't think I need to see you to the door, Harrington."

McKay stood as well. "No, sir, I can find my way. But I hope you'll do just one thing—I hope you'll listen to her. I hope you'll give her that much. If you do, I know you'll find that Pup's decision to leave her job has nothing whatsoever to do with me."

Nick was so still he could have been made of stone. McKay didn't say another word but turned to the door. Nick didn't believe for a moment that McKay wasn't the reason . . . but if he didn't buy that argument, why couldn't he get the words from his mind? Nick eventually went back to his desk, but more than an hour passed before he got any work done.

Out in the hallway, McKay walked slowly back to his own office and shut the door. He didn't think he'd lost his job, but it was probably pretty close. He didn't return to Carlyle's office but he could have. Whether or not he and Pup had a future together, he would need to take the position in Boulder for the future security of his job.

The kitchen at the Wallace household was a busy place. Pup had taken it into her head to bake for McKay. Miranda was dubious but let her at it. However, when she watched the second eggshell go into the bowl, she had to step in.

"That's two," she said firmly.

"Did I drop another one?" Pup scrutinized the bowl and saw it, fishing it out with a long spoon.

"Now what else have you put in there when I wasn't looking?"

The younger woman sighed. "I don't know. Why did I think that being in love would suddenly make me a good cook?"

Delighted laughter came from the doorway. Camille had come in just in time to hear this.

"You can laugh, Camille," Pup told her with a frown. "You bake and cook well. Nick's never found an eggshell in his muffin."

"What I don't understand," Camille replied, still amused as she joined them and looked into the bowl, "is why this sudden urge?"

"I just think McKay would enjoy it."

"Tell me something, Callie; has Mr. Harrington already tasted your cooking?"

"Yes. Many times."

Camille shrugged as if the point was already made.

"What am I missing?"

The mistress of the household shook her head in tender exasperation. "He's already fallen for you, Callie. There must be something else that attracts him."

Pup just stood there. Camille had never seen her like this. She was always so sure of herself, never at a loss. Now she stood over a large batter bowl and looked uncertainly down at the contents. Earlier she'd seen her at one of the front windows, looking out like a child waiting for her papa to come up the walk.

"I guess I'll just clean this up and forget it."

"No, you won't," Miranda cut in. "I'll clean it up, and I'll even make something out of it. That way you can tell Mr. Harrington that you helped."

The phrase made Pup feel like a five-year-old, but she wasn't going to turn down the offer. She thanked the competent cook and housekeeper and left the room with Camille. The older woman spoke as soon as they were in the dining room. She had been laughing and having fun in the kitchen, but now her voice was serious. It brought Pup firmly back to earth.

"Will you help me with something today, Callie?"

"Sure. Anything."

"Will you help me find a church?"

Pup could have wept. *Here is my friend searching desperately to understand what is going on inside of her, and all I can think about is McKay,* she thought. *Camille is right. McKay doesn't care if I can cook.*

"I know of a church for you," Pup said softly. "And I'm sorry I didn't think of it before."

"Do you really, Callie?" Camille's face was full of yearning and hope.

"Yes. It's the church McKay attends. He told me about it."
She had a sudden thought. "Go get ready to go out, Camille.
I'll tell Miranda we're leaving."

"Where are we going?"

"The church. I'm not sure of the name, but Adair
MacKinnon is the pastor. We'll find it today, and then come
Sunday morning, you'll know right where it is."

Camille, as refined a lady as had ever graced the streets of
Denver, looked like an excited child. Her mouth opened but
no words came out.

"I'll be right back!" she finally managed, grabbing the
front of her skirt and taking the stairs on a run.

Pup returned to the kitchen, and noticing that Miranda
had already cleaned up her cooking disaster, informed the
housekeeper of their plans. When she went to get her own
things, Camille was already descending the stairs. Seeing how
thrilled Camille was, Pup wasted no time. A moment later the
women went out the front door.

"Do you think this is it?"

"Yes," Pup answered, her eyes on the tall stone building
with the short round steeple. She turned and paid the hack
driver, thanking him kindly before he went on his way.

"Should you have done that?" Camille asked as the carriage pulled away. Camille led something of a sheltered life,
making it easy for her to forget how adept Pup was at taking
care of herself.

"Let the driver go?"

"Yes. What if no one is here?"

Pup was not sure why, but even though it was a Friday
morning, she believed the church would be open. She did not
admit this to Camille; instead, she replied, "We'll just go up

and check the door." Her voice was matter-of-fact. "If it's locked, we'll sit here on this bench and talk awhile."

"How will we get home?" Camille asked, thankful that it seemed to be a safe neighborhood.

"Just like we got here. We'll walk up the street until we spot a hack for rent." Pup looked into her eyes and smiled. "Come on, let's go try the door."

Camille's heart pounded in her chest as they mounted the steps, and she thought it might stop altogether when, with a low groan, the heavy wooden door opened under Pup's hand. She pulled it wide so Camille could enter in front of her, and with only the slightest hesitation, they walked in.

The interior was a pleasant surprise. It was well lit with huge side windows, and the wood of the pews and pulpit was a light, warm brown. It wasn't a huge church, seating perhaps 120 people, with a choir loft behind the pulpit that would seat about 20 more. The women were walking slowly up the center aisle when a deep voice filled the room.

"Good morning, ladies."

Both women stopped. Coming down the aisle toward them was a large man, his broad, smiling face instantly putting them at ease.

"Good morning," Pup answered; Camille seemed incapable of speech.

"I'm Pastor Adair MacKinnon." He put his hand out. "Welcome."

"Thank you," Pup replied, shaking his hand. "My name is Callie Jennings, and this is my friend, Mrs. Camille Wallace."

Adair shook Camille's hand as well.

"What brings you to the Barton Street Bible Church this morning?"

"A friend of mine, McKay Harrington, attends here, and he told me about it."

"Ah, McKay." Adair knew he was meeting the woman herself. "How is McKay?"

"He's doing well. I saw him last night."

Adair's smile encompassed them. "Do you ladies live here in Denver?"

Pup looked to Camille, thinking she would at last speak up, but she still stood like a small, uncertain child.

"Mrs. Wallace lives here," Pup filled in. "I'm just visiting from Boulder."

"Boulder. That's a pretty area."

"Yes, it is. Pastor MacKinnon, what time do services start on Sunday?" Pup asked.

"Ten o'clock. Do you think you might be joining us?"

Refusing to answer, this time Pup looked to Camille. Camille didn't seem to notice—her eyes were still on the pastor. He was regarding her as well.

"I have questions," she stated softly.

"Oh? That's all right." The pastor's voice was welcoming. "About the church?"

"No. About Christ and salvation." It had clearly cost her to say the words, and Pup wanted to thank the man when he smiled.

"Will you come and sit for a time, ladies?"

Camille looked at Pup for the first time since entering. The younger woman nodded her head, and both followed the pastor as he led the way to the front. He directed them to the first pew. They sat side-by-side and watched as he brought a chair over from under one of the windows. He put the chair in front of them and sat down. Pup didn't know where he had gotten it, but there was also a Bible in his hand.

"Now then, Mrs. Wallace, what can I help you with?"

Nerves overcame her. Fiddling with the rings on her hands, she managed to ask, "Is it really so simple as belief? I've read parts of my Bible just recently, and it talks about belief in Jesus Christ. Is the path to God so simple?"

The pastor looked at her with serious eyes, his mind moving fast. "Your question is a good one, Mrs. Wallace, and I want to answer you honestly—even if it's not what you want to hear. Are you willing for this?"

Camille nodded without hesitation.

"It's a serious move, salvation is. It's more than just agreement or acknowledgment. The person you're putting your trust into is not a treasured aunt or cousin, it's the God of the universe. And He's going to have expectations. He's going to help you, but there will still be costs—sometimes dear ones. The path is narrow. Anything that comes between you and making God your God has got to be moved aside. Belief, yes, Mrs. Wallace, but I'd be leading you down a rosy path if I didn't tell you there's more, much more."

"In other words there might be some who won't be pleased with my decision?"

"Exactly. And your life may not be comfortable because of that. When Jesus preached and taught in the different towns, He confounded people. They were flabbergasted at what He was asking them to give up and to do. It's no less true today, even though we can't look Him in the eyes or touch His hand."

"So I should give great thought to this?"

"I think great thought on this matter would be very wise indeed."

She was silent for a time, but Pup noticed some of the apprehension had left her face. "If I don't believe today, this moment with you," she finally asked, "can I still come on Sunday?"

"Absolutely, Mrs. Wallace." His warm smile was genuine. "It would be our pleasure to have you—visiting like you have today or joining us for services. And I am available if you have more questions."

Camille wanted to weep with relief. She knew what was holding her back, and indeed it still was, but knowing that she would be welcome here took a great load from her shoulders.

Camille stood, now more in charge than Pup.

"Thank you, Pastor MacKinnon. I shall be here Sunday."

"I'll look forward to it."

Pup shook his hand as well, and Camille led the way back up the aisle toward the door. Once outside they stood and surveyed the street. Pup looked at her friend and found her face resolute.

"I've never done a thing in all my married life without Nick's permission, Callie," she told her quietly. "He's never had any interest in church, and I've gone along because I was comfortable doing so. I can't think what he'll say when I tell him I'm coming Sunday, but I'm going to do this, I'm going to do exactly what Pastor MacKinnon suggested. I'm going to give this great thought and make sure I know what I'm doing."

Pup squeezed her hand but didn't speak. Pastor MacKinnon's words had touched her as well. She needed constant reminders that her God was the God of the universe. She couldn't hear it often enough. Her heart was humbled and awed, and she asked God to strengthen her in His grace and to help her understand Him more and more. Indeed, she was so intent on her prayers that she was barely aware of Camille leading them down the street and when she saw a carriage, even waving the driver to the curb.

45

Pup had prayed about Nick's response off and on all afternoon. She had felt herself beginning to worry and worked at not trying to do God's job. Camille spent quite a bit of time in her room, and Pup had prayed for her as well. Now, however, the only person on her mind was Nick. The moment was upon her. Nick had been in fine humor during dinner, and Pup knew she was going to have to put up or shut up.

He surprised her by speaking first. "I talked to McKay today." They were in the living room with Camille. The calm demeanor of the trio belied the tension each was feeling.

"Oh," Pup responded uncertainly, "how was he?"

"Fine. We talked about you," the man admitted. "He seems to be under the impression that you want to leave the treasury department—" Nick paused. "That is what you've been trying to tell me, is it not?"

"Yes, Nick."

He nodded. "According to McKay, it has nothing to do with him."

Pup had been praying all day for an opening, and the Lord had just laid one in her lap.

"I've never met a man like McKay Harrington," she admitted. "I don't think I need to tell you that I'm in love with him, and I know he loves me."

A look of impatience crossed Nick's face, but Pup ignored it. Glancing at Camille, who had not said a word, Pup continued.

"I don't know if I can explain this, Nick, but I feel as though I live a lie. McKay has never pressured me in any way, but he has reminded me of what I've been missing in my life by leaving Jesus Christ out of everything I do. I know you don't agree with my beliefs, and my understanding of some of them is coming rather slowly, but I know I can't keep on this way."

"Keep on what way?" Nick still didn't see. "What is so awful about your life?"

"Do you remember Mrs. Meyer, Nick—the woman at the boardinghouse? She thinks Bryan Daniels is dead." Pup shook her head sadly. "Bryan Daniels never existed, but we let her think he did and then hurt her by saying he died. That's what's so bad about my life, Nick, the constant lies and fabrications. I can't be me; I can't reach out to people and be Pup or Callie Jennings."

"You want to leave the treasury, but you'll go on using a name that's not even yours?" He was getting angry and did nothing to hide that fact. He hoped to put her in her place with that accusation, but she surprised him.

"I've given a lot of thought to that, Nick, and I'm going to stay Callie Jennings—not because I want to play games, but because there are people who would like to see me dead. Not Pup Jennings specifically, but the characters I played. To change my name suddenly would draw undue attention that might make its way back to the wrong person. My life might be cut short, so I'm keeping the name for my own protection."

This sobered Nick in an instant, his anger evaporating. He didn't know why he was fighting this so much. When she'd been trapped inside that house, her cover seriously blown for the first time, Nick had told himself he'd never let her do another job, and here he was giving her a terrible time over wanting just that.

"There's more, Nick," Pup continued amid his confused thoughts. "I want to be able to stay home. I want to get back to Boulder and just live there, not worrying about checking the post office and getting back on the train. That isn't to say I've lived an awful life, but because I think God has more for me, it's a life I am done with."

"But McKay Harrington doesn't figure into any of this?" Nick's voice was calmer.

"God used McKay in a wonderful way in my life. Long before McKay showed any signs of caring for me romantically, he showed me that he cared for my spiritual welfare. When I was little more than a stranger, he and his parents offered me genuine friendship. In the process, I saw the way they lived. I knew my life was missing something.

"I hope you don't take this personally, Nick, because that's not what this is about. No one could ask for better friends than you and Camille, and as my boss you took care of me like a treasured child. But I have to leave this now. I'm not leaving the Wallaces; I'm leaving the treasury department."

"The Duncan Phipps case is a very exciting note on which to end," Nick responded calmly and logically. "What if you change your mind? What if just living in Boulder is not enough?"

"I guess I'll tackle that if and when it happens. I think I'll be fine; indeed, I think I'll be more than fine. Right now I'm not looking that far ahead. Right now I just want to leave here with your friendship, knowing I'll be welcomed back at anytime."

She thought they would be hashing this over for hours, but already Nick's face had changed. He wasn't angry or closed off. He was the Nick of old—open and ready to listen to anything she had to say.

"Will you miss it?" This was the first question Camille had asked.

Pup smiled. "I'm sure a part of me will, but I'm very excited about the changes I'll be making, too. When I feel the need to be a blonde, I'll stop in and put on the wig."

Camille smiled tenderly at her. She had handled it all so well, and Nick looked as though he was going to be all right.

"So what's going on with you and McKay?" Nick asked, the other issue already laid to rest. "If you're so crazy about the man, why are you leaving?"

"Because it's time for me to go home. He's coming in the morning to take me to the train station. From that point, we'll write and make plans to see each other. I think he'll come to Boulder when he can, and I'll visit him here until we're sure what we want to do."

"That's another part I don't understand. If you're in love, what's to figure out?"

Pup thought it a good question and answered carefully.

"Today is August 2. On April 23, McKay came to the cabin and Govern shot him. That's not even four months, Nick. I don't want to rush this. I want to be with McKay more than anyone else in the world, but I don't want to hurry into anything. I don't want to be in a panic. I have so much to take in, so much to learn, and I want to take time for all of it."

Nick nodded. His heart was suddenly lighter than it had been in weeks. The case had been on his mind but so had this woman. The terror that she would be hurt had receded. It was going to be okay.

"Are we going to be invited to the wedding?" Nick inquired to cover his feelings.

Pup stared at him, her gaze as direct as ever. "Who else would walk me down the aisle?"

Nick had to shut his eyes. She was so special. Camille was right. They probably wouldn't have had the same relationship with her if she'd actually been their daughter, but he was going to miss her as if she were his own, and it already hurt so much.

"I'm tired," Nick said, his eyes displaying that fact. "This whole thing has worn me out."

"How is the case coming together?" Pup asked, not sure he had been referring to the Duncan Phipps case but nonetheless curious.

"The files were worth their weight in gold, and so was the gold we found."

"Gold?" Pup was alert.

"That's right. Those stairs led to a small attic room that had no other access, not even a window. Inside was a safe. At first we thought we might need to blast it, but our locksmith got it open."

"And inside you found gold?" Camille was all ears as well.

Nick nodded. "Numerous bars. We certainly have no way of proving that Phipps came by it illegally, but neither will he be able to say that he can't make good on his phony mining stocks or bad accounts."

"When is his arraignment?"

"Monday," Nick told them. "Jubal's is Tuesday."

Pup looked preoccupied on this announcement, so Camille asked if she was all right.

"I think so," she said, but looked uncertain. "Maybe I shouldn't leave tomorrow; maybe I should stay for Tuesday."

"Go home," Nick said to her, knowing it was what she needed to hear. "If you want to write Jubal a note, I'll see that he gets it, but you've got that look about you that always tells me when you need to go home."

Pup looked at him. He was right; she needed to go. "Thank you, Nick."

With that he stood and came over to kiss her cheek.

"I'm going to bed," he announced. "What time do you leave in the morning?"

"I told McKay to come at 7:15."

"I'll be down to see you off. Are you coming, Camie?"

"Right behind you."

Mrs. Wallace rose gracefully to her feet and kissed Pup goodnight as well. Nick secured the downstairs, while Pup and Camille walked upstairs to their rooms. Once behind closed doors, Pup readied for bed, but she did not turn her lantern out until she had written a letter to Jubal. She kept it short but honest, telling him she was praying for him, and even writing out two verses of Scripture for him. She fell asleep praying that they would somehow touch his heart.

Pup was completely ready when McKay arrived in the morning. She had an extra bag with her, since she didn't know how soon she'd be coming back. Her heart clenched with pain when she saw McKay's face and thought about how hard it would be to say goodbye.

"Are you all set?"

"Almost," she told him softly, smiling when he bent slightly to kiss her cheek. "I need to say goodbye to Nick and Camille."

"All right. I'll take your things to the carriage."

McKay started to pick up both bags, but a hand was there ahead of him. He looked up to see Nick.

"I'll help you with this."

McKay nodded, and both men walked out with just one satchel each. McKay stowed the first one in the back and stepped aside for Nick to do the same. He then looked at the man who could make or break him in his career with the treasury.

"Carlyle tells me he's offered you another post."

"Yes, sir. Just yesterday."

"Does Pup know?"

"Not yet."

"We'll miss you here," Nick told him.

"Thank you, sir. The feeling is mutual."

Nick put his hand out.

"Take good care of her."

McKay shook the hand offered to him. "You can count on that, sir."

Nick turned back to the door, and McKay stayed by the carriage, watching him go. It was the last thing he'd expected, and his relief was great. He had thought Nick might confront him again, but things must have gone well the evening before.

Inside, Camille held onto Pup, her arms warm and tender.

"You'll be back soon?

"Yes," Pup assured her, "and you know I'll write."

"Be thinking of me, Callie. I'm going to tell Nick today about wanting to go to church in the morning."

Pup stepped back so she could see her face.

"I'll pray for you, Camille. Every day I'll ask God to show you more. And I'll pray that Nick will know a hunger as strong as yours."

Again the women hugged, and a moment later Nick was there. Camille walked them to the door but remained inside as Nick took Pup onto the front porch.

"You'll stay in touch?"

"Yes. You, too?"

"Yes. I told him to take good care of you."

Pup smiled. "My father's been dead for more than 13 years, Nick, but I know he would be so pleased with how much you care."

Nick took her into his arms, having to remind himself that he could see her with just a few hours' travel. His throat still felt tight, but her close proximity made what would have been an almost unbearable situation something he could cope with. A moment later she stepped away and went down the steps to McKay and the carriage. He helped her aboard, and she turned to wave as the wheels were set into motion.

"Are you all right?" was McKay's first question.

"Yes. It's a lot of goodbyes for one day, but I think I'll make it."

McKay took her hand and didn't press her. Pup thought of all the things she could say and how short the time was, but nothing would come. She relished the feel of McKay's large hand covering hers and tried not to think of how soon she might be snowed in at the cabin, unable to communicate with him.

The train station came into view, and they still hadn't spoken. When the carriage stopped, McKay helped her alight and told her he would go to the ticket counter. A platform attendant saw to the bags, and Pup stood alone, her eyes trying to pick out McKay in the crowd. He was back at her side in record time. When she thought he might want to spend these last minutes alone, just enjoying each other, he surprised her by handing her one of the bags.

"Can you carry this?"

"Of course."

"Okay, we'd better get in and find a seat."

Pup frowned at him but did as she was told. Indeed, she had no choice. McKay hustled her through the crowd and up the stairs so quickly that she couldn't say a word. Once in the car, he ushered her toward an empty seat in the rear.

"This looks good," he said as he began to stow the bags. "Sit here."

Pup sat down but only stared up at him, not really seeing what he was doing. Confused, she spoke when he finally sat beside her.

"Are you going to Boulder?" She framed the question at last.

"Yes."

"You are?" she questioned again, her eyes huge.

"I have to," he told her simply. "I've been offered a job there, and I have to check it out."

414

At first she said nothing. She studied his face. It was neither teasing nor serious. He merely returned her scrutiny.

"You're going to work in Boulder?"

"If I take the job."

She blinked. "You're going to live and work in Boulder, Colorado?"

"That's about right."

"Oh, McKay," she breathed, her voice barely above a whisper. "How dare you tell me such a thing when I can't kiss you."

McKay glanced around. There were people everywhere. He looked back, a playful glint in his eye.

"No one's looking," he whispered back. "Go ahead and kiss me."

She could only stare into the eyes that smiled so impishly into her own. *Boulder. He was coming to live in Boulder!*

"Do you have any idea what I feel for you?" she asked.

He picked up her hand. "I think I can imagine."

She couldn't say anything. She couldn't think. Breathing was even an effort. Wanting to know how and when this had happened, she could not even form the words. He was coming with her. She had been forced to say goodbye to Nick and Camille but not to McKay. He was moving to Boulder, and Pup knew deep in her heart that God would bless them. She still couldn't speak, but as she looked into the eyes that stared back at her so tenderly, her heart had one more whisper.

There's not another man like you in all the earth, McKay Harrington, and one day you'll be all mine.

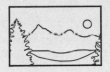

46

Boulder
Two months later

"Are you all set?" Travis asked Pup and McKay as they stood at the train station.

"I think so," McKay answered, reaching under his jacket to withdraw the train tickets from his shirt pocket.

"I hope the weather is good for you," Rebecca said with a smile, shifting Kaitlin in her arms.

"I don't know," Pup answered her friend, a sparkle lighting her eyes. "It's always fun to have an excuse to curl up by the fire with a book."

The women shared a conspiring smile.

It had been Travis' turn to take the children in to school. With the baby so young, Rebecca did not often join him so early in the day, but when she learned that McKay and Pup were leaving for Longmont that morning, she came in so the five of them could have breakfast together before they caught their train. They often shared meals on the weekends, but coming for breakfast was a different sort of treat.

Pup gave Rebecca a hug and looked down at the youngest Buchanan.

"Are you going to miss me, Katie?" she inquired of her. Kaitlin smiled into the familiar face, and Pup grinned in return. She wanted to take her into her arms, to hold her one last time, but time was working against them.

The whistle blew, and McKay caught Pup around the waist. They moved off with a final word of goodbye and wishes for a wonderful time in Longmont. Pup and McKay boarded the train amid excitement, their hearts pounding with anticipation of time together and a break in routine. They talked for a time and then sat back to enjoy the ride. McKay had a book along, and while Pup did, too, she also had a few letters to read. They spent the trip in short conversations or with their heads bent over the words in their hands.

Longmont

"What did Camille's letter say?"

It was just a few hours later, and they were at the livery. McKay had just helped Pup into the buggy and started toward his parents' home. The posting in Boulder had wanted him to begin immediately. Carlyle had okayed the swift transfer, and McKay had negotiated with his new superior for the two-week leave he had coming. Vacation was granted to him at the beginning of October, and McKay and Pup planned to spend at least ten days of that time with his parents.

Pup dug the letters from her bag.

"She says she loves the church," Pup filled him in and began to quote: "'The Lord is showing me all kinds of wonderful things. I had no idea how much I could learn from the psalms. I've explained my conversion to Nick, and while he admits he doesn't understand, he did come to church with me twice. He enjoys Pastor MacKinnon, and they've had some good conversations.'"

"That's great," McKay commented, waiting for her to read more. Once Camille's letter was back in the safety of its envelope, Pup told him she'd also had one from Jubal. Her brother, now serving his 15-year jail sentence, never had a lot to say but always thanked her for writing.

"How is he?" McKay asked.

"About the same." She fell silent for a moment. "I can still see his face at the trial, McKay, and all I could do was pray that he would turn to the Lord. I wish he'd comment on the verses I always write out."

"Give him time, Pup. Maybe you'll have a chance to really talk when you see him at the end of the month."

Pup nodded in agreement and then fell quiet, her heart praying about the days they would spend in Longmont. She had no wish to overwhelm McKay's parents, and she wanted things to start well. At the moment she hoped and prayed that they hadn't invited family in to greet them or planned to take them to town for dinner. They were at the house before Pup knew it, but she was ready—eager even—to see and talk with them.

They took the buggy and horse to the barn and then went to the kitchen door. Both Harry and Liz were right there and came straight to the door as soon as they realized McKay and Pup had arrived. They both took Pup and their son into their arms, Liz's eyes suspiciously moist when she saw the radiant looks on their faces.

They were in love; it was impossible to miss. McKay had written to her and even managed to visit once. Pup's name had been on his lips the entire weekend and prominent throughout every letter, but other than saying they wanted to come for a long visit, he'd never actually come out and said what their plans were. Pup had not been back to visit since the first time.

"Come in and sit down," Liz now bid them, wanting to know everything but forcing herself not to ask. She led the way to the living room.

"Did you want anything to eat or drink?"

"I'm fine," Pup told her.

"Nothing for me, thanks, Mom," McKay said, sinking onto the couch next to Pup, his hand finding hers.

"How was the train?" Harry asked as usual. He didn't travel much and enjoyed the thought of getting on at the station and heading off to new places.

"It was fine. No delays. It's certainly easier to come from Boulder than it was to come from Denver."

"I'll bet. How's the job?"

"Good. The cold weather was a little rough when I had to track a man into the mountains two weeks ago, but it's a great job. My supervisor is a fair man, and he's hinted that when Mark Wesley transfers to Evans, he has me in mind for Mark's position."

"That's excellent. Are you still living over the general store?"

"Yes, but I think I found a house. It's on the edge of town, a little way out, but that's what I was looking for. The downstairs has a parlor, large kitchen, and dining room, and upstairs there are three small bedrooms with built-in closets."

"Is it yours if you want it?"

"Yes, it is. It isn't for sale, but the rent is reasonable."

Liz suddenly smiled. "It's so good to have you here. How long can you stay?"

"I think about ten days."

Liz beamed at them; this was more than she'd expected. "I made myself not plan a host of activities, but if you're going to be here that long, the family will want to see you."

"That's fine, Mom. Just as long as we can take it easy today."

"We knew you would feel that way," Harry inserted. "We don't have anything planned and can spend the day doing anything you want."

His words caused Pup and McKay to exchange a look.

"I'm glad to hear that." McKay's voice was so serious that it was Harry and Liz's turn to share a glance.

"Is something wrong, Mickey?" his father asked.

"No, Dad, but Callie and I have wanted to talk to you for some time, and we thought this trip would be the right time."

"Of course," Harry replied without hesitation. "As I said, we have no plans beyond anything you want to do."

McKay nodded. He knew they would understand. A moment later, Pup's hand still in his own, he began.

"I haven't come right out and asked Callie to marry me, but we've been doing a lot of talking about it, and even met with Pastor Henley a few times." McKay looked over at her and smiled. "One of the things we wanted to do first was get to know each other better, not just each other, but our families and church families. When Callie was here before, there was so much I couldn't tell you, and now we want to do that so you'll know Callie a little bit better. It's especially important to Callie."

Harry and Liz looked to her. "We want you to know, Callie," Harry said before McKay could go on, "that you don't have to do anything to gain our approval."

"Thank you, Harry," she said gratefully. "I understand that, but there have been a lot of events in my life I've had to keep secret. Some of them will always remain secrets, but there are some things I want to tell."

"Is it about your family, Callie?" Liz asked compassionately.

"It starts there," Pup admitted, realizing the explanation might take a while. "Or I guess I should say it starts with the war. I was 15 when the war was half over. I wasn't willful, but I'd been raised to have a mind and opinion of my own, and I decided I believed in the war enough that I wanted to get involved. So with my mother's help, I cut my hair off, climbed into some of my brother's clothes, and went off to fight."

The color drained from Liz's face, and Pup smiled at her in understanding.

"At times it was horrendous. I didn't think I'd be able to stand it, but I stayed. My name was Peter Crandall and my commanding officer was Nick Wallace."

"Nick Wallace? From the treasury?" Harry asked.

"Yes. The same man. The end of the war came and those of us who'd signed on in Denver came home. Nick went back to his job with the treasury, and he asked me if I'd like to work for him. I told him no and went home, but my father had died, and my brothers had gotten wild and started running around. In order to take care of my mother, I went back to Nick, still dressed as Peter, and asked if he could still use me. When he learned I was a woman, he set me up as an undercover agent."

She could see that she had stunned them speechless, but their looks were open. It wasn't as hard to talk about as she had imagined, so she went on with some ease.

"From there I lost track of how many identities I assumed. My disguises were all stored at Nick's house. His wife, Camille, and I became very close, and when notified of a job, I would report there. Usually Camille would cut my hair off, and I'd head out as a man."

"Oh, Callie." Liz's hand had come to her mouth. "Not your beautiful curls!"

"Do you remember the bonfire?" Pup asked quietly.

Liz's eyes became huge and Pup nodded.

"I'd started a job in May, so my hair was still pretty short."

"And this, Callie," Liz asked as she pointed to her head, "is this your hair now?"

"It was before Camille Wallace had it made into a wig," McKay supplied with a smile.

Pup turned to him. "Should I show them?"

"It's up to you. It's shorter than the wig but already longer than it was."

Pup reached for the wig. Both Liz and Harry stared in amazement. Her head was covered with black, curly ringlets.

"How long will it be before you can go without the wig?" Harry wished to know.

"Hopefully by Christmas."

The wig seemed to uncork the Harringtons' questions. Over the next two hours Pup revealed more, and many questions were asked and answered. Not only did she explain Peter Crandall, but also Bryan Daniels and Morton Barnes and the role she played in Longmont. She went on to tell how her brothers had been involved, and also the way Nick had used her to crack the Duncan Phipps case. She understood how much her work had helped rid Colorado of crime, but she also told them about her conviction before the Lord to become herself again.

"Callie Jennings isn't my real name," she added. "It's Andrea May Hackett." She had stunned them again but went on to explain the importance of staying Callie. She also explained her feelings about the way she'd deceived people. Although they'd laughed today over some of her past antics, her decision never to mislead people again was a serious one. Harry and Liz agreed with her wholeheartedly.

"Don't forget the last disguise," McKay prompted her, wishing his parents could have seen her in the costume that had so taken him by surprise. "The one with the blonde wig and maid's uniform."

"Inga," Pup supplied.

"Inga?" Liz asked, eyes still wide.

"Yah. Das me, Inga."

Both Harry and Liz burst out in laughter. Pup laughed with them and looked over to find McKay's eyes fixed on her. She grinned at him, and although noticing his intent gaze, she didn't comment.

"What did Inga do?" Harry asked, as intrigued as he'd been all afternoon.

"She got into the Phipps mansion as a maid. It took a few days to penetrate Duncan's private office, but there was valuable information there. I can't say too much, but the case should be open and shut because of it."

"Oh, Callie," Liz said on a sigh; she looked almost drained. "We had no idea, but we're so pleased that you could tell us."

"I hated not telling you before, and then when I had to leave so suddenly, I thought you would never want to see me again."

"We can't say we understood," Harry told her, "because we didn't, not really. But we weren't angry, and Mickey explained that you didn't have a choice."

"Thank you, Harry. Thank you, Liz." She felt as if a weight had been taken from her shoulders.

"I think we all need a little something to eat and drink. I know I do," Liz proclaimed and stood. "Harry, will you help me?"

"Indeed I will."

Husband and wife exited. They had no more walked from the room than McKay grabbed Pup and kissed her.

"Talk like Inga again," he said when he raised his head.

"I won't," she told him on a laugh, but he kissed her again anyhow. There was little Pup enjoyed more than McKay's kisses, but now was not the time or place. She wriggled from his arms and stood. He reached for her again, but she evaded him, moving around the back of the sofa. McKay stood as well, never taking his eyes off of her.

"Go ahead, Pup," he cajoled softly, "talk like Inga."

She laughed but still refused. He started toward her and she darted away.

"What has come over you, McKay Harrington?" she asked, her eyes huge.

"I just realized how much fun being married to you is going to be," he said softly as he circled the sofa.

"Well, we're not married yet, so you just stay over there."

She was roundly ignored. This time he literally jumped over the back of the davenport to get at her, but she somehow escaped his arms. When they faced each other again, his eyes narrowed and Pup shook her head. She darted toward the front door and all but ran to the kitchen.

Liz and Harry looked up when she entered so suddenly, but she drew up short and gave them a nervous smile, stopping just inside the kitchen door. They smiled in return when McKay followed close at her heels. He wasn't moving as fast, but it was clear who his prey was. They didn't continue to stare at them, so McKay stepped close to her side, slipped an arm around her waist, and whispered in her ear.

"I'll take this up with you later," he warned her softly, and pressed a kiss to her temple. Pup only smiled.

The chase over, they both helped with the meal. An hour later the four of them sat down to a wonderful feast. The fellowship was beyond sweet. Pup felt free to leave her wig off the rest of the evening, and her heart swelled with thanks to God who had brought her to this precious place and these days of rest and communion. McKay's heart was feeling no less full as he watched his parents with the woman he loved. It was to be the start of a wonderful ten days for all of them.

As often happened when they were at the Harringtons for the evening, McKay and Pup had gone out by the lake and were watching the sun rapidly drop behind the mountains. Seeing it, they were both reminded that their stay was drawing to a close. McKay held Pup's hand, content for a time to just stand with her in silence.

"Have you enjoyed your stay?"

"Oh, yes," she told him and meant it. "I'll miss your parents when we go home to Boulder." Her voice was rather sad, her eyes still on the water.

"I love you," he told her and watched as she turned to him. "Will you be my wife?"

McKay knew that if he lived to be 90 he would never forget her answer. Her eyes sparkled with pleasure, but she bit her lip over the wonderful question, her eyes on his. He held his breath, suddenly unsure of what she might say.

"I'll marry you, McKay," she said softly, "but I do have one request."

"Anything." McKay kept his voice light but felt as if his heart had stopped.

"Can we wait until I can go without my wig?"

His relief was so great that he laughed and hugged her.

"I take it that means you can wait for my hair."

"You name the date, and I'll be there," he told her. Pup hugged him fiercely and gladly accepted his kiss when he bent his head. McKay broke apart long enough to study her face and hair.

"How much time are we talking about here?" He suddenly realized what he had agreed to.

Pup laughed in delight and kissed him again. McKay's worry about the time went up like a puff of smoke. It didn't matter when. God had taken them this far; He would take them the rest of the way. And the journey would be everything they'd hoped for and more.

Epilogue

Boulder
Six years later

McKay dished some food into Daniel Harrington's plate and watched as his son's three-year-old hands went to work, not seeing any need for ceremony until his father handed him a spoon. McKay made sure a few proper bites went down and then turned to his oldest child, five-year-old Grace. She was working on a slice of apple, a piece stuck at an odd angle in her mouth. McKay's heart smiled. Sitting right next to her plate was the front tooth that had fallen out of her mouth just that morning.

"How's it coming?" he asked.

"Okay. It feels funny."

"Before you know it, they'll all be out and you'll have to live on soup."

This earned him a smile so like his wife's that for a moment he stared at her. He realized then that it was going to be hard to head back to Boulder. They were all at the cabin and had been for more than a week. In just a few days McKay's vacation would end, and they would all go back to their house in town. Although they missed the church family and the Boulder townsfolk, the quiet of the hills and lazy days in the woods would be hard to leave.

McKay's eyes were still on Grace when 18-month-old Melissa, the youngest of the Harrington children, started to hum from her place in the high chair. She had taken a long nap and was in a fine mood, dark eyes bright, cheeks rosy. Putting some apple slices and a few pieces of chicken on her tray, McKay wondered if she would ever fall asleep that night. Days filled with playing in the sun and swimming in Lake Anne made for great sleep, unless of course you took a two-hour nap.

427

It wasn't that long until the children's bedtime, so McKay decided he would have to do something to wear Melissa out. Pup would have had ideas, but at the moment she was taking some time on her own. She had left the cabin just before dinner, telling McKay and the children that she was not hungry. McKay assumed she had gone for a walk.

Daniel chose that moment to slosh the contents of his cup onto the table. McKay grabbed the washcloth and was seeing to the mess when someone knocked at the door. McKay answered it and blinked in surprise. A man bearing a striking resemblance to Morton Barnes stood on the doorstep.

"Is Gracie Harrington here?" the man asked in a rusty voice.

"Yes," McKay smiled. No one called their daughter Gracie; she would be delighted with her mother's latest disguise and use of that name.

"I'm the Tooth Trader. I need to see Gracie."

McKay opened the door wide, his smile huge. His welcome didn't penetrate the Tooth Trader's look, however; Pup was taking her role seriously.

"Grace," her father called. The children had all turned and were staring at the stranger in their midst. Grace and Daniel giggled, but both played along. "There's someone here to see you."

"Are you Gracie?" a voice that sounded nothing like Pup's asked of Daniel. He giggled and pointed at his sister.

"You're Gracie?" Pup deliberately looked at Melissa. "You're kinda little to be losing teeth."

"No," Grace spoke up. The man was looking for her, and she had to help him. "I'm Grace Harrington."

The Tooth Trader looked to her in surprise, his eyes narrowing as if in concentration.

"I'm here about the tooth."

Grace only stared at her mother in awe. If she hadn't seen her eyes, she would never have guessed.

"You have lost a tooth, haven't you?"

Her small mouth still open in surprise, Grace got hold of herself, picked up the tooth, and held it out in her palm. Pup bent low over the proffered item.

"There it is all right. Are you sure this came out of your mouth?"

With her free hand Grace pulled down her lower lip in order to display the gaping hole in the front line of teeth.

"Oh, yeah," Pup said, inspecting the mouth as though looking for gold. "It's your tooth all right. What'll you take for it?"

Grace's eyes saucered when Pup pulled some coins from "his" pocket. She was a bright girl and knew in an instant that she was supposed to trade for the tooth. The bargaining began. At first the trader tried to get it for free, but Grace was firm, and at last had talked her way into three whole cents. Her brother, who knew those coins from seeing similar ones in his father's pocket and from buying candy at the general store, looked on in excitement. Having been left momentarily alone, Melissa was fending for herself. The dark-haired toddler had climbed from her chair and was now kneeling in McKay's seat. Happily working on her father's dinner, she was giving little notice to the evening's charade.

"Well, I'd better go," the Tooth Trader announced. "You send for me if any more teeth fall out."

Clutching the precious coins, Grace nodded, her eyes still shining with delight. Pup pocketed the tooth and turned toward the door. McKay, always slightly in awe that she hadn't lost her touch after all these years, stood aside. His eyes told her that he'd have grabbed this tooth trader and kissed her if the children hadn't been watching. A moment later she was out the door, walking in character until she was at the edge of the house, where she removed her hat and rushed to the stable to change back into her dress.

Grace was a nonstop talker after that, so excited that dinner was forgotten. McKay tried to rescue some of his dinner, but Melissa, having gotten that far without being stopped, assumed it was all hers. McKay simply joined her and tried to salvage at least part of his meal. It set the tone for an evening of high spirits. Pup wandered back just ten minutes later and had to steady herself when her daughter came at her full force. With Grace's arms still wrapped around Pup's legs, she looked up at her mother.

"That was fun, Mama. Thank you."

Pup looked tenderly into her eyes. "Did it take away some of the pain of losing it?"

Grace nodded happily, the morning's discomfort gone. They both went to the table. Pup ate a little but wasn't very hungry. All Daniel and Grace wanted to do was talk about the tooth trader. Pup listened in delight and then exclaimed, "How will we ever top this?"

"I guess we'll all have to take a swim," McKay suggested, also thinking this would wear out Melissa.

"After dinner?" Grace's eyes gave testimony to the rare treat.

"Right now," Pup agreed. "Before the sun drops too much."

Ten minutes later McKay and the children were in the lake. Her skirt hiked up and feet bare, Pup splashed on the beach with Daniel. Melissa was in her father's arms. Already a good swimmer, Grace was paddling along near him. They lasted until it was nearly dark. McKay finally called Grace from the water and sent her and Daniel ahead. He spoke to Pup with Melissa on one arm and another around his wife.

"Why don't you grab your robe and come back down and bathe."

"I was going to work on the dishes."

"I can do that."

"What about the children?" McKay always put them to bed.

"I'll do that, too. You come down and take a long bath, and I'll see you when you come up."

Whenever the children went to bed early, Pup and McKay bathed together, but tonight McKay wanted to give Pup more time on her own, since the early evening had been spent preparing for the Tooth Trader. She agreed and thanked him with a kiss, slipped inside and into her robe, and came out with the soap and a piece of toweling. McKay told a Bible story to his children and then put them to bed. He did the dishes quickly and was in bed when he heard Pup come in the door.

She went to the children's room, to kiss them he was sure, and on her way back out he heard a bump. A low groan then came to his ears. She came limping into the bedroom.

"The kitchen table?" he asked from his place against the pillows.

"I think so. It's pretty dark out there." Pup sat with her back against the footboard and brought her legs up so she could examine the injured toe. She no more had it on the bed when McKay captured her foot and rubbed gently. She looked at him, expecting to find him bent over the foot, but he was looking at her.

"Is there something on your mind?"

"Just you," he said, smiling.

Pup's answering smile was tender.

"You were good tonight," he commented.

"Do you think she was pleased?"

"Oh, yes, she was thrilled."

Pup sighed with pleasure.

"Do you miss it?" he asked for the first time in many years. She knew exactly what he meant.

"Not at all," she said honestly. "I couldn't stand to leave you and the children, and now when I'm in the mood, I can join The Boulder Company."

Boulder had a repertory group which put on a large production every October. The year before Pup had played the heroine. Her monologue, spoken while she'd been tied to the authentic-looking railroad tracks on stage, had moved the audience to hysterical tears. They had talked about it for weeks.

"Come join me," McKay invited, and Pup moved to the head of the bed and climbed beneath the covers. Her hair was still damp and her cool skin felt wonderful as McKay cuddled her close, his cheek against her hair. There was no need for words. It was a lovely close to the day, but also a normal one. They were a man and woman in love, loved by God, and blessed by Him in an abundance of ways.

Years ago McKay had known that this journey with the wife God had given him would be more than he could ever hope or pray for. And God, who loved to give to His children, had gone far beyond his wildest dreams. If McKay was ever tempted to doubt, he had only to look into his wife's face or the faces of the three children who looked just like her. The truth stared him in the face every day. God had been good to them.